THE TWIN SISTER

PAIGE DEARTH

Copyright © [2024] by Paige Dearth

All rights reserved. No portion of this book may be reproduced in any form without written permission from the publisher or author, except as permitted by U.S. copyright law.

ISBN 9798987144770 (Paperback)
ISBN 9798987144787 (Hardcover)

Dirt On The Author

Born and raised in Plymouth Meeting, a small town west of Philadelphia, Paige Dearth was a victim of child abuse and spent her early years yearning desperately for a better life. Living through the fear and isolation that marked her youth, she found a way of coping with the trauma: she developed the ability to dream up stories grounded in reality that would provide her with a creative outlet when she finally embarked on a series of novels. Paige's debut novel, Believe Like A Child, is the darkest version of the life she imagines she would have been doomed to lead had fate not intervened just in the nick of time. The beginning of Believe Like A Child is based on Paige's life while the remainder of the book is fiction. Paige writes real-life horror and refers to her work as Fiction with Meaning. She hopes that awareness through fiction creates prevention.

Connect With Paige

Sign Up For New Book Releases At Paige's Website:

PaigeDearth.com

Find All Of Paige's Books On Amazon:

Amazon.com

Follow Paige At:

Facebook: facebook.com/paigedearth

Instagram: paigedearth

Goodreads

X: @paigedearth

More books by Paige

Home Street Home Series (can be read in any order):
Believe Like A Child
When Smiles Fade
One Among Us
Mean Little People
Never Be Alone
My Final Breath

Rainey Paxton Series (must be read in order):
A Little Pinprick
A Little High
Girls Missing
Girls Found

Raven Ledger Duet (must be read in order):
The Shooter's Sister
The Twin Sister

For the love of my life, the one I grew from scratch.
Love, Mom

Acknowledgements

For all of you, like me, who've had your heart broken by someone you loved and thought you knew. Then they revealed themselves as a stranger, someone appalling. Just know, you now have room in your heart to find other people who will love you wholly.

To my honey. With you, I am home.

xo

The Twin Sister

Raven was at Allegheny High School. At first, she stood still with her hands clenched and eyes scanning her surroundings. She heard a noise and started running down a hallway. The sound of her sneakers slapping on the tile floor was secondary to her heartbeat pounding in her ears. She looked over her shoulder and saw the masked man rushing forward with his gun aimed at her. She turned right and opened the first classroom door she came to. She stepped inside, closing the door quietly and pressing her forehead against the wood of the door. She could hear his footsteps coming closer. She turned to look for a place to hide. The grisly sight took her breath away.

Raven's eyes widened when she saw Addie sitting in the corner of the room with her hands wrapped around her knees, rocking. She called out, but her best friend couldn't hear her over the deafening sounds of people crying and howling, reaching with limp arms for help.

She was confused, squinting through the thick noise, like when we turn the car radio down to see street signs better. There was a woman next to Addie, holding her. Raven tried to get to them, but she couldn't move past all the dead and dying people. Bodies were everywhere. Some people were barely alive, reaching out to her for help. The color red was endless—the color of death.

Raven took a few steps forward, still screaming Addie's name. Finally, her friend looked up. Her face was covered in blood. Her eyes were wide and flat. Raven looked at the person sitting next to Addie, holding her only friend. It was Mrs. Fisher, Raven's favorite teacher, the woman who had helped free her from Sable's house.

Mrs. Fisher had a bullet wound in the center of her forehead. Raven breathed a sigh of relief. The teacher had survived, and Addie had lived, too. It was a miracle. Maybe her life could be whole again. That she could go on and do the things she'd planned with both by her side.

Suddenly, all the screaming and crying stopped. Chills crept up Raven's spine from the eerie silence. Something was wrong. She frantically looked around the room. Then in the corner, she saw the man dressed in black. His ski mask was in place, his rifle dangling by his side. He was walking as if he were at the park on a beautiful spring morning. The fear of entrapment escalated inside of her.

She shook it off and replaced her fear with rage. *Who do you think you are? Look what you've done to all these people.*

Raven's stomach was twisted with spasms, and she pressed her palms against it, trying to untangle the pain.

Matthew was moving toward her faster now. He walked with the gait of a common street thug—a boy with a gun—the only power he possessed.

She wouldn't let Addie and Mrs. Fisher die—not again. This time she'd give her own life. She'd been given a second chance. Her head snapped to the two people she loved, and her mouth dropped open when her eyes pored over their lifeless bodies, heaped on top of each other.

Raven dropped to her knees and pressed her hands over her face. "Noooooooo," she shrieked.

She crawled on her hands and knees, trying to dodge the people sprawled out under her. She kept her eyes on the floor, the empty stares of people no longer there. The journey across the room seemed to take forever, as though a million years had passed.

She looked back over her shoulder and saw Matthew coming at her in his full murderer gear. Her stomach retched, and she moved quicker. When she reached Addie and Mrs. Fisher, they were already gone. But still, she sat with her back to them, arms spread open, protecting them against her brother.

Matthew approached with swiftness and placed the end of his rifle against her head. His eyes looked like two pools of black ink. She was shaking violently and looked down at her hands. One of them was holding the gun he'd given her. She lifted it quickly and shot her brother. He fell backward and she rushed forward, putting her body over his.

"Why?" she screamed hysterically.

She pounded on his chest, on his heart that was no longer beating, screaming at him, berating him, professing her eternal hatred for him.

"You ruined all these lives and mine, too!" she yelled.

Matthew's eyes opened, and he glared at her one last time.

***

Raven's eyes snapped open, and she was in her bed at the shelter. She was covered in sweat, and tears were streaming down her face. Her stomach was burning, and she could barely breathe. She sat up and took in several long breaths through her nose.

"It was only a dream," she murmured to herself.

It was one version of the most terrible day of her life. Raven would continue to have recurring nightmares and live those horrible moments for a long time to come.

Chapter One

The week following the school shooting, Raven Ledger thought her life was over. She found herself alone, shunned from the community where she'd lived for ten years. Going out in public had become dangerous for her. On top of being fearful for her life, she carried guilt for her brother's senseless crime and sympathy for the victims and their families.

She grappled with unrelenting hate for her brother, the boy she'd loved a week ago. She struggled to forget the brother she knew and see the demon he had become. It was difficult to hate Matthew after loving him for so long. A fond memory of Matthew would randomly pop into her mind, making her question what she knew now. It was a constant internal battle between love and hate, good and evil, life and death.

Then would come the bursts of self-pity: she was alone and rejected by those around her. She believed the worst thing in life, equal to being unloved, was to be unwanted.

Since the school shootings, her life had become miserable. She was constantly battling the media who wanted to exploit her. She knew speaking to them, telling everyone how sorry she was, would lead the Kensington Hoods to her. Five of the victims were associated with the gang and killed by her brother, and they held her accountable for the murders.

Matthew had altered the lives of many families. The tragedy played out on the news—and the world watched as mourners attended twenty-one funerals. The people in her hometown of Kensington, Philadelphia, whether there was a direct relationship with the victims or not, blamed her. They wanted to see Raven punished for her brother's sins.

Risking her safety, Raven had attended the funerals to respect those who had perished at her brother's hands. She lived in the shadows, wearing a disguise as she watched families bury their teenage children and children bury their mothers or fathers. She wanted to tell the mourners how sorry she was for what happened to the people they loved.

Raven wore her hair tucked under a baseball cap, oversized clothes, and sunglasses. She looked more like a boy, and when she took off her costume after returning to the youth shelter, she saw a pathetic, useless girl in the mirror, who carried her brother's weight in guilt on her back.

Raven had attended the last funeral where she said goodbye to her only friend Addie. As she stood in line for the bus that would bring her back to the shelter, she heard a girl yelling with red-hot anger. Her head lifted toward the familiar voice.

"There's that motherfucking bitch. She's getting on the bus," Blanco yelled to four other girls. "She thinks she can hide from us. That whore needs to pay for our dead brothers and sisters."

Raven pushed forward, the last to step onto the bus. She whipped her sunglasses off and looked into the bus driver's eyes. "Close the door!" she screamed in a frantic tone. "Drive. Hurry! Please!"

The driver, an older woman, looked in the direction of where Raven was pointing. She knew the area well and quickly closed the door, peeling away from the bus stop.

"Sit down," the driver said in a steady voice.

Raven plopped in the seat behind the woman. She slouched as they drove by Blanco and her friends. She watched as Blanco screamed and waved her hands. Her heart fluttered and her stomach spun with nausea.

If Blanco gets her hands on me, she will kill me.

Seeing the uncontrollable rage on Blanco's face was an awakening. It differed from when they lived at Sable's. Blanco had the same angry look, but now, she could see the teen was bloodthirsty. Raven cringed remembering the savage beatings she'd endured from the girl. Now, Blanco's lips were pulled back to bare her teeth, and she could hear the guttural roar that strung out Raven's name as the bus pulled away.

Raven returned to the youth shelter with her hands still shaking. She kept looking over her shoulder and into the dark corners of the shelter, waiting for Blanco to be there.

Paula, Addie's mom, had been right. The Kensington Hoods and Sisterhoods were hunting her. The street gang blamed Raven for what Matthew had done, and while she knew it wasn't true and that she had taken no part in it, Raven couldn't blame people for hating her.

As time moved forward, Raven's anger and bewilderment grew. She hated being held accountable for something she didn't do. Yet, when her bitterness grew toward those who hated her and blamed her, she would force herself to remember that day in school. It kept her grounded and focused on who mattered—the families of those who lost their loved ones. She thought about the victims every day and inside every minute.

Through it all, there was no room for her grief. Matthew had stolen that from her, too.

***

Raven had been hiding in the shelter, a recluse that only traveled for necessities at night. She would ride the bus to places outside of the immediate neighborhood to buy necessities. She had been afraid to step outside in broad daylight since seeing Blanco.

Six weeks after the shootings, Raven turned eighteen. It was the day after her birthday that the news was blaring on the television. The youth shelter residents were all watching, and then, Raven's face filled the screen.

"Holy shit," Pam, one resident stated. She turned to Raven. "That's you. Your brother is the one who shot up that school?"

Raven's skin blistered under her clothing. Ignoring the girl, Raven went to look for a staff member.

"Jerry?"

The twenty-five-year-old Black man smiled at her. "Oh, hey, Raven. What's up?"

Raven crossed her arms over her stomach and her eyes welled.

Jerry rushed to her. "Are you okay? Come on. Let's go into the office." He led her a few feet away and, once inside, closed the door. "Did something happen with one of the other residents?"

Raven shook her head. She pulled in deep breaths to squelch her emotions. "I turned eighteen yesterday. My picture was on the news just now . . . and a picture of my brother. They know who I am."

"Oh no." He put his hand over his forehead. "We should've anticipated that. All right. Here's what I'm going to do. I'll call Officer Townsend. You remember the police officer that originally brought you here?"

Raven nodded. "Yeah, I liked her." Tears streaked down her cheeks, and she brushed them away.

Jerry's eyes saddened. "Caitlin Townsend is a good egg. She has a lot of compassion for people."

"Okay, but what can she do about it?" Raven asked. She wanted an immediate solution. She needed something—anything to make her heart stop pounding in quick, hard thuds.

Jerry shoved his hands into his pant pockets. "Well, I think she can help us figure out how to protect you."

"How? The whole place knows who I am now," she stated with annoyance. She leaned into Jerry. "I know that people blame me, and if I try, I can understand why they do. But we both know I have a gang in Kensington looking for me. Now that my identity has been leaked and the girls here know who I am, they'll be coming for me."

Jerry jerked his head back. "Okay. Sit tight and I'll call Caitlin." He walked to the door and looked over his shoulder. "Stay here and keep the door closed." Then he was gone.

As Raven sat alone in the room, she was convinced there was nowhere she'd be able to hide to remain safe . . . alive. She longed for a friendly face . . . someone she could trust. But the safety and security she'd built for herself was gone. Everything that belonged to her had vanished in fourteen minutes on a beautiful spring morning.

Chapter Two

Raven sat across from Officer Townsend and Jerry. Her belly was flip-flopping, and her legs were bouncing under the table. She kept looking into the room where the other residents were sitting. They were whispering to each other, and she worried that one of them was affiliated with the Kensington gang.

Raven looked back at the policewoman. "Where am I gonna go? I don't have any family. No friends," she cried.

Townsend touched her arm. "Raven, I know this is very difficult for you."

Raven stood. "You do? Did your brother walk into a high school and kill a bunch of people for no good reason?" Her voice was mixed with anger and sarcasm.

"No. Look, Raven, I'm trying to help you here. If you'd rather I'd go . . ."

"No." Raven's tone was remorseful. She sat again, closer to the woman this time. "I'm sorry. I don't mean to be an asshole. I can't figure out what I'm supposed to do or who I'm supposed to be now."

Officer Townsend placed a hand over Raven's. "Okay. Here's what we're going to do. There is a shelter in South Philadelphia. There are very few people who know about it." Then she dropped her eyes to the table.

Raven's eyebrows lifted and a wave of panic pulsed through her. "What's the catch?"

"It's a shelter for women who were convicted of violent crimes. A place where they stay after they're done serving their prison sentence."

Raven shook her head in disbelief. "What kind of violent crimes?" Her eyes were wide, and she crossed her arms over her chest.

"The worst kind of crime. Women who killed their children. Women who took part in breaking and entering that resulted in murder. Arsonists and armed robbers. Those kinds of women. Generally, the people of our society who lacked good judgment and morals when they committed their crimes. While they've served their time and have presumably been rehabilitated, you need to know this so you can understand and be careful if you go there."

"So, we are talking about women who are like my brother." Raven pressed her back against the chair. She raked her fingers through her hair. Then she blew out a long breath, emptying her lungs along with her fear into the room. "Isn't it dangerous to be around people like them?"

"Yes, it is. But I think it's more dangerous for you to be here . . . in the same neighborhood as the Kensington Hoods and Sisterhoods. The thing about the other shelter is that it's kept secret because of the people who live there. Like you, they are people who others want to hurt. So you have a much better chance of staying hidden there."

"Officer Townsend, I don't know if I have the stomach for something like that—to be around people who have done those things."

The woman stood. "I understand. But right now, it's the safest alternative I have to offer you."

Raven's eyes moved to Jerry's, and he lifted his chin in agreement. "It's dangerous for you and all of the residents if you stay here," he admitted. "I think Caitlin has come up with a good option." He gave her a sympathetic smile. "It's worth a try."

Raven dragged her eyes back to the officer. "So if they were in prison, then are these women older than me?"

"Yes. They are mostly women in their twenties and thirties."

"Well," Raven said, running a hand across her forehead, "what if there are women from the Kensington Sisterhoods there?"

Officer Townsend shook her head. "I wouldn't have picked that shelter if I thought there were gang members there. These are women who had no criminal history before committing their crimes. They've had no previous affiliations with gangs or cartels. That includes the time that they were incarcerated. That's a requirement for placement at this shelter."

"Um, that doesn't make any sense. How does the shelter know for sure these women aren't associated with gangs or cartels?"

"Well, the police are the only people who place the women there. We use intelligence to determine if a woman has a history with gangs or cartels. Nothing is a hundred percent certain, but we do our best. We are as thorough as possible. We haven't had a breach yet. For the most part, these women have nowhere else to go after they've served their time." She tilted her head. "Even they deserve a second chance."

Raven's eyes moved to the floor. "I get it, but it sounds dangerous to live with women who've committed violent crimes. I just got out of high school. I haven't even lived yet."

"I understand. But again, my point is that the women who live there are looking to stay hidden, the same as you. I think you'll find that some of the women there are quite nice. I hope that because you are younger, one or two of them will want to look after you, and they'll be protective."

Raven rubbed her eyes with the butt of her palms. "Okay, I'll go. I don't have much of a choice. Do I?" She didn't need an answer to her question; she already knew.

Officer Townsend glanced at the girl. "Good. I was hoping you'd go. I called them before I came here to see you. Someone left three days ago. They're expecting you."

Raven stood and strode to the door. "I'll grab my things. Would you be able to give me a ride there?"

Townsend nodded. "Yes, that was my plan. Raven, I think it's the best place for you to be right now. For your protection. The people who run the shelter are outstanding. Many of them are ex-military and retired police. They know how to protect the shelter and the people in it."

***

Thirty minutes later, Raven stepped outside with Officer Townsend. She was surprised when there wasn't a squad car waiting. Instead, the policewoman led her to her personal vehicle.

"How come we're riding in this car? Isn't it safer to be in a police car?" Raven asked. Her eyes were bouncing around, looking for who might be lurking.

"It's not a good idea to show up in a police car to the shelter since it's not well-known. We have to use discretion when we go there," she explained.

"Right, that makes sense." Raven rubbed the back of her stiff neck. "Do you think this is ever going to end for me? Will I be looking over my shoulder for the rest of my life?"

The officer didn't know what the future held for the girl and didn't want to give her false hope. She pinched her lips together. "There are some people who have very long memories. They're usually the more volatile folks like the girls looking for you from the Kensington Sisterhoods. But I hope that someday you'll be able to put this behind you."

Raven stared out the front window and shook her head. "No. I'm not looking to forget what happened or put it behind me. I'm willing to live with it here." She patted her chest over her heart. "It's important that I never forget all the people that my brother killed. What I want is to stop being hunted and hated by people that know nothing about me." She turned her head and looked out the passenger window. "I killed my brother, and even though it was the right thing to do, it still hurts. But see, I'm not supposed to grieve, so I've held all my feelings in. My grief insults people . . . and oddly, I understand that."

Officer Townsend glanced at her. "Raven, that's heavy stuff for a person your age. Everyone has a right to grieve a loss. You have a right to grieve the death of your brother," she hedged.

Raven widened her eyes. "No, I could never. It would be wrong. Matthew destroyed so many lives, including mine. I hate him . . . I hate what he did. I despise what he made me do to him to prevent more people from dying. I was there. He was heartless and cruel. I'll never forgive him. If my brother had loved me, he would've told me his plan . . . given me a chance to stop him. Do you get that, Officer Townsend? Does it make sense? Because sometimes, I feel like I'm going crazy. There was a time not too long ago when I adored Matthew. What he did changed everything for me and in me."

The officer nodded. "It does make sense, Raven. Hey, listen," she said, patting the girl's hand. "How about from now on you call me Caitlin?"

Raven smirked. "Sure. Will you be able to stay with me a while—at the new shelter?"

"I can stay with you while they process you in, but then I have to get going."

Raven let out a sigh of relief. "Caitlin, thanks for listening to me. I haven't had anyone to talk to since this happened. I've been very lonely."

"Sure thing. I'm always here if you need me."

Raven settled back against the leather seat, watching Kensington zoom by, as she left it behind her.

Chapter Three

As Raven left North Philly and crossed into South Philly, there was a drastic change in the scenery. She looked around her, amazed. It was nice compared to where she'd been living. It was a thriving neighborhood. South Philly was teeming with people walking the streets. Couples holding hands, parents with small children, elderly people sitting in clusters drinking coffee and laughing. They were shopping and sitting outside of cafés and restaurants.

She stared out the passenger window. "I had no idea South Philly was this nice. How can I have lived this close my whole life and not know it was so . . . normal here? A twenty-minute car ride changes everything." She turned her head to face Caitlin. "It's beautiful."

Caitlin chuckled. "Well, fewer drug addicts and alcoholics are hanging on the streets, but trust me, you can find the same trouble here that you can find in North Philly. There are criminals here, too, and of course, the Italian mob has a huge presence."

"Yeah, I heard about that. But it looks like I can walk down the street without dodging bodies. Or the worst is when I would get used needles stuck in the soles of my sneakers." She let out a low whistle. "Man, who knew it could be this nice?"

"I agree. It's a big difference from where you were living. Don't get confused, there are certain sections of South Philly where the homeless are concentrated. But overall, the areas with the highest homelessness and the most crime are in North Philly, then Center City." Caitlin pulled in a breath through her nose. "The area you'll be staying in is on the fringe of Center City."

Raven leaned her head to the side. "What are you saying? Is that bad?"

Caitlin shrugged. "It's not bad, but it isn't like this neighborhood."

"Well, that sucks." The girl smiled. "I'll still be closer to South Philly, though. At least it'll be easier to visit."

Caitlin put on her turn signal and made a right onto a street. "You'll still be in South Philly but not as nice as this part. Maybe someday you'll live in the better area of South Philly and things will be more pleasant for you than they are today. You need to have goals," she sang with a smile.

Raven huffed. "Yeah, all I'm trying to do is get by . . . not get strung up by a lynch mob. That's it. It's that simple."

Ten minutes later, Caitlin parked her car next to a curb. "Here we are."

Raven looked around. She'd noticed how the neighborhood was more run-down. It still wasn't as bad as North Philly, but it wasn't like the heart of South Philly. Her eyes darted around. More homeless people milled about and slept on the sidewalks. There were no restaurants or cute cafés here. It was more industrial. Rigid. Depressing.

***

Raven stood inside the entrance of the one-story shelter. She looked at the sign above the door, Last Call. She followed Caitlin through a security door where they were buzzed in.

They entered into a large open sitting area. It was institutional, but not sterile, with its plastic chairs and futon couches. A large television sat in front of the rows of folding chairs. To the left and right were doors leading to bedrooms.

Raven was checked in and given a card to swipe to leave and enter the shelter.

Then the woman on the other side of the desk kept her eyes on a paper in front of her. She ground out in a smoker's throaty voice, "Okay, here are the rules: no visitors, don't tell anyone where you're staying, no drinking or drugs on the premises. Don't steal anyone's stuff or you'll be thrown out. Don't lie to any of the people running the shelter. No violence, weapons, or any form of aggression will be tolerated."

Raven fidgeted in her chair, not because she'd have to refrain or work hard not to break the rules, but because she'd be living among women who needed those rules. It was frightening.

She looked at Caitlin and blinked rapidly. "Are you sure this is the right place for me?" she whispered.

Caitlin pulled her to the side. "Yes, I'm sure. Look, go with the flow. Be yourself. These women have spent years in prison. All they want is to go on with their lives. I'm not saying they'll all be nice, but at least give them a chance."

"You're right. I'm acting like they're bad people the same way strangers are treating me."

Caitlin lifted her finger in the air, pointing into Raven's face. "Oh, that's not what I'm saying at all. These women have done unthinkable things. You're not the same as the women who live here. I'm telling you to be open, but guarded. Do you understand?"

Raven nodded. "I spent seven years with an evil foster mother . . . I understand."

"Good."

When the paperwork was complete, a woman entered the room where Raven and Caitlin had been waiting.

"Hello, I'm Meg. I work here at the shelter," she said, extending her hand to Raven.

"I'm Raven," she mumbled.

"Yep, I know who you are. Your brother was the school shooter at Allegheny High School."

Raven visibly cringed. "Um, I . . . um, yeah."

"Okay, well, it's clear that makes you uncomfortable, and that's understandable. But in here, you need to learn to sit with that dark cloud hanging over your head. Everyone living in this shelter has a black cloud following them. Don't let them tell you anything different. Your face is plastered all over the news, so it won't be easy to hide who you are. But here's the thing, most of these women are so ashamed of what they've done that they won't even know how to handle you."

Raven's eyebrows pulled together. "What do you mean? Handle me?"

Meg nodded. "Yeah, it's no different in here than it is on the streets, in corporations, even the government. Everyone in here is in a pecking order. Women who killed kids are at the bottom along with sex traffickers. Above them are breaking and entering, which ended in murder or kidnapping. Above them are arsonists. And those at the top of the hierarchy are the women who beat, stabbed, or shot their lovers to death for various reasons. But don't be mistaken, all the women sleeping within these walls are prone to violence."

Raven clutched her hands together tighter and stared at her fingertips. "Are you saying this is like being in prison?"

"No. Of course it isn't. You can leave the shelter between certain hours. Exceptions will be made if you have a job with odd hours. You can shower whenever you want, and while we have scheduled meals for breakfast, lunch, and dinner, the chow hall is open to get coffee, water, soda, and some apples and bananas all the time."

The girl nodded. A trickle of relief ran through her.

Meg lifted a mug of coffee to her lips and took a sip. "So, we have all of these women who are criminals and have spent time in some very rough prisons. Then there's you. Let's see, you have a brother who committed mass murder at a high school, but the police have determined you had nothing to do with what he did. A lot of these women have school-age children, so they relate to the suffering of the families in Kensington. The fact that you killed your brother will give you a higher ranking, more pull, so to speak. Keep that in mind . . . Use it to your advantage."

"Meg, I had to kill my twin brother to stop him from killing more people. Honestly, I didn't know how else to make him stop. How am I supposed to use that to help me?"

Meg moved closer to the girl. "By telling the women in here that you weren't about to let one more person die. That you understood these were other people's kids, and that you weren't about to sit by and let him continue. That it didn't matter that it was your brother. Understand?"

Raven nodded but her hands were shaking. "I'm nervous," she admitted.

"Of course you are," Meg stated lightly. "Try to relax. You'll do fine here. If anyone gives you crap, you see whoever is on duty. We are all capable of handling these women, and you'll learn how to do the same."

Raven tilted her head. "I don't want to learn how to handle other people. I want to get on with my life." She glanced at Caitlin. Raven still wasn't sure that she had come to the right place.

Meg clapped her hands together.

On edge, Raven jumped in her seat.

"Are you ready to meet your roommate? It's two women to a room here. I think you'll like the person we paired you with," Meg explained.

Raven followed Meg from the office into the common room. Her heart quickened. As she walked through, the women watched her. Some faces looked friendly, and others looked deadly.

Raven straightened her spine and pulled her shoulders back. She was trying to look confident to the women who already knew too much about her.

Chapter Four

Raven followed Meg into room number eight. Inside the bedroom, there were two beds pushed up against the right and left walls. There was a nightstand and dresser for each occupant. It was not fancy, and the bed was actually a cot, like at Sable's house, but it was much more private than the open arrangement at the youth shelter.

"Dalton, this is Raven Ledger." Meg turned to Raven. "This is Dalton Harris."

Dalton was lying on her back, holding a photograph in her hand. She looked Raven up and down. Then her eyes shot to Meg. "She rooming with me?"

Meg nodded. "She could use someone to show her around. She'll need to know where the bathroom and chow room is."

Dalton chuckled. "We call it the cafeteria, not the chow room."

Meg pinched her lips together. "When you spend time in the Marines, we call it chow. You know that group of people who fight for your country and all of your freedoms. Chow room means food. We'd eat and keep on protecting this country."

Dalton saluted her in a mocking gesture. "Well, I wish you had fought for my freedom from prison," she cackled. She sat upright. "Come on, Meg. You know I'm messing with you."

Meg gave her a terse smile. "Military people don't like to be messed with. Anyway, you'll show Raven around then?"

"Yeah, I'll show . . . Wait a minute." She wagged a finger at Raven. "Ain't you that girl whose brother shot up that school?"

Raven's heart dropped to the pit of her stomach. "Yes."

Dalton tapped her index finger on her chin. "Didn't you wipe him out? You shot him with his gun," she chuckled.

Raven nodded. "That's right. I killed him so other kids didn't have to die."

"Yeah, your high school picture was on the news this morning. I heard about all the shit that happened. The news showed pictures of all the people who were murdered. I was watching that shit with the other women. Some people think you saved lives, but there are a whole bunch of them who think you helped that prick and plugged him so he wouldn't rat you out. So did you help him?"

Raven narrowed her eyes. "I killed him, didn't I? I would never kill anyone, let alone my brother if I didn't have to. As for knowing what he was going to do, I had no idea—"

Dalton cut her off. "But ain't you two twins? Aren't twins supposed to know that shit? You know, get weird vibes or some of that telepathy?"

Raven pushed her long brown hair over her shoulders and focused her fiery green eyes on Dalton. She was putting on a show, but she would not be intimidated.

Raven shrugged. "I didn't get a vibe," she stated firmly. "All I knew was to pull the trigger to stop him." She turned her back on Dalton and moved to the dresser. She plopped her canvas bag on the top, unzipped it, and started putting clothes in the drawers.

Dalton stood and took a few steps closer to the girl. "Ah right. I feel you. But you know, the women in here are gonna have a lot of questions for you. It ain't easy to understand how someone can murder all those people."

"I didn't do it. You need to get that through your head," Raven barked, annoyed at the accusation. She held eye contact with Dalton. "Besides, I have a lot of questions for you, too." She leaned closer to Dalton. "So here's what I will tell you. When you can figure out why my brother murdered all those people, then you can explain it to me. I don't fucking know how he could do it either, and I'm sick of people asking me to explain it."

Some of Raven's bravado came from Meg's warning, but an intolerance and imbalance were brewing in her belly. That a woman who had committed a serious crime thought she owed *her* an explanation pissed her off.

Meg and Caitlin had watched the exchange. Both women held small grins on their lips. They could see that Raven could hold her own.

"All right," Meg interrupted. "So you're good?"

Raven nodded. "I'm fine."

"Great," Meg mumbled, leaving the room.

The girl finished unpacking her bag and went over to Caitlin. "Come on. I'll walk you out."

As the two women left the room, Raven looked over her shoulder at Dalton. "I'll be right back. We can talk some more."

Dalton put her hand at the base of her neck. "Yeah, sure. I'll show you around, too." Her demeanor had turned from cocky to accommodating.

Outside, Caitlin opened her arms, and Raven stepped into them. "You did good with Dalton. You're quite the actor."

Raven pulled her head back. "That wasn't all an act. I meant what I said. I'm tired of having to defend myself, and I'm not about to do it here. I want to be left alone to find my way. I don't think that's too much to ask."

As Raven walked back into the building, she hoped to have the courage and strength to make it to the next part of her life.

***

It was thirty minutes later when Raven returned to her room. Dalton was sitting on her bed, waiting for her.

"Listen, I didn't mean nothing by asking those questions," Dalton admitted.

Raven met her eyes. "It's fine. I'll get over it. Like you said, there's going to be a lot more questions from the other women in here."

"Did Meg warn you, too?" she asked with a smirk.

Raven relaxed her shoulders and smiled back. "Yeah, she told me because I'm all over the news. But I got mad at you because I'm tired of being the target for something I didn't do."

"Yeah, shit. I get that. And you know, I remember having my face all over the news, too. Man, they were some tough days. I couldn't go nowhere without people yelling at me or throwing things at me. My husband was a popular man in our neighborhood."

Raven sat on her cot. "Why? What did you do to your husband?"

"I killed that ugly prick. The bastard had beaten me for the first two years of our marriage. I was scared to death of that asshole. Then, one night he came home with another man." She moved her gaze away from Raven. "He forced me to have sex with random dudes for money. He brought home guys on the block or that he found in nearby bars. They'd come into my house, and he'd let them do whatever they wanted to me."

Raven's hand flew to her mouth. "O my God. I-I-I can't even imagine something like that happening."

Dalton chuckled. "Me neither... until it did. My old man was a gambler. He took out a lot of loans with the different mobs. He'd borrow money from the Italian mob to pay what he owed to the Irish mob and then do it again in reverse. He'd skim some money, pay some back, and lose it gambling until he dove deeper and deeper into debt. So he'd bring in these guys and get paid for the things he forced me to do."

"Why didn't you run away?" Raven asked.

"Yeah, lots of people ask me that question. I've asked myself that question, too. I was brainwashed, too scared he'd find me and kill me. He beat me all the time, and he'd let those guys who screwed me beat me, too ... if that's what they paid for." She shook her head. "It was bad. I don't have a good reason for staying other than I was more afraid of what he'd do to me if I left him than if I stayed with him."

Raven moved to Dalton's cot.

The woman wrinkled her forehead when the girl made the move but said nothing. "You sure do get comfortable real fast. I didn't invite you onto my cot."

"Oh, I can go back to my own," she said, blushing and rising to her feet.

"Nah, it's okay. You can sit next to me."

Raven sat down again. She gave Dalton a side-glance. "Is it okay if I ask how you killed your husband?"

Indifferent, Dalton shrugged. "I waited until he was asleep. Then I grabbed the biggest knife I could find in the kitchen drawer and I slit his throat. He didn't die right away, so I stabbed him in the chest another five times. I wasn't letting that motherfucker walk outta there alive. Nope. I sure wasn't."

"How long were you in prison?"

Dalton scratched her head as if counting the time. "Ten years. I was twenty-one when I got sent inside."

"Twenty-one! How old were you when you got married?"

Dalton tilted her head. "Ah, I was a bitty baby. About the same age as you are now. See, I married him the day I turned eighteen; he was thirty-three. Shortly after my twentieth birthday, he started bringing those guys home to fuck me. I killed him nine months after it started. I couldn't take it anymore."

"When did you get out of prison?" Raven asked. She was so curious about the woman.

"A month ago," Dalton stated.

"So you're thirty-one?"

"That's right."

Raven shook her head. "Jeez, I thought my life was the only shit show. Was prison awful?"

"Girl, please. You have no idea. That ain't no place you ever wanna be."

Raven stood and leaned against her dresser. "Are you going to show me around this place? I have to pee."

Dalton got up and moved to the door. "Yep, I was waiting on your slow ass," she said with a smile.

She let Dalton go first and followed closely behind her.

When Raven walked into the common room, she immediately knew there would be obstacles she'd need to face head-on.

Chapter Five

Inside the common room, Raven's eyes were cast downward. She was hoping no one would notice her. Her ears filled with the murmuring of the other women. Her eyes lifted and she found eighteen women staring at her. She glared back, taking in the different faces—most friendly but some not so much.

Several excruciating seconds ticked by until a burly woman stood from her seat. "You that crazy bitch that killed her crazier brother?"

Raven remained still as though her feet were mounted in cement. "Ex-ex-excuse me?"

"Ex-ex-excuse m-m-m-me," the woman mocked. "What? Did I stutter?"

A burst of adrenaline rushed through her veins and filled her to the brim with anger. She assessed the woman. *A little older than me.* Her dull black hair hung to the center of her back. She was sloppy and unkempt inside her wrinkled clothing.

Raven lifted her chin. "Yeah, I killed my brother. But I did it to save people. How about you? Have you killed anyone?"

"Oh shit," Dalton whispered in Raven's ear. "Nobody fucks with Sloane."

Raven's head snapped toward Dalton. Her eyes were wide and her mouth was gaping open. She looked over at Sloane heading in her direction.

Don't panic, Ledger, she told herself.

"Who the fuck do you think you're talking to?" Sloane barked inches from her face.

Raven put her palms up. "Look, you insulted me first. You can't say nasty shit to me and then get insulted when I come at you. You know, you're gonna get the same respect you're putting out." She held her ground, back erect and face fixed in a scowl.

Sloane narrowed her eyes and watched Raven. Sloane's face was etched with hard lines . . . lines caused by a rough life. "You better watch yourself. You're barking up the wrong bitch tree, little girl. I don't take no shit from nobody," Sloane stated, cocking her head to the side.

Dalton put her arm between the two young women. "Sloane, she didn't mean nothing by it. Damn, girl, cut her a break. She just got here," she reasoned.

"Oh yeah, Dalton? What's she doing here? Huh? She didn't spend no time in prison. What? Now they're bringing in killers that ain't done their time on the inside like the rest of us?"

Raven glared at Sloane. "I'm here because I need a place to stay. I ain't no different than you. I had bad things happen to me. I don't know your story, but I'm guessing you had a shitty life, too."

Sloane's frown eased. She glanced down at her old sneakers. "Yeah, I had a hard life. So what?" She fanned a hand over the room. "We all had a hard life. That's why we did things to people." She pointed into Raven's face. "You keep yourself in check."

Sloane turned and went back to the women she'd been sitting with. She gave her friend next to her a high five and sat down.

Dalton grabbed Raven's hand and pulled her toward the cafeteria. When they were out of earshot, she leaned into the girl. "All right, listen to me good. You need to be careful with some of these women. See Sloane, she got mad at her parents because they wouldn't continue to fund her drug habit and she set their house on fire while they were sleeping. They both got out, but not without severe injuries. She's someone you need to avoid."

"How old is she?" Raven asked, barely listening and still seething with anger.

"Sloane is twenty-three. She got lucky her parents didn't die in the fire. She was only seventeen when she did it. She ended up serving six years. Two in juvie and four in a women's prison somewhere in western Pennsylvania."

"Why is she so rude? She's finally out of prison and can move on with her life."

Dalton sighed. "I don't know. She's had a tough life. She says her parents ruined her. She started doing drugs when she was fourteen. By the time she turned seventeen, she was already locked up . . . She grew up on drugs, crime, and prison. Prison life is hard for those of us who made it to twenty on the outside; it's unbearable for kids who hardly know their asses from a hole in the ground. She hasn't been out in the world yet. Went from home to prison to here. Those prisons are battlegrounds. They aren't meant for regular folks."

Regular folks? Are you kidding?

"Oh, well, it sounds like Sloane has been through a lot. I understand it. That sucks for her."

Dalton stopped walking, her sneakers squeaking to a halt on the tile floor. "It sounds like you feel bad for her. That girl will carve you into a million pieces. Honey, she ain't someone you should have sympathy for. She also has two women who hang out with her here. The three of them are violent, they feed off of each other, and all of them have committed senseless crimes."

Raven tilted her head. "Are there crimes that aren't senseless?"

Dalton scoffed. "Yeah. Killing your abusive husband that turned you into a prostitute in your own home."

The girl nodded. "Yeah, I see your point. But . . . but . . ."

"But what?"

"But did you ever tell the police what was happening to you? Getting your husband arrested so that you wouldn't have to spend time in prison for him, too."

Dalton looked away from Raven, her embarrassment reddening her cheeks. "Sure. I thought about it. Then I thought about what would happen to me if he found out. If they didn't arrest him. If he was a free man, I'd be on the run or worse yet, stuck living with him. See, you don't know because you haven't been there."

Raven jerked her head back. "It's true that I don't know about someone making me have sex with men. But I know all about having to tell secrets that are supposed to never leave the house and being beaten."

Dalton shifted her gaze back to the girl. "Oh yeah?"

Raven nodded. "Yeah."

Dalton grabbed her hand. "There's a lot more to Raven Ledger than meets the eye. Is that what you're saying?"

"Something like that," Raven stated with a smile.

Chapter Six

Over the next week, Raven tried to settle into the Last Call. She did her best to make it a temporary home. She wasn't different than the other women, after all; Raven had shot and killed her brother. She knew what it was like to take someone else's life. The difference between her and some of the others was living with the memories of having to watch innocent people die.

She had heeded Dalton's warning to steer clear of Sloane, but the news reports about the school shootings were endless, which brought attention to her every day. It was a constant reminder that her brother had betrayed and destroyed an entire community. His goal had been met. Sloane reminded her daily that she must have the same insane blood pumping through her veins, and that was a reason for the others to watch her.

Matthew's repulsive crime had left behind him the fourth-worst deadly school shooting in America. He had taken twenty-one souls that day, and the media frenzy was relentless. The news fed off of the victims, the victims' families, and communities across the country. Given the opportunity, many people would spew venom about how much they hated Matthew and the family who raised him. They interviewed many young men and staff from the boys home where he lived. As ratings went up, so did the anxiety of parents across the nation.

It had been a little more than two weeks since the shootings. Philadelphia was reeling from the tragedy that occurred in their backyard, and the streets of Kensington were still buzzing with hateful energy for the shooter and his sister. Unable to watch another second of the news, Raven went into the office and sat across from Meg.

The woman looked up from a crossword puzzle she was solving. "Hey."

"Hi," Raven said, leaning her elbows on the table between them. "I need a break from this place."

Meg put down her pen. "You've been here a week. Most of the women out there have been here for months."

"I know," Raven moaned. "But I don't wanna sit around here and watch TV all day. I need to get a job so that I can save money and get a place of my own. That was my plan before my brother screwed it up for me."

Meg sneered. "Okay, so you'll look for a job then." She reached behind her and grabbed the local paper. She flipped through the thin pages and turned the paper around for Raven. "Here's the Help Wanted section. Go through and see if you qualify for any of them."

Raven pulled the paper toward her. She ran her finger down the ads.

Meanwhile, Meg went back to her puzzle.

Twenty minutes later, Raven looked at the woman. "Okay," she said, moving to the edge of her chair. "There are four jobs I think I can do. Two are at fast-food restaurants. There's a cashier position at the Dollar General, and"—she lifted her finger in the air and broadened her smile—"there's a job as a barback. I don't know what that is, but it says no experience is necessary. The only thing about that one is the hours. Two to eleven."

"First things first. A barback is like a bartender's personal helper. You would make sure all the bartenders have clean glasses, enough garnishes, and ice. They also bring liquor bottles and beer when they run low. The nice thing about a barback is if you're good, those bartenders will give you excellent tips."

Raven looked at the ad, then up at Meg. "How do you know so much about it?"

"I was a barback out of high school before I joined the Marines."

"Oh. So you think I should apply for it then?" Raven asked.

"Yeah, why not? Out of the four jobs you mentioned, that'll be the highest paying one. Where's it at?"

"Guilty Pleasure," she read from the newspaper.

"Oh shit. Okay," Meg said in a snarky tone, shaking her head.

"What?"

Meg lifted her nose into the air. "Guilty Pleasure is a gentleman's club. Look, there isn't anything wrong with it, but you will be around a lot of horny men and women who are barely dressed."

Raven tilted her head. "What do you mean?" she asked in an uncertain tone.

"It's a strip bar," Meg stated.

Raven's eyebrows squished together for a prolonged moment. Then she leaned forward. "Ooh. You mean where girls dance naked."

"Well, it depends on the club. Most of them are topless but not completely naked. They do wear dental floss up the crack of their asses," she said, belting out a laugh.

Raven smiled but didn't get what was so funny. "So I should work there?"

Meg gave her a shrug. "I mean, it's a strip club. If you're into that kind of thing, then I guess you should." She looked away from Raven. "Try not to become a stripper, though," she griped.

"Why are you saying it like that? What's wrong with being a stripper? It's better than being the shooter's sister," she stated sarcastically.

Often the women who lived and worked at the shelter were quick to pass judgment. Raven couldn't understand it. None of them were perfect, and they had all made mistakes. She learned that no matter what a person did or sacrificed, it was never enough for some people. Those were the people who ignored reality because they found contentment in the lies they told themselves.

Raven sat against the back of her chair. "I'm going down to Guilty Pleasure tomorrow and applying."

Meg pursed her lips. "That's fine. But make sure you prepare yourself."

"For what?"

Meg huffed. "Desperate guys and women grinding on anything that breathes." Her eyes were wide and her nostrils flared.

Raven was confused by the woman's reaction. "You were just telling me being a barback was good, and now you seem angry. Do you have something against strippers or the guys that go there? Or are you trying to warn me that it might not be safe?"

Meg's lips moved into a cocky smile. "No, not really. I, um, I had a guy in the Marines . . . He went to those places all the time. Ended up leaving me for some filthy stripper."

"Hm. Okay. How do you know she was a skank?"

Meg's eyes moved to the right, taking in a black-and-white picture of an old barn on the wall, then back at Raven. "Because what kind of a woman takes her clothes off for men, then turns around and steals my boyfriend?"

Raven's smile wavered. She was conflicted between telling Meg she was a jealous ex-girlfriend and not wanting to make any more enemies at the shelter.

"What if your boyfriend was meant to meet her so you can find someone better than him?"

Meg pointed her index finger at Raven. "That's bullshit." The woman's jaw clenched, and she rubbed the side of her face as if trying to keep her nerves in check.

"Right. Okay, well, it's in the past." Raven filled her cheeks with air and blew it loudly into the room. "I'm gonna head out." She gestured with her thumb toward the door. Then she stood. "Thanks for your help. I'll let you know how it goes."

Meg's face looked like she was smelling poop. Her nose and forehead were wrinkled, and her hand was pressed tightly over her mouth. "Yeah, sure. Let me know."

As Raven hightailed it back to her room, she realized there were many volatile women inside the shelter, and it wasn't limited to the ones who lived there.

Chapter Seven

Raven walked into Guilty Pleasure at six o'clock in the evening. The club was half-full with mostly men and a few women. There was a long bar to her right, multiple stages in the middle, and a red door trimmed in lights to the left.

Raven's eyes scanned the bar. Her gaze fell on a businessman sitting at the end, arms on the wooden surface, hunched over his almost empty drink and bellowing out a slur for a refill. She moved to the bar slowly. The bartender looked up and gave her a warm smile that helped ease her nerves. She sat on one of the stools and watched as the young man mixed several drinks.

Finally, the bartender walked over to her. He threw down a cocktail napkin, leaned onto his elbow, and gave her a grin. "I'll need to see some ID."

"Oh," Raven said anxiously. "I don't have any. I-I-I'm not here to drink. I'm here for the barback job . . . the one in the newspaper?"

"You eighteen?" he asked swiftly.

Raven nodded. "Yeah, I turned eighteen last week."

"I'll go let the boss know you're here to see him. You want a soda?"

She let out a tense giggle. "Sure."

He spun away but then turned back to her. "I'm Santino. And you are?"

"Um. Yeah, I'm Raven Ledger."

Santino scrunched his brows together. "Ledger. I've heard that name before. Are you famous or something? A porn star maybe."

Raven's heart made a full stop in her chest. There was an unbearable heat lighting up her face.

He stared at her with a serious expression and then started laughing. "I'm only teasing you."

"Oh, okay." She lowered her face slightly so that her hair fell forward. Her hands were fidgeting with the cocktail napkin as she willed him to go away before he could remember where he'd heard her name. *Please don't recognize me.*

Santino pushed off the bar. "All right. You drink your soda, and I'll go tell Victor you're here to see him."

A few minutes later a man dressed in a black suit, white shirt, and black tie swaggered up to the bar and stood next to Raven.

Victor took her in. He liked what he saw. He looked into her eyes. "I'm Victor, and Santino tells me you're Raven Ledger."

"Yes." She pressed the word through her teeth to portray confidence and not let him see she was falling apart inside.

He moved closer to her. "This is the first and last time you'll have a soda at the bar. Until you're twenty-one, you can eat and drink in the break room in the back. Come on, follow me."

Raven glanced at Santino, who flashed her a smile and twirled the towel in his hand. She slid off the stool and followed Victor into the back. Victor was in his early fifties. He was well groomed with a full head of hair and a slim, muscular physique. Victor didn't walk; he strutted, with his shoulders shimmying from side to side. As she followed behind him, she couldn't help but smile at the way he sashayed across the floor like he was a model walking the runway.

Victor stood to the side of his office door. "Go in and have a seat. You want another soda?"

She shook her head. "I'm good."

"Great, then let's get started." He shut the office door and sat behind his desk. "Have you ever done barback work?"

"No, but I worked in a deli last summer. I had to prep all the vegetables, take care of cutting the rolls, clean up at the end of my shift—that kind of stuff."

"All right. That's a good start. You'll be cutting all the garnishes for the drinks. You also need to carry some heavier things," he said, looking at her arms.

"Oh, that's no problem." She followed his gaze to her thin arms. "I'm stronger than I look."

"Do you think you'll be comfortable in this environment? Santino said you turned eighteen last week, so I assume you've never been in a strip club before." He raised his eyebrows, waiting for an answer.

Raven fidgeted in her chair under his fixed eyes. "I think I'll be fine . . . I mean, I've never been in a place like this, but I had a friend that was a prostitute when I was little."

Victor let out a laugh. The first time he'd smiled since they met twenty minutes prior. "Okay, I like you, kid. But to be clear, there's no prostitution going on in my place. Here's what I'm going to do. I'll hire you on a trial basis. If you make it through the first week and I like your work, then I'll give you the job. I'll pay you five bucks an hour under the table." He leaned across the desk. "That means tax-free."

Recalling the same conversation with Ava when she worked at the deli, Raven giggled. "I know."

"Good. You can start tomorrow. Be here by two tomorrow afternoon. You enter through the alley. There's a doorbell. Ring it and one of the bouncers will let you in." He stood to indicate the interview was over.

Raven moved to the door quickly.

"Hey, one more thing," his deep voice ground out.

She turned back to him, and he looked her up and down. "You look like a size small."

He took a few steps to a closet and pulled out a pair of short shorts and a midriff top. *Guilty Pleasure* sparkled in rhinestones across the front of the skimpy shirt.

"If you're working here, you need to look like an accessory to my girls."

"Your girls?"

"Yeah, the ones on stage that keep money in all of our pockets. See you tomorrow. Two sharp. Don't be late. I don't like people being late. It's a sign of disrespect." He guided her out of his office and shut the door behind her.

Inside the bar again, Raven's mind was whirling. Her eyes roamed over the room. Young and old men sat at tables flanked by scantily dressed women. The girls were young, all in their early twenties. They giggled and smiled, but underneath that thin layer, Raven recognized the pain hidden by the masks they wore. It was the pain of life, of facing adversity and being forced to confront it head-on to survive.

Looking down at the tiny outfit she was holding in her hands, she shook her head. She looked back at the girls: topless and wearing only a G-string. She hugged the outfit to her chest. She, too, would do what was necessary to give herself a better life.

Chapter Eight

Raven sat with Dalton at the women's shelter after they had eaten breakfast the next morning.

"I think I'm gonna like working at Guilty Pleasure. Santino—he's the bartender—was really nice, and he's so cute. Victor is the boss, and he was kind of uppity, but he has a soft side to him, too."

"That's great. I'm happy for you," Dalton said with sincerity. "I think . . ."

Before Dalton finished her sentence, Sloane moseyed up to the table. She plopped down next to Raven and leaned into her.

"Where'd you go last night?" Sloane asked in a low growl.

"Why do you care?"

Sloane gave her a wicked smirk. "Don't be nasty. I'm only trying to get to know you. So where were you?"

Raven lifted her chin. "I went to apply for a job."

Sloane chuckled. "Must be nice to live here and be able to go out onto the streets like you ain't in hiding like the rest of us. Maybe you should be sticking around this shithole, so nobody follows your crazy ass back here."

Raven angled her body toward the girl. "Maybe you should mind your own business. I know you think you're tough and all, but I've lived with a few monsters that would put you to shame. They wouldn't dream of lighting my house on fire. They would beat me to death while my eyes were wide open."

Sloane scoffed. "And what? You think that makes you some rough, tough tumbler?"

"No. Not really. But it does help me notice a bully when I meet one. This isn't prison. This is a shelter where we have a chance to make our lives better. If you wanna fight, move to Kensington. There are plenty of people there who will give you a run for your money. But beware—they won't put up with any shit," Raven fired back.

Sloane moved her face closer to Raven's. "So did you find a job?" she asked in a caustic tone.

Raven's eyes pivoted to Dalton's. "Yeah, I did. In a bar in South Philly."

"Oh yeah?" Sloane grunted. "What bar?"

Raven looked her square in the eyes. "Guilty Pleasure."

"Holy shit," Sloane cackled, throwing her head back. "What? Now you're a stripper. No ass or tits. Ain't nobody gonna give you any tips. You may as well hang up your thong now."

"I'm not stripping. I got a job as a barback."

Sloane cracked a grin. "Oh yeah? That sounds like a good job for me. Maybe you can get me a job there. We can work together, and you can give me half your tips," she taunted, baring her teeth.

Raven shook her head. "I don't think so. I like to keep my enemies at a distance."

Raven was already regretting sharing so much information with Sloane. The woman couldn't be trusted.

Dalton picked up her tray and stood. "This girl talk is nice and all," she said. "But I gotta go. I have shit to do. I'm studying to take some tests for college."

Raven smiled at Dalton while Sloane flipped her the middle finger. When the older woman was gone, Raven placed her hand on the base of her neck preparing herself to make one final attempt at peace between them.

"I'm curious, Sloane. Why did you try to kill your parents? I've been told it's because they wouldn't give you money to buy drugs, is that true?"

Sloane glanced down at her hands and back up with eyes blazing. "Fuck you. That's what everybody kicks around. But I'm sure you know there's always more to a story than people are willing to admit."

"Yeah, I do. That's why I'm asking you about it." Raven was fighting the urge to slap the woman.

Sloane leaned her head to one side. "Why would I tell you anything? It ain't like I know you, and it certainly ain't like I wanna be your friend."

Raven shrugged. "Because we might find out that we get along. I don't want to fight. You and me are the closest in age, and I thought you could use someone to talk to. I know I can. I mean, I can talk to Dalton, but she's a lot older than me. She's more like a mom."

Sloane rolled her eyes. "Bitch, I'm five years older than you. I ain't no teenybopper."

Raven looked away from the girl. "I know. But the way I see it is you'd be more like my older sister. Five years is nothing. What I don't have in time compared to you, I have in maturity," she cracked sarcastically.

Sloane glared at her, but Raven returned a smile.

Raven was determined not to let the woman ruin her only chance to get on her feet. "So are we cool?" she asked.

Sloane gave her a nod and smiled back at her.

Ah, I'm breaking through to Sloane.

Raven didn't know Sloane well enough yet to understand that her smile was cunning, and Sloane was happy imagining breaking Raven.

Chapter Nine

The next afternoon at ten minutes to two, Raven pressed the doorbell in the back alley of Guilty Pleasure. She anxiously rocked from foot to foot while waiting for someone to open the door.

The door swung open and a bulky man filled the entire opening. He was over six feet tall and plump with muscles. He had jet-black hair and brown eyes. He stared down at her. The man looked like he'd stepped out of Italy and into the club.

"Who the hell are you?" he demanded in an intimidating voice.

"I'm, I'm Raven. V-v-victor told me to be here by two t-t-today," she stuttered.

Her eyes were glued to his massive arms. His biceps were so large that his arms stuck out at an angle by his sides, and she was certain that he couldn't press them flat to his body if he tried.

The man gave her a grin. "I'm messin' with you. I know who you are. I know everything going on around here. Come in."

She hurried past him and into a cold room filled with kegs and cases of beer. She stopped short and looked at him.

He narrowed his eyes at her. "Ah right. I'm Nick. I keep this place free of assholes. You're working with Santino tonight. He came in early to train you, so don't make him regret it. He's out at the bar waiting for you."

Raven shook her head. "You don't have to worry. I'll learn everything fast. I swear." She looked around the refrigerated room. "How do I get to the bar from here?"

Nick rolled his eyes and let out a loud sigh. "See that door there?" he asked but didn't wait for her to answer. "Go through that, down the hall past the dressing room, and hang a left. There'll be another door that brings you into the bar."

Without waiting for Raven to respond, he left her standing there. She crossed her arms over her chest and shivered from the cold. She made her way through the first door.

That was easy enough.

Then as she walked down the hall, she heard several female voices. She came to an open door on the right and looked inside at a group of young women. Some were naked while others were topless. Her mouth dropped open and she slowed her pace.

"Ooooh," one girl crowed at her. "You like the view, honey?" She lifted her boobs toward the door.

The blood rushed to Raven's face so fast she thought her ears would catch on fire.

"Come in here," the girl said. She was a short, thin Hispanic girl.

Raven walked into the dressing room with six girls watching her.

"What are you doing here? You auditioning with Victor? Victor gonna dicker?" she cackled.

Raven shook her head. "N-no. I'm the new barback."

"Oh, baby," the girl crooned. She moved closer to Raven, too close, and touched her long brown hair. "You're too pretty to be a barback. Maybe you and me can dance together."

Four of the girls watching were laughing, but the fifth girl approached Raven. "Knock it off, Bebe. Leave her alone."

Bebe hiked her hands up on her hips. "Lexie, don't get all motherly again. The last time you did that, you ended up on the wrong side of Victor. Remember?"

Lexie flicked a wrist at her. "Shut up, Bebe. Mind your own business. You came in early to learn how to dance the pole better and I'm gonna teach you. But you gotta shut that piehole."

Bebe playfully smacked Lexie's butt and walked back to her dressing table.

Lexie gave Raven her attention. "Don't mind Bebe. She's bitchy to everyone, so don't take it personally. I'm Lexie," she stated, sticking her hand out.

Raven placed her hand in the older girl's. "I'm Raven."

Lexie grinned. "Well, welcome to Guilty Pleasure. Did Victor give you a uniform? You need to change into one before I bring you onto the floor."

Raven grimaced. She leaned her face closer. "I have it on under my clothes."

Lexie grinned. "Oh, okay. Well, you can leave your clothes in my locker. I'll give you the combination. We can share."

"Thanks," Raven said and followed Lexie over to a bank of lockers.

"Come on," Lexie urged. "You don't wanna be late on your first day."

Raven took off her oversized T-shirt and baggy sweatpants. She stood before Lexie with her arms crossed over her chest.

"Come on now, doll. You look fabulous."

Raven lowered her chin to her chest. "I don't feel fabulous . . . I feel naked."

Lexie laughed. "Oh, listen. In this club, there's a big difference between wearing a tiny outfit and being naked. Don't confuse the two." She grabbed Raven's hand and walked toward the door. She stopped and placed her hands on Raven's shoulders. "You lift your head high and show the boys what you're made of. You wanna be so confident that you scare them a little."

This made Raven smile. "Okay, I'll try."

"You have a good teacher tonight. Santino is a nice guy, but he likes to sleep around. So use caution with him."

Lexie started to walk out of the dressing room, but Raven didn't move. The young woman turned back. "Hurry or you'll be late. Victor is a stickler about being on time."

Raven put her hands up to her own chest, and Lexie looked down at her naked breasts. "Oh, Santino has seen these boobs about a million times." She smiled at the girl. "But for you, I'll put my robe on." She grabbed a scanty silk robe from the back of a chair and slid it over her shoulders, leaving the front open to expose her cleavage.

As Raven followed Lexie out to the club floor, she lifted her head and straightened her back, already grateful to have met Lexie.

Chapter Ten

"Oh, look who's back," Santino cooed with a sexy grin as Raven approached him.

Flattered, Raven's knees wobbled, and she nibbled her bottom lip. Then she let out an awkward giggle. "Yeah, here I am," she said, trying to sound poised. "I hear that I'll be working with you tonight . . . You're going to show me stuff."

O my God, I sound like a geek.

Santino chuckled. "I'll show you anything you want." His eyes scanned her from head to toe. The tiny outfit she was wearing complemented her slender eighteen-year-old body.

"Okay, that's enough," Lexie cut in. She shot Santino a dismissive glance. "Lay off the new girl. She's a barback. She didn't come here to strip." Lexie gave Raven a side-glance. "Remember, he sleeps around."

Raven giggled. She loved the straightforward way Lexie dealt with people. "I'll remember."

"Hey now," Santino sang. "I'm a good catch."

"No, you'd be good to catch something from." Lexie pointed at Santino. "I'm going to leave her in your capable hands. Do not disappoint me. I know where you work."

Raven watched Lexie as she walked away. Once she was gone, she turned to Santino. "So where do you want me to start?"

He waved her back behind the bar. "I want to go over the glass situation first. Then we'll talk about the other stuff. Rule number one, never run out of glasses and hard liquor behind this bar. The three Ns are the most important part of your job. No glasses. No booze. No money."

Raven smiled. "Got it."

As she was stocking the shelves with glasses from the back, Santino was taking inventory of the open liquor bottles. "So, I was right. You are kind of famous."

A blast of adrenaline, like a jolt of electricity, ran through her body. She didn't answer. She focused on lining up the glasses perfectly.

"Are you ignoring me?" he asked.

She was squatting and raised her eyes to meet his. "Are you my boss?"

He shrugged. "Not really. I'm more like your partner. The only boss around this place is Victor."

"Then, yes, I'm ignoring you," she said.

"Wow. I just got shut down by the new girl."

Raven smiled to herself. *That's right. There's a new girl in town.*

"I see how it is," Santino pressed. He got closer to her and lowered his voice. "I won't tell nobody, but they'll put it together soon enough."

She avoided eye contact. "For real?"

"Yeah. People will be curious about you once they know."

Raven sat on her butt. "You don't think Victor will fire me?"

"He told me you're on a week's trial, so technically he hasn't hired you yet. But if he did . . . No, I don't think he'd fire you. Victor isn't that kind of guy."

Raven nodded. Her heart was racing and her stomach was churning. She got onto her knees and started filling the lower shelves with more glasses.

"Okay, so I guess we aren't talking about it," he said, mocking himself.

She stopped and stood next to him. "Santino, every time people find out who I am, they want me to talk about it. I want this job and so I'll tell you this. That was the worst day of my life. I loved my brother . . . so much. Then when I saw him for the monster he was, I hated him. I had to kill him to stop him. A day doesn't go by that I don't think about those two or three minutes of my life. They dominate me. All I want to do is try my best to move on and live as normal as possible. I have no family, and my brother killed my only friend."

Raven turned away and went back to working on the glasses. Santino watched after her. He turned and looked into the empty club, then knelt next to her.

"I didn't know. I'm sorry about what happened to you. I'll do whatever I can to keep things good for you here. Some of the girls can be mean."

She pressed her lips together. "Thank you. Now I wanna learn this job so in a week from now, Victor will be begging me to stay." Then she gave him a full-blown Raven Ledger smile.

***

By six that evening, the club was jumping. Raven was running between the kitchen and the bar. She was going into the back for more glasses when a man stepped in front of her.

"Hey, beautiful," he groaned.

"Hi, I need to get through. I'm working." *No glasses. No booze. No money.*

"I know you're working. I've been watching you. In fact, I can't take my eyes off of you. But instead of carrying shit back and forth to the bar, I think you'd be better up on that stage. You sure as hell would make a lot more money," he chuckled.

Raven looked over at a young woman lying on the stage. She was arching her back. Her feet were strapped into six-inch heels. Her ankles were pressing together, dangling in midair, her legs rotating in circles.

Raven looked back at the man. "That's not my thing. Please let me by."

She tried to veer to the right, but he stepped in her way. Raven pivoted to the left, and he did it again. Then he took her into a bear hug as she thrashed against him.

"Hey, Charles," Lexie's voice sang. "Leave my girl alone. She's working." The young woman was standing next to him, rubbing her hand up and down his right arm. "She's a barback, and you're gonna get her fired. If you get her fired, then I'll be very, very mad at you. I'd probably stop doing private dances for you. I mean, you know Victor doesn't make us do lap dances for anyone that makes us uncomfortable. Do you want me to be uncomfortable with you?" She put her arms around his waist. As she did this, he let go of Raven, and she hurried away.

When Raven got into the back, she took a moment to catch her breath. She lifted a rack of beer mugs, and as she turned to go back, Victor was in the doorway.

"How's it going?" he asked.

She was still jittery from the overly forward fellow. "It's going good. Santino has been teaching me what to do."

"I meant Charles, the guy who grabbed you out there." He threw a thumb over his shoulder. "Our bouncer told me what he did."

"Oh, I'm fine. Lexie helped me out."

Victor nodded. "That's good. But as you become more comfortable, I need to know you can get yourself out of those situations. I want you to talk to Lexie—get advice from her on how to handle some of them. They're mostly decent guys, but just like in our personal lives, we always have a few assholes around. Charles is one of them."

Raven looked down at her worn sneakers, and Victor's eyes followed her gaze.

"Yeah, that's another thing. Get yourself a pair of nice sneakers."

Her eyes tore up to his. "I don't have money for that right now. If you decide to give me a job here, then I'll save for them and that'll be the first thing I buy."

Victor gave her a curt nod and left her standing there.

***

As Raven hustled back and forth for the remainder of the night. She quickly realized it wasn't a bad job, and she liked moving around a lot. Lost in her thoughts, Victor approached her as she was carrying a case of beer to the bar.

"I'm going to need you here late on Friday and Saturday nights, six to two a.m. Is that going to be a problem for you?"

Raven looked him in the eyes. "No. That's not a problem at all." She gave him a quick smile and rushed away to deliver the case of beer.

Santino was waiting for her and took the case from her grip. He looked her over as she handed him the beer bottles to put into the cooler.

Santino cleared his throat. "Victor came and asked me how you're doing. I told him I don't know how we ever ran this place without you."

She paused, blushing and wringing her hands together. "Thanks, I appreciate it. He asked me, well, kind of told me, that I have to work six to closing this Friday and Saturday."

"Oh," he said, placing his hand over his heart. "That's a great sign. Victor doesn't invite anyone who isn't good to work during prime hours. That's the time when we make a lot of money. I guess you have me to thank for that."

Raven cocked her hip and gave him a smirk. "You're the best." She meant it. It was nice to have the sense of being wanted and needed. She already knew she'd be willing to sacrifice to work at Guilty Pleasure.

Chapter Eleven

Back at the shelter that night, Raven went to her room and took off her T-shirt and sweatpants. She froze when her door flung open.

Sloane walked into the room unannounced. She stopped dead in her tracks and stared at Raven's body. Her dull black hair hung over her face, and her flat gray eyes scanned the girl.

"What are you doing?" Raven screeched. She was standing in her Guilty Pleasure uniform and quickly covered her chest. "Get out!"

"Oh, no shit," Sloane scoffed. "You're a killer and a hoe." She forced out a condescending laugh. "What? Your raggedy ass is stripping already? You can't keep up as a barback? Ain't nobody believed you were doing that anyway. We all know you're a whore with those pathetic pimples for tits. Look at your flat-ass chest in that shirt."

Raven dropped her arms to her sides. She pushed her chest out. It was true, she had small breasts, but she also had wicked curves and tight, toned skin.

"Get out of my room, Sloane. You are such an asshole." Her voice was deep and menacing.

Sloane charged her, and Raven started swinging. Within seconds, the two were wrestling on the floor. By the time Dalton made it to the door from the common room, Sloane was sitting on Raven's stomach, slapping her in the face.

Raven bucked her hips and Sloane flew forward.

Dalton got between them. "Stop it!" She looked at Sloane, then her head snapped toward Raven. "What the fuck are you two doing?"

Raven flattened her hair. "She started it." She stood, and Dalton took in the girl's outfit.

"Go back to your room, Sloane," Dalton said dryly.

"Go fuck yourself, Dalton. You ain't the boss of me," Sloane growled in response. She rose to her feet, pushed Raven in the chest, and walked out the door. She spun back to face them and pointed her index finger at Raven. "You better check yourself, whore."

When Sloane was gone, Raven collapsed on her cot. She rubbed the side of her face where Sloane had hit her.

"How did you guys end up in a fight . . . rolling around on the floor like two grizzly bears wrestling in the wild?" Dalton asked calmly.

Raven lifted her shoulders back and pointed at her chest. "I got a job at Guilty Pleasure. Apparently, that pisses her off."

Dalton sat next to Raven. "Everyone thinks you're stripping. Are you?"

The girl shook her head. "I'm a barback. I don't even have a job there yet. I'm on a one-week trial."

"Doesn't it bother you to be in that place with all those men drooling over women? Demeaning them?" Dalton asked.

"You know, it takes getting used to. But only because I've never been around it. What I saw tonight was grown women doing what they want to. I met a few of them. They're strong women with even stronger opinions. They don't take shit from nobody."

Raven looked down at the rhinestones on her shirt. Then her eyes moved to Dalton's. "You know what bothers me, though? To be living here with a bunch of volatile women who have proven to be violent, like Sloane. Why does she care what I do to make money?"

Dalton patted Raven's bare thigh. "Maybe she was a stripper at some point and had a bad experience. She was hooked on drugs. In and out of her parents' house. Who knows? She's such a hothead that you can't even ask her or have a serious conversation with her."

"I'm waiting for her to set my bed on fire while I'm sleeping," Raven admitted grimly.

Dalton widened her eyes. "No, she wouldn't do that here."

"Oh," Raven said, bounding to her feet, "she wouldn't? She came at me two minutes ago because of the uniform I was wearing. I think there's something else going on with her, and I need to stay ahead of her crazy ass."

Dalton gave the girl a quirky grin. "How do you plan on doing that?"

Raven shrugged. "The women around here are willing to gossip about anything. Someone has to have the scoop on her. I'm the only one she's targeting. It doesn't make any sense."

"It makes perfect sense to me. You're the only one that stands up to her. Everyone else doesn't think she's worth the time or grief. That's the point you're missing."

Raven pursed her lips. "I'm not letting anyone push me around ever again." She was quiet for several seconds. "Maybe I should ask Sloane why she hates me so much."

Dalton pulled her blanket back and slipped onto her cot. "I get that you want to know, but I don't know how much you'll get out of her. Sloane is nuts. She's not worth the trouble."

Raven dressed in pajamas and lay on top of her covers. Her hands were linked behind her head as she stared at the ceiling. Her thoughts wandered back to the shootings, as they often did. She remembered the last time her brother looked into her face. A grin had slithered over his lips, thinking she'd never pull the trigger. In the moment right before she killed him, Raven saw in his loveless eyes he was about to kill her. That moment, his look, made her heart shatter into a million pieces that would never fit back together.

Matthew didn't drag me to hell with him, and neither will anyone else.

***

The next morning at breakfast, Raven grabbed her tray and plopped down across from Sloane. She stared at the girl. She didn't blink or smile or say hello.

Sloane glared back at her. "You need to get away from me and go back to your roomie over there," she said, pointing at Dalton.

"No. I'm not leaving. Not until you tell me why you hate me so much. All you're doing is trying to make my life harder, but it isn't working." She leaned up on her elbows. "I want to know why. That way, maybe I can do something about it," she stated in an even voice.

Sloane dragged her hands through her dry black hair. She jammed her tray away from her. Her fingers were retracting, becoming claw-like. "I don't like that you get to live here without serving your time in prison like the rest of us," she hissed in a scathing tone. "You ain't different than any of us. You fucking killed somebody—shot him right through the heart." She leaned across the table to get closer to Raven. "I didn't even kill nobody and I had to do my time. You? Look at you. Your brother shot up a whole school and then you murdered him. You probably killed him so he wouldn't tell anyone you helped him. But you get to come here and act like you're some kind of hero or something. Do you understand that everyone sees you and your brother the same? You should've killed yourself with that gun while you had the chance."

Raven gasped at the harsh words. Her mouth was hanging open. "So you're mad at me because I didn't go to prison? Let me tell you something, Sloane. I built my own prison and I've been living in it since the day of the shootings. You had someone lock you up, but me, I locked myself up. And now, all I'm trying to do is unlock the cage I've put myself in."

Sloane let out an icy cackle. "How? By becoming a stripper? Is that how you're unlocking your fucking cage?" Sloane stood and addressed the room full of women. "Did everyone know that Ledger is working at Guilty Pleasure?" She turned to Raven. "You think that's trying to make yourself better? Well, let me tell you something. They'll be turning your ass out onto the street for ten-dollar blow jobs in a month."

Raven stood, leaving her tray of food on the table. "You're a rotten, horrible, mean person."

Sloane straightened her back to meet Raven's height. "Oh yeah? I ain't half as mean as the Kensington Sisterhoods."

Raven's whole body stiffened. She clutched at her gut, rushing away to the bathroom and into a stall, where she puked. Then she sat next to the toilet.

There was a soft knock on the stall door. "Raven?" Dalton said in a kind voice.

"Yeah?"

"Are you okay?"

Raven stood on shaky legs and unlocked the door. When she pulled it open, Dalton's posture was hunched and her fingers were pinching at the skin on the base of her throat. The girl looked her over.

"You don't need to worry," Raven stated. "I'm okay. I think Sloane knows the Kensington Sisterhoods. She's going to tell them I'm here. I'm going to have to leave right away. Like today. It'll be dangerous for everyone if they come here looking for me."

Dalton shook her head. "That's not true. I don't think she knows them at all. On the news yesterday, there was some reporter that said several gang members from the Kensington Hoods and Sisterhoods were murdered by your brother. She's using the information to scare you."

"Really?" Raven asked, her voice breaking.

Dalton gathered the girl up in her arms. "Really," she whispered.

As Raven walked back to her room with Dalton, she realized there was a lot to learn before she could function in her small world with people who wanted to destroy her.

Chapter Twelve

Later that morning, Raven and Dalton sauntered into the common room. As soon as they sat down, Trudy, a woman watching Raven from across the room, walked over to them.

Trudy was a Black woman who, by anyone's standards, fought like a professional boxer. She was beautiful on the outside with long brown hair and eyes the color of honey. But inside, she'd kill without hesitation to protect herself or someone she loved.

Trudy approached the two young women. She stopped in front of Raven, blocking her view of the television. "Sloane said you planned the school shooting. That true?"

In disbelief, like she had been slapped across the face, Raven gave her an unfocused gaze, blinking rapidly. "Sloane is a liar. Are you kidding right now?"

"No, I ain't fucking kidding. I ain't got time to come over and ask you questions if I already know the answer. I don't know you from nobody. So what you tell me, I'll believe, unless I find a reason not to," Trudy explained.

Annoyed she had to explain herself again, Raven gave her a curt, tight nod. "Okay, then. I had no idea my brother was going to kill people." She dragged her eyes to Trudy's. "If I knew, I would've called the police, told someone who could've helped. I would've done something. Matthew took two people from me that I loved. He also killed my mom, who was a terrible mother, but she was the only living relative I had left."

Trudy's pinched lips evolved into a pucker as she weighed the girl's words with the seriousness in her eyes and face. "All right then. I believe you. Now let me tell you about Sloane. That bitch is a whole other animal. She don't believe not a single word that comes rushing outta your mouth. But me and my friends over there"—she looked sideways at a group of three women watching them—"we believe you. See now, that's my magic power. I can tell when people are lying." She glanced at Dalton. "She ain't lying."

Dalton gave her a shrug. "No shit, Trudy. Stop acting like you got some crystal ball hidden up your ass or something. Leave her alone now. You got what you wanted out of her."

Trudy glared at Dalton and then turned to leave.

"No, wait!" Raven said, getting to her feet and facing the woman. "Thank you for believing me."

Dalton rolled her eyes. "Girl, please."

Trudy put her hand over Raven's shoulder. "See now, you don't need to thank me. You need to go on about your way." She walked the girl several feet away from Dalton. "I'm gonna keep my eyes on Sloane for you. My friends over there are gonna do the same. There ain't nothing wrong with Dalton, though she thinks because she's older than most of them here that she's got saying power."

Raven smiled. "Dalton's been nice to me."

"I'm sure she has been. She's probably mighty happy that you came 'cause she didn't have no friends before you got here. Anyway, I'm a few years older than she is and I know better than her. I was in prison for killing my brother, too, but it was different than you."

Raven rubbed her arms anxiously. "Why did you kill your brother?"

"Hm." She shook her head. "Boy raped the shit outta me. I was seventeen years old. I ain't never been with a man either. He threw me down like a dog and took me from every which way for hours. That night I pulled the refrigerator out and cut that wire plugged into the wall. While he was sound asleep, I wrapped that cord around his neck as gently as I could and twisted that bitch so fast, he died before he got it undid."

Raven's mouth dropped open. "Oh, I'm so sorry that happened to you." She tilted her head to the side. "Why would you go to prison if your brother raped you?"

Trudy shook her head. "I didn't have no proof. I was too dumb then to go to the hospital and let the doctor look at me right after it happened. The judge only knew what they heard. That by the time the paramedics arrived, my brother was dead as a doornail. The cord was still wrapped around his throat, and I tied that motherfucker off in a tight knot just in case he came back to life, like in the movies. No, siree, I wasn't taking no chances. The judge didn't believe he raped me because of how I killed him—and because I did it so quick after I claimed he had his way with me. So the prosecutor convinced them I was an evil person who killed for the thrill of it. The prosecutor argued I was a danger and menace to society and I needed juvie to put me on the right path. His argument convinced the judge people that I was guilty and that I needed to be locked up. I got sent to adult prison after I turned eighteen, and that's where I learned how to fight for what was right and just." She made two fists and lifted them into the air.

"What about your mom or dad? Didn't they stand up for you in court . . . tell the judge you were innocent?"

"Nah, they loved that boy of theirs. Lots of people choose sides without wanting to know the whole story. It happens all the time in this world. Some things are too ugly for people to believe, so they pretend it ain't so." She dragged her eyes to Raven's. "I'm not proud of what I did to my brother, but I ain't ashamed of it either. I told that judge he could put me in prison 'cause I wasn't sorry and I'd do it again. I would've only served a couple years, but then I went and got caught as an accomplice to killing some rotten bitch that raped a new girl in prison."

"Wow," Raven breathed, looking down at her feet. "You spent more time in prison to help another woman." She lifted her face. "That makes you a superhero."

Trudy beamed with pride. "That's right, sweetie. I like that. I'm a superhero." Her face got serious again. "I understand more than most people in this whole fucking town what you've been through. I loved my brother before he assaulted me. He was the only person I considered family. Is that how it was for you?"

Raven nodded. "We lived apart from the time we were ten until seventeen. But still, he was the only family I had left. He would . . . help me. He'd listen to me. Then it all turned sour, and I still can't figure out how."

Trudy patted the girl's shoulder. "Sometimes we don't know why people do nasty things to hurt others. I think it's mostly 'cause they only care about themselves and how they feel. Then they turn around and make their bad behavior everyone else's fault but their own. It don't make no sense, and I don't worry about understanding it no more—used to drive me crazy trying to figure it out. One day it hit me, my brother was a lousy motherfucker his whole life, and I never saw it until I did. You ever think that about your brother?"

Raven shook her head. "No, I never did. Matthew was different, odd, but he wasn't hateful or cruel. He didn't have a bad temper." She shrugged.

"But what do I know? He turned around and did the worst thing anyone can do. So I question everything I knew about him and everything I know about myself."

"Yeah, it's a bitch to wrestle with how someone you loved, your flesh and blood, can turn out to be the worst person in your life. That's some fucked-up bullshit. It messes with your head until you're able to clear out the drama. Then everything is crystal clear."

Raven pushed her hair behind her ears. She lowered her voice to a whisper. "At night, when I'm lying in bed, I can still see his face in the last second of life. He was going to kill me if I hadn't killed him first. He raised the rifle . . ." Her breath hitched.

She couldn't finish her sentence. Saying the words out loud to a stranger was too hard. She'd barely been able to admit it to herself.

Trudy pulled the girl to her and looked out into the room. Several women were watching them. "Come on," she said in the girl's ear. "Let's go to my room where we can have some privacy. These bitches ain't got nothing better to do than watch other people suffer."

As Raven allowed the woman to guide her away, she looked over her shoulder at Dalton. The woman looked back at her, shaking her head. But Raven knew in the deepest part of her soul that Trudy was the person she needed.

Chapter Thirteen

"Come and sit down on my bed," Trudy offered.

As soon as Raven was inside Trudy's room, she broke down in tears. Her breath sucked in and pushed out. A soft moan from somewhere deep inside of her released through her parted lips. Her head was hanging, her shoulders rising and falling with each new sob.

Trudy sat next to Raven and rubbed her back. "It's okay, sweetie. You let that shit out. I know what it's like to have someone else's rot lay inside your gut, eating you up every day. You ain't gotta do that no more. It's time for you to let that go . . . Let your brother go, too."

Raven's eyes moved to Trudy. "That's so hard to do. I never got a say in what happened to my life. Matthew did what he did and ruined everything I knew. Now, he's dead because I killed him, and everyone thinks I'm the bad person."

Trudy lifted the girl's chin with her index finger. "It don't matter what people think about you. Knowing the truth, knowing what really happened is all that counts. The rest of it is all noise. People like to have something to fester on and be negative about. They like to talk and gossip and tell each other what they would've done if it was them instead of you on the receiving end. That's a bunch of bullshit. Cowards flapping their lips. They ain't you. Your brother took most of you. Don't let the bystanders take the rest."

Raven pushed herself back on the bed and put her back against the wall. "It's not that easy." She glanced at the woman. "There are people involved . . . bad people."

"What do you mean by that?" Trudy asked, moving next to Raven.

Raven let out a loud sigh. "My brother killed five gang members from the Kensington Hoods and Sisterhoods."

Trudy pressed her lips together. "I see. So they want you to pay for what he's done. 'Cause in gang life, it ain't an eye for an eye; it's a life for a broken fingernail. I know all about those thug-ass bitches." She went quiet, pulling up her courage. "My brother was a Kensington Hood."

Raven gasped. Her hand flew to her neck. "O my God, Trudy. Please don't tell anyone that I'm here."

"Sweetie, I hate those bastards. While my brother was his own person and made the choices he did, those goons taught him how to close his heart. Take whatever he wanted. Kill whenever he wanted. I ain't no gang sympathizer. I did my share of protecting myself from them in prison. That's why I learned to fight," Trudy admitted.

"Wait! You were in prison with the Kensington Sisterhoods?" Raven asked, mortified by the idea.

Trudy gave her head an exaggerated nod. "I sure was. I killed one of their brothers. It didn't matter none that he was my brother by blood. They thought I should pay for what I'd done to him. They gave no mind to the fact that he forced himself on me. That's something the gang will overlook as long as it ain't one of their own."

Raven's eyes grew wider. "Weren't you afraid you'd get stanked?"

Trudy let out a hearty laugh. "You mean shanked?"

Raven chuckled. "Yeah, shanked."

Trudy nudged the girl with her shoulder. "Girl, good thing your skinny ass never ended up in the can."

Raven turned her head and stared into the woman's eyes. "How long did you have to live like that in prison?"

"It started about a week after I got to adult prison. Once word got out who I was, then it was almost immediately. Don't get me wrong, I'm strong. I always have been. And athletic, too. Let's not forget that I choked my brother to death with a cord, and he had about fifty pounds on me. But when I get crossed, something in me changes. I go from sweet Trudy"—she framed her face with her hands and smiled—"to Trudy, the Tasmanian devil, and I take out everything in my path. I don't look for trouble, but the minute I think I'm being threatened, it's all over."

"Weren't you afraid those gang members were gonna kill you in the shower or while you slept? How could you live like that?" Raven asked.

Her curiosity was piqued, and she wanted to know everything Trudy had done to survive. Maybe she'd get pointers on how to protect herself.

"At first, I was afraid. But then I learned there were only three Kensington Sisterhoods in that prison. So I made it a point to have three times the number of friends. I schmoozed the meanest bitches in that hole." She shook her head and a smile lifted her lips at the memory of the women. "I sure did. The meanest motherfuckers I could find."

"They protected you?"

"Well." Trudy gave her a side-glance. "We protected each other. Everyone in prison has got an enemy or two. There ain't no getting around that . . . all those women locked up together. All that estrogen. A hundred bitches getting their periods at the same time. People with cramps and migraines from menstruating. There's bound to be some friction among all that womanhood."

Raven smiled. "Yeah, when I lived in foster care, there were six of us, and it seemed like three or four always had our periods together. Everybody moaned and griped. I took some pain relievers and kept on going."

Trudy cocked her head. "Some women ain't got it that easy. When I was young, I used to be in bed for two days. I got over that right quick in juvie, 'cause they don't let you lay around unless you got a fever or you're puking or shittin' your pants."

Raven gathered her hair to one side and pulled at the ends. "Jail sounds worse than foster care."

"Oh, child, you have no idea. Those places ain't meant for normal people. But those women, the ones who became my friends, taught me things I didn't know. There's always some good we can get outta even the worst situations."

Raven smiled. "What did they teach you?"

Trudy smirked. "Well, for starters, they taught me that being a woman is a privilege and that no man should stomp on my body or my rights. That's why they taught me how to fight. I can knock a man's block off if I need to. I go to the gym every day to keep up my strength and speed. Anyway, those women taught me that a bloodline don't make us family. Your family are the people that stick by you. They're always on your side because they know your heart. There are a lot of fake-ass pricks out there. You ain't one of those kind, though. I know you're loyal till the end."

Raven rested her head on Trudy's shoulder. She didn't know the woman well enough to take such liberties, but something about her made Raven want to be closer.

Trudy reached her hand up and patted the girl's cheek gently. "You gonna be okay." The older woman smiled. "I can teach you how to fight. That's something I can give you."

Raven's head popped up. "Really? You'd do that?"

"'Course I would. Ain't gonna help much if you're looking down the barrel of a gun, but if you ain't, it'll give you a fighting chance."

"I would like that. Can we start tomorrow?"

Trudy nodded. "I go to the gym at six, so you gotta get up early."

"No problem." A surge of strength and acceptance rushed through her veins. "I know what it's like to have a gun pointed in my face. That's what my brother did to me. It's still hard to believe sometimes."

"Sweetie, it hasn't been that long . . . What, a few months have passed?"

"Three months, but it seems like three years."

Trudy took Raven's hand. "Give it time, sweetie. Things have a way of working their way out. In the meantime, you do what's right for you. And you see that Sloane? You stay away from her."

Chapter Fourteen

When Raven wasn't working at Guilty Pleasure, she spent her time with Trudy. While she and Dalton remained roommates and friends, Trudy gave the girl the courage and will to move forward and stepped in as a mother to the young teen.

"Hey, Trudy, what's shaking?" Raven sang as she walked into the woman's room at the shelter.

Trudy shook her butt and pointed her finger at it. "That's what's shaking. Right there. That fine ass of mine. How was work last night?"

Raven flopped on Trudy's bed. "Well, it was good until two dancers got into a fistfight. I almost had to jump in to help the smaller one."

The older woman pressed her lips into a thin line. "I ain't teaching you how to fight so you can get involved in other people's stuff."

Raven scoffed. "What? You helped the girl that got raped in prison."

"Girl, you best mind yourself. First off, smartass, you ain't living in prison. Even if you were, just because I do something don't mean that you ought to do it. I want you to learn from my mistakes, not repeat them." She opened her eyes wider. "So don't question me."

The girl lifted her head and gave the woman her attention. She moved to the edge of the bed, her toes bouncing on the floor. "I'm sorry, Trudy. I didn't mean anything by it."

Trudy ruffled Raven's hair. "Don't get all worked up. But I'm telling you like it is. See, what I do and what I did ain't what I want for you. I like that you're a nice person . . . calm and eager to get on with your life. I'm teaching you things to help you get there, not to change the path that you're on."

"I know, but ever since I was young, I stuck up for people who were weaker than me," Raven explained.

"I like that about you, but you did those things to help other kids. Like that disgusting thug, Blanco, who you told me about. The bitch hunting you wouldn't be alive if you didn't defend her. She best hope I never meet her ass in a dark alley." Trudy rubbed her palms on her jeans. "See, you have to watch who you defend in life. That girl ought to be on the ground, kissing your feet. She should've told the world that you saved her. Instead, she's embarrassed 'cause she wasn't as strong as you. You had to save her and that pisses her off. Which reminds me, Sloane say anything more about the gang?"

Raven brushed her hair from her face and rolled her eyes. "Sloane gives me a daily reminder that she'll tell them, but I think she's losing some of her steam." Raven's voice got giddy. "I think she's afraid of you."

"Bitch better be afraid of me. She best stop being a pain in the ass, too, with all that threatening she's been doing. Someday her fat ass will be sitting on the streets. She ain't got no goals or ambition. All she wants to do is sit around and talk about other people. Do I need to have a talk with her about you?"

Raven shook her head. "It'll only make things worse."

"Ah right. I'll keep it to myself." Trudy took Raven into an embrace. "You're gonna be okay, you hear?"

Raven nodded. "Yeah, I hear."

She looked the younger girl in the eyes. "You know, I ain't gonna be here much longer."

Raven's mouth dropped open. "What do you mean?"

"Well, I've been here going on six months. I've been working a job for a while, saving up so I can get a place. This shelter has a one-year limit. I don't wanna wait that long. Some of the people I work with live in West Philly. They say it's nice there."

Raven shook her head. "That's not what I heard. I heard West Philly is dangerous."

"Sweetie, you lived in North Philly for ten years. There ain't no place more dangerous than that drug-infested town. Damn, I feel sorry for those people who have lived there their whole lives. Now they got addicts coming from all over the country to be there. Like it's a fucking tourist attraction. It ain't cool," Trudy stated.

"You're right. I remember seeing the old people who were stuck there. They would come into the deli for a hoagie and complain to the owner about the neighborhood. I know how it is to live somewhere that makes you afraid." Raven walked to the bedroom door. "I'm going down to get lunch. I have to be at Guilty Pleasure by two today. I'm freaking working until two in the morning. I love working there, but I hate doing twelve-hour shifts."

"You hate doing twelve hours, or you hate coming home at two in the morning when the streets are dark and there ain't no traffic around?"

Raven smiled. "Yeah, that. It makes me nervous sometimes."

"I'll wait up for you then. You let me know what time the bus drops you off on the corner and I'll be there," Trudy offered.

"Yeah, right," Raven laughed.

"I ain't messing with you. Just say the word."

Raven moved back into the room and hugged the woman. "You're the best-unrelated mom I've ever had."

Trudy hugged the girl closer. "You remember, Trudy will always love you."

Raven closed her eyes and took in the moment. This was what she'd lacked from her mother, and she was grateful this woman stepped into the role, if only temporarily.

Chapter Fifteen

That afternoon when Raven arrived at Guilty Pleasure, she found Santino behind the bar taking inventory.

"Hey, Santino, I'm ready to get started."

Santino pulled a few almost empty liquor bottles from a shelf and placed them on top of the bar. "Hey, how's it going? We have a big night. I hope you're up for it."

Raven pulled her head back. "You hope I'm up for what? What's so special about tonight?"

He grinned. "Oh, the fun I have in store for you. Someone booked a bachelor party. They'll be over in the private area. Bachelor parties are the best and the worst, so when we get them, we need to balance their needs against the other people in the bar."

She let out a soft giggle. "Okay, that makes sense, I guess. But what's the best and worst part?"

"Well, the best is that everyone working will get big tips tonight. Guys are very generous with a friend who's getting married, so they'll pay anything to show their buddy a good time. That includes having servers make them a priority, and they do that by tipping throughout the night. Then because they're a big party, there'll be a gratuity added to their check for food and drinks. Now, the worst part about a bachelor party is they all get too drunk and act stupid," he explained.

Santino pointed across the room to a section of the bar that sat a foot above the rest of the room and was partitioned off with a metal railing.

"They'll be up in the VIP section tonight. I'm going to need you to cut bags of lemons and limes. Fill cups with cherries . . . Let's see, what else?" he said, tapping his chin with his index finger. "Oh, right. Lorenzo, our dishwasher, called out sick. This is the third time he called out on a Saturday night. Victor needs you to step in and help. One of the waitresses will help you if she isn't too busy, but don't count on it. Oh, and make sure you keep up with bussing the tables for this party. Expect them to be rowdy. The bouncers will have eyes on them constantly, but don't get offended because they're bound to get vulgar."

Raven lifted her eyebrows. "What do you mean by vulgar?" She didn't wait for an answer. "I'm not putting up with guys touching me like the strippers do. You know what? I'm gonna tell Victor that I need to wear my jeans tonight so I'm not traipsing around with my ass hanging out of those ridiculous shorts."

Santino's eyebrows pulled together. "You're not telling Victor anything. These guys are in it for the whole go-go bar experience." He rested his elbow against the bar and softened his tone. "Listen, I know the dude that's hosting the bachelor party. He comes from big money. We will be well taken care of. You won't be sorry. All you need to do is play it cool, do your work, and you'll go home with a pocket full of money. Trust me." He lifted the bottles from the bar to carry them into the back. "I almost forgot. Be nice."

Raven's eyes lit up. "I have no idea why you're saying that. I'm nice to everyone."

"Until they touch you or say something offensive," he remarked.

"That's right. I'm not here to be harassed."

Santino let out a loud chuckle. "We work in a strip club, not an all-night diner. Get a grip, Ledger."

Raven shook her head. "I'm not letting anyone touch me or pull me on their lap or touch my hair . . . you know, like some of the pervs in here try to do."

"Of course you're not. You know Victor doesn't allow that with any of his employees outside of his dancers. He'd never keep this place staffed if he did."

Raven started cleaning the bar. "That's true. Hey, do you know when Lexie is coming in?"

"She's here already. She's in the dressing room. I'll walk you back to the kitchen and show you how to take care of the dishes. Then you can go find her."

He started walking, and Raven followed. "Now, once you load the dishes, they clean themselves, then you need to put them away. Do not piss off Guido. He's the angriest chef I've ever known. Anyway, he'll be a complete asshole if he decides you're incompetent. He's always looking for reasons to say people suck," Santino warned her.

"Oh, okay. Thanks for that. No pressure," she giggled. "Guido is always nice to me."

"That's because you haven't had to do work for him. You'll see."

Bebe approached the two as they were walking. She stumbled up on them. "Hey, it's the new girl," she bellowed. Her voice was dripping in sarcasm.

The two stopped walking. Raven's leg muscles tightened and she shook out her hands. Bebe was an annoying person, and that hadn't changed since the first time she met her. Lexie had stepped in twice when Bebe confronted Raven for no good reason.

"Hey, Bebe," Raven said unenthusiastically. "You know, I think I've been here long enough not to be called the new girl anymore."

Raven gave Santino a side-glance. His jaw was tight and veins were protruding on his forehead. Whatever was going on, he was not happy.

The negative tension between Santino and Bebe was noticeable. To diffuse the situation, Raven plastered a fake smile on her face. "How's it going, Bebe?"

"Not that great, *Raven*. It'll go better when you get the fuck away from my guy," Bebe barked.

Raven's head snapped in Santino's direction, and she turned back to Bebe. "We aren't doing anything. We work together. In case you forgot, he's a bartender and I'm a fucking barback. If you have an issue with that, then you should take it up with Victor. I'm sure he'd be thrilled to know you're putting your love life before his business while you're working."

"Oh, go screw yourself. I'm not falling for that shit. Are you trying to tell me that you two are all business? That you aren't having sex? *We're just bartender and barback*," Bebe sang in a mocking tone. The girl glared at Santino. "This is it? You want her over me?" She waved her hand in the air, up and down the front of Raven. "Are you blind?"

Santino stepped closer to her. "Bebe, you're out of line. And I can tell you're drunk again. You better go into the dressing room and sleep it off before Victor sees you."

"Kiss my ass, Santino. Answer the question." She sneered at Raven and then pressed her face closer to Santino. "Is she trying to get into your pants or what?"

"Stop it," Raven said in an even tone. "I'm here working, the same as you. I haven't done anything wrong, and I don't want to date Santino. My job is to support his job. It's as simple as that."

Santino leaned into Raven. "How about if you go into the kitchen? Go talk to Guido and he'll give you the rundown on how to take care of things for him."

Bebe touched her index finger to Raven's sternum. "Yeah, go into the kitchen, skank. That's what skanks do—they clean other people's shit."

Raven narrowed her eyes at the girl. Then the tight lines on her face eased. She realized there was no reason to argue with Bebe. Santino was right. Now that Bebe was closer to her, she could smell the alcohol on her breath.

Raven shifted her eyes back to Santino. "I don't know what's going on with you two, but you need to make it clear that I haven't done anything. That you and me aren't a thing," she said and walked away, leaving the two standing there.

As she stomped into the kitchen, she murmured to herself, "Go screw yourself, Bebe. You're another Blanco, a jealous girl who is nothing but a bitch and a bully."

Chapter Sixteen

Raven was exhausted halfway through her shift that night. All the men at the bachelor party were rowdy and messy, spilling drinks and dropping food. One of them threw up under a table, leaving Raven to clean the mess.

With the smell of bile stuck in her nose, she made her way over to the bar. She leaned in to get Santino's attention, and he moved toward her while shaking a drink.

"What's up?" he asked.

"I have a guy in the VIP area puking. Can you cut back on the alcohol for the bachelor boys? I don't need them all blowing chunks."

Santino twisted the tops off three beer bottles. "Which one barfed?"

Raven looked over her shoulder. "The guy in the red shirt lying across the small sofa. He's trashed."

"Ah right, I'll let the servers know. Can you go to the front door and tell Rocco his bouncers need to check on that guy?"

"Sure," she yelled over the music that started again. "But why don't we tell his buddies to take him home?"

"Because." He gave her a sexy, toothy smile. "We're making a shit ton of money right now. Their bill is enormous, and we still have a few hours to go." He pulled a bottle of water from the cooler below him. "Bring this over to one of his friends and tell them the dude needs to drink it. I'll flag him, and our bouncers will make sure he's good until he leaves." He made eye contact with a guy at the bar waving a twenty-dollar bill at him. "I'll be right with you." Turning back to Raven, he gave her a smirk. "I'm too busy right now . . . I gotta go. Drop off the water and talk to Rocco before you do anything else."

Raven nodded. After delivering the water, she set off to the front door to find the head bouncer, Rocco. She liked him. He was a big guy with a broad chest and well-defined muscles. His Italian heritage showed in his olive skin tone and brown eyes. He had thick, black hair, and the first thing you noticed about him was his confidence, which overshadowed all of his good looks. On her way to him, she glanced over at the stage, and Lexie, who was dancing, pointed at her and smiled. Raven gave her a wave and hurried by.

"Rocco, there's a guy with the private party that puked under one of the tables. Santino sent me over to tell you about it."

Rocco looked toward the VIP area, shook his head, and grunted. "Man, these fucking guys are so stupid. They come in here, get trashed, spend all of their money, and don't remember what they did the next day." He moved his eyes to hers. "Did I ever tell you that bouncing is like being a parent with a young child? You spend your entire time making sure nobody kills themselves."

Raven's eyes brightened and she giggled. She loved the way Rocco saw things for what they were. "The good news is he's the only one who drank too much so far."

Rocco crossed his arms over his chest. "Ah right. Did Santino say he'll let the servers know he's flagged?"

"Yeah, and I told him not to put too much alcohol in their drinks because the rest of them are getting drunk, too."

Rocco tapped his forehead and then pointed at her. "See, you're a smart girl. You gotta lot of potential."

Raven beamed. "Thanks. Now all I have to do is figure out what I want to do with all that potential."

Rocco gave her a warm grin. "Hey, listen. How come you don't wanna dance? You got the looks. You got the body. You could make enough money in six months to help you get a place, maybe go to college."

She choked out a nervous chuckle. "Um, no way. That's not me. I could never go up there and take my clothes off. I hate being the center of attention. Besides, I can't dance, and I hate the way some of these guys look at the girls."

"Aw, that ain't nothing. Ninety-nine percent are a bunch of guys who enjoy looking at beautiful women. Most of 'em are lonely and they come here, make friends, and come back to share some laughs. It ain't all about topless girls dancing."

Raven shrugged. "Yeah, I guess. But why not meet people at a regular bar?"

Rocco wagged his finger. "Because in here, they can be themselves. Beyond these walls, people judge everything about a person. How they look. How they talk. How much money they make. They end up pretending they're someone they ain't. Let me ask you a question. What are you making as a barback? Five bucks an hour?"

Raven grimaced. "Yeah, plus whatever the servers and bartenders tip me," she added as though it would matter.

"Do you know what those dancers make an hour?"

She shook her head.

"They make anywhere between a hundred to three hundred bucks an hour."

Her mouth dropped open. "What? No way. You're kidding, right?"

Rocco chuckled. "Why the hell would I kid about that? And it's all in cash, too. Ask Lexie. She'll tell you."

Raven blushed. "Wow, that's a lot of money." She watched the stage. Pandora, an Indian woman, was dancing. She flowed like water through a stream. Raven pointed. "Pandora is one of the best dancers here. She's so . . . I don't know, graceful."

Rocco's eyes pivoted to the stage and back at the girl. "Pandora wanted to be some kinda famous ballerina. Then she got hurt and those snooty people told her to hang up her tutu. I agree with you, though. She's got better moves than all the girls in here."

Raven looked across the room to the VIP area. Three of the tables were covered with glasses. "I have to go bus those tables before those guys break all the glasses and Victor skins me alive or, even worse, fires me."

"See, if you was dancing, you wouldn't have to worry about that," he commented.

Raven put her hands on her hips. "You're supposed to make sure I do good, not try to get me to be a stripper."

"You're right, but I know you wanna get a place of your own and all. I ain't trying to talk you into nothing . . . even though I guess it sounds like that's what I was trying to do. I like you. You know that. You got a lot more sense than any eighteen-year-old I've ever met. From now on, I promise I won't say nothing about you dancing."

She patted his thick arm. "Thanks, Rocco. Stay cool."

Raven strutted away. She thought Rocco was a great guy, but like so many others in the club, they focused on the business of making money. It wasn't the first time one of the bar employees encouraged Raven to dance.

She'd imagined how great it would be to earn more money, but it wasn't her thing. She had often watched the dancers in awe. They had charisma and self-assurance. They seemed on top of the world.

While Raven wanted all those things, she'd have to find them in her own way. Raven knew in her heart there was something and someone out there for her. But taking her clothes off and dancing on a stage wasn't the answer. She wanted more from life. She *needed* more, and at some point, she'd have to decide how much she would give of herself to get it.

Chapter Seventeen

Raven entered the shelter at three in the morning. The television in the common room was on, and the only person sitting there was Trudy. The older woman looked over her shoulder, then stood. "Raven, come in here. We need to talk."

Raven shuffled over. She was tired, and all she could think about was lying in her bed. "Hey, Trudy. I had a hard shift at work . . . a dumb bachelor party. I'm really tired. Can we talk in the morning?"

Trudy shook her head. "No, we need to talk now."

As Raven got closer, she could see the lines around Trudy's eyes and mouth. "What's wrong? Did something happen?"

"Sloane was shooting her mouth off tonight. She vowed to get you when you least expect it. You need to be careful coming home from work—in my head, that's when it'll be easier to attack you."

"Attack me?" Raven let out a moan. "I don't even know why we are in this war. I never did anything to her. So what are you saying? She's going to be waiting in the dark to jump out and kill me?"

Trudy tilted her head. "I don't know how she's planning on doing it, sweetie. All I know is when someone the likes of Sloane shoots off her mouth, it's a warning sign. I was in prison with women like her." Trudy tapped her finger on her skull. "Sloane is off. She ain't right. Her brain don't work like normal people."

Raven shook her head. "You mean she's sick?"

"Sloane is a paranoid schizophrenic. She's delusional. You understand?"

Raven stared at her. She had some sense of what Trudy was saying but didn't completely know all the facts. "I think you're saying she can't control herself. Right?"

Trudy put her hand on the base of her neck. "Here's the thing, once Sloane believes something to be true, she can't be convinced different. Even if you prove to her that she's wrong, like with hard evidence. Some people with her condition have hallucinations. Her roommate was telling me that Sloane sees and hears things that ain't there. She considers you a threat." The woman shook her head. "Not sure why. I've been told she thinks you're a spy. Ain't no telling where she came up with that nonsense."

"Why would her roommate tell *you* all of that about her?"

"Because there was an incident tonight." Trudy shoved her hands into her front pockets. "That's the thing. Most of us in this joint knew nothing about her problem until tonight. We were in the middle of dinner when Sloane stood on her table and started screaming. First, she stripped down to her bare ass. Then she was throwing food and stomping her feet. Yelling about some men that were coming for her 'cause you called them. Anyway, they called an ambulance and when they checked her room, they found all her medication hidden in her top drawer. Her meds keep her stable. Doesn't look like she's taken them for a while."

"Are they keeping her in the hospital?"

Trudy nodded. "Probably for a few days, then she'll be back."

"What should I do?"

"You need to be careful. You have no idea what she's done in her delusional state."

"Like what? What are you worried about?"

"I don't know, Raven. I mean, she tried to burn her parents to death. Imagine what she'd do to someone she ain't related to. Besides, you don't know what she'll do when she gets out. All I'm saying is you need to watch your back. I'm gonna be watching your back, too."

Raven hugged the woman. "Thank you, Trudy. I have to get out of here as soon as possible."

"You and me both, sister. You'll have some time to relax before they send her back here from the hospital. Hopefully, they'll regulate her crazy ass first," she mused.

***

Six days later, while Raven was watching television, she looked up and saw Sloane walking into the common room. She had been released from the hospital an hour earlier. She was alone. Taking long strides through the room.

Sloane's two friends rushed forward to embrace her. The rest of the women were not happy that Sloane was back. They had all gossiped about her while she was gone. The consensus was to stay on her good side in case she went off the deep end again.

Raven remained rooted to her seat.

Trudy was standing across the room, and her eyes searched Raven's face. Then she lifted her chin toward her bedroom.

Raven got to her feet and headed in the same direction Trudy was walking.

"What? You ain't gonna say hello to me, Ledger?" Sloane's voice chirped.

Raven turned, and she could see Sloane was trying to look friendly, but beyond the plastic smile, her eyes were narrowed and her pupils dilated.

"I was giving you time to settle in. How are you, Sloane?"

"I'm fine. Why wouldn't I be?" she snapped.

Raven raised her palms in the air. "I didn't mean anything by it. I was only asking."

Sloane moved closer to Raven in slow, deliberate steps. When she was only a foot away, she bared her teeth at the girl. "Don't think because I was away that I forgot about you. These bitches all think I'm crazy. But I'm not. I know exactly what I'm doing. I've managed to fool every fucking one of them. So know this . . . I plan to kill you." She licked her lips in a grotesque manner that made Raven cringe.

"You have no reason to want to kill me," Raven hissed. Then she straightened her back and smiled at Sloane. "I'm sure you're happy to be back."

"Fucking right, I am. I came back here to finish what I started. I like to see things through to the bitter end. You know what I'm talking about, right?"

"Not really," she commented and walked around the woman, leaving her standing in the common room.

Raven found Trudy in her room and closed the door. "Sloane told me that everyone thinks she's crazy, but that she knows exactly what she's doing. I think she faked the whole episode last week."

Raven was pacing the bedroom. She was twisting her fingers together and biting her bottom lip. "Well, say something."

Trudy approached the girl. "Sweetie, I don't know what to say other than it's hard to tell what the truth is. The woman has some serious issues. You need to keep away from her."

"Sloane told me that she came back here to finish what she started."

"With you?" Trudy said, puffing out her chest.

"Yes."

Trudy sighed. "I won't let her do anything to you if it's within my control. I can't initiate because I don't wanna go back to prison. I hated that fucking place."

"No, I would never want you to go back to prison. I was only telling you because I don't have anyone else to tell. Well, I mean, Dalton knows the way I feel about what Sloane did last week. I thought I should tell her in case Sloane sets our room on fire," Raven explained.

"You need a plan to get outta here. It ain't good for you or any of us. How about those people at Guilty Pleasure? Maybe you can room with one of the women who work there."

"Yeah, that's a good idea. I'll talk to Lexie tonight."

"Good," Trudy commented. "I wanna put this flame out before it gets started. You talk to your girl Lexie and let me know what happens."

Suddenly, Raven went from being uncertain of her future to fearing it.

Chapter Eighteen

As soon as Raven got to work that night, she rushed through the club looking for Lexie. She found her in the dressing room and dragged a chair next to her.

"Hey, girl," Lexie sang, giving Raven a huge smile.

"Hi."

"Uh-oh. What's wrong? You don't look so good."

Raven scooted her chair closer, not wanting the other girls to overhear their conversation. "I'm having a problem at the shelter, and I need to get out of there before something bad happens."

"Are you in danger?"

Raven nodded. "Yes. Remember I told you about Sloane? How she's always starting trouble with me?"

Lexie nodded. "The maniac who tried to barbeque her parents while they were sleeping?"

"Yeah, her."

Raven relayed the story, and when she was finished, she sat back in her chair. "So, I was wondering if you needed a roommate."

Lexie's eyes grew wide. "Oh. Well, I already live with somebody, but you can crash on my sofa for a week or two . . . until you find something permanent."

Raven's chest fell, but she nodded. "I have close to a thousand dollars saved to get my own place. Do you think that's enough?"

Lexie cocked her head to the side. "Sure, if you can find someone renting a room in their house or someone who wants to share an apartment. But you have to be careful who you live with. Otherwise, you'll be screwed for the length of the lease. I'd stick with renting a room. That way you can move if you don't like it. That's what I did."

"Then, yes. I'd love to crash on your sofa," Raven said. She was smiling, but Lexie noticed the short, quick breaths she was taking.

"All right. How about if you bring your stuff in tomorrow and we can go to my apartment at the end of our shift?"

Raven stood and leaned over Lexie, giving her a tight hug. "Thanks, Lexie. I swear, you won't even know I'm there."

Lexie scrunched her brow. "I'm not worried about that. I want you to be happy and safe. You've already been through a lot this year, and I'm happy to help."

Raven had an extra bounce in her step on her way to the bar.

Santino observed her coming toward him. "Well, you're in a good mood."

Raven smiled and moved behind the bar. "Lexie said I can live with her for a couple of weeks until I can find my own place. I'll probably rent a room somewhere because I can't afford an apartment."

Santino patted her shoulder. "Good for you. Things aren't working out too well at the shelter?"

Raven pushed her hair from her face. "Things are kind of crappy there right now. One of the women threatened to kill me. She's super aggressive, but screw her, I'm out of there tomorrow."

"I hate bitches that threaten people. It's good you're moving on. I'm happy for you. Now can we get to work? Since you need money more than ever, you have to try to keep up," he teased.

Except for Lexie and Santino, the other employees thought Raven was staying with a family member. They were the only two she entrusted with where she was living. She took comfort in them knowing.

***

The next morning, after telling the staff member on duty she was leaving, Raven set out to find Trudy. She sat at the table across from her in the cafeteria.

Trudy looked up from her food with Raven watching her. The girl's face was shining, her eyes were bright, and her smile was authentic.

"Good morning, Miss Raven."

"Good morning." She held her happiness in check.

"What's going on? You're actin' way too giddy for this time in the morning," Trudy grumbled.

"I am giddy." Raven glanced at Trudy's friend sitting next to her.

Trudy picked up her tray. "Ah right. Come on. Let's go find us somewhere quiet."

Raven followed the older woman. Inside Trudy's bedroom, Raven let out a random giggle.

"What the hell is goin' on with you?" Trudy asked, smirking at the joy on the girl's face.

Raven pulled in a long breath. Her chest expanded as her lungs filled with air then she blew it out. "I found a place to stay. Tonight when I leave for work, I'm taking all my stuff with me. Lexie, my friend from the bar, is going to let me sleep on her sofa for a couple of weeks while I find a room to rent."

Trudy hesitated, and her forehead creased with worry lines. "Okay, a couple means two to *me*. What if you don't find a room by then?"

The question took Raven by surprise. "Wh-wh . . . I'll find one. It's not that hard, right?"

Trudy shrugged. "What the hell do I know about finding a room? I'm asking you. You only have a couple of weeks, so you have to know where you're going next. I know I told you to talk to those girls about a living arrangement, but I meant a permanent one. I know you're young and nobody gave you any guidance, but when you make a life decision, you gotta remember to think about it in a bigger way. Like where will you be in three weeks after your time runs out? How will you get to work? Will you need a new job closer to your place? I expect you to always have a plan. These are the things my prison mom taught me. That's what I called her. She schooled me on life . . . same woman who taught me how to street fight."

Raven's shoulders rolled forward. "Why does life always gotta be so hard? I don't know all the answers, but I'll figure something out."

Trudy pinched her lips together. "Well, you best have something figured out in the next forty-eight hours. That's gotta be your goal."

Raven nodded, as her face flushed from the blood rushing to it. Even though she and Lexie talked about this, it didn't seem as critical. Now, she realized she made a promise with a time stamp on it.

Raven sat on Trudy's cot and closed her eyes. She told herself that things would work out in her favor, as she did her best not to panic. She thought about it logically. She'd take one step at a time. A place to live long-term was her priority now. She had no idea where to start, but she pressed her shoulders back and gathered her courage. Like many things in her life, she would accept the challenge and overcome the obstacles.

Chapter Nineteen

The next day, as Raven approached her bedroom, Sloane was blocking the doorway. "Everybody's talking . . . saying you're leaving today. Where are you running to, bitch?" Sloane yelled.

Raven drew some satisfaction that the woman was annoyed about her actions. "Get out of the way, Sloane."

"I ain't moving. You want me to get outta the way, then you can make me."

Sloane came flying forward as Dalton pushed the woman from behind. "What's your problem, Sloane? She's leaving. You should be happy. You hate her so much and now you ain't gotta see her no more."

Raven stood to the side of her bedroom door, and Sloane moved toward her. Out of the corner of Raven's eye, she saw movement and turned her head. Trudy's friends were heading right toward them.

"Come on now, Sloane," Trudy's friend said. "Let her through. You can come with us to have a cup of coffee."

Sloane hesitated at first, but seeing the hardness on their faces, she followed the women. She looked at Raven over her shoulder. "I ain't done with you yet."

With Sloane gone, Raven rushed into her room and grabbed the familiar bag that Evelyn, her first temporary foster mom, had given her when she was eight years old. She took a second to appreciate the bag. She ran her hand over the pink, orange, yellow, and purple flowers. The bag gave her belonging and comfort. It had been the only constant in her life.

"You sure do love that bag," Dalton commented.

Raven looked at the object fondly. "I can hear laughter and comfort of the past in this bag. It's the only thing that has stayed with me since I was a kid. I walked through hell with it. It's like an old friend. Does that sound crazy?"

"Nah, that ain't crazy. It's like how I drool over that picture I look at every day. It's a reminder of better times."

Raven shoved her belongings into the bag. Then she lifted the mattress from her cot where she kept the money she saved. She lifted the white envelope, but it was flat. She opened the envelope. It was empty.

"All my money is gone," she murmured, the moment not quite real.

As her reality seeped in, Raven dropped to her knees and covered her head with her hands. A sob broke loose. Her money, the money she needed to start her life, had vanished. Her guts twisted as anger and disappointment battled inside of her.

Dalton squatted next to her. "It's gonna be okay. You'll be all right."

Raven couldn't hear her roommate. She was swimming inside her sorrow. She went down on the floor and rolled onto her side. Her knees came up to meet her chest, and as she wrapped her arms around them, she roared out a cry of distress. She was inconsolable thinking about the thousand dollars that had been stolen . . . after how hard she'd saved it. After several minutes, she stood and steadied herself. Then she left her room as Dalton watched in horror.

Raven rushed into the cafeteria where Sloane was leaning against a counter with her two friends.

"I know you stole my money," Raven screamed. Her eyes were bloodshot, and tears streaked her face. "Where is it?"

Sloane sneered at her. "I have no idea what you're talking about. Even if I did, I'd never tell you."

Raven narrowed her eyes and rolled her hands into fists. "Let me tell you something, you piece of shit. You will never keep me down. You will never beat me. You took everything I worked for, and even with all of my money gone, I will make it through this. I'm not like you. I'm not weak and pathetic. You're going straight to hell."

Sloane stood stiffly, staring into Raven's eyes. Her mouth was slightly open and then it turned upward into a depraved grin. "Good luck with all that. I might go to hell, but you're going to go *through* hell. They'll be dragging you by your hair over the hot coals and broken glass. You'll be sorry you ever met me."

"I already am." Raven stomped out of the cafeteria.

Back in her room, Raven threw herself onto her cot.

Dalton was sitting up. Her head dropped to the side, and there was sadness in her eyes. "Let me guess. She denied taking your money?" Dalton asked.

Raven nodded and continued to cry. "It was so hard to save that much money. I didn't buy myself hardly anything. I can't believe it's all gone."

"I'm sorry this happened to you. But look on the bright side, you're getting out of here. You're gonna do something better, and you'll be safer."

Raven stood and lifted her duffel bag onto her shoulder. Then she held her arms open.

"I can't believe you're leaving," Dalton said, sniffling and embracing the girl. "You haven't even been here that long."

"I know, but it's time for me to go. You said so yourself. I can't stay here and put up with Sloane anymore. It's too much, and I deserve better. Besides, I work so much you probably won't even notice I'm gone." She was teary-eyed and trying to lighten Dalton's mood. "But it doesn't mean I'll never see you again. We can get together anytime we want."

Dalton nodded. "Yeah, sure. You know me. I'm not so good at keeping up with relationships." She shook her head, thinking of herself. "You came after me and you're leaving already. You've been here for what? Two months?"

Raven gave her a sad smile. "Almost three now. Look, you'll find something better. I know you're going to make it."

"Ah right." She sat on her bed. Sad and nervous, Dalton gripped her knees with her hands. "I don't do well with goodbyes." She cast her eyes down to her lap. "You should get going. I don't wanna drag it out. Take care."

"I will. You do the same. I'll see you again soon."

Raven walked out of the room. She went through the shelter to find Trudy. After saying goodbye to a few people, she found the older woman alone in the cafeteria, drinking coffee.

Raven put her bag on top of the table and sat next to the woman. Then she placed a hand on the woman's back.

"I heard you got all your money stolen," Trudy said.

Raven nodded, the emptiness of loss burning in her belly.

Trudy reached into her pocket and gave the girl fifty dollars. "It's all I can spare. I wish it was more."

"No, Trudy. I can't take your money," she said, shaking her head.

"Sure you can. I'll be pissed if you don't take it. I ain't about to send you into the world without a dollar in your pocket."

Raven took the bills and shoved them into her duffel bag. "Thank you."

Trudy gave her a terse grin. Inside, her heart broke that the girl was hit with the blow of losing her hard-earned money. "So you're all packed?"

Trudy's voice was even and tight. There were deep lines on the sides of her eyes, and her mouth was turned downward. Sadness was draped over her like dark clouds on a dreary, stormy day. She'd miss the girl beyond what even Raven could imagine.

"Yeah, I'm ready to go. I came to find you so I can tell you how much I appreciate your help over the past six weeks. You're a smart lady, and I'm gonna miss you so much." She had a ball in her throat, and she tried to swallow it back. She couldn't hold in the tears any longer.

"Oh, come on now, sweetie. Ain't no need to cry." Trudy's eyes were filled, and the inside of her chest was sizzling. "It won't be the same here without you. Try and think of it like you're off to a new adventure."

Raven nodded, but choked by unhappiness, she couldn't get any words out of her mouth.

"Change is hard," Trudy said, swiping at her tears and taking the girl's hand. "Once again, you're doing something to keep others safe . . . you know, the other women in here. But this time, it's also for yourself because you deserve better than the crap you're getting from Sloane. This will stop all that nonsense with her . . . for you and all of us."

Raven nodded and dipped her chin to her chest. "I know. And I'm happy about going somewhere new. But I don't know how I'll get along without you."

"Ah, hogwash. You ain't gonna miss me because this isn't the last time you'll see me. Once you settle, I'll need your phone number and I'll call you up. We'll get together. We can hang out and talk like we've been doing. You can call me here. Don't forget. Okay?"

Trudy put a hand on Raven's cheek and looked into her eyes. "There's something real important I want you to remember. When you're out there in the world, you're gonna have ups and downs. That's a part of life, so don't think you're being singled out for having to struggle at times."

Raven rested her head on the woman's shoulder.

Trudy stroked her hair. "Here's what you gotta keep in the front of your mind at all times. You keep your eyes on the bad people, the ones that steal your joy and don't want you to succeed. They work hard to get a lot of your attention. They need your energy to feed their ugliness, so they suck the good right the hell outta you. That's how they keep you down. But, at the same time, you need to keep your heart open to the good people. Those people will lift you up so you can do what God meant for you. They are the ones that will be there when you need them most. Hang on to those motherfuckers 'cause they ain't easy to come by. Otherwise, you'll miss the greatest opportunities to love and be loved."

Raven hugged the woman tighter. "I'll remember."

Trudy pushed her back at arm's length. "You promise?"

"Yes, I'll never forget it or any of the other things you taught me. Will you do me a favor?"

Trudy filled her mouth with air, puffing out her cheeks, then blew it out loudly. "Now what?"

"Will you keep an eye on Dalton? She doesn't have anybody. She gets lonely like the rest of us. Except she's not that good at making friends."

"Mmm, why do you have to go and give me the shit jobs?"

Raven stood and pulled Trudy to her feet. "Because you're the strongest woman in here. The strongest woman I know. You're the only person who can handle it. Besides, you know I can't trust any of the other bitches in this place," she teased, trying to lighten their solemn mood.

The two shared a teary-eyed laugh.

"I'll see you soon," Raven said, lifting her bag.

"You bet. Be good. Be fierce. Be a motherfucking warrior out there."

Raven gave her one last watery smile before she left the woman there alone, hanging on to a cold cup of coffee.

***

On Raven's way out of the shelter, Sloane grabbed her by the arm. "So, you ain't gonna tell me where you're going?"

"Um, no, because it isn't any of your business. You already took all of my money; you're not getting another thing out of me," she said, standing her ground and baring her teeth.

"Maybe you got family somewhere you're gonna go suck off of. I bet they're all rotten pieces of shit like you," Sloane said with her face snarled.

"Yeah, you're brilliant. You've figured out my whole life. Actually, you remind me of some of my family, especially the ones that were total assholes. Just think, now you'll need to find someone else to push around. Let go of me." Raven yanked her arm from the girl's grip. "Have a nice life, Sloane."

"Fuck you," the woman spat. "Don't think I'm gonna forget about you because you ain't here no more. I'll never forget that dumbass Raven Ledger got a break without having to serve her time in prison like the rest of us. I'm coming for you. You can count on it!" she screamed.

Raven took satisfaction that Sloane was angered over her departure. It wasn't worth the money that was stolen, but it was a small payback.

Raven stopped suddenly. She couldn't leave without saying what was in her heart. She spun on her. "You know, Sloane, I'll never understand why my life makes you so mad. What do you care whether I went to prison or not? My situation was different. I killed someone to save other people, which means I'm nothing like you, nothing at all. So get that through your thick skull."

Sloane ran her tongue over her teeth. "This ain't over. You think you're gonna waltz outta here without paying the consequences. You ain't. Go on and leave now. Go find your pathetic life, but don't get too comfortable. Because I'm coming for you. Someday, maybe not today, maybe tomorrow or next month, who knows." She belted out a cackle. "But I will destroy you. I don't care where you try to hide from me."

"You're insane," Raven stated and walked away.

Raven's stomach churned. As she walked out onto the street, she acknowledged that Sloane robbed her of the moment. That precious, rare flash of freedom only felt a few times in adult life.

Chapter Twenty

When Raven got to Guilty Pleasure, she barreled into the dressing room and placed her duffel bag on the table. She caught the attention of a few dancers, who eyed her up.

"What's up with the bag? Are you dancing now?" Bebe fired at her.

Raven's eyebrows lifted. "Oh no. No, I'm not dancing. This is my stuff—"

"Stuff?" Bebe screeched. "Stuff for what?"

Raven put her hands on her hips. "It's my clothes. Why do you care what's in my bag?"

Bebe crept closer, wearing only a thong. "I care if you got things in there that you plan on wearing to seduce my boyfriend."

As Raven opened her mouth to argue with Bebe, Lexie walked into the room.

"Bebe, get over yourself," Lexie barked at her. She stood inches from the girl and lifted a finger into the air. "One, Santino isn't your boyfriend. You're making that shit up in your head." She lifted a second finger. "Two, if Raven was gonna seduce him, she wouldn't need a dumb costume. And three, mind your own fucking business."

Bebe stared into Lexie's eyes, but the woman didn't flinch.

"You can look at me all you want, Bebe. You don't scare me, and it doesn't change a thing. Stop picking on people who aren't doing you any harm." She turned to Raven. "Come on. Bring your things over to my locker."

Raven walked beside Lexie. "Hell, I left one asshole at the shelter to come here and find another one waiting for me. I can't stand Bebe," she mumbled.

Lexie rolled her eyes. "Fuck these bitches. Don't give Bebe any of your energy. She's always lashing out at people. Bebe is miserable. Some of the men that come in here like to be bossed around and treated like dirt—it's some kind of mommy thing. If it wasn't for them, she'd have no clients."

"So," Raven said, changing the subject. "Thanks again for letting me stay at your place."

Lexie picked up the heaviness in Raven's tone.

"Did something happen with Sloane again?"

Raven nodded and her tears fell quickly. "I saved a thousand bucks and she stole it." She lifted her hands into the air. "I'm not telling you that to get more time on your sofa. If I save almost everything I earn for the next two weeks, I think I can have enough money to get a room, like we talked about."

Lexie put a hand on her shoulder. "Don't worry. I'll talk to Santino and the servers about a bigger cut of the tips. That's the one thing we can do for each other when we're hitting a rough spot."

Raven gave her a weak smile. "Really?"

"Yes, really."

"But won't they be annoyed that they're giving me more of their money?"

Lexie shook her head. "*Most* of us here are like family. There are only a few assholes." She shot a searing glance in Bebe's direction. "Now you better get out on the floor before Santino sends a search party for you."

***

It was past three in the morning when Raven stepped into Lexie's apartment. She stood inside the door and took in the enormous room. When Lexie said she lived in an apartment, Raven had expected a tiny place, like the projects she lived in with her mother and Matthew.

Lexie's apartment was more like a small house. The living room had two sofas, multiple chairs, a large coffee table, and end tables. The entire room was done in black and white with splashes of hot pink pillows accessorizing and giving the room a burst of color.

"Wow. This is beautiful."

Lexie grinned. "Thanks. I bought it a couple of years ago. I have a roommate who's an accountant. She pays half the mortgage and bills."

"She's okay with me staying here?"

"Yeah, I talked to her. She knows it's only temporary."

Raven nodded. "How many bedrooms are there?"

Lexie walked over to her sofa and sat down. "I have two bedrooms and two bathrooms. My roommate's daughter sleeps in the second bedroom."

"Oh," Raven said, confused. She squinted at her friend. "Then where does your roommate sleep?"

"Carla sleeps in my bed . . . with me."

Raven walked over to the sofa and sat next to Lexie. "Carla?"

"Yep, she's my girlfriend," Lexie admitted.

"Wait. You're gay?"

"I am. I don't tell the girls at work because I don't want my regulars to find out."

"Okay," Raven said, smiling and turning her body toward her friend. "You have to tell me how you can dance at a bar and not even like men."

"Oh, honey, I never said I don't like men. I adore men. I don't want to sleep with them, that's all. I'm attracted to women. I used to sleep with men until I met Carla five years ago."

Raven was shocked by Lexie's honesty. "Good for you. You're doing what makes you happy, and you don't care what anyone thinks."

"I am happy, and someday you'll be happy, too. I'm sure of it." She slapped her hands on her thighs. "I'm going to bed. Be prepared . . . In a few hours, there'll be a flurry of noise and activity as Carla and her daughter get ready to leave. Try your best to sleep through it."

"No problem. I'm a heavy sleeper. I'll be fine."

Alone in Lexie's plush living room, Raven fought the anxiety building inside of her since she discovered her money had been stolen. She needed to find somewhere to go soon. She hoped to stay close to work because Guilty Pleasure had become more to her than a job; it had become a place where she had family.

Chapter Twenty-One

Three days later, the strip club was packed with customers. It was a Saturday night, and the club was running drink specials. Raven was rushing around, stocking the bar, clearing tables, and running tubs of glasses back to the dishwasher. Even Guido, the grumpiest chef in South Philadelphia, took a second to tell Raven she was doing a great job.

She was coming from the kitchen with a rack of tall glasses when someone smacked her butt. Her head whipped sideways and she gave the guy a dirty look. "Don't touch me."

Raven moved to the bar, unloaded the glasses, and headed back toward the kitchen again. She stopped in the bathroom before going to the kitchen for more glasses. She passed the DJ booth and entered the darkened hall that led to the ladies' room.

As she rounded the corner, someone grabbed her arm and brought her to a sudden stop. "I said don't touch me," she growled.

She whipped around and faced a man she didn't recognize. He was in his early twenties. He had short blond hair and brown eyes. There was a spider tattoo on the side of his left eye.

"Where you goin'?" he asked.

"I-I-I have to get to the kitchen. The ch-chef is waiting for me. He'll send someone to look for me if I'm not there in a few seconds."

"Oh? Is that right? I don't believe you." He put his face close to Raven's, pressed his lips outward into an O, and sucked the air from her mouth. "See, I've been looking for you, Raven Ledger."

Her hackles went up. No one called her by her first and last name. "Who are you?"

The young man put his hand over her mouth and pulled her farther into the dark hall only lit by black light bulbs. Raven's eyes were bulging as she tried to twist away from him, but his other arm was strapped around her waist, holding her against his body. Then he let out a low, quick whistle.

From the shadows came three people. As they got closer, Raven could see one of them was a girl. As she approached, Raven choked on her saliva.

"You thought we wouldn't find you, but you were wrong," Blanco hissed through clenched teeth.

Raven was frantically trying to break free.

"That guy holding you—guess who he is?" Blanco said, flicking the girl's forehead. "Let me give you a clue. Remember when your brother was in the classroom, killing my brothers and sisters? Well, two boys were begging for their lives. One of those boys, Scott, has a brother in the Kensington Hoods. The dude holding you is Scully. That's his older brother."

Raven was trying to shake her head. She was attempting to speak through the fingers pressing her lips into her teeth. Tears streamed down her face.

I'm screwed. I'm gonna die.

The gang members didn't notice Lorenzo the dishwasher had strolled by the entrance to the kitchen. He paused and looked into the deep dimness of the hall. He could see the man with a hand covering Raven's mouth. He stood still hoping they wouldn't see him.

When Blanco punched Raven in the face, Lorenzo ran to get Rocco.

Raven reeled backward as pain washed over her and blood oozed from her nose.

"Let's go. Take her out the back," Blanco ordered.

"Nah, you ain't taking her nowhere."

Blanco's head snapped toward a man's voice. It was Rocco.

Rocco moved into the hall slowly, a gun in his right hand hanging down by his side. Behind Rocco were three more bouncers. They moved toward them at a steady pace.

When Rocco was standing next to Scully, he looked into the young man's eyes. "You need to let her go if you wanna get outta here alive."

Scully scoffed. "Get the fuck away from me, you pasta-eatin' motherfucker."

Rocco lifted his arm and pressed his gun against Scully's forehead. "Let her go."

Blanco and the two other gang members all had their guns pulled. Aiming them at Rocco.

Rocco's bouncers had their guns pointed at the gang members. It was a standoff until one bouncer yelled something in Italian and three more big guys approached from the opposite side of the hall.

"Now you're gonna let her go, you maggot-eatin' motherfucker?"

Scully took his hand away from Raven's mouth. Then he pulled his arm from her waist and shoved her forward with all his weight. Raven landed face-first into the wall on the other side of the hall.

Scully turned and looked into Rocco's eyes. "This ain't between you and me. This is between that piece of shit right there," he growled, pointing at Raven on the floor holding her face, "and the Kensington Hoods."

Rocco pulled his shoulders back. "Oh yeah. Why is that? What could she have done that you got some kind of fucking vendetta against her?"

"Her brother killed my blood brother," Scully snapped.

"So what? That wasn't her. She ain't got nothing to do with what her brother did. What are you, stupid or something?" Rocco asked in an even, cold tone.

Scully pointed his index finger a few inches from Rocco's face. "Let me tell you something. I don't know how you goombahs do it here in South Philly, but my pack does it different. It's an eye for an eye, bitch. She had to know what he was doing. But you know what? Even if she didn't, it's her life for my brother's." He held his hands out, palms up. "Simple as that."

"There ain't nothing simple about what you're doing to her. Now, I'm gonna give you a chance to leave. And when you do, don't ever come back here."

Scully gave him a wicked smile.

"See now," Rocco said, cocking his gun. "When you smile at me like that, I get the urge to smash my fist into your face, stomp on it with my boot, and let your gangster bitch here blow me while you're passed out on the floor."

Blanco flinched but quickly regained composure. She straightened her back and stuck out her chest. "You'd have to kill me before you stick anything that belongs to you into my mouth."

"Okay, that's fine." Rocco gave her a sinister smile. "We can make that happen. Now, this is enough talking." He lifted his free hand, and the large bouncers converged on the group of gangsters. "These are my friends. They're gonna make sure you get outta the bar without causing a scene."

The bouncers surrounded the group.

Before they left, Raven used the wall to get to her feet. There was blood running from her nose, over her mouth, and down her neck. She stepped into Blanco. "I saved your life that day. You know I did, but you aren't willing to let anyone else know that. I remember the look on your face. You were scared like I was. You aren't the fearless girl you pretend to be."

Blanco hacked up phlegm and spit in Raven's face.

Raven instinctively swung her arm and hit Blanco in the face with an open hand. Then she turned and walked away, heading into the dressing room.

Rocco lifted his chin, and one of his bouncers stayed with Raven, following her to safety.

Chapter Twenty-Two

Inside the dressing room, Raven collapsed on a chair.

The girls fell silent when they saw her bloodied face. Several dancers rushed to her side, offering their help. She looked around her at the chaos she was causing. This was not how she pictured her new start, and her intuition told her there would be more pain coming her way.

By now, Raven's face and cropped shirt were covered in blood. Some girls returned to their makeup tables, while a few still rallied around her.

"What the hell happened to you?" Moxie asked. She was a stripper who liked Raven.

"It's a long story," she rattled through swollen lips.

"Well, are you okay? Do you need a doctor or something?"

Rocco's voice boomed from behind them. "Nah, she'll be fine. She might need a rabies shot from the rat that hit her." He approached and held out a hand. "Somebody give me tissues."

Rocco dabbed at the blood coming from her nose. He could see that it wasn't broken. He lifted her top lip gently. "You're lucky. You still got all your teeth. Nothing lost there."

As Rocco was finishing, Lexie came rushing into the room. "Raven! Are you okay?"

The girl nodded, and Lexie knelt in front of her. Then she looked up at Rocco. "Where's Victor?"

"He's in his office, Lex. He already knows what happened."

"You guys are going to take care of her?" Lexie asked.

"If you're asking if we're gonna get her outta here safe, the answer is yes," Rocco stated.

Lexie stood and grabbed Rocco's hand. She led him a few feet away from the other girls. "Raven is staying at my place right now. She was looking for something more permanent."

Rocco shook his head. "She ain't staying at your place no more. Get your shit together and I'll have one of the guys drive you there to get her stuff."

"I can't throw her out, Rocco. Look at her," Lexie argued.

"I know she's your friend. Look, I like her, too, but wherever she goes, those goons will follow. You're putting yourself and anyone else who lives with you at risk. Is that what you wanna do?"

Lexie shook her head, thinking of Carla and her young daughter. "No, of course not, but we can't abandon Raven either."

"Ain't nobody gonna abandon her. Victor has an idea. It won't be long-term, but it'll get her outta this club. We can't jeopardize the whole place for one person. You know how this goes."

"Yes, I do. That's why I'm worried. What's the plan?"

"You don't need to know that, Lex. A car will be out back for you in ten minutes. Get your shit together and get out there."

***

Forty-five minutes later, when Lexie returned to the club, Raven was sitting in a chair in the dressing room. Lexie placed the girl's duffel bag next to her.

"Raven, I'm sorry. It wasn't my idea for you to leave my place."

Raven looked up. Her eyes were already bruising. She had used the club shower to wash away the blood, and Moxie had helped her put her jeans and T-shirt back on.

"I know. Rocco filled me in, and he's right. I would never be able to live with myself if anything happened to you or your family because I brought them to your house."

Lexie burst into tears. "Oh, Raven. I'm heartbroken. I can't believe this is happening to you." She hugged the girl gingerly, mindful of her injuries.

"Yeah, me too. I appreciate you being my friend. I'm leaving soon. Victor has a plan for me."

Lexie nodded and took the girl into her arms. "You be careful."

"I will," Raven said. Then she left the dressing room to find Santino.

All eyes were on her as she walked through the bar with her face mangled. She could see the sympathy for her in their faces, accompanied by relief it wasn't them.

Chapter Twenty-Three

After all the plans were arranged for Raven, Victor marched onto the main floor and strode to the bar, taking long, heavy steps to where the girl was standing with Santino.

"Raven, let's go."

Her eyes grew wide. She was still shaken from the altercation. "Wh-where am I going?"

"I'm taking you out of here. I'm sorry. I think you're a nice kid and a damn good worker, but I won't have gangs taking over my bar. I have other employees to think about. I have my business to take care of."

Raven pulled at the hem of her T-shirt. "Victor, I don't have anywhere else to go. I gave up my room at the place I was staying. They'll find me again. I'm sure they're going to follow me. They're going to kill me next time."

Victor's eyes softened as he thought about his daughter. "Look, I know who you are. I've always known. I know where you live, too. I know almost everything about all my employees whether they tell me or not." He paused and looked her over. "Even though it was your brother who killed five of their gang members, people like that can't be reasoned with. Revenge is lifeblood for them." He looked down at his shoes and his hand grazed over the outside of his jacket to the gun he kept there. He glanced at her again. "I can keep you safe for a few days. I know of a motel where you can stay . . . until you can find somewhere else to live."

Raven peeked at Santino. "I need to go back to where I was staying and talk to someone before I disappear off the face of the earth." She squinted through her swollen eyes. "Please, Victor. I have to warn someone close to me."

"Look, I think it's stupid, but if you want to go, then I can't stop you. I won't let one of my bouncers take you there, I can't put them in that kind of danger, and I can't send ten guys with you. I need to know, these Kensington Hoods, how did they know where to find you tonight?"

She shrugged and her eyes swelled with tears. "There's a woman who lives in the shelter. She hates me and she's crazy. I think she might've told them where I work. I don't know for sure. That's why I have to go back."

Victor shoved his hands into his front pockets. "For fuck's sake, Raven. Can this be any more complicated? I'm sure you can call whoever it is you need to warn. You have to cut and run," he said in a heated tone, scowling at her. "I think you're putting yourself in the line of fire if you go back now."

Raven shook her head. "I know you're right, Victor. I can't leave and not tell my friend. There's a woman at the shelter, and I'm afraid they'll hurt her to try and find me. I'll go and talk to her. I'll come back here after. Would that be okay?"

"That's fine by me, but don't bring those thugs back here again. You understand?"

Raven shrank away.

Santino stepped closer to the owner. "Come on, Victor. She had no way of knowing they were going to come in here looking for her tonight. She can't guarantee they won't come back. But here's the thing." He looked at Raven. "When you go to the shelter, you should tell the bitch that ratted you out that Victor fired you because the gang came into his club. Tell her you hate her and that you'll have to live on the streets. That might throw them off your trail for a week or so. Hopefully, it'll keep them from coming back here."

"Good thinking," Victor complimented. "Fine, Raven. Go." He pulled a twenty-dollar bill from his wallet. "Take a taxi to the fucking shelter and get back here as fast as you can."

"Victor?" Santino said in a sharp tone to get his attention. "I'm going to ride with her. She can't go alone . . . She doesn't have a fighting chance by herself. I'll be back within the hour." He looked around the bar and the crowd had thinned out since the altercation with the Kensington gang. "You all right with that?"

Victor looked at Raven and then turned his attention to Santino. "As long as the other bartenders can cover for you. But I want you back here within the hour. I don't need one more goddamn person to worry about."

THE TWIN SISTER

***

A short time later, the taxi pulled over a block from the shelter.

Raven grabbed the handle. "You stay here, Santino. I'm going to run down, and I'll be back in ten minutes."

"No. I'm coming with you."

She leaned across the seat, moving her face closer to his. "You can't. Stay here. I'll be quick." She put her mouth next to his ear. "Don't let this taxi leave. Okay?"

Santino regarded her for a prolonged moment. "Fine. But you have ten minutes before I come down there."

***

Raven walked through the front door of the shelter and saw the receptionist behind the glass.

"Hey, Raven. What are you doing here? Lilly told me you don't live here anymore. You moved out three days ago. Found another place to live."

Raven gave her a swollen-face smile. "I did. But I went out to the gym with Trudy, and she put my ID in her pocket. I forgot to get it from her. I'll only be a minute, or you can ask her to come out here."

The woman moved closer to the bulletproof glass. "What happened to your face?"

"Oh, two guys at the bar got into a fight and I jumped between them. It was so stupid."

The woman watched her for a moment, then pressed a button on the side of her desk. "Be quick."

Raven pulled the door open that led to the common room. It wasn't yet midnight, and several women were watching television. Raven tried to go unnoticed as she crept along the wall and into Trudy's room.

"Trudy?" she whispered in a panicked tone.

Trudy sat up in her bed. She blinked and rubbed the sleep from her eyes. "What are you doing here?"

"I came to warn you. It's about Sloane. She sent the Kensington Hoods to the club. I came back to tell you I have to leave Lexie's place. I don't know where I'm going, but I didn't want you to worry about me."

"Why the hell didn't you just call here? Why would you risk your ass like this?"

Raven's shoulders rolled forward and her head hung. The hot tears burned her eyes and stung her scraped skin. "Because."

Trudy was on her feet. She put her hands on the girl's shoulders. "Because why, sweetie?"

"Because I'm scared. I'm all alone. I don't know where I'm going or what I'm doing. I like all those people at Guilty Pleasure, but they ain't you. Besides, the owner is giving me a place to stay for a couple of days. Then I'm on my own."

"All right now," Trudy said, pulling the girl to her. "I want you to call here as soon as you land somewhere. But be careful what you tell the person when they answer the phone."

Raven nodded. "You need to watch your back. I was thinking . . . what if Sloane tells the gang to go after you to get to me?"

"She won't."

Raven tilted her head. "How do you know that?"

"Because it'll be the biggest mistake she ever makes. I'll make sure of it."

Raven gave the woman another hug. "I have to go. Someone is waiting for me. I'll call you."

Then the girl rushed from Trudy's room. She had exited the building when she saw Sloane coming at her from across the street. Raven's eyes darted around.

"Bitch, you can stop looking for your skank friends. They ain't here to help you."

Raven pushed Sloane in the chest to back her up a few feet. Sloane stumbled a few steps back and then caught her balance.

Raven didn't hesitate. She swung, punching Sloane on the tip of her jaw.

Sloane fell to the sidewalk on her knees. She looked up at Raven with unfocused eyes.

Raven jumped on Sloane's back and punched her hard. *Left, right, left, right.* Exactly the way Trudy had taught her to fight.

Raven stopped only for a second. Sloane was attempting to cover her face, but Raven was relentless. "Are you done trying to ruin my life?" she screamed.

Raven was still swinging when someone put their hands under her arms and lifted her to her feet. She turned and looked into Dalton's concerned gaze.

"What the hell are you doing?" Dalton asked as she dragged Raven away from Sloane by her wrists.

"See my face? Sloane did this to me. She let the Kensington Hoods know where I work. I'm tired of this crap. I won't let her get away with putting my life in danger anymore." Raven was breathing hard, and sweat dripped down the sides of her face. She pointed at Sloane, who was slumped over on the sidewalk.

"There are other ways to handle this shit."

Raven moved her face closer to Dalton so she could get a better look at what Scully did to her. "Like what? Wait for them to hunt me? Wait for them to kill me next time? I won't do that. Ever."

Dalton nodded. "Okay, I get you. I know how it is to be beaten." She looked over at Sloane still a bit dazed. "But go now and leave this piece of shit behind you."

"Okay," Raven agreed evenly. She took a few steps over to Sloane and squatted next to her. She glared through puffy, bruised eyes at the traitor.

Sloane narrowed her eyes and gave her a clipped smile. "I want you to know those Kensington Hoods weren't so hard to find. In fact, it was easy. You should've seen the look on their faces when I told them I knew exactly where you were. I'm surprised you're still breathing. You can bet they'll be back to finish what they started."

Raven rolled her eyes and cocked her head. "What? Are you the devil's lackey now? You're a loser, Sloane. You put my life in danger and everyone that was in the bar tonight."

Sloane swallowed hard. Then she shook it off and snickered. "You think I give a shit about anybody at Guilty Pleasure? 'Cause if you do, then you're more clueless than I thought. I hope the rotten Kensington Hoods go there looking for you again. See, I'm on their good side, I led them to you."

Raven cackled. "You're so eager to hurt me that you don't care who else has to suffer. But guess what? That gang isn't particular about who they kill. They might decide you're an idiot, which they probably will very soon since they got bitch-slapped at the club. I sure hope you warned them about the bouncers and security there. Oh! You knew nothing about that, did you? You sent them into a lion's den."

Raven's stomach was spinning. She and Sloane had been at each other's throats. Now, there was a chance they'd be hunted by the same aggressors. Raven knew Blanco well enough to understand that Sloane would be blamed for sending them into an impossible situation at the bar.

Sloane stood. "I hope those Hoods fucking kill you. Everyone knows you should've died in that school right next to your brother."

Raven scoffed. "That's rich coming from a woman who tried to burn her parents to death." Raven's mouth twisted upward on one side. "You need to get out of this shelter before they come looking for you."

Then Raven put her face closer to Sloane's and smiled in the most pleasant way. "Oh, and it doesn't matter that I got fired from Guilty Pleasure tonight because unlike you, I have other plans . . . you know, more options available to me since I've never been in jail," she said, ensuring her words twisted like a knife in Sloane's heart.

Raven stood. Then she walked away from the shelter toward the taxi at the end of the block. Right before she got there, she heard footsteps striking the sidewalk behind her. She glanced over her shoulder and heard Blanco scream her name.

Raven flung the back door open and dove into the back seat.

Santino leaned up on the front seat. "Go! Man, go!" he yelled, banging on the plexiglass that separated them.

The taxi driver looked to his left and saw the angry group running at them. He stepped on the brake, put the car in drive, and pressed on the gas. The tires spun and smoked billowed out right before the car jerked into motion and they sped away.

Chapter Twenty-Four

"What the hell happened?" Santino hissed, in a reserved tone so the driver wouldn't overhear him.

"I have no idea. They showed up out of nowhere. I got in a fight with Sloane or I would've been out of there sooner." She leaned her head against the back seat of the car, still breathing heavily. She rolled her face toward Santino. "I'm scared. Victor is sending me to a motel," she whispered.

"Victor has a friend who owns a few motels. Sometimes he does this for a dancer if they're being chased by their abusive boyfriends. I don't know which one you're going to, and it doesn't matter. I think it's a good idea. Victor is smart that way, and he wouldn't put you somewhere they can find you. He's got people that work for him all over the place. I would trust him."

"Victor has people? What kind of people?"

Santino ran a hand through his hair. "People he can rely on in tough situations. He has a couple of personal bodyguards, too. There can be some jealous boyfriends or husbands of the dancers that go after him. It's already happened three times. Plus, he's worth *a lot* of money. Guilty Pleasure rakes in bundles of cash every night. He keeps it upscale, you know, with a real chef and all, for a reason. Not only does he get male travelers, but he also has a lot of regulars who come from the outskirts of the city. You know, businessmen who are entertaining clients. A good meal, strong drinks, and a show."

Raven nodded. "I appreciate what he's doing for me, but I'm nervous. What if it's a dangerous place?"

Santino grabbed her hand. "It might be, but it doesn't matter. You can't get too comfortable at the motel anyway. When Victor says a couple of days, that's exactly what he means. Use the time to figure out where you're going next. That's the only thing that matters."

Raven looked down, and her hair fell over her face. "I didn't get to tell you. Sloane stole all the money I saved. A thousand bucks." Her voice broke.

Santino moved closer and put his arm over her shoulder. "I have a little money stashed aside. I can lend it to you. I don't have much, but I can come up with three, maybe four hundred dollars. I can let you borrow it for a couple of weeks."

Raven shook her head. "Thank you. I can't take your money because I can't pay you back."

"I'm sorry. I wish I could give it to you, but I have rent and bills due..."

She let out a loud breath. "It's fine. You don't owe me anything. Something will come to me." She looked at him with fear in her swollen eyes. "I'll do whatever I need to."

At the time, Raven meant it.

Chapter Twenty-Five

When Raven and Santino returned to Guilty Pleasure, Victor was waiting for them. "We need to go right now," he told Raven.

She opened her arms and hugged Santino. "Thanks for everything." Her voice hitched. "I hope we meet again someday."

Santino held her tighter. "You take care of yourself. You'll see your way through it. You're smart and capable. You remember that, okay?"

Tears dribbled down Raven's face as she nodded. She'd miss seeing Santino. She turned to leave, and Lexie was standing behind her.

"You weren't gonna leave without saying goodbye to me, were you?" the woman asked.

"Oh, Lexie." She threw herself into the woman's arms. "I don't want to leave. I wish I could stay. Will I see you again?"

Lexie put her at arm's length. "I sure as hell hope so. But if we don't see each other again, you remember that you are much bigger than the problems your brother created for you. Be strong, don't take any shit, and don't let the assholes drag you down to their level." She gave her a sad smile and handed Raven her familiar duffel bag. Lexie leaned forward, kissed Raven on the cheek, and rushed away.

***

As Raven sat in the back of Victor's car, she hung her head to hide the silent tears that fell. Rocco was in the front passenger seat, and he looked over his shoulder at her.

"You okay back there?" he asked.

Raven nodded but wouldn't look at him.

Victor glanced at her in his rearview mirror. "Raven, I've paid for the motel room for five nights, longer than I originally told you. That should give you enough time to find a place to live. Do you have any money?"

"No. All my money was stolen by the woman who let the gang know where I work."

Victor raised his eyebrows. "Oh yeah? What is this woman's name?"

Raven lifted her head. She was worried Victor would go after Sloane. She wanted no part in getting revenge on the woman. She didn't need another thing to weigh heavy on her brain or one more reason to carry the burden of guilt.

"Oh, it doesn't matter. She's . . . she's messed up in the head."

Victor's eyes narrowed as he watched the road in front of him. "It matters to me, Raven. I'm only asking so I can make certain this woman doesn't come looking for your job after you're gone," he lied.

"But you're not going to look for her?"

"No," Victor said with definitiveness. "I have better things to do with my time than search for some rotten broad that sent a bunch of thugs to make trouble at my bar."

"Her name is Sloane Mathers. She hated me from the second I walked into the shelter. She was pissed because I didn't go to jail for killing my brother. She's a jealous woman. We've never gotten along," Raven admitted.

"Well, Sloane sounds like the kind of woman I'd like to ram in the face. The kind of girl that would sell her soul to get even," Victor ranted.

"She's an unhappy person," Raven said. "You're not going to do anything to her, right?"

"Of course I'm not. I'm not an animal. I don't give a shit about that bitch, but if she shows up at my club, then she's going to have a problem," Victor vowed.

But Victor wasn't the man who forgot things easily. He didn't care that Sloane was trying to hurt Raven. When she sent the Kensington Hoods to his bar, Sloane had crossed the line, and she would eventually pay for her bad choice.

Raven leaned back and closed her eyes. She listened to the hum of Victor's tires against the road and was lulled into a semi-sleep state.

"We're here," Victor said. He had parked the car at the motel and was looking into the back seat at Raven sleeping. "Hey! Raven."

Her eyes popped open. "Oh, sorry," she said, sitting up straight.

She looked around her. There was a single-story, L-shaped building with twenty entry doors. Tall weeds were poking up through the cracked blacktop. The *E* in the motel sign was burned out, and the office looked like it was haunted, with its eerie yellow light casting a menacing glow through the dirty front window. The place looked abandoned except for there being seven cars in the worn parking lot scattered in front of motel doors.

"I know it isn't fancy, but it's a place for you to sleep and shower," Victor stated matter-of-factly as he observed the horrified look on her face. "You should prepare yourself, though . . . This place brings in a lot of riffraff. But it was the only motel I could get without going into West or North Philly." He watched her, waiting to see that she understood. She didn't.

She squinted at him. "Should I be scared? Is it a dangerous motel?"

Victor nodded. "It could be dangerous if you get involved with the people who rent rooms here. That's why it's important to pay attention to everything going on around you. You should stay inside at night and proceed with caution during the day."

"Oh," Raven gasped. "That's scary. Are you sure there isn't another place I could stay? Another motel close by?"

He shook his head. "I told you already, this is the best I could get last minute. I'm trying to help out here. I could've told you to leave tonight and not done anything more. I'm doing this because I think you're a nice girl. You have a good mind, and your heart is in the right place. I feel sorry for you. So, you'll need to go with it."

Raven's hand floated to the base of her neck. "You're right. This is all coming at me so fast, and I appreciate everything you've done to help. But . . . but what if something happens? Like what if someone does something bad to me while I'm here?"

"Then you should call the cops. Don't expect them to get here quickly, though. They aren't that responsive to this area of town." Victor got out of his car and opened the back door for her.

She got out, heaving her duffel bag behind her. He reached into his pant pocket and brought out a key with a large plastic tag on it. The number 7 was stenciled in black paint. He handed her the key and pointed to the door in front of the car.

"All right." He reached into his other pant pocket and pulled out a wad of money. "Here's your last paycheck." He counted off two hundred dollars, at least one hundred more than he owed her. "Get some food and spend this money wisely. Remember, I paid for five nights. Mind your own business. Do you understand me? Do not get involved with the people staying here and you'll be fine."

Raven looked down. The large plastic key ring filled her palm, and she curled her fingers around it. She looked up at Victor. "Thanks for helping. I loved working at your bar."

Victor shuffled his feet and looked away from her. "Okay, kid. I have to go."

Victor was rarely emotional about anything that didn't involve his wife, daughter, or his bar. But he had a soft spot for Raven. Maybe it was her innocence or her unwillingness to do whatever it took to fit in with the crowd. He wasn't sure and couldn't place his finger on the source, but he instinctively knew the girl had good intentions.

"Take care of yourself," he said, getting back into his car.

Rocco got out of the car and looked at her over the roof. "Hey, Raven. You're gonna do good shit in the world. Go out and make me proud." He smiled at her.

Raven's heart cracked in half. "Thank you, Rocco. Stay cool."

She stood on the battered pavement as Victor pulled away. She turned toward her motel room, inserted the key, and stepped inside. Her hand scraped along the wall of the dark room until it hit a switch. A light fixture with a burnt orange globe shone over a fake wood table and two chairs. The door closed behind her and she threw the extra lock on.

She placed her duffel bag on the small table and walked to the bed. The filthy carpet sucked at her sneakers. The room smelled of mold and stale liquor. A faint aroma of cigarette smoke clung inside the heavy, burlap-type curtains. She pulled the thin comforter back. The top side was an orange-and-brown checker, and the bottom side was a white pilling fiber.

Leaving the bed, she took slow steps to the bathroom. Flipping on the light, it had a filthy sink, toilet, and bathtub-shower combo with black mildew covering the edges of the tub and the grout between the tiles on the wall.

Raven turned the water on in the sink. At first, the water ran in a rust color, but after a minute, it came out clear. She cupped her hands together and splashed water on her face. Two towels were sitting on top of the toilet tank. With her face dripping wet, she grabbed one. It was stiff and scratchy, so she patted it lightly against her painful flesh.

While the Last Call was a shelter and provided few luxury items, it was a more sterile environment, clean, compared to the motel room that needed scrubbing, remodeling, or maybe being demolished and rebuilt.

"What a fucking dump," she said to herself.

Back in the bedroom, Raven turned on the television and kicked off her sneakers. It seemed like a million years had passed since she had watched television on her own. She watched an old sitcom on one of the four channels she could get at the motel.

As she lay in bed watching a show, her eyes got heavy, and without fighting it, she fell into a deep sleep.

Chapter Twenty-Six

It was the middle of the night when Raven was woken by heavy banging. At first, she thought someone was knocking on her motel door and her heart fired away like a string of firecrackers in her chest—*boom, boom, boom, pow, pow, pow!*

Then she heard it again and realized it was somewhere nearby. Relieved, she crept from the bed with her bare feet pressing into the sticky carpet. Pulling her toes from the carpet was a reminder the motel was not a place that she'd want to remain too long. The motel was for the downtrodden and lost people—like herself, the people who belonged nowhere. She took careful steps over to the window. Not to be noticed, she lifted the edge of the curtain carefully. Two doors down, a large, burly man with long, wild hair knocked on the door of room 9.

"Open the fucking door, Monica. I swear to God, I'll break it down if you don't," he yelled. Then he pounded on the metal door several more times and kicked the bottom with his boot.

Finally, Raven could see the light from the room casting out into the parking lot, and she knew the door was open. Raven couldn't see who was on the inside, but she watched the big man raise his fists and rush forward. There were muffled screams. The sounds of a woman being beaten, the sounds her mother used to make when Gage beat her.

Raven moved to her bed and sat on the edge. *I should help her.*

Victor's warning pressed to the forefront of her mind. *Do not get involved with the people staying here.* The last thing she needed was to get kicked out of the motel or, worse yet, have someone tell the Kensington Hoods where they could find her.

Raven pulled the covers up, but she couldn't sleep. All she could do was imagine what was happening in the motel room two doors down. *What if that man kills that woman and I lay here doing nothing?*

She stayed in bed with the television off, listening for proof that the woman was still alive. Two hours later, Raven heard the man's voice again. She threw the grimy covers back and rushed to the window. She watched.

"I'm going to get smokes. I'm gonna leave the room key here, and when I come back, you better open this fucking door. Do not make me wait." He got into a beat-up pickup truck parked in front of the room, started the engine, and took off.

Raven slipped her feet into her sneakers, grabbed her room key, and rushed to the woman's door. She knocked lightly and the door opened almost immediately. Standing in front of her was a young woman, a little older than her, with a bloody nose and swollen face to match her own. The woman's fear was visible. She was gripping the doorframe and was shaking uncontrollably. Her face was ashen under the blood and bruises.

"O my God, are you okay?" Raven gushed.

The girl flinched. "Wh-who are y-you?" the girl mumbled through swollen lips.

"I'm Raven." She pointed toward her room. "I'm in room 7."

"I'm Monica," the girl stated.

Raven took in the girl's injuries. "I heard that man screaming at you. I think you might need stitches above your right eye."

Monica shook her head wildly. "No. No, you can't say anything to anyone. Bull will kill me." She stepped back from the doorway in jerky movements.

"Okay. I won't tell anyone. I promise," Raven assured her. "Is Bull your husband?"

Monica shook her head spastically. She pressed her hands inside her front pockets. Then she ran them through her hair before crossing them over her chest. She couldn't settle, anticipating his return. "He's my boyfriend, but he's not very friendly. Actually, he's a big dick. I met him six months ago, and I moved in with him. He thinks he owns me." Tears dribbled down her cheeks. "The problem is, he does own me. I can't get away from him. I ran this morning, came here, and he found me."

"Wow. That's messed up. Listen, maybe I can help figure out a plan to get you away from Bull."

"That's not possible," she uttered.

Raven moved closer to the girl and lowered her voice. "I think it's possible. Do you want to go to my room? He won't find you there. We'll just stay inside."

"If we can't stay inside forever, he'll find me. This is the second time I ran. I can't hide from him no matter how hard I try," Monica cried.

"How does he keep finding you?"

Monica shook her head. "The first time I went to his mother's house . . . 'cause I don't have any family. She called him and he beat me right in front of her. This time I thought I was being smart. But being dumb, I used his credit card to rent the room and he found out because I paid for two weeks thinking I could get on my feet in that time. His credit card company called him. I never even thought about the credit card company doing that."

"Oh," Raven said, trying to sound casual. Even she knew it would be a stupid move to use an abusive boyfriend's credit card, she remained quiet, not wanting to make it worse for Monica.

Raven looked behind her. She, too, was now paranoid that Bull would return. "I really think you should come to my room."

"Why do you want to get involved? Bull will kill you if he finds out you helped me."

Raven winced. She didn't want to hear that, and she had to gather her courage not to walk away and leave the girl standing there. "I know what it's like to need help. I understand what it is to be invisible. To be worthless. I'm trying to give you a hand. I don't have any family. I've had some people help me along the way, though. Like the room I'm in." She gestured with her head toward her room. "My old boss paid for it."

"He did?" Monica's eyes grew larger. "Is he coming back to . . . you know?"

Raven watched the young woman for a second, then it sunk in. "Oh no. We don't like each other or anything. He was helping me out of a bad situation. He was being nice since he won't let me work at his bar no more."

"Well, why won't he let you work for him, but he helped you rent a room?" Monica asked. "That doesn't make any sense."

Raven looked away from her.

"Sorry, is that why your face is fucked up?" Monica asked in a regretful tone.

Raven moved her eyes back to the girl. "Yeah, I got into a fight at his bar. Not a boyfriend, though." She knew she'd already said too much. "Listen, if you're going to come down, you should do it now. Before Bull gets back."

Monica nodded, went deeper into the room, and grabbed her purse. She stepped outside, and they walked beside each other to Raven's room.

Raven assessed the empty-handed girl. "Don't you have any clothes with you?"

Monica nodded. "There's no time for that. He'll be back any minute."

"Right," Raven stated, hurrying to her door.

Inside the room, Monica sat on the bed as Raven wet a washcloth and dabbed at the girl's cuts and bruises. They had turned on the television and both were trying to relax, but waiting for the inevitable return of Monica's boyfriend had them both on edge . . . like rogue electrical wires zapping through the air.

They heard Bull screaming before the banging started.

"Hey!" another male voice hollered from one room. "Shut the fuck up!"

"Fuck you!" Bull yelled back. "Come out here and I'll beat the living shit outta you." That was followed by Bull pounding his fists and kicking his feet against the door.

Raven shut off the lights and the television. She cracked the curtain and put one eye at the edge. Bull was out of control, punching, spitting, and kicking the door as he threatened Monica's life.

After several minutes, the office manager rushed past Raven's window. He was a big, stocky man himself. As he moved by, Raven saw the handgun tucked into the back of his pants.

"Hey, you need to leave."

"Kiss my ass," Bull fired back. "I ain't leaving until I get in this room and get my girl."

"We've already called the police, asshole. You need to get in your truck and go, or your ass is gonna end up in jail," the man warned.

"I don't give a shit about the police. That bitch on the other side of this door"—he smashed his fist into the door again—"she stole my credit card to rent this room. Yeah, bring the police so I can have her filthy, lying, cheating, stealing ass put in jail." He turned and rammed his elbow into the door several times. "You fucking thief! You whore! When I get my hands on you, I'm gonna snap your fucking neck!"

Raven turned away from the window and saw Monica on the bed, knees pulled up, hands over her ears, rocking. She rushed over to her.

"Monica, you're going to be okay. Someone who works here is out there. He said they called the police. Once the police come, you can grab your things and get out of here. This is your chance," Raven encouraged.

Monica shook her head. "I have nowhere to go."

"You can go to a women's shelter or . . . or a homeless shelter."

Monica looked up at her with swollen eyes. "Will you go with me? You said you don't have any family."

Raven's mouth dropped open. It hit her like a bucket of cold water in the face. She was advising this girl where to go when she would face the same problem in five days. With the wind knocked out of her, she sat on the edge of the bed, not knowing how to answer the girl.

"I don't know. I need time to think," Raven said after a minute had passed.

I don't take my own advice, but here I am, telling Monica what to do.

The reality of her situation crashed in on her.

I'll be on the streets in five days.

Chapter Twenty-Seven

Monica was up on her knees, shimmying toward the bottom of the mattress, moving closer to Raven. She would not give up. Being alone was Monica's worst fear and the reason she had failed relationships and was attracted to men who weren't good for her.

"We can go to a shelter together. You know, look out for each other," Monica said in a pleading tone.

Raven's shoulders rolled forward, and her neck was bent. She was uncertain and still had time to make her decision. "I don't know. I mean, w-we just met, and I haven't thought about where I'm going next. I just got here."

"But we are both alone in the world. We can be each other's family. We can start over. Please," the girl begged, tears dripping from her eyes.

Raven stood and walked to the window. She peeked out and saw two police cars behind Bull's pickup truck. Bull was on the pavement, a lit cigarette in one hand and the other hand jammed into his jeans pocket. She couldn't hear what they were saying, but Bull appeared calm.

"The police are here. They're talking to Bull," Raven said, changing the subject.

Monica rose from the bed and sprang forward, not seeming to mind the gooeyness of the carpet between her toes. She crouched next to Raven. "Let me see."

Monica peered outside, the lights on the side of the motel room doors providing enough brightness for her to see the policemen and her boyfriend. "Bull's explaining his way out of being an asshole. I can tell by the way he's standing. He does this all the time. He completely loses control with me and then in front of other people he acts like he's the most rational person I've ever met."

"How long has he been beating you?"

Monica scrunched her brow. "It started about two weeks after I moved in with him." She lowered her head in shame. "I know . . . lame."

"Did you try to leave after the first time he beat you?" Raven asked.

She shook her head. "It's a shitty game. He'll be nice, like a knight in shining armor nice. After I'm all in love with him, he starts blaming me for everything. When I stand up for myself, he beats me. Then the cycle starts all over again." She turned and looked into Raven's eyes. "Sometimes I think I'm crazy. Other times, I believe him . . . that it's all my fault. And then, there are times when I realize he is the most toxic person I've ever known. Even worse than my parents, and they were terrible people."

Raven raked her fingers through her hair. "I know what you mean. My dad was great, but he died when I was young. My mom hurt me without ever laying a finger on me. She didn't do any parenting. She didn't protect me or my brother the way we needed her to."

"Wait! You have a brother? Is he cute?" Monica was already thinking maybe she'd like him, and they could hook up. "We should go to his place. Will he let us crash there for a while?" Monica asked.

Monica's desperation to get away from Bull was intense. Her nervous energy filled the room and made it impossible for Raven to think straight, and now she was asking about Matthew.

Raven shook her head. "I told you I don't have a family. My brother died in March."

Disappointed, Monica's chest caved. "Oh, man. That sucks. I'm sorry to hear that. How'd he die?"

Raven looked away. "I don't wanna talk about it."

"Oh, okay. I'm sorry if I upset you. What about your mom? Maybe we can crash at her place for a while."

"My mom is dead, too," Raven murmured.

"Shit. Sorry."

Raven stood and paced. "Like I said, I don't have any family. And you know, I don't want to talk about any of them right now. It's sad and disturbing. I have a lot of other shit to figure out."

Monica rubbed her forehead. "So any chance I can stay here with you until you have to leave? It'll give me a little time to figure out something. Plus, maybe by then, you'll come with me." She gave Raven a half-cocked smile. "Please. I'm not too proud to beg," she joked.

Raven strode over to her duffel bag. She pulled out a stale soft pretzel and ripped it in half. "Here you go. It's not much, but it's all I have right now. I'll go out in the morning and buy us some food. Do you have any money?"

Monica reached into her pocket and pulled out two twenty-dollar bills. "I snatched them from Bull a week ago. He didn't even notice. Bull drinks a lot, so he doesn't keep track of things too good."

Raven gave her a side-glance. "He seems to keep good track of you."

Monica smirked. "Yeah, that's because he doesn't like to be alone. If I'd known that, I would've never moved in with him. His wife left him, ran, and took his kid. He wasn't able to find them. I had no idea I'd pay the consequences for her running out on him. He never told me about her until after I was living in his place. He's freaking obsessed."

"Bull sounds like an asshole. How old is he?"

"He's thirty-three." She looked down at her hands. "I'm twenty," Monica said, blushing. "I never should've got with him. But I thought I was in love with him and that he'd take care of me. Look where that got me." She waved her hand over her swollen, bruised face.

Raven pulled back the pilling comforter and then the sheet. She kicked off her sneakers and slid under the covers. "You can stay here with me until I have to leave. I'm not promising that I'll go with you . . . I need time. I don't want to end up putting myself in a bad situation."

Raven's thoughts were on the Kensington Hoods and Sisterhoods. She needed to avoid them. She didn't want to go to a known shelter because the odds were they might recognize her. Raven thought she needed to find a shelter off the beaten path . . . something for people who had resigned themselves to living on the streets. People who had accepted their fate and would live out the rest of their days alone.

Chapter Twenty-Eight

On the sixth day, Raven and Monica snuck out of the motel early in the morning, while it was still dark outside. Raven found a shelter near the Philadelphia airport. It wasn't in the mainstream of the city. There were eighteen miles between the shelter and North Philly, but only a third of that distance from South Philly. She thought it was the perfect solution.

They took two buses to reach the shelter. They stood in front of a sign: My Doorstep. Underneath the name it read, *A Stepping Stone to a Life Worth Living*.

"This is it," Raven said. She looked up at the run-down single home.

The brick exterior was being strangled by wild vines, the front door needed paint, and the railing was falling away from the cement steps leading to the house. Raven took it all in.

"It sure doesn't look like a stepping stone," Raven commented.

Monica smirked. "Yeah, it's more like a big, ugly, broken boulder."

The two girls laughed and nudged each other. They had gotten close after spending five days together locked in the depressing motel room. But Raven hadn't talked about her brother. She had rationalized there was no reason for Monica to know.

"Okay, we need to go knock on the door," Raven said, her eyes glued to the shambles of the home. "Of all the places I could've picked, this had to be the one that I thought would be perfect. I'm sure glad we came together."

"Yeah, no kidding. It looks like a house from a horror movie," Monica whispered. "You can thank me for nagging you to come with me. You almost went off on your own until I lured you in with my good looks and charm. Good thing for you, I came along."

"You came along? I'm the one who risked my ass walking down to your room and rescued you from your bad mistake. But *I'm* the lucky one." Raven chuckled. "You're broke, remember?"

Monica weaved her arm through Raven's. "I remember. But what I lack in funds, I make up for in personality."

Raven giggled. "Come on." She tightened her arm and dragged the girl forward. Standing on the top step, she rang the bell on the side of the door and looked at her new friend.

A woman, who was close to six feet tall, pulled the door open. "Can I help you?"

Raven inched closer to Monica. "We're looking for a shelter to stay in. And we were, well, we were hoping you could help us."

The woman had a stern face. Her lips locked into a permanent frown, her eyebrows pulled together, and her nose was turned up at the tip. She was a big lady, not only tall but thick . . . built more like a man. After what seemed an eternity to Raven, the woman stepped aside and let them in.

Raven stood in the entryway, taking in the dark paneled walls and matching wood floors. She turned back to the woman. "I'm Raven Ledger, and this is my friend Monica Garcia."

The woman took in Raven's milky skin and green eyes. Then she scrutinized Monica's brown, Hispanic skin with matching brown eyes. "I'm Cassidy. I run the place. You two know that this is a coed shelter—that means both men and women live here."

Raven nodded. "Yes, ma'am, we know."

"I am not *ma'am*. I have a name and I told it to you already. You are to call me Cassidy if you want me to respond to you."

"Oh, I'm sorry," Raven mumbled. She shot Monica a helpless look.

Cassidy planted her hands on her broad hips. "That aside, the reason I told you about it being coed is because we don't allow residents to fraternize. We don't tolerate lovers quarreling here or being obscene in public spaces."

Monica nodded. "That's cool. So, what do we need to do to stay here? Do you got a room for us?"

"You mean to say, do I *have* a room for you, not *got*. It all depends on my assessment." The woman tilted her head, ignoring Raven. "Why is your face bruised?"

Already insulted that the woman mocked how she spoke, Monica's eyes narrowed. "My boyfriend did it," she snapped.

"I hope your boyfriend didn't follow you here," Cassidy said, lifting the blind on the front window and looking out.

Raven spoke up. "No, he didn't follow us. He doesn't know where Monica is. We thought this was a safe place to stay and we could get off the streets."

"Young lady, that's exactly what this place is."

Raven pulled her shoulders back and lifted her chin. "Don't call me young lady. I told you my name is Raven, and if you expect me to answer you, you'll use it. Isn't that the rule?"

Cassidy's face puckered with annoyance. "You need to understand that several other people live here, and I'm not about to jeopardize their safety because your friend has a boyfriend problem. Did her boyfriend beat you, too? Is that why you have matching faces?"

Raven grabbed Monica by the hand. "Let's go. I don't think this is the right place for us."

"Well," Cassidy huffed. "That's the first intelligent thing you've said so far."

Raven shook her head and walked to the front door. "You don't need to be so rude." She pulled it open and stepped outside with Monica following her.

"What an asshole," Raven commented.

"Yeah, but now where are we gonna go?"

Raven shrugged. "I have no idea, but we'll figure it out."

The girls walked toward South Philadelphia. Neither of them knew where they'd end up, but the one thing Raven took comfort in was that she wasn't alone. She knew that the closer she got to North Philly, the higher the chance someone would recognize her and tell the gang. She also realized her options were limited unless she wanted to live on the streets, which she hadn't the first clue how to do.

"We need to look for another shelter. Maybe one closer to Center City," Raven remarked.

"Oh, I know! There's a place I heard about in North Philly. It's some kind of old church or bank that people sleep in."

Raven stopped walking and shook her head. "No, North Philly is out. It's too dangerous there."

Monica looked around them. The streets were filled with trash. They were in an industrial part of town. Old factories and plants that only used a portion of their capacity. "It doesn't look too safe here either. Let's go check it out and if we don't like it, then we can find somewhere else."

"I'm not going to North Philly! I can't go there. If that's what you want, then go!" Raven's hands were shaking.

"Hey," Monica said, her voice becoming soft. "What's going on? We don't have to go there, okay?"

Raven closed her eyes and nodded. "Yeah, good. I'm sure we can find something in Center City. There's a lot more places than out here. Let's catch the bus, but after this, we have to watch our money. We're spending it too fast."

***

Forty-five minutes later, the girls sat on a bus heading back into the city. Raven looked out the window and watched the scenery pass.

After a while, Monica leaned her upper body against the side of Raven's. "Are you going to tell me why you freaked out about going to North Philly?"

Raven gave her a side-glance. She found herself conflicted. She liked having someone to figure out her next steps with, a friend like Addie had been. But guilt gnawed at her gut for holding back the secret that could put Monica at risk now that they were going back into the heart of the city. It was only fair that she let her know the danger she'd be in by hanging with her. She turned and rested her back against the side of the bus window.

Raven took a deep breath. Her anxiety was heightened. Her fear of Monica wanting to ditch her was getting the better of her.

"Did you hear about the shootings at Allegheny High School?"

Chapter Twenty-Nine

Raven told Monica what happened on the day of the school shooting.

Raven lowered her face. "So yeah, it was my brother who killed all those people." She sat still and waited for the fallout.

"So you have no idea how many people you saved. It's not just the ones in the classroom. He could've kept killing other people in the school." Monica paused for a moment and then she patted Raven on the leg. "Shit, girl. Your brother's a fucking asshole. But you ain't your brother. And that gang? They're a bunch of losers."

Raven released an audible sigh. "So I guess we both have people hunting us."

Monica pinched her lips together. "Yeah, I guess we do. So now what?"

Raven looked down at her hands and shrugged. "We find a place to stay. Get jobs. Then we can rent an apartment." She scoffed. "Maybe we should move to another state. We'd probably be safer that way."

"Hey, that's not a bad idea. We'll save as much money as we can. Then we'll move down south, where it's warm. We can strut around in bikinis and drink piña coladas on the beach," Monica offered.

Raven grinned. "Sounds cool. I like that idea. Look at us, planning for our future and shit. I'm glad we met. When I was working at Guilty Pleasure, there were a few people I got close to. I miss them."

"Wait! Go back," Monica said. "You worked at Guilty Pleasure?" She looked over her shoulder and then angled her body toward Raven. Her eyes were bright, and she wore a mischievous smile. "Were you a stripper? You can get another job and make a ton of money."

Raven rolled her eyes. "Yeah, right. Are you out of your mind? Do I look like someone who can be a stripper? I guarantee you there's not a man on this earth that would pay to watch me wiggle my butt." She pulled on her oversized sweatshirt. "I wear my clothes too baggy for that shit anyway," she teased.

"Shut up, I think you're hot. Hey, maybe we can get jobs stripping together," Monica stated. "Those girls make a lot of money. Plus, it would be fun."

Raven nudged her. "No way. That doesn't sound like fun to me. I've seen those girls, and they have to fake being happy all the time. I was a barback there and I loved my job."

"Did you have to wear one of those teeny-weeny uniforms?" she asked, pressing her thumb and index finger close together.

Raven scoffed. "Yes. I hated it."

Monica sat back. "Well, I was never a stripper, but I did some things in high school with the boys for money . . . to get away from my parents."

"Things? What kind of things?"

"Sex things. You know, a little of this and a little of that."

Raven leaned her head to the side. "Are you saying you kinda prostituted?"

"Well, when you say it that way, it makes it sound disgusting. It wasn't like that. I only did it with boys I liked."

Raven put her hand on Monica's shoulder. "I didn't mean anything by it. When I was eight years old, my only friend was a prostitute on Kensington Avenue. Her name was Skye. I still think about her sometimes. But back to you. Things must've been really bad at your house to make you do those things."

"You have no idea. My parents were freaks. They were swingers, you know, who liked to have sex with other couples. It's all they cared about . . . finding the couples, making sure there was plenty of booze, and picking sexy outfits . . . I was nonexistent. My mom wasn't even sure if my dad was really my dad. So I needed money to move out after high school. It wasn't hard for me to let boys pay me to have fun. I was raised in a home where sex was normal—having sex with many people was even more normal."

"That's crazy. So your parents had sex with other couples in your house? Where you could see them? What was that like?" Raven asked gently.

"Well, let's see. Imagine you're nine and the first time you learn about sex is walking into your living room where your mom is bent over the sofa with some stranger behind her. There were people everywhere having sex. It didn't matter what kind—regular, oral, anal. I literally shrieked and no one stopped. It was like I wasn't there."

Raven covered her mouth with her hand. "Did your parents talk to you about it after?"

"Are you kidding? No, they did it more after I saw them the first time. It was sickening, and it happened a lot. We rarely ate dinner together, and I had to spend most of my time in my bedroom with the door locked. I was afraid someone from their kinky group would sneak in," Monica explained. "So, that's how I got the idea to make money from the boys at school. I know it's strange, but I had to get out of there." She rubbed her arms nervously. "I left the day after I graduated high school. I disappeared and never contacted them again. And you know what?"

Raven shook her head as Monica's heartbreak unfolded.

"They never looked for me." Her voice hitched. "They never reported me missing. I don't have any memories of being loved by them. I was a mistake." Monica stared into the distance.

Raven put her arm around the girl and pulled her closer. "You weren't a mistake. Where would I be at this minute if Monica Garcia wasn't in the world? I'll tell you where—all alone with my two hundred bucks and no one to talk to."

Monica chuckled and rested her head on her friend's shoulder. "I've never had a best friend before . . . you know, a girl. I think if you keep up the good work, I might hire you for the job. It doesn't pay anything, though."

Chapter Thirty

Raven dashed up the block to Center City House, a shelter they found in a phone book. It was two o'clock in the afternoon by the time the girls arrived. As they got closer, they both looked at each other, eyes wide and lips pursed. A long line of people extended the entire block, around the corner, and halfway down the next block.

Raven leaned into Monica. "You get in line and I'm gonna find out what's going on . . . make sure we're at the right place."

As Raven approached the front of the line, the homeless people waiting eyed her suspiciously.

An old white man looked at her. His face was snarled with annoyance. He had a long gray beard and a bushy mustache with matching eyebrows. "Hey! You! Get to the back of the line."

Raven turned to the man, blinking rapidly.

"Yeah, you! The blinker. Wait your fucking turn."

"Oh, shut up, Howard," a Black woman yelled. "Have you seen her around? 'Cause I haven't seen her before. She don't know what's going on." The woman turned to Raven. "Honey, are you lost or something?"

Raven inched closer to the woman, aware that everyone near was watching her. "Me and my friend need a place to stay. Is this the line for the shelter?"

"See, Howard? You son of a bitch, she's never been here before. You need to stop being such a miserable old coot. Try to remember when you were"—she turned back to Raven—"how old are you?"

"Eighteen."

The woman's eyes bounced to Howard again. "Try to remember when you were eighteen, and you still had all your hair and teeth." She grabbed Raven's hand, and the girl fought her instinct to pull away. "Don't pay him no mind. He's grumpy with everyone."

A few people close to the duo nodded.

"Listen here, I'm Bitsy. What's your name, honey?"

"I'm Raven." She nervously pointed down the block. "My friend Monica is in the back of the line, around the corner."

"Well, Raven, I'd let you in with me 'cept it'll cause a damn riot."

"What's everyone waiting for?" Raven asked.

"Oh, the doors open at four. We start lining up around noon to be sure to get a bed." She leaned in closer. "The line is pretty long most days. I don't know if you and your friend will make it in here tonight. This here," she said, pointing to the front door, "it's the best shelter in the city. They got decent food, and they keep the bathrooms clean. You still have to keep an eye on your stuff. Even the people who work here can't control the thieves."

Raven winced. "The thieves? How do we protect our stuff?"

"First off, you never, ever leave your things alone. One of you always has to be in charge of them. Now, see here, if you get inside today, you find me. I'll show you the ropes. If you don't get in today, which I suspect you won't, come back here by noon tomorrow to get in line."

Raven's eyes shot downward to the sidewalk. "But if we don't get in, we don't have anywhere to sleep tonight."

Bitsy put her arm around Raven's shoulder and pulled her in to whisper in her ear. "If you don't make it in, then you go to the Market Street train station. You stay there as long as you can. Hide in the bathroom stalls. They won't come looking for you in there. In the morning, you wanna be out of the station by eight, before the rush of people come through. But don't go telling everybody 'cause it'll get overcrowded. That's my first backup when I don't get a bed."

***

After two hours of waiting in line and another thirty minutes for the line to move to the door, Raven and Monica were twenty feet from entering when the Center City House met capacity.

"Sorry, folks," a young man announced. "We have all we can take tonight. There's a shelter on Broad Street and another one on Walnut Street you can try. Everyone have a good night and stay safe."

Raven's heart sank to her stomach. Not only because they didn't get in, but also because she had wanted to talk to Bitsy more. She could tell the woman had a lot of street experience and could guide her.

"Shit. Let's go." Raven grabbed Monica's hand and headed down the block. They stood on the corner with a crowd of people. Raven eyed up a man in a business suit standing next to them. "Excuse me. Can you tell us how to get to the train station on Market Street?"

The man looked them up and down. Then he glanced at the duffel bag over Raven's shoulder. "Are you two lost?"

Embarrassed, Raven's face glimmered in a pink tone. "Yes, sir."

He nodded. "Go down two more blocks. Take a right on Market and follow it to the train station. It'll be on your left. Good luck to you both."

Raven gave him a fleeting smile as she rushed away.

"How do you know that woman Bitsy isn't sending us on a wild goose chase?" Monica asked with skepticism.

Raven shrugged. "I don't. It's the feeling I got from her. Besides, so what if she's wrong? We don't have anywhere to go, so at least we can hang out in the train station for a few hours."

"Okay, fine. But I hope we don't end up swimming with the fishes," Monica commented.

"You spent too much time with Bull. People our age don't talk like that."

Monica chuckled. "Like you'd know."

"Hey, I grew up with a bunch of teenagers who were older than me. Plus, most of them were either gang members or related to someone in a gang. They would say they're going to 'off people' but they never mentioned fishes."

Monica rolled her eyes. "I'm hungry," she whined.

"Yeah, me too. We have to be careful with our money. How about if we grab a slice of pizza or split a burger and fries?" Raven offered.

"Pizza. But I want my own slice."

Raven grabbed her hand and stopped short. She pointed above them. "Pizza it is," she sang as they looked up at a pizzeria sign hanging over their heads.

When they entered the restaurant, the smell of freshly baked dough filled the air, enticing their appetite. Raven's belly rumbled and her mouth watered. There was a man behind the counter, spinning dough on one fist, then placing it on a pizza tray and pressing the edges to form a crust. Raven had hunger pains watching him ladle on the tomato sauce and then cover it with a thick layer of mozzarella cheese.

This was the first time they were eating since they'd split a bagel in the morning. She squeezed the wad of money in her pocket. It was getting smaller, and worry burrowed itself under her skin.

We need jobs and a place to stay before winter sets in.

Chapter Thirty-One

Inside the train station, the girls planted themselves on a bench near a bathroom farthest from all the hustle and bustle of travelers.

Raven crouched against the hard wood of the bench. "All right. Tomorrow, we need to get to the shelter by noon. But we also have to figure out how to make money."

"Sure, but I don't know what I can do. I ain't got any skills. Well, I guess I could be a hooker," she joked.

"There's something wrong with you," Raven said, opening her eyes wider. "You're twenty years old and never had a job?"

Monica shook her head. "After high school, I slept on a friend's sofa for a couple of months, then I met my first boyfriend. He was almost as big of an asshole as Bull."

"So what? You lived with that guy, too?"

Monica smirked. "Yeah, girl. That's why I go for the older dudes. They have their own places and jobs. I'd never be with a guy that didn't make money."

"But *you* don't make money," Raven said incredulously.

"I know. That's exactly why I need my man to make money." Monica giggled.

"You're too much. I've had two jobs. I worked in a deli the summer between my junior and senior years of high school. I didn't have any experience, but the people who owned the place taught me how to do things. Ava was a cool woman. She didn't take shit from nobody."

"What did you do there?"

"Cut veggies and rolls and stuff," Raven said.

Monica faked a yawn. "That sounds boring as shit."

Raven nudged her with her knee. "Okay, so what is it you want to do?"

Monica shrugged. "I don't know. Sell houses or something. I need a job where I get paid a lot of money."

"Right." Raven grinned. "A girl who has never worked a day in her life and has no particular experience. Ha!"

Monica flipped her hair. "That's right. A girl has to dream big."

Raven nodded. "That's great. But until you can make a whole lot of money, what can you do in the meantime?"

Monica cuddled closer and gave her an impish grin. "You can work, and I can be your sugar mama."

"Listen, sister. I don't need to be someone's sugar mama. I need a job and a place to live. So do you. Now you have to get serious."

Monica let her arms and legs flop to the sides, for dramatic effect, to show she was already exhausted. "Fine. Maybe I can get a job at a salon washing hair."

"That's a good idea," Raven stated. "I think I'm gonna stick with food. Between working at the deli and being a barback, I should be able to find something."

As the girls were chatting, a young man wandered over to them. "Hey," he said, taking them in, trying to assess their state. "How are you girls doing?"

Raven's face was blank. "We're fine. Do you need something?"

"Well, it's funny you should ask," he said. "I'm Yost. I was wondering if you had any cash you can spare. I figure two pretty girls like you can make a lot of money panhandling."

Monica let out a flattered giggle, but Raven's face remained set in stone.

"No," Raven stated. "We don't have any extra cash, Yost. If we did, we wouldn't be sitting on this bench. We'd be somewhere getting ready to have a nice dinner. Anything else?"

Raven was curt, but she'd learned from the strippers at Guilty Pleasure that some men were hustlers. She was letting Yost know that they wouldn't make a good target.

"Whoa!" Yost said, backing up and lifting his palms toward her in a theatrical move. "I was only trying to be friendly. You ain't gotta get all jacked up."

Sitting on the bench, Raven didn't like her vantage point. She stood and faced him. Even though she was at least six inches shorter, she straightened her spine.

"I'm not all jacked up, Yost. But here's the thing . . . If you were being friendly, you might come over and introduce yourself. But you wouldn't come over and ask for money. That's not friendly; that's a taker. You're not impressing either of us." She glanced at Monica batting her eyelashes at Yost.

"Okay, I'll move on then," he said. He put his hand out to Monica, and she shook it. "Your friend is kind of irritable. What's your name, beautiful?"

"Monica Garcia," she sang like a canary. Her eyes dragged over to Raven scowling at her. "Anyway, you better go now. You've managed to piss off my friend," she giggled.

Yost bent at the waist and lowered his face to Monica's. "Your friend looks like she was born pissed off," he whispered.

Overhearing him, Raven stepped closer. "Beat it, Yost."

He leaned in farther and kissed Monica on the cheek. "I hope to see you later, Monica Garcia. I'm always around . . . either here or along the Schuylkill River Trail."

"Where's that?" Monica asked, adding a touch more innocence to her expression.

"To your left when you leave the station. Ask anybody and they'll point you in the right direction. That's where I party."

"Do you live there, too?" Monica asked.

"No, I live where I drop at night." He smiled.

"Okay," Raven interrupted. "That's great, Yost. Bye."

As Yost sauntered away, both girls watched him.

"Why were you so mean?" Monica asked.

"I wasn't mean. I was protecting us. Unlike you, who felt the need to flirt with him."

Monica's face lit up. "Oh, you have no idea. I love to flirt. I mean, honestly, Yost is cute but he's too young, has no job, and nowhere to live. Like I said, I only go for older dudes."

Raven grabbed Monica's hand and pulled her into the bathroom. They took the largest stall farthest from the door and settled on the floor.

"I ca-can't live like this," Monica admitted.

"This isn't how we're going to live, but for now, for tonight, it's what we have to do. Tomorrow will be better."

Monica leaned her head on Raven's shoulder. "Promise?"

"I promise," Raven said, but even as the words squeaked through her lips, she knew there was no way she could guarantee a better tomorrow, no matter how much she wanted it to be true.

Raven rested the back of her head against the wall. *I will do something with my life,* she told herself.

She couldn't know the people she would meet and the things that awaited her.

Chapter Thirty-Two

As Raven was leaving the train station the next morning with Monica, she caught a glimpse of Yost watching them from across the terminal. She slowed her pace, keeping her eyes on the boy.

Monica was still half asleep, dragging her feet over the tile floor and yawning. "Why do you have that look on your face?" she asked, studying the deep creases between Raven's eyes.

"Because Yost is watching us. I don't like that guy. You need to stay away from him. He gives me a bad feeling," Raven warned.

Monica caught Yost's gaze and raised her eyebrows at him, then focused on her friend. "You're way too paranoid. Yost is a player. He's looking to get a piece of ass and score some money."

Raven stopped walking. "How do you know that's all he wants? I sense something darker from him."

Monica shook her head. "'Cause he's playing my game. I don't play it with little boys like him, though."

"He's playing your game? What does that mean?"

Monica batted her eyelashes at Raven. "It means that I lure men in the same way he's trying to lure us in. Well, not you, me. You know, schmooze and flatter. Show off my bubbling personality. He thinks I've fallen for his fake charm, but I see right through him and now I'm messing with him because it's fun."

Raven huffed. "That sounds exhausting. Besides, you're nothing like him. You're kind and funny. I think you're a good person."

"Yeah." She blushed. "Thanks. I don't hear that too often. I guess you're right. I'm not all about playing games. I mean, I did love Bull . . . I still do."

Raven's head snapped in Monica's direction. "That's not what I meant. Bull was unkind to you. He mistreated you, Monica. So it scares me when you say you still love him."

Monica lowered her face. "You're right. I always look past the pain. That's what I learned to do when I was a kid—to ignore the things that hurt me. I dwell on the moment I first met Bull. He was nice, funny, and caring. But don't worry, next time I'll do better. I've decided that I'm going to be attracted to good guys from now on."

Raven gave her a sad smile. "You decided? Is that a thing?"

"Yeah, see, I'm always attracted to the bad boys. The guys that get in fistfights all the time or if something bad happens, they flip out. It turns me on." She gave Raven a silly grin and lifted her finger into the air. "But that's not going to turn me on anymore." She let out a giggle.

"You're so full of crap. You can't even say it without laughing at your own bullshit," Raven teased.

She crinkled her nose. "It's true, though. I like those badass types, you know? Rough and tough. I can't get enough of 'em."

Raven threw an arm over Monica's shoulders as they continued to walk. "Seriously. I saw what Bull did to you. I know how much he hurt you physically and mentally. Aren't you afraid that you'll end up with someone like him again?"

Monica turned her head away, avoiding eye contact. "I don't know how to take care of myself. I'm not like you. I don't wanna work and earn my own money. I don't want to figure out where to live or rent an apartment or whatever. I want to hang around the house and cook some food. You know, I never wanted to have a career or anything."

Raven realized that like her, Monica was looking to be nurtured and cared for. It was an effect of being denied their basic needs as children.

Raven grabbed the girl's hand and held it tight. "Hey, you have a lot to offer. You've never worked. You might like it. You're very sociable, and people like you. Maybe you work for a while and get some skills. Then you can move to some kind of office job where you'd meet a guy that has his act together . . . He can still be older," she added.

Monica hadn't learned responsibility from her parents. She wasn't ready to succumb to societal norms. "Meh, sounds like a lot of work to me when I can walk into a bar, slam back some shots, and find a man to take me home. Enough about me. What's our plan today?"

Raven squeezed Monica's hand tighter as they walked up Market Street like two lifelong friends. "Eat. Look for jobs and get to the shelter by noon."

"Oh boy. I might die from excitement," Monica moaned.

Raven pulled in a long breath through her nose. The smell of freshly brewed coffee rose above the car fumes and the grease from a fast-food restaurant across the street. As they stood on a corner, waiting to cross the street, Raven couldn't help but envy the young women in business suits, wearing their sneakers as they powered through the city streets. They had what she wanted the most, somewhere to go.

***

By noon, Raven and Monica were standing in line at the shelter. It was a chilly fall day, and Raven was freezing with no winter clothing.

"We need to get off the streets before it gets colder," Raven said, pulling the hood up on her sweatshirt.

"Before it gets colder? I need to get into a place sooner than that. I'm talking tomorrow," Monica commented.

Raven's belly rumbled. They'd been sharing meals to stretch their money, and she looked forward to getting dinner at the shelter that night. As she stood in line, she looked behind her, and fewer than ten feet back was Bitsy.

"Hold my place," she said loud enough so the person in front and behind them heard her. "I have someone I need to go see."

"Who? That lady you met, Itty Bitty?"

Raven gave her an edgy grin. "Stop it. It's Bitsy and you know it. Keep my place. I'll leave my bag here with you."

A few seconds later, Raven approached the older woman. "Bitsy? Hi, we met yesterday."

"Oh, sweetie, I remember you." Her voice got deep. "You didn't make it in last night, did you?"

Raven shook her head. "We used your backup plan."

"How was it?"

"It was a place to stay, but no food or bed or shower. You know," Raven offered.

"Oh, I sure do. You in line?" She looked behind her, and the line was almost to the end of the block.

"Yeah, up there." Raven pointed. "My friend is saving our spot."

Bitsy craned her neck to see Monica, who was staring back at her. "Oh, I see. Let's sit together at dinner tonight. We can talk. I can give you girls some pointers. Has your friend ever been homeless before?"

Raven shook her head.

"Ah right then. I'll see if I can help you two out."

"Thanks, Bitsy."

"Sure thing. Now, when you get inside, you need to write your name on a piece of paper and pin it to your cot."

Raven leaned her head to the side. "Okay, will they give us paper and stuff inside?"

"Oh, sweetie. The homeless have to keep paper and pen at all times." The woman reached into one of her two bags. She pulled out a piece of looseleaf paper and handed the girl an extra pen. "You can keep the pen, but you gotta buy your own paper if you lose your tag. You can rip this in half and put your name on one and your friend's name on the other." She opened a change purse. "Here, use these safety pins to attach the paper."

"So we hold a cot by pinning our names on it, and everyone is going to think that's okay?"

"Most of us do it, so most of us know. Remember, you can't leave your belongings behind, so you have to claim your space somehow. It works ninety-five percent of the time," Bitsy added.

"What about the other five percent? What do we do if someone takes our cots?"

"You walk around until you find an empty one. But don't count on sleeping near your friend 'cause you won't find two together."

"Okay, thanks. We'll see you inside."

***

After Raven and Monica located two cots next to each other, they sat down and waited for dinner.

Raven watched the people around her. There were all ages and races. There were men, women, and children. It was a mosh pit of warriors doing what they could to survive.

"I hate this place already," Monica whispered.

"We haven't been here long enough for you to know if you hate it."

Monica shook her head. "Raven, look at these people. Some of them are like zombies."

Raven's eyes widened. "Yeah, well, I think a lot of people have had it hard. I bet many of them have been living on the streets for a long time. This is our second day, and we're already tired of it. Six months from now, we'll look like zombies, too."

Monica raised a finger in the air. "Yes, exactly. That goes back to the point I made earlier. I'm not a person who can live on the streets. I want a kitchen, a bathroom, and a shower." She moved her face closer to Raven's and lowered her voice. "And I don't wanna have to pin my name to a borrowed cot."

Raven pressed the heel of her hand against her forehead. She wasn't happy about their circumstances, but she would sacrifice until they got on their feet. "Give it a little time, will you?" she pleaded.

But instead of a reply, Monica laid her head on the pillow and closed her eyes.

It's only the second day and I'm already losing her, Raven thought with growing concern.

Chapter Thirty-Three

An hour later, Raven followed the crowd to the next room where dinner was being served. She pulled Monica along by her hand.

"What's wrong with you? We're going to get an actual dinner tonight," Raven said, as they shuffled closer to the front of the food line. "You've been complaining about wanting to eat since we left the motel. This is our chance to get a real meal that we don't have to share."

"I know. I'm sorry. All these people are freaking me out. What if I'm like twenty-eight years old and still sleeping in a shelter? Look around you, Raven, this could be your future," the girl whispered in a panicked tone.

"You need to stop it," Raven said firmly. "This is not a forever thing for us. Okay? Besides, you have to admit, it's better than being at the train station last night next to a toilet where people shit." She gave her friend a playful poke with her elbow.

Monica burst into a smile. "Yeah, I'll give you that. I was not happy sleeping next to a toilet."

Raven turned her face toward the girl. "You know, you're pretty picky for a girl who has no money and no job." She jabbed her again with an elbow.

"That's the thing." Monica put her arm around Raven's lower back. "I think in my past life I was super rich and famous or something."

Raven scoffed. "Yeah, right. Listen, I understand this is hard . . . Being displaced is awful. But we've both been through bad things and have come through the other side. We don't have to stay homeless if we decide we're gonna do something different. At least we have each other. Look at how many of these people are alone," she pointed out.

Monica's smile dropped. Her voice turned serious. "I'm afraid."

"Afraid of what?" Raven asked, getting closer to the girl.

"I'm afraid this is all my life will amount to. I wanna be a mom. I wanna have lots of babies. I always dreamed of creating the family I never had."

Raven hugged the girl. "If that's what you want, you'll get it."

"Oh, right. Like you don't think I'm lame for wanting to spit out kids?"

Raven shook her head. "Why would I think that?"

"Well, for starters, you keep talking about what we're gonna do to make money and how we're going to find a place to live. Where I'm like, shit, let me find a man and I don't have to do none of that stuff."

Raven's eyes met her friends. "I don't want to depend on someone else to keep me housed and fed. I grew up in the foster care system. I want to do this on my own." She smirked. "Now, I'm not saying I wouldn't take some help, but for the most part, I need to do this for me."

"See, that's what makes you special." Monica laced her fingers through Raven's. "You're strong, and you want control. That's cool. But it's not for me."

Raven lifted their joined hands and pressed them against her cheek. "It's not a big deal that we want different things. You want to be a mom and have a big family, and I want to make lots of money. We'll both get what we want, but right now we are in this together, right? That's what we agreed to before we left the motel."

Monica looked at her feet. "Yeah, sure. That's what we promised each other." She lifted her face. "I don't know how long I can do this. That's all I'm saying. I don't have the stomach for this shit."

Raven glanced at her new friend. The two had only known each other for a week, and while they'd grown close, she knew it took a lot longer to learn things about the way a person thinks and behaves. Apprehension crept up her spine as she feared being alone on the streets. Then she pushed the dark thoughts away, refusing to believe them.

***

Twenty minutes later, Raven and Monica were walking with full trays of food when Bitsy stood and waved her arms.

"Over there," Raven said, leaning into her friend. "That's Bitsy."

Monica grimaced. "She's so much older than us."

"Yeah, that's the point. She knows more than we do."

Raven placed her tray down across from the older woman and smiled brightly. "Bitsy, this is my friend, Monica."

Monica flashed a quick smile. Then she picked up her fork. She pushed through the pile of mashed potatoes and smelled them before putting some in her mouth.

"The food is pretty good here, ain't it?" Bitsy asked Monica.

Monica glanced at the woman. "Yeah, it's not bad."

"So, Bitsy," Raven said, distracting the woman from Monica's lack of enthusiasm. "How long have you been homeless?"

The woman closed her eyes for a prolonged moment. "I've been living on the streets since I was sixteen."

Raven's eyes bulged and her mouth dropped open. "How old are you?"

"I turned forty-two a month ago."

"Wait! You've been homeless for twenty-six years?" Raven asked in an incredulous tone.

Bitsy chuckled. "No, darlin'. Over the years I've had places to live for a stretch. I'd say about eight or nine of those years I spent living inside. Me and various homeless friends would get jobs and rent a place together. Then one of us would lose our job and we'd be back out on the streets again."

Bitsy's casualness about being homeless stunned Raven. "But . . . um, well . . ." The girl's voice trailed off. She didn't want to be rude or inconsiderate to the nice lady. She put a forkful of peas into her mouth and chewed slowly.

Bitsy chuckled. "I think I know what you were gonna say. You're curious how I can let myself go back on the streets after I got off of 'em? Right?"

"Yeah. I mean, wasn't that hard to leave a comfortable place?"

Bitsy shrugged. "All change is hard, but that doesn't mean we ain't gotta do it. As far as going back to being homeless, everyone takes it differently. It all depends on the kind of person you are. I hated coming back to the streets every single time. I liked having a place of my own. When I was much younger, I did some hooking, without a pimp, of course, because I could never have some dude up my ass telling me what to do. Then I got too old to attract enough men to keep my belly full, so I took on odd jobs . . . you know, short-order cook, cleaning, fast-food places. But none of those jobs paid enough money for me to have a place of my own."

Raven leaned forward on her elbows. "So if me and Monica get jobs, we should be able to get an apartment. Since there are two of us. Right?"

Bitsy shook her head. "Things ain't that simple. See, a job wants you to work during the day into the early night. But if you're staying in shelters while you're trying to save money, then you have to be in line early to get a bed. Take this place for example. Where are you getting a job that's done before noon? You ain't. Every time I got off the streets, I had to sleep on buses, trains, doorways, wherever I could find so that I could work my eight-hour shift during regular time."

"Okay, we're never getting off the streets," Monica stated. "Are you kidding us right now?"

Raven was left with the same impression, but she didn't want to believe it.

Bitsy shook her head and put a piece of meatloaf into her mouth. "Nope. I ain't kidding. This shit is fucked up. It's a hard cycle to get out of. My advice to you, since you're both young, is to go home and live with your parents. Get a job and move out the right way."

Raven squinted, crinkling her brow. "Neither of us has a family to go home to."

"Hm. Well, that's a shame. Just like me, I didn't have no one by the time I was sixteen. I think there are some things you can do. Maybe a youth shelter would be better for you."

Raven looked at Monica with a hopeful smile. "Yeah. A youth shelter. We haven't tried that yet. I stayed in one right after . . . high school."

Monica shook her head. "Sure, sounds great, but I'll be twenty-one soon."

Raven cocked her head to the side. "How soon?"

"In a month." Monica rested her fork on the tray and pushed the leftover food away from her. She looked at Bitsy. "Is that too old for a youth shelter?"

Bitsy nodded. "Especially in this part of the city."

"But in other parts of the city, her age would be okay?" Raven asked eagerly.

Bitsy shrugged. "I ain't got no idea. You'll need to figure that one out. But my guess is they're all about the same."

Monica pushed her hair from her face. "Well, that's great. Is there anything else you can think of?"

Bitsy nibbled her bottom lip. "Churches. Some churches open their doors to us in the winter. It's kind of nice being in God's house, especially during the holidays. Plus," she added with wide eyes, "people are a lot more generous that time of year." Bitsy took a bite of her dinner roll. "Of course, you can always panhandle . . . beg for money."

Raven was discouraged by the options that Bitsy was offering. Still, she would do whatever it took to get off the streets, but she hoped that Monica had the same conviction.

Chapter Thirty-Four

The next morning, Raven and Monica left the shelter after eating breakfast and showering. They walked for a few blocks in silence. Both were contemplating how to get out of the situation they found themselves in.

Raven turned to her friend. "I'm going to put some job applications in today. You can, too."

Monica looked around them. "Okay. I guess."

A few minutes later, Raven went into an upscale clothing boutique. She drew in a breath of the expensive honey-soaked floral perfume. There was a plush sofa with two matching chairs on either side in the middle of the store. The clothes were hung, spaced, and organized. Everything had a place, and Raven reveled in the luxury that surrounded her. She would've loved to afford to shop there.

The woman behind the counter looked up when the bell on the door dinged. Her eyes rolled over Raven, stopped for a moment on her duffel bag, and continued down to her worn canvas sneakers.

"Hi, I'd like to fill out a job application," she said in a cheery voice.

The woman plastered a forced grin on her face. "I see. Do you have any experience in retail?"

Raven squinted at her. "Huh?"

"Have you ever sold merchandise in a store before?"

"Oh." Raven shook her head. "No. But I worked in a deli and a bar, so I learn fast."

The woman didn't hesitate. "I'm sorry. You seem like a nice young lady, but we don't have any open positions right now. I would suggest getting some retail experience, then come back and see us."

"How do I get retail experience if you won't hire me because I don't have any?"

The woman gave her a dry smile. "You work at Dollar General or a larger retailer, like a department store. A place where they have time to train you."

Raven nodded. "Okay. Thanks." She turned and left the store deflated.

As the morning wore on and it got closer to noon, Raven started to worry. Not only did she not find anyone willing to give her a job, but Monica wasn't even trying to find work. All she did was complain that she wasn't feeling well.

***

Over the next week, Raven and Monica were stuck in a cycle that lacked opportunity. They left the shelter in the morning, looked for work, and headed back to the shelter by noon to stand in line for four hours. It was a bleak existence, and Raven knew it had to change before they got too deep into it.

It was late on a Tuesday morning when Raven sat on a curb, weary and discouraged. Monica plopped down next to her.

Raven glanced at her. "It's no use. We're never going to find jobs. Lugging our duffel bags around and wearing clothes that need to be washed." She looked at the passing cars. "We look homeless, and that means people automatically won't trust us in their stores."

Monica nodded. "Look, we tried. That has to count for something. Right? I must've filled out at least ten applications. It's like the people hiring have homeless radar. How many applications did you fill out?"

Raven shrugged. "I lost count. I was talking to this young guy at the shelter. He said we should try some of the cheap motels. They like to hire people to clean rooms or who are willing to work overnight. I thought maybe I'd give that a go."

Monica wrinkled her nose. "Ew, not me. I don't wanna work at a motel."

As the girls sat there, basking in their misery, they didn't see Yost approaching them. He came on them fast, grabbed Monica's bag, and took off down the block.

"Stop! Come back here, Yost!" Raven yelled. She bounded to her feet, held her duffel bag tight to her shoulder, and ran after him while Monica was a solid half block behind them.

Raven ran as fast as her feet would carry her, but she knew that she couldn't catch him. After three blocks, she stopped dead, unable to breathe. She bent over with her hands on her thighs, trying to fill her lungs with oxygen.

"That fucking asshole," Monica said, coming up behind her, also gasping for air. The girls stood together for a moment, dazed, as they allowed their hearts to slow.

Raven swallowed twice. "What did you lose?"

"All of my clothes. My money. I had twenty-six bucks left. He also got my gold necklace. I forgot to put it back on this morning after I showered." Monica's head dropped in defeat. "This can't get any worse."

Raven moved into her, wrapped her arms around the girl's shoulders, and pulled her into a hug.

Monica, tired of being strong, lost control of her emotions. She clung to Raven and cried. "I hate that boy. I hate this city. I hate being homeless. I hate everything about my life right now."

Raven rubbed the girl's back. "It'll be okay. We can replace the money."

Monica jerked her head back. Her eyes were red and snot was dripping from her nose. "How, Raven? How are we going to replace the money? We've been out here for a week and neither of us is any better off than when we started." She shook her head vigorously. "Besides, I'll never replace the necklace. Bull gave that to me the night he asked me to move in with him."

Raven held her closer. "I swear, I'll buy you a new one when I get a job. We'll get you something even better. Okay?" She dipped her head down to meet the girl's eyes.

Monica nodded, but her fire and determination, the little she had left, were gone.

Raven could see the vacant, disengaged look in her eyes. She understood what she was seeing—a girl who could watch but could not see, a girl who could hear but could not listen. A life so heavy with misfortune that she could no longer hide her pain behind the disguise she wore to deceive people. She knew that girl. She'd been that girl.

Monica had the look people get when they realize they'd betrayed themselves and are left with desperation. An emotion that causes people to do things out of despair, things that can bring them the greatest harm.

Chapter Thirty-Five

Raven and Monica were in line at the Center City House shelter later that same day.

Raven was standing with her back against the brick wall, and Monica was on the sidewalk curled onto her side, sleeping. Bitsy was right in front of them in line. She looked the two girls over, first at Raven, then Monica. Her eyes narrowed and she nudged Raven.

"What's wrong with Monica?" Bitsy whispered.

"She's depressed. We can't find work and then her bag got stolen today. A guy ripped it right off of her shoulder."

Raven looked down at her friend, and there was a searing pain in her heart. They had both been suffocating in uncertainty, and the incident diminished what little hope they had left. She knew Monica had lost the fight and brazenness she had when they began their journey more than a week ago.

Bitsy shook her head. "Mm, mm, mm. That's a damn shame. Did she know the person who robbed her? You ever seen them before?"

Raven nodded. "Some douchebag named Yost. We met him at the train station that first night."

"Yost?" Bitsy pinched her lips together and shook her head. "That rotten prick. I know him. He's a troublemaker for sure. He don't care about nobody but himself. He thinks he's a real charmer and a looker, too." She paused, tilted her head, and grinned. "Well, don't get me wrong, he is handsome for a boy his age, but he certainly ain't got the personality to match."

Raven grimaced. "I don't think people who are ugly on the inside can be handsome or beautiful. They all look rotten to me. I told Monica I didn't like him the first time we met him. I got this nauseating swirling in the pit of my stomach when I spotted him staring at us the next morning. Monica said he was harmless." She looked down at her hands. "She's really upset by it. She spent the rest of the morning on her own . . . said she needed to walk it off."

"Maybe you should talk to her. See if she's doing any better. Sometimes when we're hurting, we want people to notice so we ain't gotta be a burden and drop our shit in their laps without an invitation. You get me?"

Raven's mind raced backward, and she pulled up the memory of Mrs. Fisher. Her beloved teacher that Matthew had killed. The woman had done to her exactly what Bitsy was suggesting now. Mrs. Fisher had opened the door and invited Raven to tell all of her secrets and had helped her navigate through the shark infested waters of her life.

The girl nodded. "Yeah, I totally get you." Raven moved closer to Monica and sat next to her on the cold sidewalk. She gently shook her shoulder. "Monica?"

The girl's eyes fluttered open. "Did something happen?" she asked in a groggy voice.

"No. Everything is fine. I want you to know I'm sorry about what happened to you. Yost will pay for what he did. What can I do to make it better?"

Monica sniffled and wiped at her nose. Her gaze was distant and empty as she looked away from her friend. Then she cleared her throat. "Yeah, thanks." She sat upright and leaned her back against the building. "I made a decision while I was walking around by myself today. I don't want you to be mad at me. Promise?"

Raven's heart turned upside down. "What?"

It was a single word laced with dread that flitted through the air and smacked the ground.

Monica twisted her hands together. "I called Bull to come and get me."

Raven's shoulders slumped forward. "What? Why would you call him? Monica, he hurt you and threatened to kill you."

Monica lifted her eyes, but she didn't look at her friend. She was stoic. A counterfeit of the person who nested inside of her. She was facing the street and spoke without emotion as if her words were meant for the rushing traffic and car horns, not Raven. "He said he misses me and that he's sorry. He promised he'll never hit me again."

Raven gave her head a slow shake. "Didn't he promise he'd never hit you before?"

Monica put her hand on Raven's leg. "He did, but this time he means it. I can tell. When he heard my voice on the phone, he started to cry." She raised her right hand into the air. "I swear. I'm not making it up."

Raven didn't believe Bull's promises. She pulled her knees to her chest and wrapped her arms around them. "What if something bad happens to you? What if he's lying?"

"He isn't lying. I know it. Nothing is going to happen to me." She pressed the heel of her palm against her chest. "I can feel it in my heart. He's like a totally different man. He's exactly like he used to be when I first met him. I think now that he knows he can lose me for good, he changed his ways."

Raven ran a shaky hand through her hair and took a deep breath trying in vain to calm her nerves. She dragged her eyes to Monica's. "People like Bull don't change their ways in a week. I don't want to be negative, but I think it's a bad idea. You told me yourself that he was super nice and then after he got you to move in with him, he completely changed."

Monica straightened her spine. "I know you're upset that I'm leaving you here all alone, and I don't blame you. I would be pissed at me, too. I get it. But I can't stay here. I can't do this anymore. I thought I could, and I wanted everything to work out. But I hate this life so much. I want stability. I want a place to live and put my stuff . . . to call home."

"I understand. That's what we all want." Raven's heart was thrashing in her chest. Her thoughts were scrambled, and she made room for the panic setting in.

Monica is right. I'll be all alone again.

"Well, I think it's a bad idea. It seems like you've made up your mind though. When are you leaving?" Raven managed, but she couldn't make eye contact with the girl again.

"He's going to be here at three. I thought it would be easier for you if the doors were almost open before I left . . . so we could spend some time together. I'm sorry to do this to you."

Raven shook her head. "I hate that I'll be alone, but I'm more worried about what you're doing to yourself."

Monica crossed her arms over her chest and sucked in her bottom lip. Monica knew her friend was right, but the part of her that craved certainty, even if it caused great pain, was in denial.

"I'll be fine," Monica grumbled.

"Does he know who I am?" Raven asked, holding her breath as she waited for the answer.

Monica shook her head. "No, I would never tell Bull your name. He thinks you're some girl I met at a shelter. I told him you meant nothing to me." She looked down at her hands. "But that isn't true. I know we've only been together for ten days, but it feels like I've loved you my whole life. Do you hate me?"

"No, are you kidding? I don't hate you. You and me are like sisters now. I'm going to miss you. But I won't lie, I'm scared for both of us. I'll be here, and you'll be there with him." She looked into her friend's eyes. "I'm afraid he'll start beating you again. I saw it with my mom. They always start up again. You admitted that to me."

Embarrassed and unsure of herself, Monica's face flushed a deep pink. "I love him."

Raven fidgeted, tugging at the bottom of her sweatshirt. She wanted to say something that would change her friend's mind, to change the course of Monica's future. Raven searched for words that would be so impactful that Monica would suddenly realize the mistake she was making by going back to Bull. Then she settled on the truth and let her thoughts glide through her lips.

"I don't know how you can love anyone that brings you so much pain. I'm scared that Bull will kill you. I saw him that night. I watched him when you were locked inside the motel room. He was fueled by uncontrollable rage."

"Yeah." Monica got to her knees and put her arms around Raven's neck. She hugged the girl closely. "I believe it's gonna be different this time," she whispered into her ear. "I think him and me are finally going to make it."

"Did you hear what I just said?"

Monica nodded. "I want to give him one more chance."

Raven wanted to shake the girl until she came to her senses. And while all of her protective instincts were firing, there was nothing she could do to stop Monica from going back to the man who abused her.

Raven and Monica sat side by side. At three o'clock, Bull's pickup truck pulled up to the curb in front of the shelter.

Monica looked over at the truck. "My ride is here." She stood and pulled Raven to her feet.

"Yeah, I guess this is it. You be safe, okay? Take care of yourself." Her voice was saturated with sadness.

Monica's breath hitched. "You too. Thanks for being a good friend . . . the best friend I've had in a long time." She turned to walk away, but Raven snatched her by the wrist.

"Are you sure about this? It's not too late to change your mind. We can leave here right now. We'll go to another part of the city and find a different shelter," Raven said in a pleading tone.

Monica gave her a dim smile and shook her head. "No, I'm sure. I want to go."

"Okay, but listen to me. The first time he puts a hand on you, promise me that you'll leave him and never look back."

Monica looked away.

"Promise me," Raven said forcefully.

"All right. I promise." She gave Raven one more quick hug and ran to the truck.

Raven's eyes settled on Bull standing beside the passenger door. When he spotted Monica running toward him, there was a scornful smile on his face. The same jacked-up nose and tight lips she'd seen on Gage's face so many times during her childhood. The look on Bull's face was one of self-gratification and victory.

Bull got exactly what he wanted, a woman crawling back to him. He didn't give a thought to what he was doing to her because he viewed Monica as his property. She was an object he rarely nurtured and would harm with a flash of bad temper.

Monica stood smiling at Bull, waiting to be received by him. Instead, he put a hand on the front of her throat. Her happy expression fell, and his eyes penetrated her self-assurance and joy, both gone in an instant. She leaned away from him. He slid his hand to the back of her neck and pulled her forward for a kiss. Then he left her standing on the sidewalk and got back into his truck.

Monica looked over her shoulder at Raven before she opened the door and climbed into Bull's truck. She gave her a fleeting smile, and then she was gone.

Raven was motionless as she watched Bull drive away with her friend.

Bitsy reached for her hand. "Are you gonna be okay, sweetie?"

Raven's eyes were damp. She looked from the empty curb to the woman. "I think that man is going to do awful things to her. She wouldn't listen to me. Monica is pretending to believe him, but she knows better. I know she only went back to him to get off the streets. He's hurt her before, and he'll do it again."

"Now, that's a mouthful of truth. A man who puts his hands on a woman ain't got no boundaries. He'll do it over and over and over again. But you gotta believe you were a good friend to her. I heard everything you said. I couldn't help but eavesdrop on you since the two of you were sitting so close. You told her what you thought, and that's the best you can do when it pertains to other people's lives. You can't make her or nobody do nothing they don't wanna do. You were brave to say the things you did, knowing she didn't wanna hear them." Bitsy rubbed the girl's hand. "How about if you and me find cots together tonight?"

Raven gave her a weak smile. "That would be nice."

At four o'clock when the door to the shelter opened and the line started moving, Raven thought about Monica and wished she was still there.

Raven would see Monica one more time, but not in person. One year later, on the front page of the *Philadelphia News Wire*. There was a picture of Monica. The headline read: *Woman found beaten to death, boyfriend is being investigated in her murder.*

Chapter Thirty-Six

The next morning, Raven woke and looked over at Bitsy. The older woman was asleep. The air from her lungs flowed past the slackened tissues of her throat, and she was vibrating out a soft snore.

Raven watched the woman for a long time. She tried to imagine how Bitsy looked when she was sixteen and first came to live on the streets. Raven wanted a full life for herself, and she couldn't help but wonder if twenty-four years from now she'd become Bitsy. This thought petrified her.

Bitsy's eyes eased open, but Raven didn't notice. She looked at the young teen lying unnaturally still.

Raven closed her eyes and sighed.

"Are you doing okay over there?" Bitsy asked, breaking the barrier of Raven's silent torment.

"Yeah, yeah, I'm fine." The words rolled off her tongue like a jackhammer—sharp, quick, precise.

Bitsy sat up. "You don't look fine." She ran her fingers through her matted hair. "You know when I was your age, I met this woman who was almost fifty years old. I remember watching her and being real scared, kind of the way your face looks right now. I thought to myself, that ain't gonna be me. But here I am."

Raven threw her legs over the cot and sat up, facing the older woman. "I wasn't judging you or nothing."

"No, sweetie, I don't think you were." She stood and moved next to Raven. "See, that woman I met when I was young, she did the best she could to help me. She suggested I go sell sex to make money. So that's what I did because that's what she did when she was younger. But after some years of being homeless, I realized that wasn't the right answer. I hoped one day I could help someone like you."

Raven gave her a deflated grin. "It must've been awful for you."

"Sure was." Bitsy shook her head. "I ain't never known anyone who wants to get paid for sex. It ain't the most pleasant thing in the world, that's for certain. But back to my story. See, you came along, and I know you're the one I'm supposed to help. And that's what I'm gonna do."

Raven scratched at the dry skin on her arms. "How are you going to do that?"

"Well, I'm gonna give you the best advice I can so you can get off the streets. The way you do that is to get a job, save money, and move the hell away from this shit."

Raven pressed the air from her lungs, and she hung her head. "I've been trying to get a job, but it's impossible. It's like the shop owners are allergic to my homelessness."

Bitsy nodded. "I understand, and that's why I wanna try to help you."

Raven had a rush of adrenaline. "That would be great. Tell me what I need to do. I swear, I won't disappoint you."

"First, let's go get breakfast. Then you can shower, and we'll head out."

"Where are we going?" Raven asked.

"Never mind all of that now. Let's just say I know a woman who owes me a favor . . . has for a long time. I'm gonna call in that favor today."

"Are you serious?" Raven threw her arms around the woman. "I don't have to do anything illegal, right?"

"Of course not. I said I'm gonna try to help you get a job, not land you in prison," Bitsy chuckled.

"Thank you so much. Is your friend close to here?"

"That's the only catch. She's in the heart of West Philly. So it's a distance from here. The shifts could change, so you might not always make it to a shelter at night. On those nights, you can ride the bus or the train to kill time until morning. There are other options I'm thinking about, too. You'll have to take it as it comes."

Raven's relief washed away. Her face went pale, and Bitsy squeezed her hand.

"Why are you turning white?"

"Because I got used to this shelter and now, I have to find another one," Raven admitted. The girl's elbows were pressed tight to her body and her breaths burst in and out.

Bitsy watched her. "You can throw your worry right out the window. I'm gonna go with you. I'll stay for a bit. Maybe a week or two until you get settled. I'm gonna show you around and you'll be set." She lifted the girl's chin with her fingers. "But I want you to hear me loud and clear. I don't ever wanna hear you say that you got used to a shelter. I can say that because I'm past my time, but you? No, siree. You're getting off these streets. You understand me?"

Raven's eyes grew wide, and she nodded. "Where did you come from? Seriously. People are usually out to hurt me, not help me."

"If you say so." The older woman smirked. "Let me tell you something I learned . . . took until I was damn near thirty to learn it. You gotta expect good people to find you and they will. If you're expecting bad people to find you, they will, too. I expect to come across people who make my life better. And here you are." She smiled at the girl. "I ain't gonna leave you flat like your friend Monica did. I know she's got her reasons, but from where I sit, that naïve girl made her life a lot more difficult. You can't be lazy to live on the streets. That's what people think—that we're here because we don't wanna work. I ain't gonna lie, that's true for some, but most of us have to work much harder to stay alive."

"This means so much to me, Bitsy. I'll do everything I can to get off the streets, and when I do, you can come live with me," Raven promised.

"Eighteen is a magical age," the woman chuckled. "See now, that's the kind of attitude I wanna hear. But let me be clear. I'm not helping you so you can pay me back. I'm helping you because I always wanted to do something bigger with my life. Everybody with a soul does, and you're my chance to do it."

Raven stared into the woman's eyes. She could see the quiet storm brewing inside of her. Bitsy was out to make a point, change a life, make a difference, and Raven was honored to be the recipient.

Chapter Thirty-Seven

When Raven left the shelter that morning, her sense of purpose was restored. Having Bitsy beside her allowed Raven to breathe easier and release some of her fear.

When they stepped off the bus in West Philly, Raven leaned into Bitsy. "There are a lot of people here."

"Yeah, that's right. There are more laborer jobs here compared to Center City. Come on now. Follow me."

Raven walked beside Bitsy for a few blocks before turning left into a cramped alley. "Where are we going?"

The woman gave her a side-glance. "To get you a job. Remember?"

Raven pointed behind them. "But what about out there on the street? It looked a lot better than back here in this dark alley."

"Hey, you said you're willing to do whatever to get your skinny ass off the streets," she said, grinning. "You might regret saying that a week from now."

"Are you going to tell me where we're going?" the teen asked.

"Right here." She had stopped in front of a large steel door.

Turning the knob, Bitsy pushed it open to a big room with cement floors and cinderblock walls. In the room were two rows of long tables. The smell hit Raven's sinuses. The stench was from all the dead fish. The putrid odor originated from the bacteria and fish enzymes. Fish heads were piled up in large trash cans. Raven watched two dozen people, chopping off heads, slitting the fish through the gut, and opening them wide. They removed all internal substances and cut out the bones in one long strip.

Bitsy waved her hands in the air and let out a howl. She rushed away from Raven and into the arms of an Italian woman.

"Oh, Felicia. I've missed you, girl," Bitsy cooed.

"How you been doing, Bitsy? Where you been? I haven't seen you in over a year. I thought you said you couldn't live without me," Felicia heckled her.

"Girl, please. Don't act like I never told you what it's like to live on the streets. Takes all your time to be homeless and have nowhere to go," Bitsy reminded her.

"Yeah, right," Felicia snapped. "Come into my office. Let's have a cup of coffee. I got some fresh donuts, too."

Bitsy turned around. "Raven!" she screamed from across the room. Then she waved the girl to her.

"Who the hell is that?" Felicia whispered before Raven was close to them.

"A girl. She's been on the streets for less than two weeks. I want her off before she gets sucked into this wretched life." Her eyes moved to Felicia's. "You need to help me do that . . . This is my favor. The one you promised me. I need you to give her a job."

Felicia pursed her lips and nodded.

"How is Enzo doing?" Bitsy asked.

"My son is good now because of you. The doctor has him on the right medication, and he's been working and saving money. He even met a girl—a nice Italian girl. She's shy and a bit homely, but we like her."

Bitsy chuckled. "A bit homely?"

Felicia nodded. Her face grew serious. "Yeah, she's bucktoothed with bulgy eyes. And she has one of those chins that don't stick out as far as the rest of her face. You know what I'm talking about?"

Bitsy nodded and chuckled. "You're still rotten. You know, looks ain't everything."

She turned toward Felicia and in unison they sang, "But they sure do help you get laid."

The two women laughed as Raven approached them.

Bitsy held her belly, still allowing the happy moment to consume her. She reached her hand out and put it on Raven's shoulder.

"This here is my friend, Raven."

Raven smiled politely. "Hello."

"How are you, hon?" Felicia asked. "I understand you're looking for work."

Raven nodded. "Yes, ma'am. I learn fast, and I'm a hard worker."

"Okay, good. You see those men and women over there?" She was pointing to the people processing the fish. "You'll learn how to do their job. It's dirty, smelly, and cold, but you'll get used to all that."

Raven fidgeted and let out a nervous giggle. The people processing the fish looked like ninjas with the way their knives sliced through the air.

"I've never cut fish before." She glanced at Bitsy for help, but Bitsy was watching Felicia.

"You don't say?" Felicia teased and shared another laugh with Bitsy. "Don't worry, kid. We'll teach you." She dragged her eyes to Bitsy. "Are you two staying together?"

"Yeah, that's the plan."

Felicia nodded. "Where you at?"

Bitsy draped her arm over the woman's shoulder. "In one of those cheap storage lockers you're gonna rent. Then we'll take over the monthly payments."

Felicia jerked her head back. "Come on, Bitsy. You know you can't live in a storage locker. That ain't allowed."

Bitsy gave her a toothy grin. "I lived in a storage locker for three months until the management caught on. I told you that story."

Felicia shook her head. "You know, you're a pain in my ass. Ah right, I'll see what I can do. How much can you afford a month?"

Bitsy's eyes glimmered. "How much are you paying my girl to gut your fish?"

Felicia eyed Raven up and down. "She ain't got no experience, and I need to train her, which takes time away from one of my workers . . ."

Bitsy shook her head. "Come out with it," she mocked her.

"I can give you thirty-six hours a week. I'll need you to work midnight to six in the morning, Monday through Saturday."

Raven nodded enthusiastically. "I can do that."

Felicia turned back to Bitsy. "I'll give her four bucks an hour. That's about six hundred twenty bucks a month."

"Okay." Bitsy nodded. "She can afford fifty bucks a month for the storage unit."

Felicia ran her hands through her hair. "Okay, I'll work it out."

Bitsy hugged the woman. "I knew you would."

"Raven, be back here at midnight," Felicia said. She turned to Bitsy. "I'll call Georgio. He'll get you the locker by noon today. You got something to sleep on?"

Bitsy shook her head.

"Ah right. Georgio will bring some stuff to the locker for you guys to use." She started to walk away and turned back. "Raven, we have a shower in the ladies' locker room, so you ain't gotta go home smelling like crotch rot at the end of your shift."

"What about me? Can I use the shower, too?" Bitsy sang, blinking her eyes at the woman.

"Fine, but don't use all the hot water. You come in with her at midnight and shower so I ain't got to answer a bunch of questions. My midnight to six shift is only four people."

"Okay, then we'll come back here at noon, and Georgio can take us to the locker."

Felicia nodded. "You're still a big pain in my ass."

Bitsy smiled. "I know. But you wouldn't have it any other way."

Outside in the alley again, Raven gave Bitsy a warm hug. "Thank you. How do you know Felicia?"

"It's a long story. We should go find a place to lounge. Then I'll let you buy me lunch with some of that money of yours." She patted the girl's shoulder. "I know this might not be what you dreamed about, but Felicia and her family are good people."

"And the storage locker?"

Bitsy smiled. "It's an old trick for an old gal."

As Raven made her way out of the alley, she was happy to have a chance at something new. The girl never suspected the secret that Bitsy was keeping from her.

Chapter Thirty-Eight

Raven sat in the back of Georgio's car, clutching her coveted duffel bag. Changes had been happening quickly since she'd left Guilty Pleasure. She looked out the car window, watching the children playing on the block and old women in coats and hats sitting on their steps. That's when it struck her that she hadn't known Bitsy long. The lady was nice, but she barely knew the woman. Now she was sitting in the back of a strange man's car.

What am I doing? I'm so desperate to be safe that I might be putting myself in danger.

"So, Raven, where are you from?" Georgio asked, breaking into her worried thoughts.

"I, um, I grew up in North Philly," she murmured. She wrung her hands together, and her eyes darted to Bitsy looking out the front window.

Is she avoiding eye contact with me?

"Oh, wow. That's a bad area." He glanced at her in the rearview mirror. "Does that mean you're a good fighter?"

Okay, odd question.

Raven's belly rose and fell. "I don't know. I guess. I've been fighting my whole life, but I never learned how to fight until I got out of high school and left North Philly."

"Oh yeah. Who taught you?" he asked.

"Hey," Bitsy cut in. "Leave my girl alone. Why you asking her so many questions? You want people all up in your ass asking you about all the girls you're screwing? No, you don't, I'm sure. How about if you ask Raven if she's hungry or something more useful."

Georgio gave Bitsy a side-glance. "Sorry. You know I didn't mean nothing by it. I was curious. I live with a mom who'd rather cut her fingers and toes off than let her kids leave home and not know where they are."

Bitsy cocked her head. "Yeah, but it still happened, though, didn't it? Enzo was gone for how long?" She tapped a finger against her forehead. "I taught you to think before you speak to homeless people. We've been through all this." She huffed.

Georgio chuckled. "Okay, you got me." He glanced at Raven in his rearview mirror again. "I don't mean to be nosey. I like to know things about people that are around my family, and Bitsy is my family."

Bitsy turned her head away from him, but a smile stretched over her lips.

Bitsy had become integrated into Georgio's family several years prior. The woman had helped Enzo, his brother, find his way home. Bitsy knew from the moment she laid eyes on Enzo he wasn't homeless. He was lost. He was a teenage boy in distress. She had spent days following Enzo around, talking to him, trying to convince Enzo that his family was worried. It was clear by his behavior and the things he shared with her during his lucid moments that the boy's family hadn't thrown him out.

Enzo would spend his days humming, rocking, and talking to people who weren't there. Then he'd have sudden outbursts of anger and self-harm. Bitsy had observed him closely and at a distance long enough to know that he wasn't addicted to drugs or alcohol. It took more than two weeks, but Bitsy eventually got Enzo to tell her where he lived. She begged for money for two days to get enough to take a taxi to his home in West Philly.

Bitsy stood on the porch of Enzo's family home, wringing her hands together. She had knocked on the front door, and a moment later Felicia answered.

"Can I help you?" Felicia asked, taking in the woman's dirty clothes and foul odor.

"Yeah. Do you have a son named Enzo?"

Felicia's eyes bulged and she pressed a hand over her mouth. She gasped and her hand fumbled down to the collar of her shirt. "Sweet Jesus, do you know where my Enzo is? Is he alive?"

Bitsy nodded. "He's okay. I've been following him for a couple of weeks now. I finally got him to trust me enough to give me your address. You can see I'm homeless, but your boy, he ain't out here because he don't have a nice home. He's out on the streets because his head ain't right. The boy don't belong out there where people will take advantage of him."

Felicia blushed as she nodded. "Yes, Enzo has issues. He's had them since he was a young boy. He stopped taking his medication—we don't know why—but the meds helped him. He was level and happy," she added quickly. "He's a good boy." The woman's voice broke, and she lowered her face.

"You ain't gotta convince me of that. I know Enzo is a nice young man. He's respectful. He don't hurt nobody . . . well, 'cept himself. He don't steal. He mostly spends time alone, stuck in his head. I couldn't get him to come here with me, so I came to bring you to him. He needs to be home with you and be the man he ought to be."

Felicia had pushed aside all of her misgivings about the unkempt vagabond. She took Bitsy into a tight embrace.

A short time later, Felicia, Bitsy, and Georgio sat on a curb beside Enzo in West Philadelphia. Enzo had agreed to go with them but only if Bitsy could go to his house too. Felicia gave the other woman a sweet smile.

"Yes, Enzo. Of course Bitsy can stay at our house."

Bitsy had returned a brief smile, but this was something she hadn't expected or mentally prepared for. It was then she decided to go only to get Enzo back home.

Bitsy had lived in Felicia's house for five weeks while Enzo was put back on his medication that leveled him. In those five weeks, the family had grown to admire the woman who'd loved Enzo and kept him safe even from himself.

Bitsy was jolted from her daydreaming when Georgio laid his hand on top of the woman's. "So, Bits, are you finally ready to get off the streets?" he asked with a big smile on his lips. He looked in his rearview mirror and gave Raven a mischievous grin.

Raven was wide-eyed and still uneasy.

"Nope. Nuh-uh. Not me. I'm too old for that shit now. I'm looking forward to staying in the storage unit you got us. I was only gonna stay long enough to get Raven settled. But now seeing you and your mom, I think I'll stay and get through the winter. Then I'll be off to something new. I've only come back here to see to it my girl gets a job for herself so she can straighten up and fly right. You know the inside lifestyle doesn't suit me, but I need a little rest. I like the closeness of a storage unit in the winter. Some of my best memories when I was in my late twenties were living in a storage locker down in West Philly. As I get older, I'm getting more and more like a bear. I wanna hunker down in the winter and wait for the first sign of spring before I show my face again. Besides, I'm tired, been for a while now, and I need a place to rest my bones." Bitsy chuckled.

Georgio patted her hand. "I hear you. I put some things for you in the locker already. I have more stuff in my trunk that my mom wanted you to have, too."

Bitsy looked over her shoulder into the back seat. "Ain't this family the best?"

Raven gave her a terse grin. "Yes. They seem really nice."

Picking up on Raven's anxiety, Bitsy's eyes lingered on the girl for a few seconds. Then she whacked Georgio in the arm. "You hear that. They seem really nice." She looked over her shoulder again. "They're the kind of people we can trust." She gave Raven a wink. "Georgio, I wanna see my boy Enzo. Where is he?"

Georgio gave her a quick glimpse. "I told him you're in town right after my mom called me today. Enzo can't wait to see you."

Bitsy faced him straight on. Her brow was wrinkled, and she gave Georgio a pained gaze.

"Come on, now. I know that look," Georgio commented. "You don't need to worry. Enzo's doing really good. He has a job and he's going to school at night to learn how to be a computer programmer."

"Oh," she gasped, putting her hand over her heart and letting her back relax into the seat. "You almost gave me a fucking heart attack. I thought something bad happened to him. You know I like my information fast and furious, not dripping outta your mouth like it's plugged with cotton." She let her head fall back. "My Enzo is doing good. Makes me so happy to know it. I wanna see him soon. You tell him I said so, too."

"You don't need to worry. He can't wait to see you either. He wants my mom to make a big dinner so you can come over and spend time with the whole family."

"That's good. How's your dad doing?"

Georgio shrugged listlessly, his lifeless eyes betraying his gloominess. "He's bedridden now."

Bitsy looked over her shoulder at Raven. "Georgio's dad had two strokes, bad ones, right before I brought Enzo home. His body has been failing ever since. Never got back to walking on his own. It's been hard on Felicia . . . on all of them."

"Oh," Raven breathed. "I'm sorry to hear about your dad."

"Yeah, thanks," Georgio mumbled.

Bitsy could see the pained expression on the young man's face. Losing his father was a big blow, and he'd taken on the role of the dominant male in the household. "See here, Georgio." Her voice was light and upbeat. "Tell your mama I want some of those homemade manicotti. Oh, and tell her I want the bresaola in the sauce with meatballs. Damn, I love that shit. Sometimes I dream of it."

This brought a smile to Georgio's lips.

As they drove the rest of the way to the storage unit, Raven listened to the two reminisce about those five weeks they lived together. Raven couldn't help but wonder how hard it must have been on Bitsy to go back on the streets after being part of their family.

***

Georgio parallel parked the car a few feet from the storage unit. He got out and looked around. Then he lifted the door and flipped on the light.

"Let's go. Make it quick," Bitsy told Raven.

The two rushed from the car and into the unit. Inside, Georgio quickly pulled the door closed.

Raven looked around the twelve-by-twelve-foot locker. It was as cold inside as it was outside, but being enclosed gave a sense of safety. She understood now why Bitsy wanted to be in it for the winter.

"What happens when it gets colder?" Raven asked.

"We'll get us some coats, and Georgio will bring us more blankets," Bitsy stated.

"And," Georgio added, "I brought you this." He opened a box and pulled out a propane heater. "The smell is awful, but it'll warm this whole space. You might need to lift the door a few inches now and again to let the smell out." He pointed to the fourteen-foot ceiling. "But the ceiling is high, and you shouldn't have a problem."

Raven put her duffel bag down and assessed the things that had been brought in for them. There were two twin mattresses on the floor with sheets and a thick comforter on top of each. There were three battery operated lanterns, two tables, and a radio. Felicia had sent over a few books and magazines to read, too.

Georgio hauled in another box from his trunk filled with drinks and snacks. "My mom thought you'd need these in case you get hungry."

"Your mom is an angel. Tonight I'm gonna walk Raven to the fish shop so she knows how to get there. After, I'm gonna go scrounge for dinner."

She walked over to Georgio and put a hand on his chest. "If you need me, knock three times, wait, and knock twice, so I know it's you on the other side of this door."

"Got it. You'll be safe here. Make sure you come and go when it's dark outside and you'll be fine. The office doesn't open until nine in the morning and is closed by five at night. With the winter biting at our asses, it'll get dark early. So there shouldn't be any problems."

Bitsy put her hands on her hips. "Oh, you don't say? You should remember I've been on the streets longer than you've been alive. You ain't gotta worry about me. I'll be fine." She hugged him. "Now, you get going so me and Raven can get settled in and relax before she's gotta go chop up fish."

Once Georgio was gone, Raven immediately started to make her bed, while Bitsy flopped onto the other mattress. She was lying flat on her back and breathing heavily.

"Hey, are you okay?" Raven asked.

The woman flipped a wrist in her direction. "Yeah, I'm fine. It's been a long day, and I didn't sleep good last night." Bitsy closed her eyes.

Raven assessed the woman. She didn't know her that well but thought she looked exhausted. She stood over her. "How about if you take my bed? It's already made, and I'll take yours," she offered.

"Well, ain't you an angel sent from heaven above? Thank you, sweetie. I'll take you up on that offer. The day sure did get the better of me . . . and you know, it's emotional seeing Georgio and Felicia. I thought about them a lot recently. They're the closest thing I have to family. Now, if you don't mind, I'm gonna take a tiny nap," the woman said.

"Yeah, of course. You should rest. I'll try to do the same."

Raven watched Bitsy climb under the comforter on the mattress and fall asleep in seconds. The woman looked at peace as her body relaxed into a dream state.

As Bitsy slept, Raven's thoughts wandered to her new job. Cutting fish didn't look easy. She was nervous she'd be clumsy with the knives and chop her hand off. She hoped that whoever would teach her had a lot of patience.

What if I can't do it? What will happen to me and Bitsy?

Then she gave herself comfort by remembering when she started working at the deli for Ava and Dante. She was as nervous then, afraid she'd fail, but had paid attention and figured it out.

THE TWIN SISTER

Starting new seems like a fun idea, but it takes work, she told herself.

Chapter Thirty-Nine

Raven arrived at the fish processing plant and was met by a man with a welcoming smile.

"Ciao. I'm Marco. Come. Come." He opened the door wider and waved her inside.

"Hi. I'm Raven. Are you the person who is going to train me? I never cut fish before, but I pick things up fast."

Marco tilted his head to the side. "No, capire."

Concern gripped her. She looked around the plant for someone who might fill the language barrier. Her eyes narrowed and she shook her head. "Um..."

Marco pointed at an American flag on the wall and shook his head.

"You don't speak *any* English?" she asked. *Holy shit.*

His smile lit up his face. "Si. No 'lish."

"Okay." She clamped her teeth down on her bottom lip and pointed to the others. "English?"

Marco's smile widened. "No."

"So what do I do?" she asked, waving her hands around the empty air. She pointed to the two people at the metal table already cutting fish.

Marco brought her to the worktable. She noticed his shoulders were hunched. A result of skinning, gutting, and filleting fish for years. She stood at the table while Marco pulled a stool out. He rested both hands on her shoulders and then pressed her down. Then he sat on the stool next to her.

"Fish, we cut." He made a scissoring motion.

Raven nodded. "Yes."

Marco walked to a cabinet and pulled out clean knives, as her eyes followed him. He was a short man with jet-black hair and brown eyes. He looked average. But his smile told her he was much more than mediocre. His smile was unique, one that was rarely found on the streets. It was genuine, and she couldn't take her eyes off of him. He was happy to be there. Happy to be working. Marco radiated joy and gratitude.

When Marco returned to the table, he handed Raven a long, sharp knife. Twisting his face, he lifted his shoulders to his ears. Marco pointed to the sharp blade. Then he ran an index finger across his throat and pointed at the knife again.

"Right. It's sharp. Okay, I'll be careful."

He laid the knife on the stainless-steel table in front of her. She grabbed the handle like it was a baseball bat and he laughed, shaking his head. "No, no," he said, grinning at her. He lifted his knife and showed her how to hold it.

Raven did the same.

"Si," he said. He tapped her shoulder and pointed to his eyes, indicating she needed to pay attention.

She nodded.

Marco put a fish in front of each of them, and she mimicked everything he did.

"I chopped mine to bits," she said out loud, laughing.

No one understood what she said. The other three workers stared at her. She looked around her when no one reacted.

Oh boy, these are gonna be long nights.

She tapped Marco on the shoulder. She pulled a fish from a basket and pointed her knife at it. Marco took her through the process again.

At 6:30 in the morning, after a hot shower, she made her way back to the storage unit. She jumped the fence in the back of the lot where no one could see her. She knocked on the door three times. Paused and knocked twice more.

When she lifted the door, Bitsy was sitting on her mattress, back against the wall, reading a magazine Felicia had sent. "Good morning, sweetie," the older woman sang. "How did it go last night?"

Raven kicked off her sneakers and flopped on her mattress, pulling the comforter over her lap. "It was okay. They all speak Italian, so it was hard to learn what I'm supposed to do."

Bitsy nodded. "Yeah, that's tough. But think of it this way, there are a lot of people who speak your language but what they're saying don't make any sense. You know who I'm talking about . . . people like your friend Monica. The girl ran right back into the arms of the man who thumped the shit outta her on a regular basis. I couldn't understand nothing she said to you about why she was going back. Besides, learning to communicate with people who don't speak your language teaches you how to express yourself in other ways."

Raven nodded. "Yeah, you're right. But it's a weird job. It's smelly and, Bitsy, the knives I have to use are so sharp I'm scared I'll cut my hand off."

"You're probably right about the knives, so it's in your best interest to learn how to handle your work tools. Don't worry about the rest—not talking to nobody or it being cold and smelly. You do your work and come back here and talk to me. There are twenty-four hours in a day, and you only spend six hours there. You do the math." She playfully nudged the girl's foot with her own. "Do yourself a favor and use those six hours to think about what you want outta your life. Let yourself dream about having things you never thought possible. I didn't do that when I was young. My mind was preoccupied with shit that didn't matter," Bitsy advised.

"Well, well, well. Look at you being all positive and shit."

Bitsy chuckled. "Who, me? Girl, I'm walking positivity. But I'm also hungry from giving all that great advice. I think we should go out and get some breakfast. What do you say?"

Raven nodded. "Yeah, I'm starving. Then I need to come back and sleep."

***

Back from breakfast, Raven pulled the door down and turned on the propane heater. She looked over and saw Bitsy place her hands on the block wall and stretch out her back.

"I need to get me some pain relievers. I got a terrible hurting in my back and neck," Bitsy commented.

"Maybe it's your mattress. Do you wanna switch?"

Bitsy glanced at the girl. "The mattress is fine. Don't worry. Go on and get some sleep. Midnight will be here before you know it."

Raven got onto her mattress. "I can run out to the store when I wake up and grab you something for your pain, so you have it before I go to work."

"That would be mighty sweet of you. I'd appreciate that. You get your rest and I'm gonna start reading this book," she said, lifting it into her hand. "When I lived with Felicia and her family, the two of us would read the same book and talk about it." She closed her eyes and shook her head. "I sure as hell miss those days."

Since Bitsy opened the door into her past, Raven stepped inside. She propped herself up on her elbow. "Why *did* you leave their house and go back to the streets? Felicia would've given you a job, and you could've gotten your own place. You said they're like family."

"Yeah, well, they are. See, the thing is while I was living there, I fell on some hard times . . . It wasn't all perfect."

"What happened?"

"Ah, I had access to alcohol. I'm a recovering alcoholic. When I went to live with them, I was still drinking a lot. I weaned off the juice slowly over the first three weeks. They didn't know I was an alcoholic. I functioned and hid it well. But you know, it was a couple of glasses of wine with dinner or a few beers with Georgio. Just enough to keep me going."

"Wow, that's hard to believe. I mean"—she held her palms out—"I believe you, but it sounds like you're talking about somebody else. You're the most responsible person I know," Raven complimented.

"I might be now, but I didn't used to be."

"So then something happened at Felicia's house while you were living there?"

Bitsy nodded and shrank into herself at the memory. "Yeah, one night Felicia threw a big party, and there was lots of beer and hard liquor. I got trashed and made a spectacle of myself. I was dancing and stripping and falling all over the place. I said some crude shit to one of Felicia's best friends. Of course, Felicia didn't throw me out or nothing, but I was burning with shame the next day when Enzo told me some of the things I did. So for the next three weeks, while Enzo's meds were kicking in, I only drank enough to keep me from withdrawing. I left as soon as I could and went straight to a detox place. There's a volunteer organization in southwest Philly. They were nice people. I stayed in that place for five nights and six days. Then I had to visit the center every day. After a month, I was in AA." She shook her head. "That whole experience changed my life." Bitsy dragged a hand across her forehead. "I'm not proud of what I did back then."

"I think it was very brave. You had a problem, and you fixed it on your own. Nobody had to force you or tell you to get help. You were embarrassed, and that's all it took."

Bitsy grinned and lifted her chin high. "You're right. Once I learned—and I mean really accepted that I couldn't change the past—the present became easier to live in. Ah right now. You better sleep. I'll be here when you get up."

Raven's heavy eyelids eased closed, and as she fell into a deep sleep, a sense of home washed over her.

Chapter Forty: One Month Later

By the end of Raven's first month at the fish processing plant, she was almost as fluent with the knives as the others. She had picked up a few words of Italian, but she mostly communicated with her coworkers by acting out her questions.

It was mid-November, and the weather was turning colder. It had been raining for two weeks straight with temperatures hovering in the high thirties.

As Raven walked home, she clung to her umbrella so the winds wouldn't whip it from her grip. The cold cut at her cheeks and bit at her chapped lips. She was breathless by the time she reached the storage unit. She bent over, and her jacket hiked up her torso. A shiver ran through her when the cold rain hit the exposed skin on her lower back above her jeans. After doing the warning knock, Raven grabbed the handle and pulled the door up.

Inside the storage unit with the door closed between her and the unrelenting, stormy wind and rain, Raven shook off her umbrella. She closed her eyes and stood still for a moment, basking in the warmth of the unit. She ran her fingers through her wet hair to get it out of her face, and that's when she saw Bitsy lying on her mattress, writhing in pain.

She rushed to the mattress and fell to her knees. "Bitsy? What's wrong?"

Bitsy moaned and looked up at the girl. She'd been crying. "It's just a little bit of pain in my back. That's all it is. I'll be okay."

"No, Bitsy, it's not okay. You've been having back pain since we got here, and it's getting worse. It's not normal the way you've been lying in bed. You hardly ever leave this storage unit. Now you're curled in a ball because the pain has gotten so bad you can't take it. You have to go to the doctor. You can't wait anymore. I think we should go to the hospital."

Bitsy shook her head. "That ain't necessary."

"Why? Why ain't it necessary to get you the relief you need? They'll give you something for the pain. They say once you break the cycle of pain, you can get back to normal," Raven reasoned.

"There ain't no getting back to normal." Bitsy flinched from another bolt of agony.

"What are you talking about?"

Raven's blood pressure was rising. She knew something needed to be done but was helpless to make it happen. She was missing a piece of the puzzle. It was all up to Bitsy. There was tension in the air. Her eyes narrowed and she looked into the woman's pained face, but Bitsy avoided her gaze. She decided on a different approach.

Raven moved onto the bed beside the older woman and gently rubbed her back. "Is there something you aren't telling me? You and me are in this together. If I was sick, you'd want to take care of me, and that's what I want to do for you," she pleaded, her voice quivering.

"Jesus, child, you're a pain in my ass. You never quit until you get what you want outta me." She rolled onto her back and looked into Raven's eyes. "I'm sick. I've been sick for a long time . . . over two years now."

The girl placed a hand on Bitsy's shoulder. Her mouth drooped and her eyes opened wide. "What does that mean? Sick how? Not like you're dying sick, right?"

Bitsy's eyes found hers. "I can't promise you that I ain't gonna die. I started with breast cancer. Then the motherfucker moved into my bones about four months ago. The doctor told me that could happen, and it did."

"What?" Raven mumbled. "You've had cancer this whole time and you didn't tell me?"

Bitsy shrugged. "Sweetie, think about it. I haven't even known you for too long. What? Five, maybe six weeks now. It wasn't something I was comfortable burdening you with. I want you to concentrate on yourself. I told myself I'd be healthy until one day I dropped dead. I figured I'd make it through the winter, till you got on your feet and found a place to live. Then I was gonna go back into Center City, to one of those hospice places. But it must be spreading a lot faster than I expected it to."

Raven choked back her tears. Looking at Bitsy now, with this information, she could see the physical effects. Bitsy was much thinner, her hair had thinned, she was always tired, and her skin and nails had no luster. All the signs were there, but she hadn't seen them.

O my God. I'm going to lose her.

Raven cleared her throat and sat up. She willed herself to be strong. She knew it wouldn't be right to make Bitsy comfort her.

The girl stroked Bitsy's hair. "Okay, you know what I think?"

"No, but I have a feeling you're gonna tell me," Bitsy murmured through another round of pain.

"I think we should take you to the hospital now. That's the only place that can help you with your pain. They'll make you more comfortable. There's no reason to put yourself through this." She leaned her head to the side. "It doesn't make sense or do either of us any good for you to lie here and suffer. Let me help you."

Knock, knock, knock. Pause. *Knock, knock.*

"Thank God." Raven got to her feet and rushed to the door. "Come in."

The door slid open and Georgio slipped inside and pulled the door down behind him. "Hey, Bitsy, my mom sent me to tell you . . ."

Raven's head snapped toward the woman. She was rolled into a fetal position, breathing through the pain. She turned back to Georgio. "Bitsy has cancer. It's bad, and she said it's moved to her bones. She's in pain. She doesn't want to go to the hospital, but I'm taking her there anyway. Will you drive us?"

"Raven!" Bitsy grunted. "Did I say you can tell people my business?"

Raven glanced at her with a scowl. "No, you didn't. But I need help and so do you."

Georgio nodded and knelt next to the mattress. "Bits?"

The woman opened her eyes and let out a moan drenched in pain.

"I'm taking you and Raven to the hospital."

Bitsy shook her head, but Georgio lifted her into his arms. He took her outside and laid her across the back seat. Raven was right behind him, covering the woman with her quilt. She slid into the front seat, and Georgio didn't waste a minute.

As Georgio sped through the city streets, Raven looked into the back seat at Bitsy. She didn't recognize the woman she'd met less than two months prior. Bitsy brought a shaky hand to her forehead as she let loose an uncontrollable whimper.

"Hang on, Bitsy. We're almost there," Raven encouraged. Her head snapped to face Georgio. "Drive faster," she hissed. Her hands curled into fists as she prayed for her friend's suffering to end.

Chapter Forty-One

Raven practically carried Bitsy into a bay at the emergency room. She propped her on the bed and then helped the woman undress. When Raven pulled Bitsy's shirt over her head, she gasped. The woman was skin and bones, and all of her ribs were prominent.

"Don't go making those sounds now," Bitsy said in a weak but defensive tone. "I didn't need you to see what's happening. I knew it was coming at me, and I wanted you to focus on yourself."

"Bitsy?" Raven's voice hitched. "We live in a twelve-foot space. How could you hide this from me? How is it even possible?"

"It wasn't that hard. Different schedules. I avoided changing when you were there. Just like you, I know how to let people see only what I want 'em to see." She pursed her lips. "We all got secrets. Ain't that right?"

Raven was too distracted by Bitsy's condition to comprehend what the woman was saying.

"I'm sorry. What did you say?" Raven asked innocently.

"I said we all got secrets."

Raven cocked her head. "What are you talking about? And where is that nurse to give you pain meds?"

Bitsy shook her head. "Don't change the subject. I'm talking about that burden you've been carrying on your back for what your brother did." The woman closed her eyes and breathed through another round of pain.

Raven stopped and stared at her. She tried to hide her shame. She pulled the thin blanket over the woman. "How long have you known about Matthew?"

"Eh, since we went to see Felicia that first day. She recognized you from the television. She said your picture was all over the news. I didn't ask her much about it 'cause I didn't want her to worry that she was hiring the wrong person. You got the police looking for you?" Bitsy asked.

Raven scoffed. "No. Of course not. The police were the only people that helped me after the shootings."

"Good. Then who you got looking for you?"

"What makes you think someone is looking for me?"

Bitsy raised her eyebrows. "I'm educated in people—from watching them—all forms of life."

The girl pulled a plastic chair close to the side of her bed. She lowered her face for a split second, then raised it again. "A gang from Kensington. Some of their people were killed."

"Mm, mm, mm. That's a damn crime that you gotta lug that shit around with you through your young life. But you'll be okay. Time will make it better. Always does."

A nurse walked into the room, and Raven stood. "She's in a lot of pain. Can you ask the doctor to give her something?"

The nurse moved to the side of Bitsy's bed and smiled at her. "I'm Nancy. I'll be your nurse in the ER. Where's your pain?"

"Good to meet ya, Nancy. The pain is in my back and neck. It's coming from my breast cancer."

"Oh, I'm so sorry to hear that. When were you diagnosed?" the nurse asked politely.

"Well, I was told I had breast cancer a little less than two years ago. It was bad. I caught it too late."

"Where did you have this diagnosis?" Nancy asked. "I'll need to get copies of your medical records."

"Here, at this hospital."

"Did you have chemo or radiation?"

Bitsy shook her head. "Nope. It was too far gone, and I decided not to have it."

"Okay, did you have any surgeries on your breasts?"

"Nope, too late for that, too," Bitsy admitted sadly.

The nurse patted her shoulder. "I'll go pull your records. Then the doctor will be right in, and we'll get you something to take care of that pain."

Bitsy nodded and closed her eyes again. As she did, Felicia walked into the bay with Georgio and Enzo.

Bitsy's eyes lit up. "Enzo. My handsome boy. Come give me some sugar. Hell, child, it looks like you've grown into a man since I saw you two weeks ago."

Enzo went to her hesitantly. His face was ashen, and he took cautious steps closer to the gurney. "You're not dying, are you?"

"Son, we all dying."

Enzo took her hand in his. "I mean right now."

Bitsy pushed a loud breath from her lungs. "No, but I'm sick. I'm real sick, Enzo."

Enzo put the bed rail down, sat in a chair next to her, and put his head on her chest like he was a small child. Bitsy stroked his hair while he cried and the others watched, trying in vain not to cry with him.

After a minute, Felicia took hold of her son's arm and pulled him to his feet. She looked at Georgio. "Take Enzo to the waiting room and stay there with him."

Finally, Bitsy was alone with Raven and Felicia.

Felicia ran her hand gently across the woman's cheek. "Georgio said it's bad. That you're in a lot of pain?"

Bitsy pulled in a breath through her nose. "Yes, it's bad. But look, I knew this thing was barreling at me. The oncologist warned me. By the time I met with him, the damn shit had spread too far. So I decided not to spend what time I had left pumping myself with chemicals."

"Bitsy," Raven cut in. "What treatment did your doctor recommend?"

"Those doctors always want you to try medicine to prolong life. That's what they're supposed to do." Bitsy shook her head. "When I asked how much longer the treatments would get me, he said six months tops. If he said six years, I might've considered it, but that ain't enough time to put myself through all that nonsense. Besides, I didn't want to walk around after the treatment waiting for it to come back and find me. This way, I knew it was there and I could deal with it better. I avoided all that psychological bullshit of waiting for the grim reaper to be around the next corner."

Raven put her hand over the woman's. "Oh, Bitsy. I wish you had told me sooner. I could've done something—I don't know—something to make you feel better, instead of you looking after me," she said in a strangled voice.

"You should've told me, too," Felicia said in a stern tone. "How dare you keep this kinda secret from me?"

Bitsy waved her off. "You got enough shit to worry about with your husband. You didn't need to be thinking about me, too. I've been fine since I got to West Philly. It's only in the last two weeks that things got bad."

The doctor walked in, and they all went silent. "Bitsy, I'm Dr. Lancer, the on-call oncologist. How are you?"

"Well." She grinned. "As you can see, I ain't doing too good today, but maybe tomorrow will be better."

Dr. Lancer patted her hand. "I've reviewed your records. You had some testing done by one of my partners. I see he explained that the cancer was fairly far gone when it was found."

Bitsy nodded. "It's in my bones now."

"I don't have those test results. Did you have them done at another facility?" he said, looking at his paperwork.

"No. I didn't get no test for that. I can feel it," Bitsy stated.

Dr. Lancer nodded. "Okay, I'd like to do some tests to be certain."

Bitsy rolled her eyes. "Doc, no disrespect, but I already feel like a city bus mowed me down, I don't wanna be poked and prodded." She turned her head and glared at Raven. "I told this young lady here that I didn't want to come to the hospital."

Dr. Lancer patted her hand. "I'll tell you what. To do the test, I will have you sedated, and we will get a bone biopsy, just to be certain." He leveled her with his gaze. "Can we agree on that approach?"

Bitsy met his gaze. "You gonna sedate me now?"

Dr. Lancer cracked a smile and shook his head. "I'm going to give you a strong painkiller now. Then we will admit you, and you'll probably have the test sometime tomorrow."

Bitsy's eyes welled. "How long I gotta stay in here? I don't do well trapped in places."

"It's hard to say right now. But at least a few days, maybe a week. We'll see how it goes."

Bitsy shook her head. "I can't stay in here. I got things to do."

"You do not," Raven stated assertively. "There's nothing you need to do right now. You need to stay here and do what the doctor says. I can't stand by and watch you suffer. I'll come every day after work and sit with you. I swear."

Felicia tapped the bed rail. "And if that don't work, I'll chain you to this goddamn bed," she added, smiling at her friend.

Bitsy turned to Dr. Lancer again. "Okay. But can you get me some pain medicine in a hurry? I can't take it no more."

"You got it," he said, squeezing her hand.

He left the room, and the nurse came back within ten minutes. "Dr. Lancer prescribed you something that's going to make you feel so much better. It might make you sleepy, too."

"I don't care if it kills me right about now. I can't take the pain."

Raven's eyes were locked on Bitsy's when the nurse pushed the clear fluid into her IV. The woman's shoulders relaxed and a few minutes later her jaw dropped open. It was the first time in hours that Raven could breathe easily.

Chapter Forty-Two

Six days later, Raven was sitting beside Bitsy's hospital bed when Dr. Lancer walked into the room during morning rounds. Bitsy's eyes were closed as she relaxed in bed.

Raven looked up from the magazine she was leafing through.

Dr. Lancer looked at Raven. "How's our patient today?"

Raven snickered. "Ornery. She fusses about everything. Mostly that she hates hospitals—not just this one, but all of them—and she wants to leave." Her tone was jovial, and as she spoke, she threw a scathing look in Bitsy's direction.

Bitsy opened her eyes and looked at the girl. "Don't listen to her, doc. She don't know shit about shit."

Dr. Lancer chuckled and moved to the side of her bed. "Seriously, how are you feeling today?"

Bitsy shrugged. "Like my insides are crawling with cancer and I'm hurtling toward death."

His mouth was downturned, and he nodded. "I'm sorry about what's going on with you. As we discussed after the results of your bone biopsy, the pain will become more persistent over time. It may come and go, but short of heavy doses of painkillers, we can only do so much to reduce the side effects of the cancer."

She nodded. "Yeah, that really sucks. I got myself a lousy hand in this game. Listen, doc, I know I'm at the end of my life. Funny how I can feel it coming at me. My body is failing, turning her fucking back on me. But doc"—she dragged her eyes to his—"I can't stand the pain, and I don't wanna spend my last days not knowing where I'm at or who is around me. I don't have that many people, but the ones I have . . . I wanna know they're there. I wanna know I ain't dying alone."

Overcome with sorrow, Raven covered her face with her hands. Then she shook it off and lifted her chin. "I'll be right here with you, Bitsy, and so will Felicia and her family. You won't be alone and don't have to suffer with all this pain. Maybe there's something else." She looked to the doctor. "Is there some kind of medicine that will help with the pain, but she won't be so out of it?"

He rocked his head from side to side. "Not really, but I think I have something that will help." He gave Bitsy a serious look. "But understand, it won't be as good as the medication you've been on. You'll still have pain if you go this route, but I can knock the edge off of it."

Bitsy nodded. "Yeah, that would be good, doc. That's what I want you to do."

As they were discussing the medication for Bitsy, Felicia walked into the room and stood by the door, listening to the conversation. She was stoic, not adding anything, knowing she would make the same request of the doctor if it were her lying in that bed.

"When can I get outta here?" Bitsy asked.

"I think tomorrow or the next day. You're going to need someone who can care for you. I want to make sure you have all the support that you'll need before I release you. Where will you be going from here?" Dr. Lancer asked.

Bitsy rubbed her palms on her thighs. "There's a hospice place in Center City. I'm going there as long as they have a bed for me."

"And if they don't?" he asked.

"If they don't, then I'll find a shelter and figure something else out," Bitsy explained.

Raven's guts were twisting. She couldn't wrap her mind around Bitsy being ill and having nowhere to go. The thought of the woman waiting on the sidewalk in the bitter cold for hours to get a bed at a shelter made her hands shake.

Felicia stepped up to the railing at her bed. "Like hell you'll go to a shelter. Not on my watch, sister. You're coming home with me. You'll stay at my house so I can keep an eye on you."

Raven let out a sigh of relief, and Bitsy's head turned in the girl's direction. "What about her?" she asked Felicia, pointing at Raven.

"Don't worry about me," Raven said hurriedly, knowing that Bitsy would be well taken care of at Felicia's house.

"Yes, her too. She'll come stay with you. I ain't stupid. I know you won't come without her. Besides, I'm gonna need Raven to help me with you."

Felicia moved her face closer and lowered her voice. "Because we both know neither of my boys are gonna be good with this dying shit."

Felicia was putting on a brave front, but her heart was splintering inside her chest. "You and Raven will take Enzo's room, and he's gonna sleep in Georgio's room," she stated.

Bitsy shook her head. "I can't put Enzo out of his room. You know that's his safe place. He likes it in there when he's feeling vulnerable." She looked at the doctor. "Close your ears, you can't hear this."

He gave her a sad smile. "Okay."

"Me and Raven are going back to the storage unit. I can be perfectly comfortable there," Bitsy stated.

Felicia hadn't taken her eyes off of Bitsy. "Over my dead body." Her voice rose and she puffed out her chest. "You ain't living out your last days in no goddamn storage unit."

Bitsy pursed her lips and shook her head. "Felicia, I appreciate what you're doing, but Raven will make sure I get the medicine I need. Right?" she asked, turning to Raven.

"Yes, of course. I'll do whatever you need me to do, but I think it's a better idea for you to stay at Felicia's . . . you know, in a real house. This is about you, Bitsy. It's not about me or Enzo." Raven kept her eyes glued to the woman's. She hoped Bitsy would see her desperation and make the right decision.

Felicia grabbed Raven's hand. "You will come to my house with Bitsy. She is no longer in control of this decision. She's so set on thinking she's a burden that she forgets the blessing she's been to all of us. Bitsy is gonna need you. She's gonna need everyone in our family. She's just too much of a fool and a hardhead to know it."

Raven watched the relief pass through Dr. Lancer as his shoulders slid away from his ears. *He must think we are all out of our minds.*

Bitsy pressed the button on her bed to sit up higher. "Felicia, I don't know who you think you're bossing around, but I don't take shit from nobody. You're acting like you don't know me. You know the kinda woman I am—independent," she snapped.

Felicia moved her face inches from Bitsy's. "I don't give a shit what kinda woman you are. If you don't let me do this for you . . ." Her voice broke and her chest heaved, no longer able to keep herself together. "Please, Bitsy, please," she managed in a strangled voice. She was crying and looked to Raven for help.

Raven swiped at her own tears. "Felicia is right. You have to go to her house. Going back to the storage unit is a bad idea. You need different things now like running water, heat . . . real meals. I can take care of you much better there."

Bitsy shook her head. "But I'm putting Enzo out."

Felicia gave her a sorrowful grin. "Bitsy, it was Enzo's idea for you to come stay with us. He and Georgio worked it out before they even talked to me."

Bitsy's tears slid down her cheeks freely. "My boy. Enzo loves me that much," she mumbled to herself. The older woman looked at Raven. "I guess we're moving inside for a while."

Raven nodded. "I guess we are," she choked out. She secretly hoped that when Bitsy said for a while, it meant a long time. Raven was not anywhere near ready to let Bitsy go.

Chapter Forty-Three

After getting Bitsy settled in Enzo's bed, Raven and Georgio went to the storage locker to remove their belongings.

"It's nice of your family to let Bitsy and me stay at your house," Raven said.

Georgio nodded. "Finding out that Bits is sick has been really hard on all of us. We haven't seen her in a long time, so you would think it would hurt less, but it doesn't. She could be gone for twenty years, and we'd still fall madly in love with her all over again. Bitsy single-handedly saved our family." He gave her a side-glance. "Once Enzo was gone and we couldn't find him, we were falling apart, bit by bit. My parents couldn't agree on anything, and it was like I no longer existed to them. We were all obsessed with finding Enzo. I resented my parents for wanting Enzo back so much. It was like I didn't matter to them. But at the same time, I missed my brother so bad I could barely function. We were all fucked up until Bitsy knocked on our door that day."

"Wow, does Bitsy know all of this?"

Georgio shrugged. "My family are big believers in showing appreciation instead of telling someone. You know, the words we speak don't always match the way we feel inside."

"Boy, do I understand that," she remarked.

He stopped at a red light and turned his head toward her. "So my mom told me who you are. How's that been going for you?"

Raven faced him. She knew eventually Felicia or Georgio would want to talk about what happened. "It's been hard."

"What was it like? You know, being in that room and watching all those people die?" he asked.

Raven lowered her eyes. "Gut-wrenching. Paralyzing. Um, horrible. Have you ever had a scary dream and you woke up screaming or crying?"

He nodded. "Yeah. When I was a kid, I did that all the time. I used to dream that werewolves were coming to eat me. My mom would shake me awake. Then the feeling of that dream would hang on for hours. My mom would lay in bed with me 'cause I was afraid to be left alone."

Raven was watching him. "That's what the day was like for me. It was a never-ending horror. I watched my brother kill people like they were nothing. He murdered my best friend and a teacher who went out of her way to help me . . . and him. He did it so casually and there was nothing I could do to stop him. Until there was." She lowered her voice. "I never really got to grieve them or say goodbye. I wasn't allowed to show grief or sorrow. So that feeling of waking up from a bad dream but still being afraid, that's what it's been like for me every day since the shootings."

"Man, that's fucked up. I'm sorry to hear that." He glanced at her. "Really. And . . . and you shot him. Right?"

She looked over at him. "Yeah. I shot him before he killed two girls who had made my life a living hell the year before."

Georgio shook his head. "I bet they were happy you were there to stop him."

"Ha! Hardly. They blamed me for the whole thing. They said I was working with him. They even told the police it was my fault. But luckily, other students survived and told the police I saved people." Raven let out a loud sigh.

"Is that why you're living on the streets?" he hedged.

She nodded. "I met Bitsy my first night on the streets. We were both going into the same shelter. She's been helping me, you know, giving me advice ever since."

The two drove the rest of the way in silence. Raven's thoughts lingered on Bitsy. She had known no one with cancer, and she didn't understand it well. But she understood that Bitsy was dying, and this gave her great angst. Thinking about going on without the woman was heartbreaking, and all she wanted was a miracle.

When Raven finished packing Bitsy's things and some of her own, she leaned her back on the wall. "So, here's the deal. I'm going to keep paying the monthly rental, but I don't want Bitsy to know about it. She's insisting that I'll be renting a room by the time she . . . she, you know. But I'm not leaving her before that time comes. I need somewhere to go afterward. I want you to keep this between us. Okay?"

Georgio nodded. "Yeah, I get it. It'll be our secret."

***

"Did you get all my shit?" Bitsy asked when Raven returned.

The woman was sitting on the sofa, swaddled in a blanket that Felicia insisted she wrap her in.

"Yes, Bitsy," Raven sang. "I got everything."

"Good. Now come over here and sit down with me. Felicia is on a damn rampage. She's insisting I gotta eat. I told her I ain't hungry, but that didn't seem to matter. She was harping the whole time you were gone about how I gotta keep my strength up."

Raven sat next to the woman. "Felicia's right. You need to eat. It'll help."

Bitsy pursed her lips. "Since when ain't you on my side?"

Raven chuckled and rested her head on Bitsy's shoulder. "I am on your side. I only care about you being comfortable and getting better."

Bitsy shook her head. "Sweetie, you need to stop thinking that way. You know I ain't gonna get better. You best wrap your head around it before it's too late."

"I'm not in denial. I know you're sick. But is it so wrong that I think that miracles can happen?"

"No," Bitsy said. "It ain't wrong, but in my situation, it's downright stupid." She gave the girl a grave look. "There ain't no miracles happening here, and when you say otherwise, you're setting me up to fail you."

Raven shook her head. "Oh no. I'm sorry. You didn't fail me. All you've ever done is help me."

"All right then." She went quiet for a few minutes, staring at the television without actually watching it. "I think we should talk about what you're going to do when I'm gone."

Raven's heart thudded. She knew this was coming but still wasn't prepared for the conversation. "Okay. Well, when you're gone, I'll move out of here and find somewhere else."

"How much money did you save?" Bitsy asked.

Raven rubbed her sweaty palms on her jeans. "About three hundred and twenty-five. I've saved everything I could. Plus, I had a hundred left over from the money I already had. All together four twenty-five."

"You done real good. Saved most of what you earned. Let's say I live another month. After expenses, you'll be able to save about three hundred more. That'll give you some cash to get a room somewhere while you work at the fish place. How's that sound?"

Raven shrugged. "It sounds like my life is gonna suck without you in it." She sniffled back the tears stinging her eyes.

"I'll always be with you. I'll be that voice in your head bugging you to do what's right for *you*. I want you to start looking for a room."

Raven nodded. "Okay, Bitsy. I will."

"How do you like your job?"

Raven shrugged. "It's okay. I mean, I won't say that I love it or see myself doing it forever. It's a dirty job. I cut up fish. It's not the most exciting, but it works for now."

"Yep, I understand that. So you best start looking for another job while you still have one."

"Yeah, sure," Raven said. "You know, you make it all sound so easy. If that's true, then why didn't you do it?"

Bitsy smiled. "Because I didn't wanna do it. I don't mind the streets. That's where you and me are different. You wanna live in a house. I see how happy you are here. You're content. So we need to make sure that's what you get."

Raven put her arms around the woman. "I'm going to miss you so much." She choked on a sob lodged in her throat.

"Yeah, sweetie. I'll miss you, too." She laid her head on Raven's shoulder, and the two sat together as time ticked away.

Chapter Forty-Four

The next morning, Raven bought a newspaper on her way home from work. She helped Bitsy into the kitchen where she spread the newspaper out on the kitchen table. The girl knew that keeping them both preoccupied was better than dwelling on the woman's imminent death.

"Oh, look. Here's one," Bitsy said in a weak voice. "It's not too far. It's closer to South Philly and it's in an okay neighborhood. You won't be able to walk to work, but you can take the bus. Ain't that big of a deal."

Raven read the ad. "No, look. It says the person is looking to share her room. I want my own." She searched the next page. "Here's one. A room about eight blocks away."

Bitsy clucked her tongue. "Yeah, I don't think that one will work. I ain't too keen on you being in that area by yourself."

Raven squinted at the woman. "Why? I've been living in bad areas my whole life. I grew up in North Philly, remember?"

"Yeah, I remember. I'm losing my life, but I ain't lost my memory. See, the thing is you wasn't a woman when you lived in North Philly. Being grown changes everything. Some men prey on women, but you ain't gonna be one of them. You hear me? That area has a lot of roamers. They're worse than some of the gangs. Take whatever they want and move on without anyone knowing who they are."

The girl chuckled. "I think I would be okay. I know how to fight." She lifted her right arm, rolled her hand into a ball, and flexed her muscles.

Bitsy assessed the girl. Then she put her fingers around Raven's thin bicep and squeezed. Hanging on to the girl's arm, she let out a weak giggle. "Who you gonna scare with this scrappy piece of meat?"

Raven pursed her lips in a theatrical move. "Hey, there's a lot of power inside these arms. Eighteen years of pent-up anger to be specific."

Bitsy shook her head and went back to scouring the paper for another five minutes before she closed her eyes.

Raven glanced at her and stood. "Come on." She put both hands out for the woman to take. "I'll help you into bed."

Bitsy pushed her hands away and her eyes opened wide. "I don't wanna go lay in no bed. I wanna be among the living for as long as I can. The day is coming at me, fast and radical like, where I won't get outta bed at all. I ain't about to rush into that."

"Still bossy, I see." Raven smirked at the woman. "Okay, I'll help you onto the sofa. Would you like some hot tea?"

"Hot tea would be real nice. Felicia bought some honey. You can make sure you put a drizzle of that in it, too."

Raven cocked her hip out. "Oh, can I now?"

Bitsy gave her a loving grin. "If you don't, I'll have to kick your scrawny, raggedy ass."

Raven laughed. She got the woman situated and went back to the kitchen to put the tea kettle on the stove. As she was waiting for the water to boil, Felicia had come home for lunch.

"How's she doing today?" Felicia whispered.

"Not that great." Raven leaned her back against the counter. "She's weaker today than she was yesterday. I don't know how it's possible to lose that much strength overnight."

"Cancer is a fucking bitch. Then there's Bitsy herself. She spent more than half her life wandering around the streets, scrounging for food and a place to sleep . . . hunkering down in places outside to fight the freezing cold and sweltering heat. The rain, the snow, the wind—that ain't easy on a body."

Felicia glanced up at the girl. The teenager held a vacant stare, and her posture was sagging against the counter.

"Raven."

The girl lifted her eyes to meet Felicia's.

"I know this ain't easy on you in a different way. When Bitsy's gone, I'll still have my two boys and husband. But I have to believe you're thinking about having no one again, and that has to weigh heavy on your heart. I can see how scary this must be for you. But you're smart and likable. You're going to be okay. I'd like to tell you that you can stay here forever, but you see how cramped we are now. I want you to know that even though you won't be in this house with us, I'll always be there for you. I really wish there was more I could do. I'm sorry I don't have something more permanent to offer you."

Raven nodded and moved to the woman. "Of course. I knew this wasn't a forever thing, and I appreciate that you let me stay with Bitsy. I don't know what I would've done if I hadn't been able to spend this time with her." She looked down at her shoes as tears seared her eyes. "I'm going to miss her so much. She's become a good friend to me, and she's like a mom." She opened her arms and hugged Felicia. "Thank you for being kind to both of us. I'll always appreciate everything you're doing."

Felicia put her at arm's length. "Bitsy told me she was gonna help you look for a room to rent . . . for after she's gone. Did you find anything?"

The girl nodded. "There's one in West Philly. It seems okay, kind of seedy. Bitsy doesn't like the area, but I think it'll be fine. I'm gonna check it out tomorrow after work."

Felicia cocked her head. "So then you'll be moving out sooner . . . before Bitsy is gone?"

Raven shrugged. "If I like it. I'm guessing the owner won't hold the room for me without knowing exactly when I can move in. Besides, I think it would be better if I did it sooner. It'll give me a chance to settle into something new but still be close enough to be here most of the time."

Raven's original plan was to move back into the storage unit, but she figured there was no harm in considering a room in a real house.

Felicia paused. She considered what the girl told her. "I'm glad you plan on being here a lot. I understand why it would be better for you to move sooner . . . to give you time to adjust. Most people your age wouldn't leave until the bitter end. You have a good head on your shoulders. But so we're talking the same language, I think you already know you don't have to leave here immediately after Bitsy's gone. It ain't like any of us mind having you around. You're a nice kid, and my family likes you," she offered.

Raven beamed. It was gratifying to hear someone say nice things to her. "Thank you." She gave the woman a grateful smile, finished making Bitsy's tea, and brought it to her.

***

It was nine in the morning the next day when Raven walked to the house in West Philly to see the room for rent. As Bitsy had warned, the neighborhood wasn't family friendly like where Felicia lived. Young and old men hung on the street corners. Some were gambling, while others smoked cigarettes and drank quarts of beer.

Why aren't these people already at work?

She dashed past a couple of groups of men who gawked at her. "Oh, hey, baby. I'll take some early morning loving," one man yelled, grabbing his crotch.

Raven hurried her pace and rushed to the address she was looking for. She swiftly climbed the three wooden steps out front and knocked on the door.

A slovenly man in his early forties pulled it open. "You Raven?" His eyes roved up and down her. Then a sleazy smile grew on his thin lips.

Raven crossed her arms over her chest, and her face was set in a hard scowl, partly from the men who had harassed her along the way and partly because the man before her was already acting like one of them. She looked the man over. His hair was shaved close to his scalp. His face was long and his upper jaw jutted forward. His teeth were severely twisted and stained yellow. She was repulsed by the enormous, silver rings jammed on his filthy fingers.

"Yeah, I'm Raven. Are you Mickey?" The question bubbled from her esophagus up her throat, hoping he wasn't the owner.

He pulled the door open wider. "Yep, that's me."

Ugh!

Mickey gestured with his hand. "Come on in." He pointed to the stairs directly inside the front door. "The room is up there."

Her eyes narrowed. "Sure. I'll follow you up."

Farther inside the house, Raven was overwhelmed with the smell of cigarette smoke, sewage, and rotten food. The heady odor swirled up her nose and down to the base of her throat. She slapped her tongue to the roof of her mouth, trying to dislodge the taste.

As Mickey stomped up the steps, Raven looked around at the mess in the living room to the right. There were pizza boxes and fast-food wrappers. In the center of the coffee table, displayed like a bouquet of flowers, stood a two-foot-tall bong.

Great, a drug house, she thought.

She noticed beer cans lying around. He had woven blankets covering his windows, which made the house dark and dreary. The only light was from the television. Her senses were heightened. She wasn't sure if it was from danger or utter disgust, but the urge to flee was rushing through her veins.

Stay with it. I only need a place to sleep, shower, and store my clothes.

"So do you live here by yourself?" Raven asked as she followed behind him. She was trying to take her mind off of the conflict turning inside of her, but the stench he left in his wake was turning her stomach.

"Sort of. I ain't got no old lady if that's what you're asking." Mickey looked over his shoulder, and as her sight was drawn to his large, crooked teeth, he gave her a wink.

Raven's insides ran cold, and she visibly shuddered. Her nose lifted and her mouth twisted.

Ew!

"H-h-how many rooms do you have?" she asked, trying to break herself out of the funk she was in.

"I got three up here. I sleep in the big one. A buddy of mine rents one, but he's hardly ever here, and then you'll be in the other. It should be a good time," he stated. "You can always stay in the big one with me if you want." He let out a throaty chuckle that rumbled the phlegm in his chest.

Having had enough of Mickey already, she paused at the top of the stairs. Raven looked at the man square in the eyes. "Look, I'm not here for anything other than to rent a room. If that's going to be a problem, I'll look for something else."

"Mmm, feisty. I like that. Come on," he stated, his shoulders drooping forward. "I'm just messing with you."

He opened the bedroom door on the right, and Raven looked in. She inched herself forward as he moved in behind her. Once inside, he closed the door.

She spun on him. "What are you doing?"

He shoved his hands into the front pockets of his filthy jeans. "Nothing. Showing the room like you wanted me to." She noticed the man had become nervous.

This asshole is nothing but a blowhard.

Raven looked around. There was a single bed, a bare mattress covered with urine stains, and a battered dresser. The only window in the room was covered with plywood.

She pointed to the window. "You can take the wood off, right?"

He shook his head. "Nah, the glass is broken. Some shit-face threw a rock through it. I'll get around to fixing it another time, but I ain't got the money right now."

"Okay." Raven walked toward the bedroom door. "Where's the bathroom?"

"Down the hall. I only got one. It's a little out of order right now, but I'll get the toilet and sink fixed once I get your first, last, and security deposit."

"Wait. The only toilet and sink aren't working?"

"Yeah, it's no big deal. I use a bucket to flush the toilet. You can use the sink in the kitchen if you really need one."

Raven jerked her head back. "Okay. Well, I'm gonna go. My mom is sick, and I need to get back to her."

He rubbed his bloated belly. "So, are you gonna rent it or what?"

Raven kept walking toward the stairs. "I don't think this is gonna work out for me."

The man grabbed her arm. "What the fuck does that mean? You think you're too good to live here?"

She ripped her arm from his grip. "No! I wouldn't be comfortable here."

He bounced his eyebrows. "You wanna see my room? We can share it, and I'll only charge you half the rent."

Without responding, Raven scampered down the steps and rushed out the door. As she walked back to Felicia's house, she stewed thinking about the repulsive man. There was nothing in the way of cheap rent other than Mickey's house of menace. But that wouldn't stop her. She'd keep looking until she found something and put Bitsy's mind at ease.

Chapter Forty-Five

Eight days later, Raven woke during the night to a gurgling sound, like someone was underwater.

Raven sat upright. "Bitsy! Are you okay?" Her words were strangled by panic.

Bitsy opened her eyes slightly, then pressed them closed again, curling her body against the pain. "No, sweetie. I think I gotta go to the hospital now."

Raven jumped from the bed, thrust the bedroom door open, and ran to Felicia's room. She almost banged on it with all of her might, then came to her senses, not wanting to alarm the entire family. Bitsy would want to go out with dignity, not bedlam. Rolling her hand into a fist, she knocked gently.

"Who is it?" Felicia gurgled in a stupor.

"It's Raven. Bitsy . . . Bitsy asked to go to the hospital now," she said as her voice broke.

Felicia flung the bedroom door open and took in Raven's anguished gaze. Raven's eyes were wild, and her fingers were clawing at the collar of her T-shirt.

"Georgio!" Felicia yelled.

He was halfway down the hall by then with Enzo on his heels. The young men had heard what Raven said. "I'm gonna bring the car out front."

"No," Felicia stated. "Call an ambulance first. If she's asking to go to the hospital, then I know she needs immediate attention. I don't want her sitting in pain in the ER waiting for the drunks and addicts to be taken care of before her." She dragged her eyes back to Raven. "Get yourself together. You can ride in the ambulance, and Georgio will take me in his car."

Raven brushed the tears from her cheeks and nodded. "Okay. Should I get Bitsy out into the living room?"

"No, there's no need for that. Leave her where she is. The paramedics will go in and get her."

Back in the bedroom, Raven pulled on a pair of jeans and tied her sneakers. Then she sat on the edge of the bed and gently ran her hand over Bitsy's hair.

"The ambulance is coming. They're going to help you. Hang in there."

Bitsy gritted her teeth and nodded. Then she used all of her might to pry her eyes open. "This is the last ride for me . . . I ain't coming back here. Do you understand?"

Raven's breath hitched. "Yeah. But Bitsy, we don't need to talk about this right now. Maybe once the doctor settles your pain, you'll see things different." Even as the teen said the words, she knew there was no truth to them. Bitsy had been deteriorating every day.

Raven kept shaking her head, a sign to Bitsy she wasn't accepting what was coming. Bitsy knew no one was ever ready for death no matter how much they prepared and told themselves it was close.

Bitsy patted the girl's hand. "Listen here. You gotta get your shit together. You know what you're saying is a bunch of nonsense. I wanna talk about you. Now, you remember who you are and what you can do with your life. This is where my journey ends and yours begins." She eked out a smile. "You have to be strong."

"I will, Bitsy. I promise," she said through teary eyes.

***

Raven sat in the back of the ambulance holding Bitsy's hand as the vehicle rushed through the city streets with lights flashing and sirens blaring. The paramedic had inserted an IV and was administering oxygen.

"We'll be at the hospital in under two minutes," he said to Raven. "Does she have a living will?"

Raven looked down into the woman's face and then up at the man trying to help. "I'm not sure. I don't even know what that is."

"It's a legal document about what measures she would want us to take to keep her alive."

Bitsy opened her eyes and looked at the paramedic. "I ain't got no living will. When it's my time, you tell those medical people to let me go in peace."

As the ambulance drew closer to the hospital, Bitsy's breathing became labored, and she groaned in dense clouds of pain. A fog of suffering had fallen over the woman, and Raven would have done anything to end the woman's torment.

"Can you give her something for the pain?" Raven asked.

The paramedic glanced at her. "We'll be at the hospital soon, and they'll make an assessment."

"Really? You can't do something right now?" Raven persisted.

The man looked at Raven. His eyes were soft, and his mouth was turned down. "It'll be okay. They're going to take good care of her. We've called it in. We relayed everything you told us about her cancer. I'm sure they'll have her records pulled by the time we get there."

Raven leaned her face closer to Bitsy. "It's just a little longer."

Bitsy gave her a weak nod. "Good."

***

The emergency room was chaotic. As Raven rushed beside the gurney through the packed waiting room, she was grateful that Felicia had called an ambulance. Inside a bay, Raven sat on a plastic chair in the corner while a nurse assessed Bitsy's condition. Finally, the nurse glanced at Raven.

"Luckily, Dr. Lancer is on-call. I've already spoken to him, and he'll be down to see Bitsy in a few minutes."

Raven nodded. She went to the side of the woman's bed. Alone in the bay, the teenager rubbed the woman's arm. "Did you hear what the nurse said? Dr. Lancer is here. He's coming to see you."

Bitsy opened her eyes. "Don't talk foolish words to me 'cause you don't know what to say. I don't wanna talk about that doctor and what he's gonna do for me. I wanna talk about you. Tell me what's going on in your head. It's hard for me to leave you this way. I can see you ain't right, and it isn't all because I'm lying here in this bed."

Raven bit her bottom lip.

"Come on, now. Tell me. Before that doctor gets here and I'm too out of it to talk."

The teen moved her face closer. "Okay. I'm really scared. I'm not sure if I believe in heaven or not. I'm scared that you'll die and I'll never see you again."

"Oh, don't be scared. Surely there's a God and heaven. I'll be up there watching you . . . so don't go doing dumb shit," she chuckled.

"Are you trying to be funny right now?"

"'Course I am. I don't wanna leave you all depressed and shit. I'd rather float outta this world on a laugh than a stream of tears. What else are you afraid of?"

Raven shook her head, then moved her eyes to Bitsy's. "I'm afraid of being all alone. I'm afraid of not having someone to love and who loves me back."

Bitsy nodded. "We're all afraid of that. But here's the thing. Loneliness ain't all about people. See, there are plenty of chumps that got lots of family and friends, but they're still all alone in the world . . . and all alone with their most private thoughts. That's what makes us lonely—our private thoughts. Not being able to share what we're thinking with people who actually give a fuck."

"But . . . but I'll have no one when you're gone."

Bitsy struggled to take the girl's hand in her own. "I'm sayin' that you need to help yourself. You need to learn how to change your thoughts so that they help you instead of hurting you. Once you get your head straight and stop worrying about being by yourself, you'll meet the right people who belong with you. How the hell do you think I brought you to me? I knew I was dying, and I needed to have someone who I could trust. And *bam*, there you were. And look at me now, dying with someone who I love by my side. Ain't nothing in life better than that."

"I'm doing that for you? Keeping you from being lonely?" Raven asked, her eyes growing wide.

"Yes, indeed. Of course you are. Being able to share this intimate time with someone I admire makes me real grateful. Someday, a long time from now, you'll learn that death is very personal. It's a solo act, and there isn't anyone who can take on your suffering. It takes courage to die slowly . . . knowing what's coming but you keep fighting the best you know how."

Tears were streaming down Raven's face.

"Put that bed rail down now," Bitsy ordered.

Once Raven had the rail down, Bitsy patted the mattress beside her. "You come lay with me. You hold on and as I leave, you take on all the good parts of me. You carry on in a way that would make me proud because no matter what happened to you before this moment, it's the moments you have left that count."

THE TWIN SISTER

Raven climbed onto the narrow gurney. She was on her side with an arm gently draped over Bitsy. There was a sense of comfort and familiarity with the older woman. She realized how much she would miss that closeness as she closed her eyes and laid her ear on Bitsy's heart.

Chapter Forty-Six

As Raven clung to Bitsy, she forced back her tears and started to hum "Amazing Grace." A song Bitsy hummed all the time. Raven didn't understand the significance, only that it was a favorite of Bitsy's, and hoped it would bring her comfort.

Dr. Lancer walked in a few minutes later and found the two lying together. "Hello."

Raven looked up at him. "Hi," she muttered and sniffled.

He stood over the bed and looked into Bitsy's eyes. "I understand you would like pain medication."

Bitsy nodded, but just barely.

"Okay. And you understand that I'll give you enough so you don't have to suffer any longer. But you also won't have much, if any, awareness."

"Yes. I don't want no more pain."

"All right. I'll give you something now to take the edge off, then we'll move you to a private room. Once you're there, I'll give you something stronger. I'll make sure you have no more pain. It'll give you some time to be with your family. They're in the waiting room." He stole a peek at Raven. "You can go with her when they take her up."

"Thank you. Will someone tell Felicia and her sons where to find us?"

"Yes, of course. I'll go talk to the nurse. She'll bring in the medication, and I'll let her know to inform the family where to find Bitsy once we have a room number to give them."

Raven watched the man. His tone was somber. There was a quiet sadness to him. He put his hand on Bitsy's. "I'll be up to see you as soon as you get to your room. Okay?"

Bitsy nodded. "Doc? How long I got?"

Dr. Lancer shook his head. "You're in the final stage. It could be an hour, or it could be a week. I have no way of knowing."

Raven's guts twisted like a hurricane spinning the hollowness, destroying her piece by piece.

Bitsy is right. Death is personal.

***

Raven noticed that with a smidge of pain medication, Bitsy stopped clenching her teeth. Seeing the woman find relief allowed Raven to find some, too.

Although she didn't understand why, she thought of the school shootings and watching people suffer as she was watching Bitsy suffer now. Images of teenagers begging and crying flashed into her memory. She thought about her childhood friend, Addie. Remembering the terrified look on her face and wanting so badly to comfort her. Bitsy was giving her the chance to do what she couldn't on that day. She was living the final moments of Bitsy's life by her side.

As she watched Bitsy closely, this was her opportunity to aid in the woman's comfort . . . to see her through, bid her farewell without fear or isolation.

They were brought up to a private room forty-five minutes later, lightning speed in hospital time. Raven walked beside the gurney as they rolled her into the room. Then she guided the woman as they moved her to a bed.

"How are you doing?" Raven asked her friend.

"Eh, I feel like shit. That medicine he gave me helped some, but it feels like someone is hitting me in the back with an axe."

Raven cringed. "Okay, Dr. Lancer said he'd be in to see you soon."

The girl pulled a chair closer to the bed. As she did, Felicia, Georgio, and Enzo walked into the room.

"There's our girl," Felicia sang in a strangled voice. "How are you, hon?"

Raven's eyes moved over the three of them. "She got a little relief, but the doctor wanted her to talk to her family before he gave her something stronger."

Felicia met Raven's gaze. "I see." She moved closer to Bitsy. "So this is it then?"

Bitsy smiled with her eyes and gave her a quick nod. "This is it, my friend."

"Well." The word caught in her throat. "There's no need to keep you suffering." She took the woman's hand. "It's been my distinct and humble pleasure to know and love you. You saved my son and my family. I'll be grateful to you for the rest of my life." She patted her own heart with her other hand. "You will live on . . . right here, Bitsy."

Bitsy smacked her dry lips together. "Oh, Felicia. We shoulda been born sisters. So different but so much alike. You take care of those boys."

Felicia nodded, and as the tears she was trying to contain slid from her eyes, she stepped back and pushed Georgio and Enzo forward.

After Georgio said a solemn goodbye, Enzo was left standing next to the dying woman.

Raven stood. "Maybe we should all step out for a minute."

Bitsy shook her head. "It's okay. You all can stay." She looked into Enzo's face. "My sweet boy. It's because of you I have this family with me now. You be a good boy and mind your mama. Understand me?"

Enzo's head was bowed. "Yes, ma'am."

"Okay, now. You take your family and go on home."

Enzo leaned over the woman and kissed her forehead. "I'll never forget you . . . or what you did for me."

"You better not forget me," she garbled, trying to lighten the moment. "My body might be leaving, but you ain't gotta worry. My spirit will be swimming inside of you. I love you, son."

"I love you, too," he blubbered, dropping his head to her chest one last time.

A moment later, Raven and Bitsy sat alone together. The only sound was the beeping of the heart monitor. As each beep screamed into the silence of the room, Raven knew it wouldn't be long before the silence took over.

Chapter Forty-Seven

Raven sat on the edge of her chair after Dr. Lancer left the room and before the nurse came back with the stronger pain medication.

"This is it," Bitsy informed her. "Once the nurse pushes that magic through my IV, I ain't gonna have my senses to talk to you no more. The doctor said so."

Raven nodded. "I want you to know that meeting you and being part of your life has changed me. I've learned a lot."

"Oh yeah? Tell me what was the most important thing you learned then." She closed her eyes and breathed through another gnawing pain.

"That I'll never be alone if I can enjoy my own company . . . to remember that being around people doesn't mean as much as being around ourselves." Raven smiled through moist eyes. "And that I'm strong, I deserve good things and good people in my life, and I can do anything."

Bitsy nodded. "That's right. You keep on fighting. You get what you want. Don't take no shit from nobody. You hear?"

"Yes." Raven brushed the woman's cheek with the back of her hand. "I know we haven't known each other that long, and don't think I'm weird, but I love you."

Bitsy smiled. This time her happiness exceeded her pain for a full second, and the older woman was filled with peace. "I love you, too, sweetie."

As the nurse entered the room, Raven gave Bitsy a loving smile.

"Are you ready?" the nurse asked Bitsy.

"Ready as I'll ever be." She turned her head and gave Raven a wink.

Raven stood over the woman's bed as her eyes eased closed and the pain medication put her at rest. An hour later, the heart monitor stopped beating. Raven collapsed in the chair and bawled over the beautiful soul she had lost from her life.

***

Raven helped plan a small service for Bitsy. When the service ended, the family went back to the house.

Felicia had paid to have Bitsy's remains cremated. They sat in an urn on a shelf in Enzo's room. Felicia thought it would be too much for her son, but he had insisted that Bitsy stay with him.

Raven was in the bedroom packing her belongings. She pulled out the duffel bag that had been following her for many years.

"What are you doing?" Felicia asked from the doorway.

Raven looked up at the woman. The girl's face was covered in grief. "I'm packing my things so I can move out."

"Where are you gonna go?"

The teen shrugged. "I kept the storage unit. I didn't want Bitsy to know."

Felicia moved into the room and sat on the bed next to the girl. She patted her leg. "You'll stay here and actively look for a place to live. Okay?"

Raven turned her head toward the woman and nodded. "I'll find something soon. I swear."

"I know you will. How about if we put a two-week goal on it? It'll give you something to work toward," Felicia offered.

The teen nodded. "Yeah, two weeks is good. I'll do my best to find something sooner."

"I know you will. Now come in the kitchen and help me get supper ready."

Raven put her duffel bag in the closet and followed Felicia. Two more weeks seemed like a lifetime to a young girl with no family and nowhere else to go.

***

Twelve days later, there was still no single room for rent in West Philly. Anxiety was building in Raven. She was jittery and on edge. She had overheard Enzo asking his mother when she was leaving so he could have his room back.

Raven walked into the kitchen. "Hi, Felicia."

"Oh, hi, hon." She turned and greeted the girl. "How's it going? You find anything that looks reasonable?"

She nodded. "Yeah, I think I may have found something," she lied.

Raven had resigned herself that she'd go back to the shelter in Center City. She could no longer see herself going back to the storage unit that she shared with Bitsy. She'd have to give up her job at the fish processing plant, and that stung. It wasn't that she loved what she was doing. She hated cleaning fish. But it was a steady job that paid.

Felicia clapped her hands together, then put them over her chest. "Oh, that's great to hear. I was getting worried there for a while. So when are you going to look at it?"

Raven smiled. "I'll call them today, but I don't want you to worry. I'll be out in two days."

Felicia's eyes softened and her mouth slightly fell open. It was a motherly look, one of concern for the girl and relief for her family.

"I want to make sure you're going to a good place. Okay? I need to know where you're going and all that," Felicia stated.

"Sure thing. I'll let you know after I call them."

Raven had no idea how she'd get out of the lie she told. But she had to think of something. Otherwise, she'd have to leave Felicia's house when the woman wasn't home, and she knew that Felicia deserved better.

Chapter Forty-Eight

"Ava's Deli," the voice screeched into the phone.

"Ava? It's me, Raven."

"Holy Mary, Mother of God. Hold on. Let me go to the back." The telephone clattered on the counter. "Hey, Dante," Ava yelled. "I gotta take this call in the back. Hang up the phone in the front and answer the other line till I get off. And don't be a dick to anyone."

Raven was holding her breath. *At least Ava didn't hang up on me.*

"Raven, where the hell are you? Are you okay?" Ava asked.

"I'm in West Philly. Ava, I need some help. I was with a homeless woman and she died of cancer, and I don't have anywhere to go." Raven choked on the words. "I'm on my own with nowhere to turn. I need someone to help me get off the streets. I thought maybe you'd have an idea."

Ava clutched the phone harder. "You listen to me. You did the right thing by calling me. You should've called sooner. Me and Dante, we know you. We know you're a good girl. We heard both sides of what happened at the high school. Some people are saying you saved those kids. That you stopped your brother. That's the truth and we know it."

"Thank you," she whispered. "I'm not sure what to do next. I'm working in West Philly, but I don't have a place to live. I saw on television that me and my brother are still being reported on the news." She huffed out a sour breath. "Plus, I know for a fact that the Kensington Hoods are looking for me. They want to kill me . . . They almost did," Raven admitted.

"Holy shit. Those lousy, good-for-nothing motherfuckers. We heard they want blood. Their thug asses are still looking for you? You gotta be careful. Are you somewhere safe?"

Raven looked into Felicia's living room and caught Enzo watching her instead of the television.

"Yes, I'm safe, but I have to move out of my current place. It's a long story." Raven let out a soft sigh. "I've been trying to find a room to rent, but the one place I went to, the guy was a total creeper. I have a couple more days here, then I need to go."

"Ah right. So you're in West Philly. I don't know any people there. I grew up in South Philly. I can help you better there. You need to look for a room there . . . Look in the newspaper."

"Okay, I will. And then I can take a bus to my job in West Philly."

"You won't need to. That's where I can help you. Here's what you're gonna do. Tomorrow, I want you to go to Ninth Street in South Philly. I want you to look for Palermo Brothers Bakery. You go in there and you ask for Maria. She's going to take care of you. She'll give you work. Tell her you're looking for a place to stay. Maybe she'll know somebody. You got a pen and paper? 'Cause you'll need to write this down."

Raven reached over the table. "Yes, go ahead."

"Okay, Ava mi ha mandato qui," she said, spelling it for her. "Questo e' un favore e un segreto."

"Um, okay. But what does this say?" Raven studied the writing on the paper. "I'm not selling her my soul, am I?" she asked, half-joking.

"Of course you're not. It says Ava sent me here. This is a favor and a secret. Maria will know what that means. She's my best friend. We grew up together in South Philly. She's probably gonna recognize you from TV, but once she knows I trust you, she'll trust you, too."

Raven's brow pulled together. "How am I supposed to talk to her after she reads this note? I don't speak Italian."

Ava chuckled. "In English. Maria is gonna take the note, read it, and destroy it. But this way, she'll know I need her to keep her fucking mouth shut about you . . . so she will. That's how us Italians do it in our neighborhood. Do you understand?"

Raven blew out a loud breath. "Yeah, I understand. But it feels weird to show up out of nowhere."

"No, it ain't weird. You walked into my deli one day hungry and with no skills outta nowhere. I hired you, and it worked out good. The same will happen in her bakery. Expect to work in the back of Maria's store. You'll probably be baking shit. That way people won't see you. But you ain't gotta worry too much. There's plenty of goombahs to watch out for Maria. Oh, that means men that are friends, people who look out for their own on the streets."

Raven's hands were slightly shaking. Partly because she was afraid to venture out on her own again and partly because she was happy that Ava was helping her.

"Are you listening to me?" Ava asked.

"Sorry. Yeah, I was thinking."

Ava sighed. "I'm happy to help. Don't embarrass me. I want you to call me in a couple of days, so I know what's going on with you. You hear me?" Ava demanded in a motherly tone.

Raven smiled through her silent tears. "Yes, I hear you. Thank you, Ava. This means a lot to me."

"It ain't no problem. I gotta go before Dante loses all my customers. You know he ain't the most pleasant person in my deli." She chuckled.

"Yeah, I remember. Hey, tell him I said hi."

"Ah right, I will. Be safe," Ava said with a tinge of worry in her tone.

When Raven hung up, she sat for a moment, thinking about how lucky she was to have at least one person from her past in her corner. She looked up at the ceiling. "Thank you, Bitsy."

Chapter Forty-Nine

The next morning after work, Raven took a cab from Felicia's house to Palermo's Brothers Bakery in South Philly. Standing on the sidewalk, she looked around at the active neighborhood. The Italian Market was jam-packed with people preparing to open stores and receive deliveries. She watched the merchants stock shelves, haul in bushels of crabs, and cut wheels of cheese. There was a mix of stores and homes. A middle-class community that bustled with people going off to work in the cold, crisp morning air.

She stepped inside the crowded bakery, and her flesh tingled with the warmth against her cold skin. She inhaled the smell of cinnamon, sugar, melted butter, and coffee. Bagels were toasting in the oven. The aromas were so potent she could practically taste the food.

Raven stood in the back of the crowd wearing a hat and sunglasses, the way Ava had instructed her to do. She could hear the mixers whirling in the back and people murmuring their appreciation for their order. When it was her turn at the counter, she looked at an older woman and handed her the note with Maria's name written on the outside.

The woman handed the note back and pointed to a table in the corner. "Take a seat. I'll tell her you're here to see her. What's your name?"

She shook her head. "I'm a friend of Ava's."

The woman gave her a curt nod, and Raven sat at the table. She waited for five minutes before Maria appeared.

Maria stood next to Raven's chair. She was tall and slender with long black hair pulled into a neat bun. She had high cheekbones and big brown eyes. Her lips were full and covered, ever so daintily, with a light pink lipstick. Maria's appearance was neat, clean, and reeked of class.

"Hello, I'm Maria Morano. How can I help you?"

"Hi," she responded, in awe of the woman's appearance. She held out the note with a shaky hand.

Maria unfolded the paper, read it, and slid it into a pocket of her expensive pants. She put her hand on Raven's shoulder. "Let's go to my office where it's private."

Raven followed the woman. Maria looked toward the front and gave a customer a bright smile and a quick wave before they disappeared into the back.

Raven was mesmerized by Maria's strong presence. The woman had a timeless elegance. She was refined and sophisticated in the way she carried herself. She was the woman people watched from afar, imagining she had a perfect life. Maria was built with beauty, strength, and confidence.

Inside the office, Maria opened her hand to a seat and Raven took it. She walked across the room and picked up a lighter. She burned the note, dropping it into a glass ashtray. She sat in the seat next to the girl.

"Take off your glasses and hat. It's distracting, and I want to see who I'm talking to," Maria said politely.

Raven took off her hat first. Her long, rich brown hair fell over her shoulders. Then she removed her sunglasses.

Maria's mouth delicately dropped open. "I recognize you. The boy who killed all those kids, Matthew Ledger—you're his sister?"

Raven wrung her fingers together. "Yeah. I'm Raven." She frowned. "Ava said you would recognize me. I'm nothing like my brother," she added quickly. Filled with uncertainty, she readjusted herself in the chair.

"I watch the news every day. I like to know what's going on in our city. But we aren't here to talk about your brother. Tell me how you know Ava." Maria's eyes were wide, and she was intently focused on Raven. She lifted a porcelain cup and took a dainty sip of coffee as she waited.

Raven pulled in a quick breath and steadied her hands. "I worked for Ava and Dante last summer. Between my junior and senior years of high school."

Maria smiled and walked to a silver coffee pot to refill her cup. "Would you like some?"

"Oh, no, thanks."

Maria returned and angled her body toward Raven. "Well, Ava is my best friend. I trust her more than my own family. If she says you should be here, then I have no doubt. You need a job, right?"

Raven nodded. "Yes. I'm living in West Philly with a very nice family right now, but I need to be out by the weekend. We had a common friend who died recently. Ava said it would be easier to rent a room in South

Philly. I couldn't find anything decent in West Philly. I'm gonna start looking today."

"That's good." She paused and smiled at her. "When can you start working?"

"I work for the woman I'm living with. I'd like to have a week . . . so I can give her some time to find someone."

Maria smirked. "Great. A thoughtful person with ambition. I like that." She stood. "Let me bring you back and introduce you to Effie. She runs the kitchen. She can be a bit fickle at times, so try not to be offended by her straightforwardness, which borders on being rude most of the time. Effie is trustworthy with all of my business matters, so you'll be safe with her." She turned and glanced over her shoulder. "I'll expect the same from you."

"Yeah, of course."

"In the mornings, we enter through the back alley. There's a bell next to the door. I'll be here at four a.m. and I'll need you here by six. You'll work until three in the afternoon most days. I pay by the hour in cash. Will that work for you?"

Raven smiled. She was thrilled to be working in a bakery, a clean and warm environment, too. "Yes, I-I-I'm good with that."

Maria stopped and let her arms drop to her sides. "Raven, you don't even know how much I'm going to pay you." She lifted her finger into the air. "Be sure of yourself and your worth. I can pay you five dollars an hour."

That's a dollar more an hour than Felicia is paying me. "Yeah, that sounds great. I appreciate everything you're doing."

Maria gave her a quick grin. "You can tell me how much you appreciate me after you spend time with Effie and learn how to deal with her temperament. She'll ask you questions about yourself. She's likely to recognize you. Effie seems to know everything going on in the entire state of Pennsylvania. But know this, you can trust her," she said, leveling Raven with her serious brown eyes.

Raven was excited and apprehensive. She loved having a new job but was hesitant about the woman called Effie. Raven straightened her spine, put on her best smile, and trailed behind Maria into the kitchen.

Chapter Fifty

Inside the kitchen of the bakery, Raven scanned the large space. There were three big ovens, an industrial size stove, a large sink, and a stainless-steel worktable. In the corner, there was a woman bent over the biggest mixer Raven had ever seen.

"Effie, this is Raven. She's going to start working here in a week. I wanted to bring her back so you two can get acquainted."

The twenty-eight-year-old Black woman kept her head down, pushing dough from the sides of the mixer. Then she flipped the switch off and lifted her head. She glanced at Raven and then looked directly at Maria.

"Get acquainted for what? I don't care who she is. What kind of experience she got? I don't need no little white girl holding me back. I got a lot of work to do here. I ain't a babysitter. Why don't you bring me someone older who knows what they're doing?" Effie fired back.

"Effie," Maria stated in an even voice. "You know that inexperienced people are like a blank canvas. That gives you the ability to mold them into anything you want. They learn your techniques and follow your instructions. Raven is willing to do that to work with you."

Effie hesitated, and then a slow smile formed on her lips. "Ah right. I forgot about that shit. It's been a long time since you hired anybody to help me with all this work you load on my back." She wagged her finger at the woman. "That's why I put up with you 'cause you got all that positive thinking bullshit going on." She dragged her eyes to Raven. "You ever work in a kitchen before?"

"I worked in a deli last summer," she said confidently.

Effie scoffed. "This ain't no deli and we ain't making a dumb sandwich. I'm making art here."

Raven nodded, remembering Maria's warning about the woman. The girl plastered a pleasant smile on her lips. "No, I'm sure this is nothing like a deli. Everything you make looks great and smells delicious."

Compliments might win her over.

Effie placed her hand on her hip. "I know that. I don't need no high schooler to tell me. And take that stupid smile off your face. That don't mean nothing to me. Come on over here. I'll show you around, but I expect you to remember things come a week from now when you get started. We'll get you an apron. I don't like people walking around my kitchen in street clothes." She glanced at Maria. "You can go. I got this."

"Okay, if you say so," Maria remarked. She gave Raven a quick nod and left them.

***

Before Raven left the bakery, Maria pulled her aside. She handed her a note card with an address and telephone number. At the bottom of the card, a name was written in meticulous handwriting: Cecilia.

"You call Cecilia at that number and talk to her. If she likes you, then she'll invite you to see her room. If she doesn't like you over the phone, then I will see who else might have availability. Cecilia is a lovely woman—someone I think can be very helpful to you."

Raven raked a hand through her hair. "Wow, thank you. I'll call her tomorrow."

"You'll need to call today. She's expecting to hear from you later." Maria gave her a terse smile. "Before long, you and I will be speaking the same language." She patted the girl on the shoulder and walked away.

***

Felicia was waiting in the living room when Raven got home. "How did it go?"

"I start in one week. Are you sure you're going to be able to find someone to replace me? I feel really bad about quitting."

Felicia flicked her wrist. "Stop. I'm happy that you have some people who can help you. My stomach has been eating itself with guilt. What about a place to live?"

Raven handed Felicia the note card, and the woman looked it over. "Well, she's Italian, that's for sure."

"How do you know that?"

Felicia pointed to the details on the card. "Her name is Cecilia, and she lives off of Ninth Street in the Italian Market. She's Italian all right."

Raven smiled at the woman. "So what does that mean?"

Felicia bunched her fingertips together on her right hand and shook it at the girl. "It means you'll be in good hands. I'd like to meet this woman to make sure, though."

Raven swallowed several times. She couldn't bring Felicia with her to see the house. After meeting Maria and promising discretion, it didn't seem like a good idea.

"Well, I need to call Cecilia first. Unless she invites me to see the place, I won't even be going. If I get invited, we can . . . we can talk about it."

"Go on then. Make your call, and I wanna listen if that's okay with you," Felicia stated.

Raven picked up the telephone hanging on the kitchen wall and dialed the number.

"Hello?" a woman grunted into the phone.

"Hi, Maria Morano gave me your telephone number. She said you're expecting my call—about the room you have for rent."

"Oh yeah? What's your name?"

"Raven."

"How old are you, Raven?"

Raven closed her eyes. "I'm eighteen?"

"Are you asking me or telling me?" the woman chuckled. "I don't have a problem with you being eighteen unless you're a degenerate. Are you a degenerate, Raven?"

"No, ma'am."

"Then we're off to a good start. My name is Cecilia. C-E-C-I-L-I-A. I want to be called by my given name and none of those nicknames like Cece . . . dumbest damn thing I've ever heard. I like people to get my name right, and I want you to know for when you write my name on my Christmas card."

Raven smiled and stifled a giggle. "Oh, sure thing. Whatever you want."

"What's your last name, Raven? So I can write it down."

"Ledger . . . Raven Ledger."

The phone went silent on the other end.

"Hello?" Raven said.

"Yeah, I'm here. You're that boy's sister?"

"Yes," Raven choked out.

"Maria left that part out, that hussy. Your name is on the news. Those reporters won't let up. Now they're interviewing the families of the people who got murdered. Mm, mm, mm," she hummed. "It's a shame what your brother did to all those people."

"Yes, it was wrong. I'm nothing like my brother. I would never hurt anyone."

"I'm sure you wouldn't. I heard some teenagers on the news sayin' they were in the class, and they might've died if you didn't shoot him. Then there's another group of people who say you helped your brother. Which is it? Did you help him or not?"

"No, ma'am. I had no id-idea." Her voice cracked as a sob got lodged in her throat.

Cecilia had knocked the wind out of her. She had thought the two were off to something good and then, *bam*, Matthew came barreling back into her life.

"Ain't no need to cry. I believe you. Kind of a tough situation he put you in, huh?"

"Worse than anyone can imagine," she mumbled.

"Well, you might be right. I'm seventy years old, so I've been through a lot of crap in my life. But I ain't had nothing like what you've been left to sleep with. So do you want to come here tomorrow and see the room?"

Raven gasped. The invitation was unexpected after talking about Matthew. "Really? You're still willing to rent to me?"

"Well, let's not get ahead of ourselves. I invited you to come look at the room, which means I wanna see you in person. There ain't nothing set in stone."

Raven smiled. "Right. Thank you. What time should I come? I work until six in the morning."

"Oh yeah? You work a late shift then?"

"Yes, I work at a fish processing plant. I start working at Palermo's Brothers Bakery next week. At that job, I'll work from six in the morning to three in the afternoon."

Cecilia let out a puff of air. "Well, thank the good Lord. I don't need you out all hours of the night and come banging back in here at the crack-ass of dawn, waking me up."

Raven let out a nervous giggle. "No, I definitely wouldn't want to disturb you when you're sleeping."

Cecilia whistled. "That's real good you have full-time work. Girls your age don't wanna put their time in no more. I hope you're getting paid well, so you can grow your nest egg."

"Well, the bakery is going to pay me the same as the job I had before the fish processing plant . . ." She cut her sentence short. *Why did I say that? Dumb. Dumb. Dumb.*

"I see. Where did you work before the fish place?"

Raven's head swam as though she had been dropped into the deep waters of the ocean. It was already bad enough, now she had to tell the woman she had worked at a strip club.

Ding. Ding. Ding. Round two.

"So, first I want to say that I was a barback. I stocked the bar, sometimes I cleaned the dishes. I also cleared dishes from the tables."

"Uh-huh. Where was this again?" Cecilia asked.

Raven understood she wasn't getting away without telling Cecilia the whole truth.

"I used to work at Guilty Pleasure," Raven said, pressing her eyes closed.

"Yeah, I know the place. It's a titty bar, right?" she chuckled.

Raven's eyes snapped open. "Yes, it is."

"But you didn't dance or show your titties?" the old woman asked in a jovial tone.

Raven slightly relaxed hearing the lightheartedness in the woman's voice. "Nope. Like I said, I was a barback. That's it."

"Okay, well good 'cause I wouldn't want none of those obsessed men coming here looking for you. A barback . . . that's okay, we all gotta make a living. Don't we?"

"Yes, ma'am, we do. So, it doesn't bother you that I worked there?"

The woman snorted. "Why would it bother me? I didn't have to work those horrible hours and clean up after a bunch of drunk men. You did."

"Okay, that's great. I'm happy to hear it. So can I come by tomorrow at two?"

"You sure can," Cecilia said. "I look forward to meeting you in person. I already know what you look like since I've seen your picture on television. Damn, every time I looked up, there you were. Those news people can't get enough of you. I must've seen you a million times. You might be the most famous person in Philly right now." She snickered.

Raven's spine bowed and her shoulders rolled over. "It's awful," she mumbled into the phone.

"Ah, don't pay it no mind. What's done is done."

After Raven hung up, her gaze fell on Felicia. "I passed the first test."

Felicia nodded. "Good."

"I'm going over to Cecilia's house tomorrow to meet her in person and check out the room."

Felicia puckered her lips. "Good for you, girl."

"Yeah, I'm excited. Now Enzo can have his room back."

Felicia nodded. "I'm happy everything is working the way you need it to. New job, new place to live. Now all you need is a hot man and you'll be all set."

Raven shook her head. "I'm not looking for a man. That's the last thing I need right now."

Felicia chuckled. "So do you like Cecilia?"

Raven smiled. "Well, she sounds bossy and kind of hard-assed. It was kind of like talking to Bitsy."

"Ah right. That's good. You'll find out more when you meet her. Look at you . . . all grown and doing shit on your own."

Raven smiled. "Yeah, I like it."

"Now, I would feel much better if I was there to see that woman's house," Felicia remarked.

"No, that would be weird. Besides, it would probably annoy her if I showed up with someone without warning her," Raven cautioned.

"You have a point. I wanna see that note card again so I can write down Cecilia's address and telephone number."

Raven giggled. "Okay, Mom. I'll write it all down for you."

"Good," Felicia said, lifting her chin. "You can never be too careful. Besides, Bitsy would skin me alive if I sent you there not knowing where you were going."

Raven's smile dipped. "I miss her so much. I'm doing exactly what she wanted me to do, though. I think she'd be proud. Hopefully, I'm gonna be renting a room. A place to call my own. I can't believe it."

Felicia leaned forward. "I never doubted for one minute that you'd find your way. This is only the beginning for you. You have so much life waiting to be snagged by the balls."

Felicia walked over to the counter and started to prepare dinner. "You can go get washed up and give me a hand."

"Right. I'll be back in a minute. Thank you, Felicia. For being there for me, I mean."

"I don't know what else you expected," Felicia chided. "I know you ain't got no family or anyone you can depend on. Besides, it warms my heart to see Bitsy's girl getting ahead."

Raven gave her a crooked smile. "Losing Bitsy was like losing a mom . . . I'm so lucky to have had her for the time I did. Soooo," she sang. She moved over to the older woman. "Maybe you can drive me over to Cecilia's house tomorrow. But you can't come in. You have to stay outside . . . as in down the block. It'll be nice knowing you're there . . . knowing that someone cares enough to wait for me."

"Great, it's settled then." She patted Raven's hand. "Make sure you wear something nice and fix your hair too."

***

Raven made her way into Enzo's bedroom and sat on the bed. She leaned down and rubbed her hand over her duffel bag. She had nervous excitement and a smile spread across her face. There was a seed of joy growing in her belly.

Keep your heart open to the good people, she remembered Bitsy saying as Raven closed her eyes and imagined the woman sitting beside her.

Chapter Fifty-One

The next day, Raven sat in the passenger seat of Felicia's car.

"Now listen," Felicia began. "These old Italian women are no joke. They like people your age to be respectful and mind them properly."

"I'm always respectful."

Felicia gave her a side-glance. "You are. I'm just reminding you. Sometimes they say shit that's, you know, judgmental 'cause you ain't Italian."

Raven scoffed. "Don't worry. I have a lot of practice in people judging me."

Felicia nodded. "I want to know you are in a safe place, with a person who will watch you and put your ass in line if need be." She smirked. Then she pointed to the right. "That's the house number. I'll let you out at the corner." She pulled over and parked. "You ready?"

Raven took in a deep breath. "Ready. Wish me luck."

She got out of the car and hurried down the sidewalk. She climbed the steps to the woman's rowhome. It was a brick building with a stubby porch and an endless sea of neighbors on either side that stretched the entire block. Cecilia's porch was tidy with old but well-maintained furniture.

Raven pressed a smile on her lips and rang the doorbell.

Cecilia opened the door, and she looked the girl up and down. "Well, you must be Raven," the woman sang. Cecilia was short with brownish skin and gray hair. Her brown eyes were round and vibrant.

"Yes. Thank you for letting me come here to meet you."

"Uh-ha. I'm glad you could make it. And you're right on time just like you said you'd be. That's a good start." Cecilia waved her in.

The inside of Cecilia's house was like stepping back into the late sixties. All of her furniture was protected by clear plastic slipcovers. There was a lot of green and gold. Her old chairs had embroidered flowers and patterns.

Her shag carpet was worn in spots but in overall good condition. The lamps had yellow and orange globes. There were mirrors and pictures of saints hanging on the walls. It was old-fashioned, but it was peaceful. Content. Home.

Raven followed Cecilia toward the kitchen and her senses came to life. The aroma of tomato, olive oil, meatballs, and spices tickled her nose. It was as good as walking into an Italian restaurant. "Wow, it smells delicious. You must be a really good cook."

"'Course I'm a good cook. What'd you expect? I'm Italian. Now, don't get me wrong." She lowered her voice as though there was someone else in the house with them. "My neighbor on this side"—she pointed to the left—"Sofia can't cook like I do. She comes from Northern Italy, and they ain't like us. They use those gamey meats." She crinkled her nose. "Nah, they don't cook like us Southern Italian women. Sofia will tell you she's the best cook on the block, but trust me, she's full of shit."

Raven had a huge smile on her face. Cecilia was warm and colorful. Full of zest.

Cecilia grabbed Raven by the wrist and led her to a four-person kitchen table. There was a pretty flower tablecloth underneath the clear plastic overlay. Raven sat and put her forearms on the table, then pulled them off, not liking the way the plastic clung to her skin.

The old woman walked to her stove. "I got a small pot of meatballs and sauce here. I got up practically in the middle of the night to make it. I'm cooking us pasta. We gotta have something to eat."

"You don't have to make me anything. It's only two o'clock. You can't eat pasta and meatballs this early."

Cecilia chuckled. "Oh, you got a lot to learn. There is no wrong time to eat pasta. In Italy, where I'm from, you can eat pasta for breakfast, lunch, and dinner."

"Oh. I didn't know. But I'm not really hungry," Raven said politely.

"Listen here, ladybug. Italians feed people. To turn down food is an insult and rude. It's like slapping Michelangelo in the face because he painted the ceiling. You have to learn that now if you're gonna live here with me. All of our neighbors are Italian. Do not go disrespecting them by turning down food. If it tastes like dog food, like Sofia's does, you tell them it's delicious. I'm the only one you won't have to lie to because I cook better than those fancy chefs in the Italian restaurants around here. Everyone on this block knows that I'm the best cook even though they won't admit it. Capiche?"

Raven stared at the woman, letting her head drift slowly to the side.

"Capiche. Understand?"

"Oh yeah. I mean yes, I understand."

"Good. You look like a smart girl, so I hope you'll be able to learn things quickly. Most of my neighbors are nosey bitches that wanna be in my business. You never tell them shit about me. What happens in my house stays in my house."

Raven nodded, surprised at her bluntness. "Um, okay. Sure. My lips are sealed." She made a locking motion over her lips. "I'm a vault."

Cecilia chuckled. "I like that. You're okay. A girl with a sense of humor will keep me amused . . . I hope. Okay, I'm just gonna make us some dishes and we can eat."

"Oh, Cecilia, I wish I knew you were making something for us." Raven looked down at her hands. "I'd love to eat with you. But I have someone waiting for me out in the car. I don't want to be rude to them."

Cecilia narrowed her eyes. "Who's waiting for you?"

"Well, my friend. Her name is Felicia. She came to make sure that you weren't an axe murderer or something," Raven admitted.

Cecilia gave her a curt nod. "Good thinking." The woman threw her hands in the air, opened a cabinet, and reached for plates. "All right, so your friend can wait another fifteen minutes while we eat. I'll send her out a couple cannoli. I made them myself. They're the best in town. How does that sound? Remember what I just said about turning down food from an Italian."

Raven smirked. "I'm sure she won't mind waiting if there are homemade cannoli at the end."

"Good. Now come and help me."

Chapter Fifty-Two

Raven held her plate while the woman piled pasta on it. She placed it down and went back to carry Cecilia's dish to the table.

"Oh, good manners. I like that. Now, go on and eat. I wanna know if you like it."

Raven took a seat. She rested her arms on the table with the plastic overlay. When she lifted her fork, her arm peeled away from the surface.

That'll take some getting used to.

"Tell me about your mother," Cecilia said. "Your brother killed her. Why?"

Raven choked on a piece of meatball. She immediately started to sweat. She hadn't expected the woman to jump into her personal life so quickly. She was hoping it would be a slower burn.

Raven swallowed and wiped her mouth. "This food is delicious."

"Thanks, ladybug, but tell me about your mom. It's important to understand your background if you're gonna be living under my roof."

"Right. So, my mom had postpartum depression after she delivered me and my brother. She got really bad and walked out on us . . . on our fifth birthday. Anyway, she came back a while later and only wanted to see me. She didn't want to see Matthew." Her eyes cast downward. "That was hard."

"That's a shame for her about the postpartum, but she was still your mom. What did your father do about it? I saw on the news he died about ten years back."

Raven closed her eyes and smiled at the memory of her father. "My dad was the best. We were poor, and he worked as many jobs as he had to so we could survive. But he was loving and caring. He took me and Matthew places and always tried to make things special for us."

Cecilia's lips turned up at the corners and she nodded. "That's where you get your heart and manners from—your father."

Raven shrugged. "Yeah, I guess."

"This brother of yours . . . was he a wild teenager? Out getting into trouble?"

She shook her head. "No, he was the opposite. Quiet. Focused. Got good grades. But he was always angry."

"Then one day, just like that." Cecilia snapped her fingers. "He lost his marbles?"

Raven looked down at her plate. "Yes. Just like that."

"Okay," Cecilia said, standing. She could see the effect it was having on the girl, bringing her head back into a dark time in her life. "That's all I need to know for now. Let me show you the room."

Raven followed the woman upstairs. The room was in the back of the house. Farthest from Cecilia's and the bathroom. There was a queen-size bed, dresser, and two nightstands. A dingy white paint covered the walls, and the bedspread was dark green. It was clean and tidy. There were sheer curtains on the one window facing the back alley in the room.

"This is nice," Raven commented.

"The bedspread is newer—bought it about three years back, but nobody has ever used it. I don't have company here. I was an only child and never had any kids of my own. This was my parents' house, and they left it to me."

Raven looked at the housecoat and slippers Cecilia was wearing.

"I'm not a spinster if that's what you're thinking. I slept around plenty in my day. I loved sex. Probably still would if I could find a suitable man," Cecilia said, opening the closet.

Raven giggled. The woman was so vibrant and honest, something she cherished in people.

Cecilia pointed inside the closet. "Hopefully, between this closet and the dresser, there's enough room for your clothes."

Raven blushed. "Yes, plenty. I don't have much."

"Okay, then. I guess we should talk about rent since you came here without knowing how much money it's gonna cost you. I was a bit surprised you didn't ask. I thought to myself she's either filthy rich or she doesn't know nothing about renting."

Why didn't I ask her that on the phone?

Raven bit the inside of her cheek. "Right, I've been so busy and all, I forgot to ask."

"So then you're loaded? Sky's the limit?"

Raven shook her head dramatically. "Oh no. That's not it at all." She lowered her face, then lifted her eyes to meet the woman's.

Cecilia was a woman who only respected truth; that was obvious to the girl.

"This is the first time I'm living on my own. I didn't know to ask. Like you said, I don't know nothing about renting."

"I see," the woman said, smirking and nodding. "You make a good point. I've never had to get my own place. I've been here my whole life." She waved her hands around the room. "I can see how that might happen. How much money do you make a month?"

Raven did a quick calculation in her head. "Almost seven hundred a month once I start working at the bakery. I can get a second job if I need to, though."

"You got any other bills?"

Raven shook her head.

"All right. How would a hundred and fifty a month work for you? That'll include electric and water, but you'll have to buy some of the food."

Raven smiled. "That sounds perfect. I'll be able to save money."

"That's right. It's exactly what I was thinking when I came up with that number. Now, I'm gonna need the first and last month's rent plus a security deposit. So you'll need to give me four hundred and fifty bucks before you can move in," Cecilia explained.

Raven crossed her arms over her stomach. "Oh. That's a lot of money. That's almost all the money I have saved. But if that's what you need, then I'll pay it."

Cecilia lifted her chin. "You got another number in mind?"

"I was thinking I could give you a hundred and fifty now," she said in an unsure voice.

"I'll tell you what. You give me two hundred and fifty. I'll hold a hundred of it and you'll get that back when you move out if there ain't any damages."

Raven bounced on her toes. "Deal." She extended her hand, and Cecilia shook it.

"Come on. Let me get you that cannoli for your friend. You'll be moving in tomorrow then?"

Raven followed behind the woman. "Yes, tomorrow is perfect."

When Raven got outside, she could barely contain her excitement. She ran to Felicia's car and flung the door open. She slid onto the front seat and presented Felicia with the cannoli.

Felicia took the paper plate and looked at it. "Looks like things went well."

"Things went great. I have a place to live, and Cecilia, she's a great cook."

"I'm sure she is," Felicia said, smiling as she pulled away from the curb.

As soon as Raven got back to Felicia's house, she called Ava to tell her the good news.

Chapter Fifty-Three

One week later, Raven rang the bell at the bakery.

Effie pulled the door open. "Good, you're on time. Best to keep it that way. I don't like my help being late."

Raven's eyebrows lifted. "Good morning, Effie."

Effie pushed her chest forward. "Morning. I gotta lot of work to do and so do you. We ain't got no time for small talk right now."

Raven moved inside. "Okay, whatever you say." She stood awkwardly waiting for instructions.

Effie huffed and rolled her eyes. "Come on now, get the lead out. If you wanna work with me, you have to learn to hustle."

The girl rushed forward. "Actually, I'm a pretty good hustler. I had one job that was really hectic." Raven chuckled. Effie didn't. "What do you want me to do first?"

Effie gave her a side-glance. "You can start by washing all those trays and bowls over there." She gestured with her head toward an enormous sink and a conveyor belt that took dishes into the dishwasher. "The mixing bowls and cookie pans need to be washed by hand. You use the dishwasher mainly for plates, mugs, and silverware."

Raven moved to the sink quickly and assessed the mess. She looked over her shoulder. "Where are the towels?"

Effie smiled, but her back was to the girl. "Towels are on the bottom shelf behind me where you'll also find your apron. You might wanna use the rubber apron so you don't get soaked cleaning all that shit."

"Thanks. So how long have you been working here?" Raven asked to break the tension.

"Oh, I see. Did I say it was time for chitchat?"

"Oh, sorry," Raven mumbled.

"Why you wanna know how long I've been working here anyway?"

Damn. Raven let out a nervous chuckle. "Um, well, I figure since we'll be spending a lot of time together, we might wanna get to know each other."

Effie stopped cutting the dough she was placing into the bread pans and gave the girl her attention. "You're right. We may as well get introduced. How about you start by telling me about that brother of yours? Then you can let me know if you got any of that same blood running through your system. 'Cause I don't plan to die in this bakery. This is my job, but it ain't my life."

Raven's mouth dropped open. "Okaaay," she drew out. "Growing up, my brother Matthew wasn't a violent person. He was grumpy and kind of dark." *Like you,* she thought. "But he wasn't evil . . . at least I didn't think he was. We always got along good. Our father died when we were eight, and our mom was sent to prison for child endangerment when we were ten. We never had a stable home life after my dad was gone."

"Well, there's lots of us that had a bad upbringing. That don't mean we go out and shoot up a damn school. And your mom? Tell me about her. She sounds like a real doozy," Effie probed.

Raven met her eyes. "My mom was terrible, damaging. She didn't protect us. And even though I know she was a horrible mother, I don't think she deserved to be murdered by my brother. While she was in prison, Matthew and me got sent to live in different homes. They were messed-up places. Matthew got picked on a lot . . . you know, beat up all the time."

Effie picked up a hunk of dough, sprinkled flour over the top, and started rolling again. "Did you get picked on and beat up a lot, too? Like your brother?"

Raven nodded. "Yeah, I took a lot of lumps."

"Go on. Tell me more."

"Well, our mom got released when we were seventeen, and eventually, we both got to move in with her. I was held up for a while by my foster mom at the time. Her name was Sable. One of the girls at the house used to call her Mummy, as in dead as fuck inside."

Effie grinned.

"She was right, too. Sable was meaner than a hungry lion. She had no soul."

"Hm. I knew a woman like that when I was growing up. I wanted to rip her head off and shit down her neck." Her eyes floated to Raven watching her with interest. "Anyway, go on with your story."

"Well, Matthew was doing good, I thought. Then my mom's boyfriend, Gage, moved in and we both stayed home less and less. Matthew killed him, too. Gage was mean. He was a dick," the girl added.

"Okay, I'm still not making no connection between your brother being an okay guy to shootin' up a whole school," Effie remarked. "How the hell does that happen?"

"That's the thing," Raven said, her voice rising. "I have no idea. There weren't any signs. Matthew kept his feelings private. He'd share some things with me, but I think he was too embarrassed to tell me what was really going on."

Effie huffed. "Still ain't making the connection between a decent boy and a boy who commits that kinda crime."

Raven nibbled on her bottom lip. "That makes two of us. I lived separately from Matthew for seven years. I saw him at school, but that was it. We grew apart. We each had our own crazy lives to deal with. I don't have an answer for you."

She sniffled, trying to hold in her tears from the pressure. She was tired of being the person who was supposed to have the answers about her brother.

The older woman glanced at her. "Ah right. Seems like you had your fill of it for now. I wanna tell you about clearing the tables out there."

Raven's shoulders fell and she let out a silent sigh of relief. "Yeah, whatever you need me to do."

As the woman instructed Raven on how to use the large plastic bin to collect dirty dishes, her mind wandered to Matthew.

I hope you're burning in hell.

Chapter Fifty-Four

At the end of the first day, Raven walked into the restaurant where Maria was wiping down counters and pulling the leftover baked goods from the shelves.

Raven cleared her throat, and the woman looked over.

"How did everything go with Effie?"

Raven shrugged. "I think it went good. I finished doing all of the dishes and she told me I could leave."

Maria smiled. "Effie hates doing the dishes. I often have to go back and help her. Otherwise, she gets very grumpy." She glanced at the extra baked goods. "We have leftover items. Would you like to take a bag with you?"

Raven moved closer. "Sure. I, um, can bring them home?"

The woman lifted her eyes. "Of course. I heard that Cecilia let you move in."

Raven nodded. "You talked to Ava?"

"Of course. I talk to her at least once a week. But you don't have to worry, I won't tell anyone your business. Ava told me the Kensington Hoods are looking for you," Maria blurted out.

The girl's stomach fell to her knees. She hadn't thought about the gang in a week. "Oh yeah. I'm sorry, it's not like they'll come here . . . At least I don't think they will. But what if they do?"

Maria laid her dishcloth on the counter and gave the girl her full attention. "I'm not worried about the Kensington Hoods. They have no place in this neighborhood and they know it, so relax."

"Yeah. But I also don't want to put Cecilia in danger. Do you think they would come to her house looking for me?"

Maria forced the air from her lungs, in the quietest, most delicate manner Raven had ever witnessed.

Maria placed a hand on her shoulder. "Here's what you need to know. Ava asked me to take care of you. She believes in you and that means everything to me. The who and what is irrelevant. You'll need to learn how to trust me as I'll have to do with you. You and Cecilia will be looked after. That's all you need to know."

Raven pressed her hands against her tummy. "Okay. But I don't get how you can be so sure that we won't have any problems with them," she stated with a hesitant smile.

Maria lifted her shoulders back and gave Raven a dazzling smile. "Remember, the who and the what is irrelevant." She grabbed the dishcloth. "Now, help me finish. Then we'll put together a box of goodies for you and Cecilia. You can come with me to drop the rest of the baked goods off at the women's shelter," she whispered. "Then I'll take you home. How does that sound?"

A warmth spread through the girl. The events over the past week were almost too good to be true. First, Cecilia had accepted her into her home, and now Maria offered Raven to join her.

"Yes, I'd love to go with you, and I'm sure Cecilia will be happy for the pastries."

Maria pursed her lips. "I don't think so. She'll probably tell you she could've made them much tastier than I do. But deep inside, she'll be happy that we thought of her."

The girl gave her a genuine smile. "I think you're right. It's cool that you donate your food to a shelter."

Maria nodded. "I'm a fortunate woman. I came from simple means and married into a family that had everything they could ever want. I was only sixteen when I met my husband." Her eyes moved to the ceiling in a dreamy state. "He swept me off my feet, but he's four years older than me. My parents didn't approve of him because I was so young." She moved her eyes back to Raven and shook her head. "When I turned eighteen, I married him, and my family disowned me because they didn't think he was the right choice for me. They didn't think he was good enough and wanted someone more . . . middle-class. Honestly, it didn't matter what they thought. I loved Salvatore so much that I couldn't imagine my life without him. My husband and his family have given me so much. They're very good to me."

"It sounds romantic," Raven commented.

"It was except for the part where my family disowned me."

Raven scrunched her brow. "You haven't talked to your mom and dad since you were eighteen?"

Maria nodded. "That's right. Sometimes, blood relatives are the real strangers. They do and say things that can't be undone. Like what your brother did to you. So see, you aren't alone with the hardship of your family's actions. We all have our difficulties. No one's life is simple, even if it looks like it is."

Raven bowed her head. "I'm sorry your parents screwed you."

Maria gave her a rueful smile. "So am I. But you know what? I rebounded from the loss and so will you. Now come on. Let's get moving so we can get out of here."

Raven followed Maria behind the counter and as she helped box leftover bakery items, her heart grew with gratitude that strangers were giving her a chance to make something of herself.

***

Maria pulled her car over in front of Cecilia's rowhome. "Okay, tell Cecilia I said hello. I'll wait until you get inside. Oh, and if the old woman tells you her pastries are better than mine, I suggest you agree with her." She turned and smiled at Raven.

"How do you know so much about Cecilia?"

Maria pursed her lips. "Cecilia has been a staple in this neighborhood for longer than I've been alive. Also, my husband runs a lot of businesses in the area, so we get to know people."

"Oh, you have other businesses?" Raven asked, surprised.

"Well, *he* does, yes. I run the bakery—that's completely mine. Salvatore takes care of all *his* businesses."

"Salvatore," the girl murmured. "That's a nice name."

The woman grinned. "Don't let the nice name fool you. I mean, he is a nice man to the people he loves, those that he lets inside his circle, but I don't think that outsiders or people who do him wrong would consider him a nice man."

Raven released a nervous giggle. She wasn't certain what that all meant, but there was a slight insinuation of criminality in Maria's words and tone.

"Okay, thanks for letting me tag along," Raven said, opening the car door. "I'll see you tomorrow . . . early."

As Raven walked up Cecilia's front porch, she was acutely aware of what was around her. Bitsy had taught her that much. Her eyes constantly scanned the street. She didn't know what she was looking for, but Maria made her wary with the spoken innuendos about the neighborhood and how her husband didn't accept people outside of his circle.

What if Salvatore doesn't accept me?

She had a hunch there was something more going on, and Raven planned to be careful about everything she said from now on.

Chapter Fifty-Five

While Raven was washing pans at the bakery one afternoon, Maria walked into the kitchen with her hands clutched together in front of her.

"Raven?"

The girl turned around. Her hair was messy from the steam coming off the hot water. "Yeah?"

"There's a woman here to see you. She said she's a police officer. Her name is Caitlin Townsend. She's waiting for you in the bakery."

Raven's eyes widened, and she stole a glance at Effie watching her.

"I'll just ask the motherfucking obvious question here," Effie yammered. "Why the hell you got the police coming to see you? Who told them you're working here?"

Raven lifted her chin. "I did. I told them about my last job too. They're still investigating what my brother did, and they need to be able to find me." She turned and looked at Maria. "I'm sorry. I had no reason not to tell them. Caitlin was the only person who helped me after the shootings when everyone else wanted me dead."

Maria shook her head. "It's not a problem. As long as you aren't in trouble, it's fine with me. I don't want them hanging around here all the time, though. My customers may start to think something is wrong."

Raven wiped her hands on her apron and walked into the bakery. "Hi," Raven said hesitantly as she approached the officer. "Is everything okay? Why are you here?"

Caitlin gave her a tight smile. "Everything is fine. It's good to see you. I came to talk to you about your brother. I have some things I want to go over with you."

Raven's heart was pounding in her chest. Anything related to her past triggered a stress response. "But I'm working right now. I already told you everything I know. What else is there to say?" she fretted.

Caitlin reached for her hand and pulled Raven down into the chair next to her. "I won't keep you long. Your manager," she said, looking in Maria's direction, "said that would be okay. I need to tell you about some things we found . . . things that Matthew wrote." She lowered her voice. "When we went into your mother's apartment, we found a journal hidden in your brother's room. I'm hoping something will jog your memory." She lifted the coffee mug Maria had given her and took a sip. "Wow, this is good coffee."

Raven's eyes were set on the woman. "Yeah, everything here is good," she said, slumping into the chair. "How bad is it? Did he say he wanted to kill me, too?"

Raven's thoughts were scrambled. She hadn't expected to see Caitlin this long after the crime. Many thoughts were racing through her head. *What if Matthew lied and wrote that she was involved with what he did?* Every time the police mentioned Matthew's name, she became paranoid. *That's what happens when people you know prove themselves to be someone you never met.*

Caitlin pulled the papers from her oversized purse. "These are copies, the originals are being held as evidence. As a bit of background, there were several more entries and lots of violent pictures that Matthew drew. However, we're hoping you can shed more light on the ones we thought were most critical."

Raven took the papers between her fingers. But Caitlin held on to them. "On second thought, I'd like to read these out loud to you . . . if you don't mind."

Raven lowered her face and laced her fingers together. "All right. Go ahead. But don't let anyone overhear you." She braced herself.

Caitlin looked down at the sheet. "Okay, the first entry is dated September 2."

> *"Gage came to our apartment. My brain-damaged mom is letting him stay. He told me that I'm a pussy and that I'm nothing. I smiled inside, though. I'll show him who I really am soon enough."*

THE TWIN SISTER

Raven put a hand over her forehead. "Okay. So Matthew knew what he was going to do almost as soon as Gage moved in with us. Is that what you're thinking?"

Caitlin nodded. "That's what we believe. That would put the timeline on the first day of your senior year. The next entry was on October 14."

> "My mom stood by while Gage beat the shit out of me because he was drunk and had nothing better to do. She's as guilty as he is."

Caitlin lifted her eyes. "This establishes the motive for your brother killing both of them before going into the school. Did he mention anything to you about this incident? Anything you can remember?"

Raven tilted her head. "Gage beat Matthew too many times to keep track. My brother told me he hated him. I mean, I knew he hated both of them. My mom gave us lots of reasons not to like her. We were both angry at her for bringing Gage back into our lives. He was a violent man." She shook her head slowly. "But I didn't know Matthew was planning to kill them. He never said anything like that. We talked about graduating and moving on. We talked about our futures. But all of those good things . . . they were all lies that Matthew told me."

Caitlin sat forward in her chair. "Raven, the entries get worse. Are you okay to keep going?"

"Will we have to talk about this another time if we stop now?"

Caitlin dipped her chin to her chest. "Yes, I'm sorry. But I'm willing to come back in a few days if that would be easier on you."

"No. I want to get this over with."

"Okay. November 1."

> "I came home late, and Gage choked me until I passed out. I woke up on the floor. I want to chew his arms off. Good thing someone is teaching me how to make people hurt the way that they hurt me."

Caitlin laid the small stack of papers on the table and folded her hands over them. "This is where I need to pause because Matthew starts referring to 'someone' but he never names the person in any of the entries. Do you have any idea who it is?"

Raven's eyes were like saucers. She was so wrapped up in her own loss and anger she didn't give it a second thought. She lifted her eyes to meet Caitlin's. "Well. There was a man. Matthew stayed at his house several nights a week. His name was Jester. I asked Matthew to let me meet him, but he wouldn't. He got mad whenever I asked about the guy. I don't know much more than that."

Caitlin scribbled the name down. "Is that it? Just Jester? Is that his first or last name?"

Raven shot her a bewildered look. "I have no idea. Do you think Jester has something to do with this?"

Raven wanted—no, *needed*—a reason why her brother murdered all those people. Absent a good reason would only mean she had loved a sick, sadistic, cold-blooded killer her whole life. That would suggest she was so blinded by wanting them to love each other that she refused to see the monster that lived inside Matthew.

Caitlin could see the conflict on the girl's face. She reached forward and took hold of Raven's hands. "You need to come to terms with what your brother did. This man, Jester, wasn't there. No one was with your brother on that day. Try to keep that in mind. Okay?"

"Yeah, sure. Easier said than done. I loved my brother my whole life. Then one day, he murdered twenty-one people out of the blue, including my two most favorite people in the world. It ain't easy to come to terms with that, trust me."

"I can only imagine. I'm sorry. Let's get the rest of this done and then you can get back to what you were doing," Caitlin said, looking into her eyes. "There are a few more. January 9."

> *"I'm being taught everything there is to know about guns and bombs. I'm going to get the attention and respect that I always deserved."*

Caitlin looked up from the paper. "Did Matthew mention where Jester lives? Was he close to your apartment? We suspect this person helped your brother buy guns illegally, and he can be arrested if we can prove it."

Holy shit, Matthew. You're such a fucking asshole.

"No. Like I said, Matthew wouldn't tell me anything about the guy. I asked him a couple of times and he blew me off."

"Raven, I need you to think really hard. Try to remember everything the two of you talked about. He may have said something without mentioning Jester by name."

Raven shook her head.

"We are almost done. February 8." Caitlin paused and took in a deep breath, hoping the girl was preparing herself.

> *"The only place for me to hide from the people who hurt me is in the darkness. Someday they will know what it's like to be me. To live in the shadows, to never have light cast upon them. They'll understand my suffering. Just like someday soon I will have the privilege of being them—of having all the power. Everyone will know me then. They'll all want to be my friend. They will find that under all the flesh that flanks my bones, I am the most dominant version of power. They'll regret not seeing the fire in me sooner. Before I deliver justice."*

Raven pressed her hands over her eyes and shuddered. She knew her brother was hurting, that he had wanted to be loved, but his words took her breath away. "I don't know him as that person," she said as a sob escaped her. Tears slid down her cheeks. "His thoughts were evil. Why?"

Caitlin shook her head. "I don't know." She was silent for several moments, allowing the girl time. "There's one more entry I'd like to read. Can you sit through one more?"

Raven swiped at the tears. "Yeah, but this is like cruel and unusual punishment. I don't understand the reason behind it," she murmured.

"It's to see if any of his writings help you remember any details that could lead us to this man who seems to have groomed him. Okay?"

Raven nodded.

"Last entry. March 14."

> *"I will be born again tomorrow. I will be famous . . . infamous. I have found a way to leave my legacy. So many people will talk about me many years after I'm gone. I've always hated this life, and my best friend has helped me with a plan to end it with a*

bang. The last person to go tomorrow will be me. I can't wait. It's what I've planned. My dreams are coming true. Farewell, motherfuckers! I'll see you bitches in hell."

Caitlin shoved the pages into her bag.

"Did Matthew talk about being famous? Did he aspire to do something bigger with his life that he thought was impossible to accomplish? Something that he'd seek outside help. Like maybe he wanted to be a Marine or Navy Seal?"

"No, nothing."

Caitlin sat back. "Someone took advantage of your brother's mental state. The last entry says it all. He had so much hate in his heart, and as a result, he was convinced he had the right to even the injustices that he perceived were lodged against him. I'm sorry to have put you through this again. If you think of anything . . . will you call me?"

"Yeah," she choked out.

The officer put her arm over the girl's shoulder. "We will continue to look for this man. I promise you that."

"Matthew was always a loner."

Grief-stricken, Raven doubled over. Her breaths came in heavy spurts. Her tears dripped from the tip of her chin onto her shirt. Her chest sucked in and pushed out radically.

Caitlin looked around and noticed Maria glaring at her.

The officer stood. "Okay. We'll end it here. Let me help you up."

"I got her," Maria said in a stern voice. She looked into Caitlin's face. "I hope this is the last time she'll need to see you. As you can see, this is hard on her."

Raven glanced at Maria. She could see the quiet storm spinning below the surface.

"Sure. Unless something important comes up, I won't be back," Caitlin promised.

With Caitlin gone, Maria rushed the girl into the kitchen. She'd looped her arm through Raven's and pulled her along.

Inside the kitchen, Effie looked up from her work. She moved to Raven quickly. "I got her from here."

Maria made eye contact and gave the woman a nod.

Effie helped Raven to a chair in the corner. She sat her down and handed her a clean kitchen towel. "This is to wipe away those tears. Are you okay?" Effie rasped.

Raven looked at her through red, blistery eyes. "No. I wish this would end already." She rolled her head away from Effie. It was a heavy moment. A time when disgust and outrage outweighed her grief. She was filled with regret for not being more persistent with Matthew about Jester. She blamed herself for not pressing her brother for more information.

So now there's some dickhead out there who taught my brother what justice looks like.

Raven pulled herself together and moved back to the sink. She'd talk to Effie in the morning. She had learned that Effie was shrewd, and she understood nuances that many people ignored. She'd ask Effie if she should worry about this Jester guy. She'd find out if she should talk to Maria. After all, Maria had connections and said she knew everyone. She had observed that Maria's connections were wide and deep. Everyone in the area and the Italian Market knew and respected the woman. She closed her eyes, and the exhaustion of the past thirty minutes took her hostage, so she focused her efforts on scrubbing.

***

At home that night, Cecilia watched Raven as she ate quietly. "Is something wrong? Something happen at work?"

Raven looked up from her plate. "Ah, it's something with my brother, that's all." She laid her fork down. "It feels like I'll never be done dealing with this . . . with what he did."

Cecilia put a piece of chicken cutlet into her mouth. "That sounds about right. You'll never get over what's happened. When bad things happen to people, it changes them. It makes us see the world as a dangerous place. You have to see the world through your own eyes. Try to think back to the day before the shooting. What were you happy about? How can you recapture the peace you had then?"

"That's just it. I can't. It's gone, and every time something new comes up about Matthew, it takes me right back to that classroom." She shook her head. "None of it makes sense."

Cecilia nodded. "That's the way hate works. People thrive on it. Almost enjoy being mad and angry all the time, but it don't make no sense to people who only want to be happy. You know, happy as you can possibly be." She patted Raven's hand. "Give it time. Things will get better."

Raven gave her a sheepish grin. She appreciated the woman trying to comfort her and give her advice. *I'm not so sure time will heal this gaping wound in my heart,* she thought.

Chapter Fifty-Six

"Good morning, Effie," Raven murmured when she walked into the kitchen the next day.

Effie was throwing a ten-pound bag of flour into the large mixer. She looked up for a split second. "Yeah, morning. Why is your face dragging down around your titties?"

Raven snickered at the comment. "I didn't sleep well."

"Hm. That's too bad. Can you get the eggs, sugar, and butter outta the fridge? Put them on the table. Then I need you to grease those bread pans."

The girl smiled. Effie was a bossy woman, but she was true to her work and never minced words. "Sure, I'm on it." Raven moved to the commercial refrigerator and pulled out the eggs and butter. "So that policewoman who came in here yesterday . . . Officer Townsend?"

Effie's brow wrinkled. "Yeah, what about her? You said you liked her, but she sure did rattle your cage."

Raven nodded. "She brought journal entries that my brother had written. She read them to me. Well, some of them."

"Oh, that doesn't sound good," she commented, breaking eggs into a bowl. Effie lifted her face and raised her eyebrows. "Your brother tried to blame you or something?"

The girl shook her head. "No. He wrote about how he was going to make people suffer. That he was going to get revenge. Most of the things he wrote were sick."

Effie's head was down again, looking into the mixer, and she pinched her lips together. "Mm, mm, mm. The world is so damn screwed up. What else he say?"

"A bunch of mean stuff. Then he kept talking about this friend of his, a grown man. Matthew never had any friends his age. And Caitlin wanted to know if I knew who this guy was . . . the guy Matthew said was teaching him things. That's when I remembered that he used to go to this man's house—you know, after my mom let Gage move back in with us."

"Hand me that butter, will you?" Effie huffed.

Raven moved around to the mixer, holding a large tray with blocks of butter. "So then Caitlin asked me about the guy's house Matthew went to. I felt so dumb that I don't know where he lived, but Matthew wouldn't talk to me about Jester. So I had no way—"

Effie had stopped dead and cut the girl off. "I'm sorry. Who'd you say?"

Raven blinked a couple of times. "Jester?"

The woman nodded. "Does that Jester live in the Strawberry Mansion section?"

Raven shrugged. "I just told you, I have no idea. Matthew never let me meet the guy, and he rarely talked about him. He told me that they had stuff in common. That's about it."

Effie walked over to the sink and washed her hands. Her brows were knotted together and her lips were pressed into a tight line.

Raven followed the woman to the sink. Effie's body language told her she'd hit a nerve. Her eyes searched the older woman's face. "What's going on? You seem upset."

"You're damn right I'm upset. Jester, if it's the same dude I know, is an evil motherfucker."

Raven's heart quickened. "What do you mean evil?"

Effie moved closer to the girl. "Jester is hateful. That man can't stand anyone who's different than him. He's got a decent amount of power in his neighborhood. He sells guns. Runs numbers. Gets his hands dirty if need be. Nobody respects him . . . even the thugs who run the streets are afraid of him."

"Why would this guy become friends with my brother then? It must be a different Jester."

"Oh yeah," Effie said, cocking out her hip. "How many goddamn people do you know with the name of Jester?"

Raven widened her eyes. "None, but it's not like I did research. I don't even know if Jester is his first or last name. It might even be a nickname or his gang member name."

Effie nodded. "They're all good points. It might be something worth the police lookin' into, though."

THE TWIN SISTER

The little hairs on Raven's arms stood up. "What do you mean? You think the police are going to talk to this guy and tell them I gave them his name?"

"Well, the police sure as hell best do something with that information. What if he's groomin' some other dumb chump?"

Raven shook her head. Her stomach was spinning. "But do you think the police will say I gave them his name? What if he comes after me?"

Effie tilted her head and pointed her finger at the girl. "That's a damn good point. You best let Maria know. About Jester, that is."

"Why would I do that? What does Maria have to do with Jester?"

"Well, if it's the same Jester I know, he'll come after you. That sick prick could come looking for you here. That could be dangerous for all of us," Effie warned.

Raven got teary-eyed. "Effie, what if I tell Maria and she fires me?" She looked at the older woman with pleading eyes, hoping for any bit of comfort. "What should I say?"

Effie huffed and rolled her eyes. "I can't be certain, but I doubt she'll fire you. Damn, she knows I like having someone to boss around. But this ain't all about you. This is about keeping her bakery and everybody in it safe. She should know, is all. Maria is good people, but she don't like to be surprised."

"I never should've told Caitlin anything," she moaned, too distraught to reflect on words she didn't mean.

"What are you talking about? You did the right fucking thing. No matter what happens with Maria. The bottom line is you can live with yourself for telling the cops about that douchebag." Effie scratched her forehead, a nervous tic she had. "Maria's gotta know. 'Cause it's awfully peculiar that your brother starts hanging out with that man, then he goes off like a whore in heat and shoots up a bunch of people like he's living in the Wild West," she added.

"Shit," Raven breathed. "You're right. I have to tell her. I'll tell her about Jester. I promise."

Effie smacked her lips together. "That's right, and you're gonna do that today. See, I like my life and I ain't ready to die. So either you tell Maria today or I have to. And if I gotta do it for you, I won't be happy about it neither. This is all part of being a grown-up."

Raven dropped her head and went over to the refrigerator. She began pulling out packs of bacon that needed to be fried for the morning rush.

All the good things that happened for me over the past two weeks are slipping through my fingers.

Chapter Fifty-Seven

When the bakery closed that day and Raven finished her work, she took a slow, agonizing walk out to the restaurant. She approached Maria standing in front of the cash register.

"Maria? Do you have a minute to talk?" Raven asked.

With her face down toward the register drawer, Maria lifted her large brown eyes to meet Raven's. "Is Effie giving you a hard time? I warned you a month ago when you took this job that you need thick skin to handle her." She smiled. "Just let it roll off your back."

Raven's mouth was downturned, and she shook her head. "No, it's not that. I wanted to talk to you about that police officer who came to see me yesterday. I need to tell you something."

Maria's hackles went up, but she nodded casually and added a one-shoulder shrug. She was well-schooled in how to hide what she was feeling.

"Okay, tell me. I'm listening," Maria stated. She went back to fiddling with the money in the drawer. A way to keep her hands occupied.

"Well, something came up while I was talking to her. I told Effie about it this morning and she thought I should tell you about it now."

Maria let out a tight-throated chuckle. "That's Effie. She pretends like we aren't a community, but she truly loves that we all take good care of each other." Then she leveled Raven with her eyes. "No more beating around the bush. Tell me what happened," she said in a stern tone.

Maria's tight jaw and penetrating gaze gave Raven chills. The girl wrung her hands together, and she told Maria about Matthew's journal entries. "So Caitlin asked me if I knew who my brother was talking about . . . the person who taught him stuff. Then I remembered some guy named Jester." She looked down at her shoes. "Effie said I should tell you because she knows a guy named Jester and he's dangerous."

Raven's head was hanging, once again overcome with shame for the crimes her brother committed. Otherwise, she would've noticed that Maria's hands were frozen in midair. Two manicured hands hovering over the open cash register drawer, coming to an abrupt halt with bills in both hands.

"Jester?" Maria murmured. "That's interesting that your brother knew him. Are you sure it's the same fellow?" She was trying to keep emotion from her voice, knowing it would only heighten the girl's anxiety.

Raven's head popped up. "That's what I said, but Effie is convinced it's probably the same person. She told me it's important for you to know, and so now I told you. I'm sorry if I'm causing you problems."

Maria nodded. "Yes, it's good you told me." After a second of gathering herself, she started recounting the money in her hand.

"So," Raven said, shuffling her feet. "Effie said that he might come here looking for me, and if it's the same Jester that she knows, it could be trouble. Not only for me but for everyone who works here."

She paused, dreading that she was about to throw away the small life that she'd built in South Philly. But she couldn't live through another murderous scene . . . And this one she *could* prevent from happening.

"I need to tell Cecilia tonight, too. You know, just in case Jester comes there looking for me. I'll need to find somewhere else to live."

Maria snickered. "No, that's not necessary. There is no need for you to tell Cecilia. I will take care of this and make sure you're both watched after. Besides, Cecilia is very well-known. She's a gunslinger . . . knows quite well how to protect herself."

"So wait," Raven said cautiously. "I'm not going to lose my job? I mean, Effie was very upset when she heard that man's name . . . said she doesn't want to die here."

The woman leaned her flawless face closer to Raven. "Effie can be a bit of a drama queen. She means well, but she's overly protective of me and my bakery . . . and now you, too. You should be honored. Effie doesn't take a liking to many people. I'm certain she wasn't suggesting you shouldn't work here anymore. In fact, she told me she likes having you here to help her."

Raven pressed her hands against her heart. "Whew! That's good to hear. I like Effie a lot, too. She acts tough, but she's a nice person. So you aren't worried about Jester?"

The woman straightened her back. "Oh, I didn't say that. I'm a bit worried. If the Jester your brother knew is the same man, then he's trouble. That brute is barely human. He's the devil. I swear that man was born without a soul." She gave her a sweet smile. "Even so, I promised Ava I would take care of you, and that's what I intend to do."

"Really?' Raven gasped.

"Yes, really. I like you. You're a nice young woman, and I think you have a lot of potential. We'll be fine. I'll put the word out on the streets, and people will keep their eyes and ears open."

Raven moved closer to the woman and lowered her voice. "Do you think I should be scared of him following me?"

Maria looked her in the eyes. "Yes, you should be. I know I'm worried about him following you. He's a menace and provides absolutely no value to society. He thrives on others' pain."

Like Matthew did when he was killing all those people.

The girl cringed. "How will I know him? I've never seen him before."

Maria opened a canvas bag and shoved a wad of bills inside. "Just look for the devil dressed in a skin suit," she cracked angrily. "Sorry. Jester is a tall white man, over six feet. He has black hair and a tattoo of a pentagram, a very thick distinct one, covering the top of his left hand."

Raven narrowed her eyes. "Pentagram?"

"You know, it's a star inside a circle," Maria stated. Then she grabbed the notepad next to her and drew it for the girl.

"What does it mean?" Raven asked.

"It is a symbol people display because they worship Satan."

Raven gasped. "Do you think my brother was worshipping the devil?"

Maria shrugged. "I have no idea. I'm merely telling you what the symbol represents. Try not to take your thoughts any further down that dark hole. All you need to do now is keep your eyes and ears open. I want you to tell me immediately if you see anyone suspicious. If you suspect Jester is following you, you are to go to a very public place and call me." She searched Raven's face. The girl was stricken with fear. "It'll be fine. I can find out if your brother had been hanging out in the Strawberry Mansion section. That's where Jester lives."

Raven raked a hand through her hair. "Nothing bad will happen to you, though . . . if you try to find out? What if Jester knows you're trying to get information?"

Maria pursed her lips. "Jester will never find out. I have ways, Raven."

"Okay," she murmured. "Thank you for looking out for me."

"It's my pleasure," Maria answered and gave her a forced smile. She needed to leave the bakery and get home. She had business to take care of now.

Raven was wound tight. She'd been hiding from the Kensington Hoods, and now there was another monster out there, and it was all because of Matthew. She shook off the heebie-jeebies that had settled in her spine and pulled her shoulders back.

Pull yourself together, Ledger.

Maria turned and grabbed a mug off of the shelf. She filled it with fresh coffee. "So that you know what to expect . . . I don't know for certain, but if I had to guess, the police will give Jester a visit. They'll ask him a bunch of questions about your brother. That will rile Jester up and he'll want to get even with someone. However, I have to believe the police are smart enough to keep you out of it. My thoughts are they'll lie and tell him your brother mentioned him by name in his journal. That would be the smart thing to do."

"I hope you're right. I hope they keep me out of it. Should I call Caitlin and ask her not to mention my name? Do you think that would help?"

Maria took a sip from the mug. "Sure, I see no harm in calling her. Beyond that, though, there's nothing you can do. You have to trust that Caitlin will protect your identity. You must go on with your life and be diligent about your safety. Know your surroundings and if something doesn't seem right, trust your instincts. Like I said, you call here."

"What if it's late at night?"

"My husband or I always answer this phone number. We have a duplicate line in our home."

Raven lifted her eyebrows. "Why?"

Maria didn't react. "Because this is our business, and we always want to make sure it's protected."

The girl nodded, but it still didn't make sense to her. *It's a bakery, not a bank.* But she decided not to push it any further. "Okay. Thanks, Maria."

The woman flashed her a smile. "Come on. I'll give you a ride back to your place."

Raven paused. "Thanks, that would be great. Do you mind picking me up and dropping me off every day for the rest of my life?" she half joked.

Maria chuckled. "Raven, I know this is alarming, but you need to trust things will work out. You'll call Caitlin when you get home, and also . . . I have your back. That's how I operate for people who I've come to care for. Let's go," she said and walked toward the door. She stopped and turned back. "Effie?" she yelled.

The woman came to the doorway of the kitchen. "Why you screaming my name? You can't have the decency to walk your skinny white ass back here no more?"

Maria gave the woman a playful smile and blew her an air kiss. "Effie, I'm driving Raven back to her place. I'll lock this door. I'll see you tomorrow."

"Yeah," Effie grumbled. "I'll be here. I'm always here. You're damn lucky to have me."

Even in distress, Raven couldn't help but smile. She realized how fortunate she was to have two strong women in her life, three counting Cecilia. Then her thoughts drifted to the mysterious man who took her brother under his wing. The last thing she wanted was to be hunted by a madman named Jester who was in love with the devil.

Chapter Fifty-Eight

That night, when Maria got home, she sat at her dining room table with her husband and son.

"You seem quiet tonight," Salvatore commented.

Maria moved the food around her plate. "Well, I have something we need to talk about."

"Okay," he said, pouring more wine into his glass, then hers. "What's going on?"

"You remember I hired that young girl? Raven Ledger?"

Salvatore nodded. "Right. Her brother was the school shooter." He shook his head. "Sick fucking world we live in. Anyway, I'm sorry to interrupt you. What about her?"

Maria swallowed a few times. "There's a good chance that her brother was hanging around with Jester, and the police know now, too."

Salvatore rested his fork on his plate. "Come again?"

His wife nodded. "You heard right. I don't know if the police are going to talk to him or not. But as you know, he could come looking for her, and I thought you should know."

He laced his fingers together, elbows on the table. "All right. I'll talk to my guys."

Maria's eyes shot to his. "Your guys? Do you think it's serious enough that it requires them and not a couple of the men under them?"

Salvatore took her hand and kissed the top. "You are my wife. There's nothing more important to me than my family. You know this. I trust my guys with my life so I can also trust them with yours."

"I promised Raven that I would protect her," she admitted.

Salvatore put her hand on the table and lifted his fork. "Of course you'll protect her. That's what we do for people who are loyal to us. Raven came to you and admitted what happened. That's the start of a good relationship."

Maria leaned into him. "Well, I think Effie may have had something to do with her spilling the beans to me."

Salvatore chuckled. "I'm sure she did."

"You'll tell your guys about Raven, too? Or do you want me to do that?"

He placed a piece of fish in his mouth, savoring the flavors. "I'll fill them in, and if they have any questions, they'll ask you." He pinched his thumb, index, and middle fingers together and lifted them into the air. "You are the most fabulous cook I know." He gave her a wink. "Don't tell my mother; she'll get her feelings hurt."

As they continued their dinner, Maria looked at her husband with great admiration. His father headed the Morano crime family. The Italian mafia was a mob family that lived and ran the streets of South Philadelphia. Someday, Salvatore would succeed Johnny as the new Godfather.

***

After dinner, Raven called the police station and asked for Caitlin.

"Raven?" Caitlin picked up the call in a breathy tone. "Is everything okay?"

"Yes, everything is fine. It's about Jester. You're not going to tell him my name, right?"

"Oh, Raven. Of course not. I should've explained that to you yesterday. We would never divulge our source."

Raven's shoulders dropped. "Okay. That's all I wanted to know."

"Try not to worry too much. Okay?"

The girl scoffed. "Yeah, right. It's not that easy to do."

"I hear you. Take care and call if you need me," Caitlin stated.

When Raven hung up the phone, she sat on the sofa and looked out the front window onto the porch. Cecilia was wrapped in her winter coat, wearing her scarf and hat, talking to Sofia. As she watched the two women chatter, she allowed herself to settle into the warmth of the home. She hoped that her life would continue on a path that would lead her to greatness and that someday soon, she'd be able to put her old life behind her for good.

Chapter Fifty-Nine

The next morning Effie was wiping her hands on her apron when Raven arrived at work. She lifted her eyes. "You told Maria about Jester, right?"

Raven nodded.

"How did it go?"

Raven approached the woman. "It went good. I was so scared she was going to fire me, but she was great about it. She was happy I told her."

"No shit. I know what's best for Maria. Next time don't question me." She smirked.

"Are you kidding? I was scared to tell her, that's all. But I'd never question you. No one in their right mind would question you. Not even Maria," Raven teased her.

"Uh-huh. Enough of your flapping lips. Get your ass moving," Effie ordered.

"Jeez." Raven smiled. "You're so bossy."

"That's right. This is my kitchen. Another thing, Maria is my people. I keep a very small circle and you ain't in it . . . yet."

Raven gave the woman her best smile. "So I'm almost in your circle?"

Effie shook her head. "Don't go getting ahead of yourself. You have a lot of road to travel before you're in."

The girl chuckled. "Whatever it takes. How did Maria get in your circle? It's not just because you work for her."

Effie tilted her head. "If it wasn't for Maria, I wouldn't be here today. I owe that woman everything."

"Why? What did she do?" the girl asked seriously.

Effie stopped working and stared at the girl, wondering if she could trust her. "I'll tell you, but if I find out you told anybody, I'll cream your ass all over this kitchen. We understand each other?"

Raven put on a serious face and nodded. *Who am I going to tell?*

"Okay, I was homeless when I was sixteen. By the time I was twenty-four, I'd been living in the streets for eight years. I was sitting right outside the door of the bakery, and the cops were cruising the streets. The other store owners don't like homeless people loiterin' on their sidewalks. They say it's bad for business."

Raven grabbed a cupcake and pulled the paper back. She was listening so intently that Effie couldn't help but smile to herself. "Where did you sleep?"

"Alleyways, doorways, train stations . . . wherever the hell I could find. It ain't as bad in the summer, but damn those cold winter days and nights, they eat away at your flesh and bones."

Raven nodded. "Yeah, I was off the streets before the dead of winter, but even late fall is tough."

Effie put her hands on her hips. "You wanna hear my story or tell yours?"

The girl's eyes grew larger. "Sorry."

"Anyway, I had been mugged and I ran from these two white dudes who stole fourteen bucks from me. It might not seem like a lot, but it was all the money I had in the world. When I couldn't run no more, I collapsed on the sidewalk outside this bakery."

"That happened to a friend of mine, too. We knew the guy. Did you know the guys that robbed you?"

Effie shook her head. "Never seen them before."

"Did they hurt you?"

"Damn straight they did. Beat the hell outta me. That's the streets. People will kill you for a worn pair of sneakers if they want 'em."

Raven took another bite of her cupcake. "So what happened?"

Effie glared at her. "I'd tell you if you stop interrupting."

"Right," the girl said with a smile.

"Well, when Maria got here at four the next morning, I was sprawled out across the front of her door. Passed out . . . all beat up . . . bleeding. I was a sorry sight," Effie explained, recalling her lowest moment.

Raven handed Effie a cupcake, and the woman peeled the paper back. She took a bite. "Maria, that skinny thing, dragged my ass inside, and that woman nursed me back to health. She put up a cot in her office. She slept on the sofa to care for me for three whole nights. During the day, her husband Salvatore would come here and check on me." She shook her head fondly. "They sure did. From that day forward, I knew they would always be my family." She lowered her voice and bounced her eyebrows. "You ain't met Salvatore yet, but holy shit, that man is easy on the eyes. He can be a force to reckon with if you cross him, but damn, he's hot. Of course, he loves me." She tapped both hands on her chest. "I'm one of his favorite people—he tells me all the time." She beamed with pride.

Raven smirked. "Does Maria know you're lusting after her husband?"

Effie flicked her wrist at the girl. "You better hush your mouth. Maria knows I think her man is a hunka, hunka burning love. That don't mean I want him." Her eyes moved away from Raven. "Besides, I'd never do anything to hurt Maria, and I won't let anyone else hurt her either."

Raven nodded. "Yeah, she's special. So after you were better, Maria gave you a job here and the rest is history. Right?" she teased, rushing to the conclusion.

Effie wagged her finger at the girl. "I'm trying to tell you a story. Don't be a smartass. But yeah, she gave me a job here and let me sleep in the office. Then her and Salvatore helped me rent an apartment a couple of miles from here. It ain't nothing fancy, but it's in a damn good neighborhood. I got plenty of room and I keep it clean like my kitchen here. I have everything I need."

Raven closed her eyes, then opened them again. "So you and Maria were really young then."

"I was twenty-four and Maria was twenty. I told her after a few months, I said, 'Maria, ain't nobody ever care for me like you. I think you're an angel sent from God.' You know what she told me?"

Raven shook her head.

"She said, 'Effie, I grew up poor and I know what it's like to live without things you want and need. I could've easily been living on the streets if things didn't work out with Salvatore, since my family disowned me because I loved him. Salvatore gave me opportunity—so that's what I can do for you. Paying it forward is very important to me.'"

Raven teared up. "Wow, I didn't expect that. Maria has helped me, too. She's been great."

"That's right. That's why she's my people, and I'll protect her till the day I die. Only damn person in the world that's ever believed in me. Yep." She nodded emphatically. "That's the real shit right there."

"I hope someday I'll have my own place, too . . . like you do. Not that I don't like living with Cecilia. She's great. Like the grandmother I've never had." She paused, looking down at her hands, and then her head snapped up. "I have an idea," Raven sang excitedly.

Effie perked up. "What?"

"Maybe you and me can be neighbors."

Effie shook her head. "I don't know about all that. You're kinda needy and sometimes a little annoying."

The two laughed. Then Effie got serious again. "Those Moranos will help you if you're good to them. But you gotta be worthy. You have to be loyal. That means do your work, keep your head down and your mouth shut."

Raven's head jerked back. "Keep my mouth shut about what? I don't even argue with *you*. I'd never argue with Maria."

Effie popped the remainder of the cupcake into her mouth. "I ain't talking about that. You gotta remember, what happens here stays here. That ain't no joke. Now get yourself together and let's get the day started."

Raven moved to her workstation, and as she worked throughout the day, she hoped that someday, she could be as independent as Effie.

Chapter Sixty

While Raven was loading dishes into the dishwasher, Maria flitted into the kitchen.

"Raven? I'd like you to learn how to work the front. You'll learn how to serve people so you can help me to take orders and work the register," Maria said.

"Whoa!" Effie butted in. "Who the fuck is gonna do the dishes if she's doing all that?"

Maria gave her a scathing look. "Effie, I need her up front part-time. You know I need to spend some more time with my son. So if it's okay with you," she said sarcastically, "I'd like to have Raven cover the store. I've offered this to you many times, and what do you always tell me?"

Effie cocked her head to the side. "I tell you I ain't puttin' up with those picky-ass people out there. I ain't got tolerance for their bullshit. But that don't mean I want you to take the girl away from me . . . I ain't looking to do more work. I'm looking to do less."

"Oh, Effie. You're impossible."

"I might be impossible," Effie fired back, "but I know what I want, and you can't run this place without me now."

Maria waltzed over to the woman and hugged her. "Well, Miss Effie, I need you to give a little on this one. Please."

"And I need you to respect your elders. You keep in mind that I'm four years older than you," Effie said, cracking a smile.

Maria walked toward the kitchen door. "Raven, if Effie can spare you, I'll need you to be up front in ten minutes."

Raven nodded. She looked from Effie to Maria, not wanting to get into the middle of things. Even though it was lighthearted, she didn't want to piss off either woman.

"Effie?" Maria said, still smiling.

"Yeah, she'll be out in ten, but I need her back here to finish her work before she goes home."

"Thank you, Effie. You're the best," Maria sang, leaving the kitchen.

***

Raven went into the bakery and stood next to Maria. She looked out the window and watched the snow falling. "Jeez, snow before Thanksgiving. That's odd."

"I don't think we're getting too much today," Maria commented, glancing outside. "On the news last night, the weatherman said it would be a hard winter. They're rarely ever right about the weather. Imagine having a job where you only have to be right fifty percent of the time."

Raven smiled. "I don't mind the snow. I like how it makes everything look clean." She turned to Maria. "Where do you want me to start?"

Maria looked over at Raven, then glanced at the tables full of people. "First go in the back, take the apron off, and fix your hair. Then I'll show you how to run the cash register. As customers come in, you can follow me while I take their orders."

Raven blushed and looked down at herself. She dealt with dirty dishes most of the day and had clothes that suited the job. She glanced at Maria. "I don't have any nice clothes."

Maria gave her a curt nod. "I have a few things at home. I think they'll fit you. I'll bring them in tomorrow."

Raven smiled. "I'd love that. You have the nicest clothes I've ever seen."

The woman pursed her lips. "I didn't always have the nicest clothes, or jewelry, or anything else for that matter. So I'm happy to share some of my things with you. Come now, go get yourself together."

***

A week later, Maria stood behind Raven as she rang up purchases.

Raven had a line of people at the counter, and Maria walked into the kitchen to talk with Effie about how they could share the girl's time. While

THE TWIN SISTER

she was gone, three nineteen-year-old boys entered the bakery. When it was their turn to order, they all glared at Raven with deadpan eyes.

Raven gave them a half smile, but the needling in her gut knew they were trouble. "Can I help you?"

"Tell her what you want, Angelo," one boy whispered and gave his friend a push forward.

Angelo swaggered up closer to Raven and leaned an elbow on the counter. "Hmmm. Let's see. What do I want?" He looked into Raven's face. His eyes were narrowed, and his upper lip was curled. He turned to his friends, "I think you guys are right." He looked at Raven again. "Ain't you that kid's sister? The one who shot up that school?"

Raven's body stiffened. She flinched, but collected herself quickly, putting on the fake armor she wore to hide her heartache. She pressed her lips into a tight smile. "I'm sorry. Is there something I can get for you?" She threw her thumb over her shoulder to the shelves behind her.

Angelo eyed her up and down, then grabbed the front of her T-shirt. He pulled her face down to meet his. "You didn't answer my question, bitch. Are you the shooter's sister? Don't lie now." He ran his wet tongue up her cheek. "We all know who you are and what you and your brother did." He let go of her shirt and grabbed a handful of her hair. He pressed her hair against his nose and took a whiff. "You smell like a killer . . . like your brother."

Raven pulled back, but the teen gripped her hair tighter, wrapping it around his fist.

"Leave me alone," her voice screeched.

One of his friends stepped forward and slapped Raven on the side of the head.

Her free arm popped up as she tried to take a swing at the second boy. Missing her target, her arms and legs went weak. She didn't know what the boys would do to her, and no one was trying to help her. Frightened, she squeezed her bladder so as not to pee herself. Then a man's voice cut through the thick tension hanging in the air.

"Hey, what the fuck you clowns doin'?"

A tall, bulky man with brown hair and large green eyes was barreling toward them.

Angelo spun toward the voice and immediately released Raven's hair. His eyes widened and he put his hands in the air. "O-o-oh, nothing. We were just messin' with her. W-w-we didn't see you sitting there, Tony. How you been?"

Tony stepped up to Angelo, then looked past him and glared at Angelo's two friends shrinking into themselves and taking small steps backward toward the door. He put his hand over the front of Angelo's neck and squeezed. "You didn't see me and Vincent sittin' there, huh? Well, then you better look closer next time. What do you think you're doing coming in here and acting like a thug? This is Maria's store." He slapped the boy on the side of the head. "You don't do that shit in here." Tony lifted his chin toward Raven. "What'd she do to you?"

Angelo shook his head. The teen was still clawing at the death grip Tony had on him. He was gurgling and trying to pry his hand away. Try as he might, he couldn't answer.

Vincent, Tony's friend, nudged him. "Tony, you gotta let go of him so he can answer."

Tony glanced at his friend and cracked a smile. "Oh, right." He let his hand drop to his side. "Go on and tell me now, what did she do to you that made you act like a dickhead? It must be something bad seeing the way you were fucking with her. Didn't your mother ever teach you not to put your hands on a woman?"

Raven stared at Tony. All of her senses were firing. She was coming down off of the fear rush from moments ago. Relief made her muscles weak . . . and her interest was piqued by the handsome man and his friend.

Angelo was trying to catch his breath. "Look, Tony. We didn't mean nothing by it. Did we, guys?" He turned to his friends, who had backed away from him already. "This girl here is the sister of that boy who killed all those kids at Allegheny High School."

Raven visibly cringed.

Tony's eyes grew wide as he moved his face closer. "And? I ain't sure what that means. Are you saying she's guilty of something? 'Cause if you are, then you better show me some proof." Tony narrowed his eyes. "Or are you saying she gotta pay for what her brother did? Is that what you're telling me, Angelo? 'Cause I seem to recall your older brother robbed a grocery store right here in South Philly earlier this year. You want me to hold you responsible for that?"

Angelo shook his head. "N-n-no," he stuttered, protecting his neck with his hands.

Tony pointed at Raven, but his eyes remained on Angelo. "Tell her you're sorry."

"I-I-I'm sorry."

"Now tell her you won't do that dumb shit again," Vincent added.

"I w-w-won't do it again."

"Nah, that ain't what Vincent said. Say exactly what he told you to say, or I'll have to break your fucking arm," Tony growled.

"I won't do that dumb shit again," Angelo blurted in a flurry of words. He turned and scowled at Raven as if she caused the situation he'd gotten himself into.

"Get outta here," Tony barked.

Angelo turned and rushed out the door. His friends were already out on the sidewalk.

Raven watched the boys through the window. Then she turned back to Tony and smiled nervously. Her hands were busy pulling on the hem of her T-shirt. She looked toward the kitchen, wishing Maria would appear.

Tony took his first step in her direction, his eyes still burning with rage.

Raven could feel her heart stop for two full seconds as her fingers burrowed deeper into the edge of the counter to stabilize herself.

Who is this guy?

Chapter Sixty-One

Tony stepped up to the counter, his face softened, and he extended his hand to Raven.

"I'm Tony Bruno, and this is my friend, Vincent DeLuca. We've been friends since we was little. He was a real asshole before he started hanging out with me, but he's ah right now." He chuckled. He leaned closer to her. "He used to beat me up when we was boys." His eyes roved over Vincent. "He ain't big enough to do that now, though."

"Go screw yourself, Tony," Vincent bantered. "I kicked your ass because someone needed to do it and I was there."

Tony punched Vincent in the arm. "Yeah, you did it 'cause you were a degenerate . . . you douchebag."

Tony turned his attention to Raven. He flashed her a sexy smile, and her eyes slid over him.

Raven's limbs were tingling, and her stomach was rolling. She'd never had this reaction to a guy before. *It's only because he put that asshole, Angelo, in his place.*

Raven couldn't dim the smile on her lips. *Jeez, Raven, you look creepy, stop smiling at the guy.* But she couldn't pull her eyes away. The two men were colorful and fun to watch.

Vincent smiled at Raven and extended his hand. "What's your name, doll?"

She pursed her lips. "Raven."

Tony looked at his friend. "You want me to tell him not to call you doll? He don't mean nothing by it. He's ignorant when it comes to women. He's a man whore." He glanced at Vincent. "I don't think she appreciates you calling her doll. She looked like she was smelling a turd when you called her that." He looked at Raven again. "Am I right?"

She blushed. "I don't like it very much." She crinkled her nose. "Hey, thanks for helping me with those guys. Um, Maria is in the back. I should go get her."

Raven wasn't sure who the two men were, but Tony knew Maria so that had to be good. She looked at the man and bit her bottom lip. Raven fought the urge to reach over the counter and run her hand over his muscly arms.

Tony noticed her checking him out. He lifted his chin. "You ain't gotta get her. She knows we were sitting back there." He pointed into the corner of the bakery. "We're good friends with her husband, Salvatore. We all grew up together."

"It must be nice to have friends from childhood. I only had one best friend growing up."

"Oh yeah? Where's she at now?" He looked around dramatically, knowing her friend wasn't there. "She go off to college or something? Anything to get outta Philly, right?"

Raven looked down at her hands. Her rich brown hair fell over her face, and she shook her head. "No. My brother killed her at the school that day."

Tony's smile evaporated. "Oh, I'm sorry to hear that. I can't imagine being without Vincent and Salvatore. I didn't mean to upset you."

Raven pursed her lips. "It's nothing you said. Those guys were another reminder of everything that I lost."

"Tony wouldn't be able to live without me," Vincent chimed in.

Tony gave him a stern look. "This ain't no time to be funny, Vincent. Aren't you hearing what we're talking about?"

Vincent's smile faded and he hung his head. "Yeah. I'm sorry, too," he offered, moving his eyes to Raven. "That kind of talk makes me uncomfortable. I was trying to lighten things up. Seems like it was getting a little depressing."

"Ah right," Tony said, looking at Vincent. "Why don't you go back and wait for me at the table or go in the kitchen and say hello to Maria and Effie? Huh? How about that?"

"Oh yeah. That's a good idea. I could use a dose of Effie. That is one sweet woman."

Raven scoffed. "Effie? Sweet? Are you kidding?"

Vincent smiled. He had a nice smile, but it didn't compare to Tony's. "By sweet I mean she thinks I'm a hunk so she's sugary sweet to me."

"Okay. I'll see you in a while then," Tony sang to move his friend along. "Don't bust Effie's balls. I don't wanna hear no shit from Salvatore again about you hitting on her."

Vincent turned and walked toward the kitchen. Then he looked over his shoulder. "Effie loves it when I hit on her. Besides, I can't help it if I'm an Italian stud that she can't keep her hands off of."

Raven laughed out loud, and Tony joined her.

When Vincent had disappeared behind the kitchen door, Tony focused on Raven again. "So how you been doing? You know, with all the shit you've probably been getting after what happened?"

She shrugged. "I'm fine. It doesn't happen all the time. Not as much as it used to anyway. Things have been better since I came to South Philly. Maria and Effie have been great. Some of the women are rude, you know the ones with school kids." She looked toward the street. "Well, and then there are people like those guys today."

"Aw, don't worry about Angelo and his goons. They ain't nothing."

Raven smirked. "But you're something, huh? I mean the way Angelo cowered when he saw it was you." She looked out at the street again. "What was that all about? Are you a cop or something?"

Tony let out a hearty chuckle. "Me? No, I ain't no cop. I manage shit."

She looked at him, eyebrows raised, anticipating he'd explain more. "Okay. That's it? What do you manage?"

"I manage people, what else?"

O my God. There's that smile again. Tony is killing me with his smile. Holy crap, those lips . . . those perfectly kissable lips.

Chapter Sixty-Two

An hour later, Raven was bustling around the bakery refilling coffee. Maria stood behind the counter watching her. The teen finished, wiped her hands on her apron, and smiled at Maria.

"So, Vincent told me you met him and Tony today?" Maria asked casually.

Raven blushed. "Yeah. They seem nice."

"Nice?" Maria scoffed. "They're two characters straight out of a sitcom." She lowered her chin to her chest. "I've known them since I was sixteen. They both have hearts made of gold for the people they love."

"Did Vincent tell you what Angelo and his friends did to me?"

Maria nodded. "People can be cruel . . . usually because they are ignorant and need to be taught things the hard way. Those young boys haven't been schooled on how to behave. They were rude and obnoxious. That's what you should remember when you think about Angelo and his friends."

"What if they come back here and do that to me again? And Tony isn't here to stop them?"

"They won't harass you again," Maria sang like a songbird.

"How do you know?"

"Because I know. Tony put an end to it," she stated confidently.

Raven frowned, not willing to push it further. "Okay. So, unless you want me to do more out here, I need to head back and help Effie before she has a fit."

"Yes, go. I'm good here."

Raven hurried to the kitchen and put on her rubber apron as she assessed the pile of dirty dishes.

"Hey!"

Raven looked over her shoulder at Effie. "Hey."

"Come over here so I can talk to you."

Raven hung her head, preparing to be berated for being in the bakery too long. "I couldn't come back any sooner, Effie. I had to wait for Maria to say it was okay," she said as she walked toward the woman.

"Oh." Effie jutted her hip out. "You think you know me now? You know what I'm gonna say? You better think again." She pinched her lips together.

Raven let out a nervous giggle. "Okay. So what's up then?"

"I wanna talk to you about Tony Bruno. I looked out there earlier. I saw you making googly eyes at him. Looking all smitten and goofy."

The blood rushed to Raven's face. "I did not." She sang the words in the high-pitched tone of someone who was embarrassed *and* guilty.

"Listen, I don't care if you like the boy, who ain't no boy, by the way. Tony's twenty-eight years old. That's ten years older than you. You're practically jailbait," she bit, looking her up and down.

"O my God, stop it." She giggled like a ten-year-old. "By the way, I'll be nineteen soon."

"That don't matter. He's older than you and got a lot more life experience. I know he don't sleep around much. I don't really understand why. All the single women around here are lusting after his handsome ass." She rolled her eyes at her own words. "But that's not the point," Effie barked.

"Okay, so what's the point then?"

"The point is, Tony is one of the most feared mafia men in Philadelphia. The most revered mobster who has ever belonged to the Morano family. The man is very powerful, especially here in South Philly. I think you should know that before you throw yourself at him and offer to have his rug rats."

"You're so charming." Raven chuckled. Then she narrowed her eyes. "You said a mobster? Tony told me he manages people."

"He manages them all right." Effie shook her head in disgust. "Open your eyes, Raven. Did you really believe him?"

"No, I guess I didn't. But I didn't give it much thought. So then Maria's husband Salvatore Morano . . . is the king?"

Effie chuckled. "Damn, you really need to get out more. Not the king, you fool, the Godfather. But no, he ain't. Salvatore's father Johnny is the Godfather. Tony and Vincent grew up with Salvatore. They are his guys, if you know what I mean."

The teen nodded. "I think I do. Like Tony and Vincent are his bodyguards?"

Effie shrugged. "Something like that, but more serious. They don't mess around, and they don't take no shit."

Raven lifted her chin. "But Tony was so nice to me."

Effie smirked. "That's right. Because Tony Bruno is also one of the nicest men you'll ever meet. Outside of the stuff he does to make money, Tony is a sucker for an underdog. He doesn't like to see people get jacked up for no good reason. That's why everyone around here loves him."

Raven's eyes flitted around the kitchen. She'd read about mobsters in books and seen them in movies she'd watched. But she never actually talked to one. With this information, she could see why Angelo was so afraid of Tony. A slow smile spread over her lips.

"Are you telling me I should stay away from Tony?" she asked.

Effie shook her head. "No, I'm trying to learn you on who you're dealing with, that's all."

"Okay, thank you."

Raven moved back to the sink and started washing the dirty pans. As she did, she thought about the unexplained things regarding Maria that now made sense. The duplicate phone line in her house, not being overly worried about Jester, and her statement that she'd tell people on the streets to keep their eyes and ears open. It was all coming together, and Raven couldn't decide if she was scared or excited to be near it all. It was nice being in with a group that protected each other. She'd spent her life being vulnerable to people stronger than her, and now, she was surrounded by the strongest people in the city of Philadelphia.

She let out a satisfied sigh and went back to washing pans.

Chapter Sixty-Three: One Month Later

Christmas in South Philadelphia was thrilling for Raven. People were happy and pleasant. There was an excitement in the air, an energy of kindness and community, unlike North Philadelphia where the mood never changed and the darkness never lifted. Even the customers at the bakery, who were normally grumpy, wore a semi smile and uttered a "Merry Christmas" after paying for their goods.

"Better get yourself ready," Effie told Raven.

"For what?"

"Tomorrow is Christmas Eve, ain't it?"

"Yeah, so what happens on Christmas Eve? Is Santa coming?" she giggled. "Oh, I hope he brings me a million dollars."

Effie lowered her face and shook her head. "Damn snot-nosed kid. Hell, you don't know nothin' . . . I gotta teach you everything." She gave her a playful smile. "That's the day we work our balls off."

Raven rolled her eyes. "I don't have balls, Effie."

The older woman scoffed. "You will tomorrow. Trust me. So here's what's gonna happen. We need to be in here by one a.m. . . . I'll pick you up on my way in."

"One in the morning? Why? That's five hours earlier than normal."

Effie was brimming with excitement but scrutinized the teen with wide eyes. She bounced on her toes and clasped her hands together. "You know those panettone cakes we make?"

"Yeah, they're delicious—part cake and part bread. Why?"

"Well," Effie said, leaning her arm against the wall. "We need to make about two hundred of them. Everyone comes in here on Christmas Eve to buy them fresh. We've been doing it for years. People place their orders months in advance. It's an all-hands-on-deck thing."

"Ooookay, what does that mean?"

"It means that you'll be baking and so will Maria. All three of us will be filling the orders to meet the demand. Maria's mother-in-law, Mrs. Morano, comes in to work the front and that ain't no small thing to have Johnny Morano's wife working with the customers. Plus, Maria will bring in a couple of kids she knows to do dishes and stuff."

"Wait, I'm being promoted from dishwasher to baker?" Raven asked, smiling.

Effie nodded. "Don't get too excited. It's only for one day." The woman poured two ten-pound bags of flour into the industrial mixer. "What'd you buy Maria for Christmas?"

Raven looked up at her with wide eyes.

"You didn't get her nothing?" Effie chided.

"I didn't know I was supposed to," she whined. "Now what am I gonna do?"

"You're gonna give me fifteen dollars and I'll put your name on the thirty-dollar gift I bought from the two of us."

Wearing a rubber apron, Raven rushed over to Effie and hugged her.

"Ew, now. Don't go hugging me when you're wearing that nasty thing," Effie insisted.

Raven held the woman tighter and clung on for a while.

Effie knew Raven was waiting to be hugged back. She put her arms around Raven's waist and hugged her closely. After a few seconds, she pulled back.

"I've never got to enjoy Christmas before—I mean, after my dad died," Raven explained.

Effie had to stifle a gasp. The girl was so honest and vulnerable, that it shook her to the core. "All right now," she barked. "Back to work. Enough of this holly-jolly bullshit."

Raven grinned and assumed her position at the sink. She started singing a Christmas song and Effie yelled from across the kitchen. "Hey, Frank Sinatra. Did you buy Cecilia something? You better say yes."

"Of course I did. That's who I'm spending Christmas with." Raven looked down at the dishes she was rinsing. A thought struck her hard. Then she wiped her hands and went back over to Effie. "Who are you spending Christmas with?"

Effie wouldn't make eye contact. "What's it matter to you?"

Raven shook her head. "You're staying home by yourself?"

"Yeah, so what? I've done it for years. It ain't no big deal."

Raven tucked her hair behind her ears. "It is to me. This will be the first Christmas I'm celebrating since I was a kid. You can't ruin it for me by making me think about you all alone. You have to eat dinner with me and Cecilia."

Effie's head snapped in the girl's direction. She bit her bottom lip. "I can't go to that old woman's house. She don't even know me."

"What are you talking about? She knows you. I complain about you every night at dinner." Raven giggled and poked the woman in the side.

"Yeah, well, she probably knows you're a whining baby and would rather listen to you moan than tell you to shut the hell up."

Raven took Effie's wrist gently in her hand. "I'm serious. We would love to have you for dinner. It'll be so much fun. Pleeeease," she begged.

"You're for real?" Effie asked.

Raven heard the hope behind the question.

"I'm totally for real. We're eating at five. Is that good for you?"

Effie nodded, misty-eyed. "Yeah, that'll be real nice. Tell Cecilia I'm bringing a fresh baked panettone. Can't even get your hands on one from Palermo Brothers, but I got connections," she joked.

"I'll tell her. I'm sure she'll be excited."

Raven walked back toward the sink.

"Raven?" Effie called.

The girl turned around. "Yeah?"

"Thank you. It's real nice of you to invite me over."

Raven was touched. She had done something good for someone she cared about. "No problem."

Now Raven had to go home and tell Cecilia they were having a guest for dinner. She hoped the woman wouldn't be upset with her. After all, she loved to show off her cooking. It was turning out to be a good Christmas, and Raven was filled with excitement and anticipation that the next few days would be spent making good memories and forgetting about the bad ones.

***

Later that night, while eating dinner, Raven rested her fork on the side of her plate and looked at Cecilia.

"What is it? Don't you like the pork?" Cecilia asked.

Raven nodded. "Are you kidding? I love it. You're the best cook in South Philly." She was buttering up the old woman, but it was true.

"Hm, okay. You're flattering me for no reason. What happened?"

"I did something today."

Cecilia cracked a smile. "Well, stop looking so dreadful, and don't keep me waiting anymore. What did you do?"

"I invited Effie here for Christmas dinner. She's all alone on Christmas . . . I couldn't stand to think of her having no one . . . and I thought it would be nice," she gushed. "I know I should've asked you first, but I got so caught up in the moment that I blurted it out."

Cecilia smiled and shook her head. "Oh please. Pull yourself together. I'm happy to have someone join us. In the old days, there were so many people in this house on Christmas you had to walk sideways. You did good. It'll be nice."

"Whew! Okay, great."

Cecilia patted the girl's hand. "Now, finish your dinner."

Raven smiled and picked up her fork. "You're really cool for . . . for . . ."

"An older person? Is that what you're trying to say?"

"Yeah."

"I know."

Raven silently counted her blessings for how good her life had become.

Chapter Sixty-Four

Effie was right. Raven had underestimated the level of energy it would take to get through Christmas Eve day. As soon as they reached the bakery, the older woman started barking orders.

"Let's go. Set the ovens and start pulling the flour and sugar from the back."

"Aye-aye, captain," Raven sang. It was exciting to be involved in something that took a group of people. Everyone working together for the same outcome. Raven lifted a ten-pound bag of flour from the back shelf and brought it into the kitchen. "How many of these do we need?"

Effie glanced at her. "All but one. Leave it for the day after Christmas. It'll keep me until we get our next delivery."

"All of them? Effie, there's like four bags back there."

"Yes, all of them. Come on, now. We need to get moving."

By the time Raven was done lugging bags of flour and sugar, she was already exhausted, and the kitchen was an amazing place of activity and scrumptious smells.

Raven had never seen or been a part of anything like it. People from different parts of Philadelphia came into the bakery to get their panettone. There was a lot of laughter and happy greetings, and for a moment, she wished the world would stay frozen in that time and space.

***

By three that afternoon, the crowds had dwindled and they were all putting things away. Maria tapped Raven on the shoulder.

"I want you and Effie to come into my office."

Raven glanced at Effie, who gave her a nod. She followed the two women inside. On Maria's desk were two gift bags.

"Merry Christmas," Maria announced, handing each a bag.

"You go first," Effie said to Raven, enjoying the glint in the girl's eyes.

Raven sat on the chair. "It's so beautiful I don't want to open it."

Effie pinched her lips together. "Well, you ain't gonna know what's inside if you don't open the damn thing. When was the last time you got a present?"

The teen lifted her eyes to the ceiling. "Hm. That's a tough one. Let's see . . . Oh, for my eighth birthday, my hooker friend, Skye—gave me finger puppets, and my dad gave me a potato head doll. I lost both presents when CPS pulled us out of my mom's care." She shook her head. "Man, I haven't thought about that in forever." Her eyes welled and she dabbed at them and looked at Effie.

"That's about as sad as it gets," Effie remarked. "Shit, I got presents from homeless people. It might've been something they found in the trash, but it was still a present." The woman shook her head and glanced at Maria.

"Well, you should open the present I bought you," Maria said, trying not to cry with Raven.

Raven pulled the paper out and inside the bag was a blue box tied with a white ribbon. She lifted and studied the package. Then she untied the bow and pulled open the lid. There was a necklace nestled on a board covered in blue velvet.

"Wow," she said, her eyes growing wide. She lifted the chain into her hands and looked at the round pendant. Engraved on the silver disk was *la famiglia*. Raven's gaze slid over to Maria.

Maria smiled, her beautiful face lighting up with genuine affection for the girl. "It means family. That's what you are to us. You're part of our family."

Overwhelmed with emotion, Raven lowered her face and placed a hand over her eyes. At first, the two women watched her. Then her shoulders shook, and a small moan escaped her as she bawled. "Th-th-th-thank you so much!" she choked out. "It's been a long time since I had a family."

Maria hurried around the desk and put her arm over Raven's shoulder. "Thank you," she said quietly. "For being loyal and trustworthy. You must read the card."

Raven's hands shook as she opened the envelope and pulled out the card. It read:

Raven, Not all families share the same blood. Real family stands by you in the good times and the bad. Welcome to the family. Love, Maria and Salvatore

Raven put her hand on her forehead. "I've never even met Salvatore." Her voice quivered. "How can he like me and not know me?" It was an innocent question.

"Salvatore knows you through me," Maria answered affectionately. "If I trust you, then he knows that you are good. It's very simple in our world when it isn't complicated. Merry Christmas, Raven."

The two hugged and then Maria put the necklace on for the teen. After Effie opened her gift and they gave Maria their joint gift, it was time to go home.

The three stood at the back door. "I'll see you both the day after Christmas. Have a wonderful holiday."

"Same to you," Effie said, hugging Maria.

"I'll see you at Cecilia's at five o'clock," Raven said to Effie.

"Yep, see you then."

As Raven walked home, she took in the Christmas lights lining the store windows and the lit trees inside the front windows of people's houses. For the first time, Raven understood why people say Christmas is magical.

Chapter Sixty-Five

After Raven and Cecilia finished eating dinner on Christmas Eve, the teenager sat in the living room with the old woman next to her and gazed at the Christmas tree. She admired the lights glistening off of the glass balls. She soaked in the peacefulness and warmth inside the home. Her eyes moved toward the top of the tree. Tucked up high was an elf with his hands sewn together and wrapped around his knees.

Cecilia had called it the knee-hugger elf. He was jolly in his red suit, white collar, and Santa hat. Decades later, people would call them Elf on the Shelf, but for Cecilia it was bittersweet. It was a nostalgic reminder of a simpler time, the people who were gone, and the years that trailed behind her.

Cecilia glanced at Raven. "The Christmas tree is like looking at the stars in the sky on a clear night. Now, as I get older, it also symbolizes the good things from my past. What do you think about as you look at our tree?"

Raven gave Cecilia a weak smile. "I was thinking about my dad. He used to have the same elf you have on your tree." She pointed to the knee-hugging elf.

"Oh yes. They were quite the rage in the good old days. The knee-hugger elves were sold in the fifties and sixties mainly to lower- and lower-middle-class families. Everyone in the neighborhood had one. We were told to place them high up in our Christmas tree so it could see the whole family during the holidays."

Raven squinted at her. "Huh?"

Cecilia nodded, her gray hair bouncing. "That's right. It would watch over everyone and bring us good luck." She found Raven's eyes. "In those days, having good luck meant the family would have great health. We cared about each other more back then. Don't get me wrong. There's nothing terrible about having money . . . until, of course, there is."

"What do you mean? I want to have a lot of money someday and I'll still care about people."

"Yes, it's very nice to have money—even a lot of it. But when people earn money by hurting others . . . well, then it becomes greed. And greed turns into hostility. The secret is, that if you have money, no one needs to know about it. Only you and maybe your husband if you're married." She laughed. "Do you see yourself marrying one day?"

Raven nodded. "Yes, and I hope to have at least two kids. I always wanted a family after my dad died. I wasn't lucky enough to find one in foster care. I met some great people along the way, but I haven't talked to any of them in a long time. I don't even know where they are."

"Well, that's because some people are meant to be in our lives for a visit and others are meant to move in permanently. Those that come for a visit either teach us how not to be or show us the best way to be."

"Yeah, well, I wish I didn't have the rotten people stop in for a visit. They brought suffering. I'll take the people who wanna move into my life permanently." She smiled at the woman. "People like you. I never had a grandmother. Well, I guess I had one, but I never met her. My parents grew up in foster care. You're the only grandmother I ever had."

Cecilia patted the teen's hand. "Yes, and I've never had children, so you fill the same need inside of me. Sometimes God brings the right people together. To get them through phases. Like you told me about your friend, Bitsy. It's very fortunate she had you in the end." She shook her finger at the girl. "That's divine intervention."

"Then I wish God had divinely intervened for me when I was a kid." She scoffed. "I know that sounds bitter, but it makes no sense why some kids suffer, some kids create the suffering for others, and some kids barely suffer at all. How do you figure that works?"

"Oh, honey. If I knew that, I'd be living in some exotic land not having to put up with my neighbor, Sofia."

Raven chuckled. "Stop. You love Sofia. I know it's true and so do you."

Cecilia nodded. "You're right, I do. But that woman has a way of getting on my nerves like no other." The old woman lifted her coffee from the end table and took a sip. "Tomorrow morning you and me will start early to prepare Christmas dinner."

"Oh man. All you people in South Philly with these early start times," she teased.

"I almost forgot. You've been up since midnight. You should go off to bed and get some sleep. I'll see you in the morning," Cecilia said.

Raven got to her feet, leaned over the woman, and hugged her. "See you in the morning. Merry Christmas, Cecilia." Then she took one last look at the lights on the tree and made a wish that her life would always be as bright and hopeful as this moment.

Chapter Sixty-Six

By the third of January, everyone was back at work and the holiday spirit was long gone, put away like the Christmas decorations until the next year.

Raven overheard customers complaining about their Christmas bills from credit card purchases. Or they were angry that they had to return to work because they enjoyed being home with their family.

Meanwhile, Raven was grateful to have a job, a place to live, and a family. Work didn't bother her. She enjoyed the social aspect, being involved with other people, and having women who gave her solid advice. It was something she'd missed her entire life.

Raven was wiping off a table when she heard the bell over the door ring. She looked over her shoulder to welcome the person, but she froze. She couldn't believe it. She pulled back her shoulders and approached the woman.

"Trudy?"

The woman narrowed her eyes. Raven could see by the condition of her clothes and dirt smears on her face that Trudy was living on the streets. The woman's stunningly beautiful face was dirty and stressed. Her long brown hair was matted and tangled, and her honey-colored eyes had lost their glimmer. Raven got closer to the woman.

"Trudy, it's me, Raven."

"Holy shit! Raven!" Trudy yelled, throwing her arms around the girl's neck. "You sure are a sight for sore eyes. What are you doing here?"

"I work here," Raven answered proudly.

"You do? Well, do you think maybe you could spare a hot cup of coffee and a bite to eat?"

"Of course. Come on." Raven grabbed the woman's hand and brought her into the kitchen. She sat her down at the four-person break table she and Effie used.

"Who do we have here?" Effie asked, eyeing the woman up and down.

"This is Trudy. We met in a shelter—the one I told you about? Anyway, Trudy kept me safe when I lived there. She's the one who taught me how to fight." Raven smiled at Effie, then raised her eyebrows, a subtle warning to be nice.

"Did she now?" Effie said, sitting next to the woman. "I'd like to thank you for helping my girl. She's a good kid. Kind of a pain in my ass sometimes, but she's grown on me."

Trudy looked at Raven and smiled. "Yes, she is worthy of all the good things that come her way. That's for sure." She opened her eyes wider. "How about that hot coffee and the food you promised?"

Raven gave her a warm smile. "Coming right up." Then she hurried out of the kitchen.

Effie's smile dropped and she stared into the woman's face. "Did you know Raven worked here?"

Trudy shook her head. "Honestly, I knew she was in South Philly, but I didn't know she was working."

"Was you looking for her today?" Effie pressed.

"Not actively, but I wouldn't have no problem if I ran into her." Trudy leaned forward. "I ain't here to hustle her if that's what you're worried about. I would never do anything to hurt Raven Ledger. I love that girl probably the same as you. All I want is something to fill my empty belly and to spend a little time with a girl I cared for not too long ago. You ain't got nothing to be concerned about with me."

"Okay, but I want you to know that Raven has a decent life now. She's got a job here with me and a place to live. She's doing good and I don't want nothing to disrupt that. She's cut out to do something better with her life. And right now, she's building good character and work ethic so it can carry her to the next destination. So, you can sit awhile, eat, and catch up. But then you gotta go, 'cause if you don't, she'll want to take care of you."

Trudy nodded. "I know what you're saying is true. It's all good. I ain't promising I'll never come back and see her again. It would be stupid of me not to want to keep in touch with the girl." She leaned forward and narrowed her eyes. "I helped her the same as you. Understand?"

Effie nodded and stood. "That's fine, but I want you to keep it real."

"You got it."

Raven rushed back into the kitchen with a huge smile. "Here you go. It's so good to see you, Trudy. How did everything work out at the Last Call?"

Trudy sipped the hot coffee and took a big bite of the blueberry muffin Raven had picked for her. She shook her head. "Man, things got all jacked up in there. I couldn't take it anymore. They put"—she lowered her voice so Effie couldn't overhear her—"too many ex-cons in one place. A short time after you left, it seemed like I was back in the can with a bunch of women fighting each other."

"What about the staff? They just let it happen?"

"Ah, several of the people changed out for younger ones. The new ones don't give a rat's ass what happens in that shelter."

Raven nodded. "So you're living on the streets then?"

"Yeah, I almost forgot how brutal the winters can be."

"There's a shelter downtown called the Center City House. I stayed there after I left the Last Call. It's pretty decent. You need to get there by noon, or you won't get a bed for the night. They have good food and hot showers. Keep your stuff with you or it'll get lifted."

Raven sat back for a moment, fondly remembering it was the same advice that Bitsy had given her.

Trudy pulled out a piece of paper and pen from her bag. "Let me write that name down."

Raven watched. "Do you have any money?"

Trudy shook her head. "Unless you call the three dollars in my pocket having money."

The teen frowned. It was painful watching Trudy suffer. Raven reached into her pocket and pulled out her twenty-dollar emergency fund money. She carried it with her daily.

"Here." She pushed the bill forward. "It's all I got on me, and I want you to take it. Use it only on things that you absolutely need."

Effie watched from the other side of the kitchen. A tinge of a smile played on her lips.

When Trudy was done with her muffin and coffee, she stood to leave. "All right. I'm gonna head to the Center City House. Man, I can't wait to get a shower tonight."

Raven stood and hugged the woman. Though Trudy smelled of urine and the sweet, pungent odor that homeless people carry from not showering regularly, she closed her arms around the woman tighter. "I made you a bag of goodies to go. Come on, I'll walk you out."

When Raven returned to the kitchen, Effie was eyeballing her.

"Why are you looking at me like that?" the teen asked.

"I see how you were with that woman. You were kind."

"Why wouldn't I be? She helped me when I needed her. She took me under her wing and made sure I was safe."

Effie nodded. "It's good to remember what people have done in the past. Most people like to pretend that the past didn't happen, that it wasn't real, and that only their fucked-up thoughts of today count."

"There's a lesson in all that, right?"

The older woman nodded. "Yes. I like that you're clear on remembering what actually happened in the past and don't make up things that never existed."

"You mean like if I decided Trudy must've done something and deserves to be homeless? Basically, thinking she's bad now and forgetting the good she has done?"

"Yep, exactly. The key to good relationships is remembering that distinction. It'll keep you grounded, too. You'll lose a friend or family member in the blink of an eye if you accuse them of doing things they've never done... or saying things they never said. But not you, Raven Ledger. Your heart is kind. People might not always see it, but I do."

Raven hugged Effie. "Did you like Trudy? What did you say to her?"

"I told her not to fuck up your life."

Raven's mouth dropped open. "No, you didn't. Trudy would never do that to me."

Effie pinched her lips and shook her head. "Yeah, well, I needed to make sure. It seems like she's ah right. She ain't as cool as me, though."

The teen laughed. "You didn't hurt her feelings, did you?" she asked, worried.

"Girl, please. I hurt everyone's feelings. Trudy ain't no exception, but I think we ended it on a good note. I saw you give her your emergency money."

Raven smiled. "Well, she was my emergency."

"You're a good egg, Ledger. Now get your ass back to work."

Chapter Sixty-Seven: Nine Months Later

Raven had tried her best to become integrated into the community. But more than a year and a half after the shootings, she was still being shunned and treated poorly by certain people who didn't trust her being in their tight-knit neighborhood.

Raven was working the counter when two women she didn't know walked into the bakery. They were in their thirties, both gossiping homemakers with school-age children. They got to the back of the line and talked loud enough so everyone could hear them.

One of the women gestured, lifting her chin in Raven's direction. "Jesus, Sienna, I heard that girl works here but I didn't believe it."

"I know, Beatrice. What is this world coming to? I think it's ridiculous. Everyone here should be upset," Sienna stated.

"Yeah, I wonder if everyone knows her brother shot up that school. She's his twin sister. You know what they say, rotten apples don't fall too far from the family nut tree." She cackled. "She's an element no one wants in their community. People like her turn good neighborhoods bad."

"I know. I'm glad we don't live here no more. I'm surprised that Maria lets her work here. I thought the Moranos cared about the community. Then they go and hire someone like her. It doesn't make any sense. I'll tell you, it's always something."

Raven had pretended not to hear them. The inside of her chest was aching and burning, as though she'd swallowed a bee hive. She filled her lungs with air, hoping to suck in patience and bravery. That was when Maria came out of the back and stood at the counter as Sienna and Beatrice approached to place their order.

"Oh, good morning, Maria," Sienna said in a nasally tone. "You look gorgeous. I'd kill for a body like yours after having a baby."

Maria gave the woman a polite smile. "Good morning, Sienna." She moved her eyes to Beatrice. "How do you like living in the suburbs?"

"Oh, it's wonderful," Beatrice sang.

"Yeah, good. What can I get for you two?"

Beatrice shot a look at Raven with her nose turned up and lips pinched together. When Maria noticed, she leaned her head to one side and stared into Beatrice's eyes. Maria watched her, unblinking, until Beatrice looked away.

When the two women left with their baked goods, Maria turned to Raven. "I heard everything that ugly rat said about you . . . and me. Some of the women who come in here, like Sienna and Beatrice, have nothing better to do with their time than to spend it acting like vicious children. You have to let people's ignorance roll off of your back, learn to ignore them."

Raven's face and neck were bright red, and she rolled her eyes. "Believe me, I'd love to. But how am I supposed to ignore people like that?"

Maria got into Raven's personal space. "Well, the thing is, you see Sienna and Beatrice?"

"Yeah."

"Everyone in the Italian Market knows that their husbands cheat on them. They know it, too. So they criticize others to make themselves feel better. They have to convince each other that people have worse lives than they do—that's how they can stay in their marriages. I find that mean people are the weakest and most troubled. It makes no sense, I know. But that's who you're dealing with. Let that information give you some perspective on how unimportant their opinion is of you."

Raven smirked. "Thanks."

As Raven went back into the kitchen to do her work, she thought about the people in her life who had treated her poorly. There was truth in Maria's words. It *was* the most damaged and pathetic people who had hurt her throughout her life.

When will people learn that they don't need to knock someone down to lift themselves up?

***

THE TWIN SISTER

It was early evening by the time Raven had washed the dishes. With more responsibilities, Raven was working longer hours like Effie. She walked to the kitchen door and glanced out the front window of the bakery. It was October and her least favorite time of year. The days were short and the sun fell early. She woke up in the dark and left work in the dark.

She had complained to Effie the day before. *'It would be fine if we were all vampires, but since we're not, we all can't be deprived of sunlight . . . and I hate it!'*

Raven was lost in thought when Effie floated up behind her.

"When you get done staring out the front window, make sure you go back and clean up that flour you spilled earlier," Effie stated.

Raven turned around. "I did clean it, Effie. I did it twice."

"Well," the woman said, shaking her head, "then you best go clean it a third time. And this time, make sure you get all the crevices clean."

"Why can't you take the towel and the bottle of cleaner and help me? I still have to put away all the utensils so we're ready for the morning."

"Oh, are you getting flip with me now? Mixing up your job and mine? I don't know why you'd do that—I ain't nothing but good to you. In case you forgot, I got my own work to do . . . I have to prep things for the morning, too, you know. I can't be doing your work on top of mine. Now go on and clean it up, like I told you to," Effie said with her hands firmly on her hips.

Raven stomped deeper into the kitchen and threw a rag down. Then she stormed over to the shelf and grabbed a bottle of cleaning fluid. After, she scrubbed at the table in exaggerated movements while scowling at Effie.

When she was finished, Raven looked up at her. "I'm sorry. I didn't mean to be rude. I had a bad day because of those two bitches, Beatrice and Sienna. Maria talked to me about it and made me feel better, but I really want to tell both of them to go fuck off. It's hard keeping my mouth shut."

"Why are you worrying about those two old hags? They don't know nothing. What did they say?"

"You know, the same stuff about my brother and I'm rotten like he was." She lowered her voice to a whisper. "And that they don't know why the Moranos let me work here if they care about the neighborhood so much."

The older woman smiled to herself. She considered Raven more like a daughter than a coworker. She was impressed that the girl kept moving forward through all the ungodly aggravating circumstances that had been thrown at her.

"Why the fuck do you care what they think?" She tapped the pendant Raven was wearing around her neck. "Family. Remember? That was given to you by Maria and Salvatore Morano. You're their family, and you're my family, and Cecilia's. You need to let it go and forget about those bitches." She turned and walked away but then stopped short. "Oh, now make sure you clean that flour up real good."

Raven rolled her eyes and wiped down the table again. Ten minutes later, Raven slogged across the kitchen. She gave Effie a passing glance. "You better make sure my cleaning is up to your liking, Queen Effie."

The woman wagged her finger. "I like that. It's got a good sound to it. You best finish up your work. I can give you a ride home tonight if you want. It's gonna storm."

"No, thanks. I don't want a ride. I'll walk. It's not far. Oh, and Effie, thanks for all those things you said about me and family. It means a lot."

Effie clucked her tongue. "It's all true. But listen, you're being downright stupid not getting a lift from me. I know you're a ten-minute walk from here, but why would you do that when I can give you a ride? Have you seen the weather forecast?"

Raven nodded. "Yeah, I saw. It's going to rain. I think the walk will do me good. I need time to myself before I go back to Cecilia's. She knows everything. It's like she's got some kind of radar . . . If I'm upset, she immediately starts asking me a million questions. I don't want to tell her about the same thing over and over again. Did I tell you someone called me the killer's twin yesterday?" She looked over her shoulder. "It makes me sick. I love this bakery and I love living at Cecilia's. I wish I could make all the dumb people shut up, though."

Effie softened and moved to the girl. She put her arm over her shoulder. "Nobody said life is easy. Try and focus on the good things you mentioned, like me and the bakery and that old lady you live with." She gave the girl a playful smile. "Better be careful. You might get so attached to me you won't wanna be without me. Now, are you sure you don't want a ride?"

Raven shook her head. "No, thank you. I'm good. And for the record, you'll never be out of my life. You're already a part of me. That means you're stuck with me for good."

Effie giggled. "Oh brother, lucky me!" She grabbed her jacket. "The weather is going to be nasty. It'll start raining soon. You're gonna regret not taking the ride home."

"I won't melt," Raven remarked.

But Raven could have no way of knowing how much she'd regret not taking Effie up on her offer.

Chapter Sixty-Eight

Raven left the bakery thirty minutes later. She left through the front where it wasn't as dark. As she stepped onto the sidewalk, the wind sliced against her face and ears. She shivered and pulled the hood of her sweatshirt up. She shoved her hands into the front pockets and walked. She couldn't shake her anger. After all this time, she wasn't willing to be bullied anymore. The more she thought about Sienna and Beatrice, the angrier she became at everyone who treated her poorly.

She was deep in thought and had stopped paying attention to where she was going several blocks back. She had wanted to walk off her frustration before it started to rain anyway. She didn't want to burden Cecilia with her day-to-day struggles with people. Cecilia was protective and would want to fix the problem for her.

As she moved farther away from the bakery, the wind cut at her exposed skin from every angle. She rolled her shoulders forward, pressed her face down, and peered up with her eyes. But the wind was making her eyes water, and she was having a hard time seeing her way. There were a few people out on the streets, but the majority had taken cover from the fast, approaching storm.

Annoyingly, the rain started. It was a drizzle that quickly turned to a steady pour. The drops hit her from the top and sides. The wind was whipping at her from all directions, and the rain pelted her from every angle. It was a storm where umbrellas are useless and having them becomes another battle.

She strained to see a few feet ahead through the falling rain. "I'm such an idiot. I should've taken that ride from Effie, but noooo, I had to be hardheaded . . . I had to walk it off," she mumbled.

Raven stood on a corner at a traffic light to cross the street. The sound of the storm was roaring in her ears. She watched the wind and rain glide across the road like it was the ocean. She was already soaked. Looking up at the street sign, she shivered.

"Shit," she whispered, realizing in her haste she had walked too many blocks down, away from where she lived.

Now she had to turn back. Wanting to return to Cecilia's house quickly, she cut through the back alleys to zigzag her way home.

Raven hustled. Her senses were firing, and she was on high alert. It was dark and windy. There were no other people around and the city seemed abandoned, like she was living in an apocalyptic movie.

Where is everybody?

An uneasiness trickled through her. Dread wrapped itself around her heavily and stuck to her like a spiderweb. She pushed the hood from her head so she could better hear the sounds of the night over the howling wind and rain. She listened intently and prayed silently not to hear any sounds coming from the darkness.

Rushing home through the back alleys, the sound of the whooshing gusts became less prominent. Now other sounds took over. The wind scraped the trash into the corners of the alley, and a mixture of leaves, paper, and discarded aluminum cans clattered against the brick walls. She heard the patter of rodents scurrying behind her. Their small feet with their sharp nails scratching over the slick pavement. She hurried her step. Her heart beat faster, and all she focused on was getting back to Cecilia's house.

A long blast of wet air pushed at her back and muffled the sounds that were so distinct only moments prior. Her feet squished around on the soggy leaves and trash in the alley. The cold rain had soaked through her sneakers and socks. The heel of her foot rubbed the back of her sneaker, and she could feel a blister forming, tearing at her skin. Ignoring her discomfort, she moved forward quickly.

Raven's heart stopped for a full second when a siren suddenly screamed its rescue call in the far-off distance. *There must be people close by.* She allowed herself to be comforted by the thought.

Raven strained to see against the driving rain. Her arms were at her sides now, hands rolled into fists. She was pumping them back and forth to help quicken her pace. She searched the dark, cold night. There was nothing, but her stomach was spinning, her warning sign that she should be afraid.

The wind stalled for a few seconds. Relieved the storm was ending, she drew a long breath allowing herself to slow down. She could hear again.

THE TWIN SISTER

Then she heard the footsteps. At first, Raven thought she'd imagined the noise. She didn't dare move. She opened her ears and listened.

O God, no.

Footsteps came closer. She could hear them clearly now. She started speed walking through the back alley, peeking over her shoulder every few seconds, waiting to see the boogeyman behind her.

Raven Ledger knew better than to cut through the back alleys on her way home at night. Regret, like an unexpected punch in the face, dropped like a boulder to the pit of her stomach.

Chapter Sixty-Nine

Raven was running, her feet and arms were pumping, but the footsteps barreling toward her were closing the distance between them. She kept slipping and sliding on the wet ground, using walls and whatever balance she could maintain not to fall flat on her face. Her feet kept hitting the shallow puddles of water that had formed on the uneven pavement. Her heart beat wildly. The thumping of her blood in her ears drowned out the heavy footfalls catching up to her. Her skin prickled and her brain was on fire.

Raven could barely catch her breath. She made crass, sharp sounds. *Inhale, exhale, inhale, exhale.*

Feet. She could hear feet slamming and sloshing over the wet ground. Whoever it was, they were almost on her now.

Fuck!

Then she heard more than one set of feet thudding behind her, in loud hammering stomps. Then there were voices. People yelling through the storm.

Raven willed her legs to pump harder, to move faster, to outrun them. But a hand grabbed the hood of her sweatshirt and ground her to a halt.

Raven spun around. She let out a scream, a wave of pent-up fear and anxiety.

"Let me go! Let me go!"

She was swinging her fists at the person holding her steady. It was a man. He was enormous. He absorbed her punches like her fists were made of cotton balls. He gripped her shoulders and smashed her up against the brick wall. She hit the wall hard. Raven wanted to believe the people inside the warm building heard her body slam against the wall and they would run outside to save her.

Raven's hands frantically searched for something in the dark to help her. She glided them over the lightly pitted texture of the brick wall and for an instant took comfort in the familiar feel. She was using the wall to support herself. She dug her fingernails into the grooves of the mortar joints between the bricks. She was winded, and the man's chest was pressed against hers. Then a voice came closer. She couldn't tell how many others. They were on her now, sneering, laughing, and encouraging violence.

"Cut her heart out, Scully," a girl yelled. "Her clock just ran out."

I know that voice.

"She don't deserve to live. You remember all our people she let her brother kill while she stood there and watched. It's time for her blood to spill . . . all of it!"

Holy shit! It's Blanco. I'm going to die in this cold, wet, dark alley.

Raven's jaw was taut as she tried to break free of the man's grip. Her legs were shaking, and she pressed her palms harder against the brick wall.

Think, Raven, think!

She knew this moment would change her life or be her death. There would be nothing in between. She had to fight them . . . all of them.

But how?

Raven drew from her inner strength, all her years of torment, building for this moment. She refused to cry. She could see three shadows behind the person holding her against the wall. Then she closed her eyes to gather her courage and when she opened them, Blanco's nose was an inch from hers.

"You thought you'd get away from the Kensington Hoods, huh? I knew we'd find you eventually. Nobody hides from us and nobody, not even Raven Ledger, gets away with murdering our own. I told you that one day I was going to kill you and now I'm here to make good on that threat."

Raven's heart thudded when she heard the snap of a switchblade springing open and then felt Blanco pressing the tip against her cheek. A trickle of warm blood trailed down her face.

"Hold on," Scully said in a raspy voice. "She ain't getting off that easy. My brother had to beg for his life before her brother shot him. She needs to suffer before we finish her off."

Scully pulled her forward and put Raven's neck in the nook of his elbow, locked between the mass of his forearm and bicep. He pressed his arm closed, like a vice, and the pressure on Raven's neck was unbearable. She flailed, her arms and legs flying spastically, trying to break free. An instant later, Blanco was throwing punches into the side of her head.

They're going to kill me.

THE TWIN SISTER

There was a moment before the world started to fade when Raven embraced death. As the seconds ticked by in slow motion, the only thing she thought about was finally being free.

Chapter Seventy

Raven was barely conscious. Scully kept pressure on her neck until her body went limp and then he released her. She dropped to the pavement like a dead weight. Then the four gang members started kicking her.

Raven could no longer absorb the pain. Her body seemed foreign and her mind drifted, like a boat sailing through fog. The intolerable pain was gone. A comforting sensation came over her, and she welcomed the relief as she left this life. Her body became weightless, as though someone had lifted her from the ground and was carrying her away. She was suddenly warm and she was being cradled, like a baby. She could breathe again. In the distance, she heard several cracks and thuds, like bones breaking under pressure.

Are those my bones?

Scully had deprived her of oxygen for a long time. She continued to fade away, barely clinging to life. Her eyelids fluttered. Then they eased closed. All the pain dissipated and relief replaced her anguish. The cold wet night no longer mattered. She allowed herself to relax into her own passing.

"Get this fuckin' trash outta here. Bring them to the warehouse. I'll be there later," a voice echoed through her head.

Is he talking about me?

"No mistakes," the voice boomed with authority.

"Yeah, we got it. Don't worry," another man chirped.

Raven was drifting from semi-conscious to unconscious. She was confused.

They're taking me somewhere that all the members can watch me die.

The smell of wet cardboard rushed into her sinuses right before she started floating away again. In her mind's eye, she saw a major street coming into view. Suddenly, cold rain dripped inside the neck of her sweatshirt, slid down her chest and over her stomach.

I don't want to feel the cold rain. I want peace.

Raven smelled the exhaust of a car as though she was sitting next to the tailpipe, inhaling its fumes. Then the *cha-chunk* sound of a car door opening.

"Lay her across the seat," the same man's voice ordered. "You got a blanket in the trunk?"

"Yeah."

"Go get it. Put it over her before she freezes to death."

Wait. Who is that? What is happening?

Raven heard the patter of feet moving to the back of the car. The trunk clicked open and banged closed. Then a moment later, she was covered with something soft, and she nestled into it.

"Let's go. Bring her to my apartment. She can't go back to the place she lives looking like this. The old woman will have a fucking heart attack. Stop on the way to my place and pick up Macie. She'll know how to take care of her."

***

A few hours later, Raven's eyes pressed open. She didn't know what was wrong at first. She had the sensation that her skin was too small to fit her face like someone had stretched it too tightly. Her vision was blurred. Then she saw a woman looking down on her. The woman's eyes widened and there was fear etched around her mouth.

"Hello, Raven. I'm Macie, Tony Bruno's sister. You're safe now," the woman said in a lullaby voice.

Tony Bruno. Oh, the guy from the bakery. The good-looking one.

Raven put her hand over her forehead. She cringed at the pain passing through her head and face. "What happened?" she mumbled.

The woman smiled at her. "Just a minute. I'll get Tony. He can fill you in much better than me."

Raven heard heavy footsteps stomping toward her.

"Hey, how are you?" Tony asked. Vincent was standing next to him. They both looked down at her like she was a specimen in a Petri dish.

It was Tony's voice I heard giving orders.

The memory was vague, but it was there. "What happened?" she asked, still disoriented.

Tony chuckled. "You had a situation. You was almost dead. Lucky for you, we was passing that alley and saw what those assholes were doing to you. I already called Maria. She knows you're here."

Raven forced her eyes open as wide as she could. "Tony Bruno and Vincent DeLuca. I remember you two . . . from the bakery last year."

Tony beamed. "That's right." He threw his thumb over his shoulder. "I know why you'd remember me, but I ain't got a clue as to why you would remember Vincent."

She licked her overly dry lips. "You were kind to me," she muttered.

Tony moved closer. "Hey, listen, those gang members really got the better of your face. It's all swollen. Those bastards looked to be taking their whole dark, pathetic, useless lives out on you."

"Right," she murmured. "The Kensington Hoods. What happened to them?"

"That ain't important right now," Tony said. "We can talk about those limp dicks later. How you feeling?"

Raven tried to sit up but, not having the strength, fell back against the soft pillows. "Like someone brought me back from the dead."

Tony nodded. "Yeah, close enough. Thank God for Macie here. She's a real saint. She can cook a meal and mend a broken bone while crocheting a blanket," he said, pointing at his sister. "She's the one who took care of you. She's gonna stay here until you're better."

"Where am I?"

"My apartment," Tony said. "Let me ask you something. What the hell were you doin' out in the rain? You were on the border of South Philly and Center City. It ain't the best part of town. Don't you know it ain't safe?"

"I was on my way home. I was mad and I walked too far. Then it started to rain. I tried to cut through the back alleys to get back to my house quicker," she explained.

"You didn't know the weather people said there was a storm coming?" he asked.

She closed her eyes. "I knew. Effie wanted to drive me home," she admitted. "But I was in a bad mood and thought I'd walk it off."

Tony glanced at Macie and back down at Raven. "Well, I hope you never do that again. You should've listened to Effie. You should always listen to Effie. That woman knows what she's doing, and she's street-smart, too. Even I wouldn't wanna be on the bad side of her."

Vincent rolled his eyes at Tony's comment.

Raven eased her head further into the pillows and pressed her palm against her aching forehead. "Can I use your telephone? I have to call the lady I live with, Cecilia. She'll be worried about me."

"You don't need to worry about that," Macie said, giving her brother a stern look. "Maria already took care of it. She told Cecilia she needed you to take a trip to New York to buy some supplies she couldn't buy here." Macie turned to Tony. "She needs to rest. She's exhausted. You two need to get out of here."

Raven reached her hand up to the woman. "There were four gang members. I knew one of them, the woman. The men? Did they . . . rape me?" She could barely get the words out.

Macie's eyes pivoted to Tony's. He shook his head.

"No," Macie said in an assuring tone. "You were fully dressed when Tony found you."

Raven dragged her eyes to Tony's. "Is that true? 'Cause you can tell me. I'd rather know."

Tony nodded. "Look, I don't know what happened to you before I got there, but I found you with your clothes on. Your jeans were soaking wet, so I can't figure how those assholes would get them down and put them back up. Macie had to cut 'em off of you."

Raven lifted the covers and looked down at herself. She was wearing a pair of flannel pajamas. "Where did these clothes come from?"

Macie smiled. "I brought them with me. Just so you know, I was alone in this room when I undressed you and put the pajamas on."

"Th-th-thank you," Raven stammered, relieved that Macie was there.

Macie narrowed her eyes at Tony, who was gawking at the girl. She hadn't seen that silly grin on his face in a long time. She wanted to smile, but this wasn't the time, so she frowned at him. Tony noticed her glaring and shoved his hands into his front pockets like a small boy being scolded by his mother.

Macie sat on the edge of the bed next to Raven. She lifted the girl's hand. "Listen, you need to rest. There's nothing for you to worry about. I will take care of whatever you need. I'm going to sleep in here with you tonight. Also, a doctor will be here in a bit to look you over . . . to make sure nothing is broken."

Raven nodded. "Thank you for staying with me." Her eyes eased closed, and she was asleep again.

THE TWIN SISTER

Raven dreamed about being back in the alley with the gang. She was panicking . . . they were touching her. She thrashed for a few moments until the doctor finished examining her while she was asleep.

When he finished, her subconscious took her to a place of comfort as her dreams turned to nothingness.

Chapter Seventy-One

Raven woke in the morning inside a peaceful room. She stared up at a bright white ceiling fifteen feet above her head.

Where am I?

She sat up slowly. Macie was sleeping on a sofa a few feet away.

Right, I'm in Tony Bruno's apartment.

Her left eye was almost swollen shut. Seeing life through a sliver was strange, but her right eye was almost open.

"Macie?" Raven murmured.

Macie's eyes popped open. "Oh, good morning."

"Good morning. I'm sorry to wake you, but I need to go to the bathroom."

Macie waved her off. "It's fine. How are you feeling?"

The right side of Raven's face lifted into a smile. The left side was puffy and bruised. "Like someone beat the crap outta me."

Macie padded across the floor in her bare feet and sat on the edge of the bed. "You'll feel better in a few days. The doctor doesn't think you need to go to the hospital unless you start vomiting or have persistent headaches. He said you are very lucky that nothing was broken."

"I slept while he examined me?" she asked, crossing her arms over her chest.

"Kind of. You fought him, so we thought you were awake, but he realized you were sleeping. I was surprised you didn't wake up, but the doctor wasn't. He explained it was most likely the physical and emotional trauma that you'd been through."

Raven slowly moved her legs over the edge of the bed. "That's crazy. I know you told me that Maria contacted Cecilia, but she probably didn't believe her." She pushed the covers off.

"You might be right, but I'm sure Maria made her feel better. She can be very convincing."

The girl lowered her eyes. "Last night is a blur, and I appreciate everything that you've done. I need to get back to Cecilia today. She's all alone there."

"All in due time. Let's give it a few days and see how you're doing. Cecilia is a lovely woman, but I don't think she'd understand if she saw you in this condition." She lowered her voice. "You haven't seen yourself in the mirror yet. Cecilia might worry that you're worse than you are."

Raven lowered her face. "So, your brother . . . Tony found me?"

Macie nodded.

"He found me and brought me here?"

"Yes. Do you remember being attacked?"

Raven nodded. "I remember. The Kensington Hoods. What happened to them? Did Tony call the police? They're going to come back for me. They're the Kensington Hoods. They hate me because my brother killed some of their members."

Macie patted her thigh. "Yes, I know the story. Tony will be in shortly, and you can ask him all the questions you want. I can hear his shower running." She leaned into Raven. "Although I have to warn you, Tony isn't very good about sharing information. He kind of hoards it. So you may have to work harder to get it out of him."

Macie helped Raven from the bed and into the bathroom.

She propped her hands on the sink and looked into the mirror. "Holy shit!"

"Yes, that's why I was saying going home to Cecilia wouldn't be a good idea."

Raven turned her head to the side. "Did I lose any teeth?" She opened her mouth as wide as she could.

"No, you didn't."

Once she was back in bed, Macie sat on the chair closest to her. "So here's our plan over the next several days. My main focus will be taking care of you and getting you back on your feet again. Your main focus will be eating and resting so that you can get better. I want you to stay in bed this morning, and if you feel up to it later, I'll help you with a shower. I'm going to make you breakfast. Do you have any special requests? I can pretty much cook everything."

"Breakfast? Shit," Raven said in a gush of air from her lungs. "What time is it?"

Macie looked at her watch. "It's eight."

"I have to go to work." Raven sat up quickly. Her head spun in dizzying circles, and she pressed her hands onto the mattress to steady herself.

"Whoa. You can't go anywhere," Macie stated.

"I know you told Maria, but that won't mean anything to Effie. If I'm still breathing, she expects me to be there." She shook her head lightly. "Effie will eat me alive. Being a no-show is about the worst thing I can do to her. I need to call her," she moaned.

"No. You're fine. Maria said she'd talk to Effie when she got in this morning. She knows you won't be able to return to work for about a week."

Raven tilted her head and gave the woman a half-cocked smile. "I think you're probably the politest person I've ever met. I wish there were more people like you. You're very calm and you have everything worked out."

Macie gave her a bright, bold smile. "That's very kind of you to say. That's where Tony and I took two different paths. I'm the nice one, and he's the hammer." She chuckled. "I love him all the same. He's a great brother. He's thoughtful and generous. He's very protective and he includes me in a lot of things. I never was a person who made friends easily. Tony has always made up for that by making me a part of his life."

At that moment, Tony sauntered into the bedroom. "Hey, Raven. How are you feeling this morning?"

"She needs time to recuperate, Tony," Macie stated and stood in front of the girl as if she were protecting her. Macie watched him closer. She could see the enamored look on his face again.

"I know, sis. I'm just asking how she's doing." He put Macie in a headlock, like a Neanderthal, and planted a kiss on her forehead. Then he dragged his dreamy green eyes to Raven.

"Well? You doing okay?"

Raven nodded. "Yeah, I'm better this morning." She pointed to Macie. "I think you better let her go."

Tony released his grip on Macie, and she flattened her hair.

Raven smiled at the two. "I have a lot of pain, but Macie is taking good care of me."

Tony smiled at Macie and playfully nudged her with his elbow. "Yeah, well, we found you on the ground, and those crazy assholes were kicking you like you were a soccer ball and they was on the Napoli team playing for the Serie A title. So I imagine you got lots of pain this morning. I ain't even gotta imagine it." He gave her a smoking-hot smile. "Believe it or not,

I used to get my ass kicked all the time when I was a kid . . . so I know what it's like."

Raven moved her good eye to meet his.

Oh man. That smile . . . and here I am looking like a one-eyed monster. Seriously?

Raven cleared her throat. "Right before you came in, I was telling Macie that Effie is going to be pissed at me. She likes me at the bakery doing my job. It makes her life easier."

"Yeah, I heard you saying that from the hallway. I ain't no eavesdropper or nothing, but you was talking loud. You probably got kicked in the ear and you can't hear so good. Is that it?" Tony moved his face closer to the side of her head as though he could see inside her ear.

Raven blushed and let out a nervous giggle. "I think you might be right. My ears are ringing."

"Yeah, that'll go away when the swelling on the side of your face does. Anyway, I talked to Maria. She understands and said she hopes you feel better. I told her you'll be out for about a week. You can't work wit' only one eye open. You'll be scaring the customers away."

Tony laughed at his own joke, and Macie gave him a scornful look, stopping him mid-laugh. "What? Come on, Macie. I don't mean nothing by it. But look at her. She's all lopsided and shit."

I'm going to die of embarrassment right here in his soft, comfortable bed, in his beautiful spare bedroom with his sister watching me.

Raven shook her head. "I'll have to go back sooner. I'll hide my deformed face in the kitchen so I don't scare people." She paused and lifted her right eyebrow at him. "Seriously, I can't afford to lose a week of pay. I appreciate it and all. I'll take today and tomorrow, but I have to get back after that."

Tony moved closer to her. "Nah, you need to get better. Sometimes, you don't know what's good for you until other people tell you." His eyes shot to his sister, who gave him a nod. "So I'm telling you to stay put for now. Don't worry about the money. There's always more money to be made."

Raven glanced around the beautiful room she was in. Then she tilted her head up. "Look, it seems like you have a lot of money with a house like this, but I don't have anything. Money doesn't follow me like that."

Tony grinned, his hazel eyes simmering. "Well, I think that's gonna change for you one day real soon. I didn't always have money. I grew up a poor bastard with an alcoholic father and a mother who was too weak to protect her own kids. Didn't we, Macie?"

His sister nodded. "Yes, but that's another story for a different book." Macie watched him with a small smile on her lips. She was amused by Tony. He was acting like a schoolboy, clutching his hands together and rocking from foot to foot.

Raven looked around the room again at the solid wood furniture and the palest orchid walls. The artwork was perfectly matched. And the four-poster bed she was in had the best mattress she'd ever felt.

"Everything in this room is so gorgeous." She pulled her eyes back to him. "And the last time I saw you, people were practically throwing themselves at your feet. You're famous here in South Philly, huh?" she asked.

"Who, me?" He pointed to himself. "No, I ain't famous, but people know who I am in this neighborhood."

She looked around at the expensive furniture again, then recalled her conversation with Effie about Tony being a mobster. "Well, this room is beautiful. Thanks for letting me stay here."

"Hey, that ain't no problem. I gotta run. I'm meeting some of the fellas for breakfast."

Raven stared at him, taking in his handsome face.

"You should lay down now," Macie stated, helping to lift her legs back onto the bed. Then she pulled the covers up.

Ah, much better.

Macie ran a soft hand over Raven's rich brown hair. "Once you can sit up without getting dizzy, then I'll help you with a shower." She looked at her brother. "I think she needs to rest now. You should go about your day. I'd like the doctor to come back and see her later while she's awake."

Tony nodded. "Okay, I'll arrange it. Anything else?"

"I left a grocery list on the kitchen counter. Can you give it to Alanzo? Tell him I need them delivered before lunch."

"Ah right. I'll take care of it." Tony moved toward the bedroom door.

"Tony?" Raven's voice cut through the warm silence of the room.

He turned around, faced her, and lifted his chin.

"Do you know who the people are that attacked me?"

Tony narrowed his eyes. "Yeah, I know them. They ain't nothing but a bunch of street thugs. They think they're badass, but they never met me and my friends before."

"Oh, you didn't do anything bad to them, right?" Raven asked with her right eye wide, anticipating his answer.

"Nah, I ain't that kind of guy. I don't touch trash unless I need to. You don't need to worry about all of that anyway. You should concentrate on getting better and we can talk about this later. I gotta run." He glanced at his sister. "You got this?"

Macie scoffed. "Yes, of course. Have a good day and stay safe."

He turned back to the door.

"Thank you, Tony," Raven said in a sweet pitch. "I appreciate you saving me last night."

Tony lifted his right arm as he walked out of the bedroom. "The pleasure was all mine, Raven Ledger," he said as he disappeared beyond the doorway, grinning from ear to ear.

When he was gone, Raven turned to Macie. "He's something else."

Macie shook her head as she fussed over Raven's covers. "You have no idea."

"I see what you're saying. He's a good brother. When he looks at you, it's like you're his favorite person in the world. He respects you. I can see that . . . even with one eye," she joked. "I was taught that having a person's respect is the most important thing we can get from someone. You're lucky."

Macie gave her a gentle smile. "Yes, Tony is a good brother and he respects me." She pinched her lips together. "He also has ways of finding out things. I can't go out on a date without him knowing everything about the man before I do. He tells me to paint my fingernails and wear makeup . . . It drives him crazy that I don't like any of that stuff."

"Why don't you like it?"

Macie shrugged. "I didn't grow up being girly. My mother never exposed me to it. She dressed me like she dressed herself—like I was a forty-year-old housewife."

"Did you get your kindness from her?"

Macie shook her head. "Like Tony said, my mother is a weak woman. I learned to be kind by watching my father be so unkind to my brother. My dad was an example of what I never wanted to be. And no matter how much my dad ridiculed or beat Tony, my brother always protected and loved me." She let out a chuckle filled with wistful memories. Then she gently guided Raven's shoulders back against the pillows. "Now, come on. Lie back. I'll go make you breakfast and bring it to you."

Raven rested her head against the pillows and closed her eyes. Macie and Tony had a strong bond, the kind of bond she had always wanted with Matthew. It was comforting to be with people who understood what it was to be given a bad hand in life. It gave her great relief to be in this house, at this time, with these two people. No matter what happened from this moment forward, Raven would always be grateful to Tony Bruno and his sister Macie.

Chapter Seventy-Two

It was two days before Raven could get out of bed to take a shower. After Macie toweled her dry, she opened and held the pajama top for her to slide on. As the fabric hit Raven's skin, the soft sensation made her blow out a breath. She hugged the garment to her body.

"Wow," Raven said with her eyes closed, absorbing the soft texture. "These are even more comfortable than the other pajamas you let me borrow."

"You aren't borrowing these. They're yours." She gave her a grin. "Maria brought you a few sets of new pajamas and underwear while you were asleep."

Raven's eyes got misty.

"What is it? Do you have pain?" Macie asked.

The teen shook her head. "I can't believe that everyone is taking care of me. I mean, you and Tony barely even know me. And Maria, she's so kind. It's not something that I'm used to. That's all."

Macie stroked the girl's back. "We're a tight-knit family. Especially those of us close to Tony, Salvatore, and Vincent. We work together and we take care of each other."

Sounds perfect.

Dressed and revived from the warm shower, Raven followed Macie out of the bedroom and into the living area of Tony's apartment.

She stopped in the living room with her mouth hanging open. A black leather sectional sofa faced the largest television Raven had ever seen. There were coffee and end tables made from metal and glass. The pictures on his walls were crafted in vibrant colors, while others were black-and-white. The placement of the artwork couldn't have been more perfect. Given Tony's rough exterior, the apartment had a masculine quality with bold edges and colors.

She spun slowly, taking in every inch of the room. The vaulted ceiling and floor-to-ceiling windows had a view of the streets of South Philadelphia. She thought it was amazing.

Her eyes slipped over Macie. "Wow, this room is beautiful. It's like an art museum."

Macie gave her a shy smile. "Thank you. I did all of Tony's decorating for him. He wouldn't know the first thing about what looked good. His only requirement was that it wasn't too girly. It took me almost two weeks to talk him into the orchid walls in the spare bedroom you're in."

Raven's eyes washed over Macie. She was a simple woman with a bland—no, forget that—matronly appearance. She had thin lips and thick eyebrows like two caterpillars were nesting above her ordinary brown eyes. Her nose was a thread away from looking like her brother's, meaning it was far too big for a woman. Then her black hair was cut short, choppy, like she did it herself. The black strands were dull, dry, and wiry. Raven had noticed her clothes were black or gray. Her pants and shirts were all too large for her. And while her appearance wasn't too memorable, the average-looking woman was sweet and kind and filled with goodness. But Raven admired her quiet strength most.

***

One week later, as Raven entered Cecilia's home, the old woman rushed from the kitchen to meet her at the door.

"I'm gonna tell you something right now," Cecilia huffed, pointing her finger at the teenager. "I know Maria lied to me. You weren't in New York buying her shit for the bakery. The whole goddamn neighborhood heard about the girl that got mugged and beat up. Do you think people are blind? They watch things through their windows. Look at you. Your face is still black and blue and you're walking like you got a peg leg under those jeans."

Raven put on her best smile. She hugged the old woman, and Cecilia clung to her tightly, as if she had returned from a long, treacherous voyage after being lost at sea.

Raven whispered in the woman's ear, "It's good to be home. I've missed you."

Cecilia pulled away and glared into her face. "Don't give me that shit. Let me take a good look at you." She walked around Raven as if she had

X-ray vision and could see through her clothes to make certain no bones or organs were damaged. "Why didn't you call me?"

"Maria talked to you, didn't she? That's what I was told."

Cecilia put her hands on her hips. "Maria ain't living in my house now, is she? Maria ain't part of my life, is she? No, she isn't. You are. I expected a phone call from you. I was worried outta my mind."

Raven nodded and wrung her hands together. She would never purposely upset or offend Cecilia. She loved the woman.

"You're right. I should've called you myself. It was thoughtless. It won't happen again."

Cecilia relaxed her tense jaw muscles. "Okay, then. Now we both know what's expected. Did you eat? I can make you bacon and eggs." She eyed the teen closely, testing her.

Raven almost said no, then quickly remembered the rule. "Oh, that would be really nice. You know me . . . I love bacon and eggs."

As Raven sat at the kitchen table, Cecilia busied herself at the stove making them breakfast. Finally, she laid a plate of food in front of the teen and stared into her eyes.

"You know, I had to hear what happened to you from that nosey, two-faced bitch, Sofia." She tipped her head in the direction of the woman's house. "That shit cooking, old hag. She loved rubbing it in my face that she knew something that I didn't—and about *you* of all things."

Raven laughed. She couldn't help it. The way the old women competed against each other was amusing, although she knew for Cecilia it was serious neighborhood business.

She leaned into the old woman. "Sofia doesn't have a thing over you."

Cecilia sat back in her chair, folding her arms over her chest. "You're right, but you remember what I told you . . . I want to hear from you. From now on, if you're gonna be late or stay out, you have to call me." Her voice softened. "And not because of Sofia. But because I was really worried about you. I could barely eat while you were gone, and you know for me, that's saying something. I even went to the bakery and spoke to Effie. That woman is something else—a whole other story."

"What did Effie say exactly?"

"At first, she had the nerve to tell me that Maria had already talked to me. Like I didn't already know that or like I have Alzheimer's or something. But I wasn't letting her off that easy. Nope. I reminded her of how we spent such a special Christmas together like we're a real family.

I told her if she planned to come back this year, she needed to spill the beans. I knew you weren't in New York." Cecilia gulped her coffee. "Then Effie tries to continue with the lie about New York and then changes the subject, ranting that you left her to do all your work." The woman clucked her tongue. "Now, I know that woman knew you were mugged, so why wouldn't she tell me? All she did was assure me you were fine."

Raven took a bite of the crispy bacon. It crumbled in her mouth, and she closed her eyes to enjoy the salty crispiness. "Effie is very loyal to Maria and very protective. Just like you are with me. I'm sure it was hard for her not to tell you, but I know you'd do the same for me. So promise you won't hold it against her."

Cecilia patted the girl's hand. "Fine. I won't hold it against her, but she better not lie to me again. Where did you stay?"

"Um, well."

"Don't *um, well* me," the old woman snapped. "Cough it up. All of a sudden, you're like a cat with a hairball stuck in its throat."

"I was at Tony Bruno's house. His sister Macie took care of me," she admitted nervously. She was waiting for the lecture.

Cecilia shook her head. "Tony Bruno. Nice young man. He's quite involved in the Morano family. But his sister Macie is a lovely girl. Not too soft on the eyes, but sweet nonetheless."

"Cecilia!" Raven shrieked with a smile. "You can't say that about her."

"Why can't I? I got eyes. We got all kinds of people in this world. Ugly, pretty, fat, skinny. When you're young you notice all that stuff because it matters more. But when you get to be my age, you learn it's how people treat others that counts the most. I'm not being mean about Macie. But let's face it, she isn't very good-looking, and the way she dresses makes her look even older than her real age." She shook her head. "I bet she's never been laid. Now her brother Tony, oofa, he's a good-looking man." She bit the skin on her hand between her thumb and index finger to symbolize how hot Tony was. "I'll tell you right now, if I was forty years younger, I'd be shaking my ass at him every chance I got."

Raven grinned and blushed. "Yeah, he's very handsome."

"Oh, do you have a crush on Tony? Me and Sofia always wondered why he don't have a girlfriend. The women his age fall all over him, but he don't give them the time of day." She covered the side of her mouth with her hand like the stove had eyes and would read her lips. "We think he must find himself those hookers. That way he doesn't need to get involved."

Raven smiled from the top of her head to her toes. Cecilia and Sofia were always imagining how everyone lived their lives. Cecilia was talented at telling stories with emotion and scandal.

Raven thought about what Cecilia said and agreed. It was odd that Tony didn't have a girlfriend.

Cecilia leaned forward and put her hand over Raven's, pulling the girl from her thoughts. "Tony is a very powerful man. He's got a lot of clout in South Philly. He's always been sweet to me and the ladies that live on this block."

"He was very nice to me, too. Tony seems like a good guy. I like that he stands up for the people who need it. Sometimes, people with a lot of 'clout'"—she air quoted the word—"they crap all over others that need help."

The old woman's eyes softened. "I bet you know a lot about that."

Raven nodded.

"These tough guys that mugged you—did Tony catch them?"

Raven gave her a shallow nod. "Tony told me he knew who they were and that he'd taken care of things. I'm sure he threatened them, and they ran back to North Philly."

"Oh," Cecilia narrowed her eyes. "You know who they are, too?"

"Yes, they're the Kensington Hoods." She sat waiting for Cecilia to freak out. She expected to be told to pack her things and find another place to live. But the woman didn't flinch.

"You don't need to worry. In this neighborhood, we protect our own. I'm sure Tony and Vincent have everything under control."

Raven pulled her head back. "What does that mean?"

"That means," Cecilia said, using her hands to push herself up from the table, "the Morano family doesn't let people like the Kensington Hoods torment us. They'll scare the shit outta them so they never wanna step foot on these streets again."

Raven didn't know if she should be scared or delighted. She knew one thing for certain . . . She was curious to know more about Tony Bruno.

Chapter Seventy-Three: The Night of the Attack

Raven didn't know that the Kensington Hoods attacking her had created a bigger problem for the Morano family. It wasn't about some girl from North Philly getting beat up in an alley. Cecilia was right—the Morano crime family didn't and wouldn't allow gangs to infiltrate their neighborhoods.

Tony seemed to be the angriest of them all. He decided to take a small army of his men to North Philly to chat with the gang leader. The Morano family had no fear of making the first move. In fact, this tactic gave their enemies pause.

After getting Raven settled at his apartment with Macie by her side, Tony placed a call to his top guy. "I need a dozen of our soldiers. I want my best and meanest. Tell everyone to be at the club in thirty minutes. We're taking a ride."

"You got it, Tony."

The club doors swung open, and Tony swaggered inside with determination. His nostrils were flared, and his jaw was set hard. The room fell silent as Tony stood before his men with Vincent beside him. "We're taking a ride to North Philly. You all heard the Kensington Hoods came in here and attacked one of Maria and Salvatore's employees. We ain't standing for that shit. We let that go and before we know we'll have 'em in here robbing old ladies and recruiting our kids."

Salvatore, who had been sitting at one table, added, "We're going to try to do this peacefully. Everyone keep that in mind. But we will not tolerate any disrespect from common street criminals. My father is counting on this group to end this before it becomes a war that the Kensington Hoods will live to regret."

As the motorcade entered North Philadelphia, heads turned. Tony was driving the black sedan leading the line of cars. As they drove deeper into gang territory, the mobsters in the cars were on high alert. The windows were rolled down and guns were at the ready. They were destined for the house where Smuggler lived. He was at the top of the Kensington Hoods food chain.

Tony pulled his car over to the side and parked. He looked at Vincent in the back seat, then over at Salvatore sitting next to him. "Me and Vincent are going to talk to Smuggler. You stay here."

Salvatore wrinkled his forehead. "Why the hell would I stay here? I'm going, too."

"No, you ain't. As heir to the throne, your father doesn't want you taking any risks."

"My father told you that I can't do my part? To protect the family?"

Tony gave him a curt nod. "Your father is protecting you. Stop being a pain in the ass. Just shut up and stay here. Does this look like a good time for you to be debatin' with me?"

Salvatore pursed his lips. "Fine. But if you're not back here in ten minutes, I'm going in there," he said, pointing to the house.

As Tony and Vincent approached the front porch, their soldiers stood ready to defend them.

Tony knocked on the door.

Smuggler pulled it open. "What are you doing here, Bruno?"

"See, you being rude to me from the start ain't gonna help you. I suggest you kill your fucking attitude. Me and Vincent wanna talk to you. Man to man. Business to business. You wanna step out here on the porch?"

Smuggler assessed the line of cars and men along his street. He looked over his shoulder. "I need eight of you." Then he stepped onto his porch with eight of his crew following. They, too, all carried guns. Smuggler spread his feet apart, his pelvis pushed forward so Tony could see the gun in the front of his pants.

Tony smiled at the man's attempt to intimidate them. *Amateur*.

"Why are you pushing your crotch out? So we can see your gun or you think this is gonna be some kind of sexual encounter? You ain't about to get a blow job if that's what you're thinking."

Smuggler shifted his feet. He was the king in North Philly, but the mob was organized and had a lot of money, power, and weapons.

"So, what do you want?" Smuggler asked, then he hacked up phlegm and spit over the railing of the porch, trying to save face.

"Four of your people came into our neighborhood tonight. They attacked a girl. I'm here to tell you if your smelly, rotten, motherfucking members put a fucking toe in our neighborhood again, it'll be the end of the Kensington Hoods." Tony stepped into him. "Capiche?"

"Hey," Smuggler growled. "Don't come to my house, in my neighborhood, on my front porch threatening my people and talking that gabagool."

Tony gave him a terse smile and lifted his chin. "Careful, Smuggler, before you find yourself burned alive in your own home, in your neighborhood, on your front porch. I ain't playing. I don't think you're bad enough to go toe to toe with us . . . and you know that, too."

"Listen, you dago bastard, I saw what you did to my four crew members. They're all fucked up. They didn't do shit to no girl. You can't fuck them up and expect we ain't gonna retaliate."

"Yeah, I can. They got their asses beat because of what I just told you they did. They attacked a girl, a young woman, in my neighborhood. Are you hard of hearing? Got too much wax in your ears? What?"

As the two men stood nose to nose, Salvatore got out of the car and walked up to them. Smuggler's shoulders rolled over when he saw the Godfather's son.

"Do we have a problem here, gentlemen?" Salvatore asked, stepping in too closely to his rival. "Smuggler, my friend Tony is only protecting what is ours. The same as you protect what is yours. The girl that your gang attacked is an employee of mine. Do you understand the implications of your actions? How that affects the Morano family to have one of their own beaten down like a stray dog in a dark alley? A woman, nonetheless. Four on one doesn't seem like fair odds to me."

Smuggler met Salvatore's gaze. "I didn't order no attack tonight. It wasn't my people. You got the wrong crew. You practically killed four of my members. You got the wrong people, bruh. That's all I got to say to you about that. You owe my crew an apology for what you did to them."

Salvatore stepped back and tilted his head in a confused manner. "Really? An apology? Well, let me be clear. There were four Kensington Hoods who hurt my employee. They were caught in the act. Now do the names Blanco and Dice ring a bell? They are the two who gave us the most information." He pursed his lips and nodded. "Those two talked because they couldn't take the pain anymore, but mainly because they were afraid to die. I suggest you give your people more training so they learn to keep their mouths shut like Scully. How is his ear by the way? Was he able to have it sewn back on?"

Smuggler drew in a long breath. His nostrils flared. "I think you better leave."

Salvatore clenched his jaw, gritted his teeth, and lifted his chin. "Don't be rude. I wasn't finished. As I was saying, I believe Blanco was in the same foster home as my employee, and Scully's brother was killed in the school shooting. Is this making things any clearer? Are you remembering any particulars right about now?"

Smuggler punched his right fist into his left palm. "Oh, are we talking about that bitch whose brother killed my members? See you shoulda said that earlier."

Salvatore shook his head. "That's what you may be talking about, but I'm talking about a girl who happens to be the sister of the school shooter. In fact, from what I understand, she actually saved a few of your . . . what do you call them? Kensington Sisterhoods? She saved the bitch that was involved tonight. It's kind of pathetic that you need to use women to protect your turf, don't you agree?" He changed his stance and placed his hand on the gun he had holstered. "The point is, *Smuggler*, a name says it all, doesn't it?" He glanced at Tony and Vincent watching everyone around them. "Anyway, I digressed."

Salvatore pulled his gun from his holster and pressed it against Smuggler's heart in one fluid motion. The Kensington Hoods all lifted their guns. Tony, Vincent, and their soldiers on the sidewalk did the same.

Salvatore pressed the gun harder against Smuggler's chest. "Keep your low-life, filthy, fucking people out of my neighborhood. Do we understand each other?"

Smuggler scoffed, and then he swallowed several times. "Yeah. I'll talk to my guys."

Salvatore bared his teeth. "Make sure you talk to your girls, too." Then he placed his gun back in the holster, turned, and returned to the car.

Tony gave Smuggler one last warning. "Don't make me have to come back here. 'Cause if I do, it ain't gonna be this civil. Understand?"

Smuggler looked over at his men and lifted his chin. His jaw jutted out. "Let's go," he ordered his crew members, and they followed him inside the house.

Tony slid behind the steering wheel and sneered at Salvatore. "Have you lost your fucking mind? What? Do you want your father to off me? Are you trying to see me dead? What the fuck was that?"

Salvatore chuckled. "Don't be so dramatic. You're not the only one that enjoys mob life."

Tony was not amused. "What the hell were you thinking?"

"I was thinking that my father doesn't get to dictate what I do. He went behind my back and told you two what I can and cannot do. I didn't like it," he stated, lifting his nose into the air.

"Oh, for fuck's sake, Salvatore. In case you haven't noticed, your father tells us all what we can and cannot do. Why do you think you're so special?" Tony argued.

Salvatore turned to face him. "I don't think I'm special. I think I'm my own person. Nobody, not even my father, is going to tell me what I can do. Why can't you understand that I don't like being treated as though I can't hold my own?"

Tony looked down at the steering wheel. "I do understand. But you gotta get it through your head that me and Vincent care about you. We wanna keep you safe. You're the future of this family, you dumb shit."

Salvatore let Tony's words simmer for a moment. Then he lowered his face. "You're right. I'm sorry. Sometimes it's hard sitting back and letting you two do all the heavy lifting."

"All right then, we agree." Tony started the car. "No more taking chances."

"Yeah, Salvatore, you jerk off," Vincent chimed in from the back seat. "Don't be a dick again."

As the three long-time friends drove back to South Philly, they laughed about all the things Salvatore said to Smuggler and reminisced about the old days when they were teenagers running numbers and collecting money for Johnny Morano. It was a much simpler time then.

Chapter Seventy-Four

Maria walked into the bakery kitchen minutes after Raven arrived at work.

"Raven, it's so nice to have you back." She glanced at Effie. "I know Effie is happy. I think she missed you while you were gone."

"Missed her? Nah, I missed her doing her job."

Raven smiled. "You're such a liar."

"How are you feeling?" Maria asked.

The teen nodded. "A lot better. Hey, thanks for those pajamas. It was really nice of you to send them to me."

"Of course. Listen, I'd like for you to stay in the kitchen until the bruises on your face are gone. I've asked my mother-in-law to come in and cover your work in the front," Maria stated.

"Are you sure it's just until my bruises go away? I don't want to lose my place in the front because of the Kensington Hoods." She glanced at Effie. "I'm hoping someday to help you run the bakery and that maybe we can get a dishwasher to replace me."

"There you go," Effie interjected. "Flying off and leaving me after I spent all this time training you."

Raven walked over to her friend. "Effie, you know I love working with you, but I'm nineteen years old. I have to think about what I'm going to be doing ten years from now."

Effie threw the dough on the metal table and started kneading it. "Yeah, well, you best be clear—you too," she said, pointing at Maria. "I'm never taking orders from her."

Raven chuckled. "As if I'd ever try to boss you around? Get real."

"Yeah, that's all I'm saying."

The teen turned back to Maria. "I've been wanting to talk to you about my future here. I'm not looking for something right this minute, but I've been trying to decide if I should go back to school or what else I can do. I want to make money—a lot of money."

Maria nodded. "First, this has nothing to do with the Kensington Hoods. It's truly about your face being bruised. Second, I understand your desire to make a better life for yourself. I think it's something we should talk about. There's no one stopping you from going to college, if that's what you want to do. In fact, I think it's a great idea."

Raven's chest fell in, and her shoulders slumped forward. "I was hoping you'd say we could figure out a future for me here."

Maria pressed her hands to her hips. "I did say that. You're not hearing me talk with certainty about exactly what that means. The truth is, I haven't given it thought. I never saw myself not working here full-time, but now that you bring it up, it might not be such a bad idea. Salvatore and I would love to have another child, and I've been avoiding it because of how much time I spend running this bakery. When I bought this place, it was much less than it is now. Don't get me wrong, it was a good bakery, but now it's thriving."

"So we can talk about it then?"

Maria nodded. "Yes, when the time is right."

Effie scoffed. "That's like a kid asking for something and the parent says, 'We'll see.' What kind of shit is that, Maria?"

"Effie, are you calling me out?" Maria said with a smirk.

"Damn tootin' I am. The girl has ambition. She wants to carry on where you'll leave off. That don't mean you won't be part of it anymore." She rolled the pin over the dough on the table. "It means you gotta give up some of your power. That's one of the hardest things in the world for business people to do. But if you don't, then you ain't gonna grow. Didn't you say you want three or four bakeries around the city?"

"Yes, I did." Maria's armor was being chipped away as Effie spoke.

"Well, you ain't gonna do that if you don't have people who can run them for you. Ain't that right?"

Maria walked over to Effie. "How come you always know what to say?"

Effie stopped rolling the dough and looked into the woman's eyes. "Because sometimes I can see what you need even though you can't. Ain't that right, Raven?"

"Yep, Effie's right."

"Usually am," Effie added.

"Don't push it," Maria remarked.

***

When Maria was gone and Raven was alone with Effie in the kitchen, she approached the woman.

"Do you really think I could run this bakery for Maria?"

Effie gave her a side-glance. "I think you can run the front. You ain't running shit back here."

"Come on, Effie. You know what I mean."

Effie threw a new batch of dough on the table. "I think you're a real smart cookie and that you can do whatever you set your mind to. You're very mature for a girl your age. That gives you an advantage over all the other dimwits your age that only care about their clothes, makeup, and boys."

Raven threw her arm over Effie's shoulders. "Thanks. And for the record, I like boys."

Effie's face lit up. She had a bright smile on her lips. "Oh yeah? Have you ever had one? Like in high school?"

The girl shook her head. "No, never."

"Are you telling me you're still a virgin?" Effie shrieked in disbelief.

"You make it sound like a crime. No, I've never been with a guy, and yes, I'm still a virgin. So what?"

"So what? All you do is come here and go home. You'll be a fifty-year-old virgin before you know it. You better go out and meet someone. You ain't gotta marry him. Just take him for a spin."

Raven wrinkled her nose. "You're so crude."

"No, baby, I'm real. So let's see . . . You got your eye on some geriatric dude on Cecilia's block? You don't wanna start there. Old men have long balls, if you know what I mean," she cackled.

Raven blushed. "Whatever. You're talking shit now."

"Oh, lord help us all. Come on, you got your eyes on anyone? I can charm them into asking you on a date."

"Noooo, I don't," she sang, overly defensive. "You're the last person I'd ask to talk to someone I had a crush on."

Effie shook her head. "Let me give you a piece of advice about South Philly men." She lowered her voice to a whisper. "There are a lot of gangsters around here. Now, don't get me wrong, they've never done me any harm. The truth is, they've helped me. But Maria got herself involved with a mafia man, and while she got everything she wants, every time Salvatore walks out the door, her heart is in her mouth until he walks back in that door again. So choose wisely and find yourself a nice boy . . . an accountant or a lawyer or something. 'Cause those mobsters—they work hard, live hard, and usually die hard."

Raven cringed. "I had no idea you thought about them that way. I never really gave it much thought, but you're right. I guess it's no different than the gangs in North Philly."

Effie shook a finger at her. "No, it's different. These Italian mobsters, girl, they know how to love. They worship their women and everything a woman has to offer," she said, holding her breasts.

Raven grinned. "You make it sound so romantic."

"Oh, those Italian men will give you plenty of romance. Except Vincent DeLuca, all he wants to do is tap it and move on to the next." She pointed a dough-covered index finger at the teen. "No lovey-dovey with Vincent. He ain't got no sense when it comes to women."

"Okay, I'll be sure to stay away from Vincent DeLuca."

"Yeah, well, I'm giving you fair warning about the mob. If you find yourself interested in dating one, you oughta sit down and talk to Maria before you even think of going out on a first date. I know she and Salvatore love each other, but her life doesn't come without a price."

"What does that mean?"

Effie scowled at her. "It means that above all else, the family comes first."

"What's wrong with that?" Raven asked, confused. "I always wanted to have a family of my own. If I did, they would come first, too."

"I'm talking about the crime family, not the family they live with."

"Oh," Raven said in a release of breath. "Like Salvatore would do something against Maria if it was good for the Morano mob?"

"No. More like if Salvatore had to choose between his mob family and his wife, then Maria would be shit out of luck. She accepted that as her fate when she married him. Don't get me wrong, he'll protect her to the bitter end, but the mob is based solely on loyalty to the organization."

Raven walked back to the sink and started loading the industrial dishwasher. She didn't know about being in love, and Effie made it sound harder than she believed it would be. Like any other teenage girl, she wondered about love and what it would be like to be with a man. She thought about how great it would be to have a person to call her own. A lifer was how she thought of them. But she was always afraid she'd pick the wrong man. She'd hoped to find someone protective and caring like her father. She had enough loss for a lifetime. She didn't want to lose in love, too.

Chapter Seventy-Five: Summer of 1986

Raven opened the front door and there stood Billy McLeary. He wore his brown hair combed over with a part an inch above his left ear. He was wearing a light blue button-down shirt with a navy bow tie. He was her height and size, thin with slender arms and feminine hands. She cringed internally at the twenty-one-year-old with whom she'd spend the next two hours. Even if Raven had a type, he wouldn't be it.

Oh no. Effie warned me that all grandmothers think their grandsons are handsome.

"Hi, Raven. I'm Billy. My grandmother is Agnes. You know, Cecilia's friend from the next block over?" He smiled at her.

Raven had to pull her eyes away from his crooked teeth stained from drinking too much coffee and not enough teeth brushing. She wore a dim grin. "Right. Billy, good to meet you. Come on in."

"Oh, okay." He stepped into the house and Raven closed the door. She turned and Cecilia was there with her eyes popping out of her head.

"You must be Billy," Cecilia said warily.

"Yes, ma'am. I brought you these." He handed Cecilia three carnations.

She was trying to keep her "I smell poop face" at bay. The face people make unintentionally when they encounter something appalling.

"Ooooh, thank you," she managed in a screechy voice. "Where are you taking Raven tonight?"

"I got us a reservation at Coletti's Café. It's really hard to get a table there." He glanced at Raven to see if she was impressed. She wasn't. "Anyway, I didn't actually get it. My father got the reservation for me. They have really delicious Italian food."

"Oh yeah?" Cecilia said, hiking her hands to her hips. "What have you eaten there?"

"Oh," he chuckled-snorted.

Raven's eyes were like saucers. *This can't be my first date ever. I'm dreaming and I will wake up any minute.*

"Well," he said, rubbing his sweaty palms on his pants. "I've never actually eaten there myself, but everyone who's anyone says it's the best Italian food in South Philly."

"Everyone who's anyone? I'm anyone and you don't hear me raving about the place."

Raven could see Cecilia was getting her hackles up. When it came to who made the best Italian food, the woman could turn into a cheetah and pounce in a second.

"Okay." Raven pulled the door open. "Let's go. We need to get to the restaurant on time."

Billy stepped onto the porch and Raven went to hug Cecilia. "O my God. What am I going to do?"

Cecilia shook her head. "Honey, I don't know. I'm so sorry. Maybe it'll get better once the two of you are alone. Jeez, you two are like night and day. That fucking Agnes told me her grandson was good-looking. I had no idea he was such a . . . what's the word? Geek. He's the most socially awkward boy I've met in two decades. Good God, that hair and those clothes—it looks like Agnes dressed him herself. A strong wind will blow him away. If there's any trouble, run, because he can't protect you unless he's got a gun hidden under his bow tie. Holy shit."

"Okay, okay. You understand that you're not helping right now? I have to get in and out of dinner quickly. I don't want to hurt his feelings." She leaned in and pecked the silky soft skin on Cecilia's cheek. "Wish me luck."

"Luck? Child, you need the holy Mother Mary herself to come down to earth and get you outta this one. Maybe he'll get sleepy and call it an early night," she cackled.

Raven smirked. "Right, not funny. Bye!"

***

Raven was sitting next to Billy at Coletti's Café. They had enjoyed a good meal, but not as good as the food Cecilia cooked, she decided. They were seated at a great table on the edge of the dance floor, and she was marveling at all the couples dancing.

"So, how long have you lived at Cecilia's?"

"Oh, um. About a year and a half. We get along really well. I think we're good for each other."

He nodded. "Yeah, my grandmother said that."

"How about you? Where do you live?" Raven asked.

"Oh, I still live with my parents and all. Once I save up enough money, I'm going to get an apartment of my own," he said proudly, holding his chin up. "One of those really expensive ones, you know, with the high ceilings.

"Yeah, great. That'll be really good for you." She looked at the dancers and back at Billy. "Do you wanna dance?"

"Oh," he chuckled-snorted again. "I don't dance. I never learned how."

"Oh." Raven watched the people milling about, having a great time. Then her attention was drawn to a few girls from across the room giggling loudly. She looked over at the door to see Tony and Vincent walk in. The girls were already flocking to them.

They were quickly brought to the best table in the restaurant, and as they waited for drinks, Tony looked around. He spotted Raven trying her best not to look in his direction, as she prayed he wouldn't see her.

"Yo," Tony said, whacking Vincent on the leg. "Look who's over there."

Vincent craned his neck and smiled. "Sweet Raven Ledger."

Tony nodded. "Who's that douchebag she's sitting with?"

"Oh, I know who he is. Let me introduce you," Vincent said, getting to his feet.

The two men walked toward their table. Billy glanced over and saw them coming toward them. He started pulling at his bow tie, suddenly needing more air, and his face went ashen.

"Well, look who it is," Vincent said, sitting down. "It's Billy McFeary. Tony? You ever meet McFeary?"

"McLeary. It's Billy McLeary," he said in a shaky voice.

Vincent rolled his head in the man's direction. "Whatever. Anyway, you know 'im, Tony. His father is Johnny Morano's accountant. What do you do again? You punch numbers on a calculator for some hotshot firm or something?"

Billy shook his head. "N-n-no. I'm a junior accountant at the McGraff firm."

"Ooooh, no shit!" Vincent said, pursing his lips and nodding. "A junior accountant, huh? I guess you're pretty smart then."

Billy plastered a fake smile on his lips. "I like to think I'm good with numbers."

"Okay, that's good to know. You ain't so good at picking out clothes, though, huh? Who does that for you?"

Billy squirmed in his seat and Raven shot Tony a scathing look. Tony lifted his hands like he was helpless.

"That's a real nice bow tie you're wearing," Vincent said, reaching over and touching it.

Raven couldn't take the nervous energy rolling off of Billy. While she wanted the night to end, she didn't want to see the grown man have a breakdown. She stood, and when she did, Tony was right next to her.

"Hi, Raven," Tony said.

His voice made her knees weak. "Hi, Tony."

"Are you on a date with Billy McFeary?"

She glanced at the man and back at Tony. "McLeary," she said in a low voice. "And yes, we are on a date. This is a blind date. We just met tonight."

"See, this is why I never go on blind dates," Vincent sang. "You never know what you're gonna get. Hey, Billy. How about you and me go to the bar and I'll buy you a drink?"

Billy's eyes lit up. "Really? You want to hang with me?"

"Yeah, sure. We can leave Raven here and Tony will look after her."

"Okay." Billy nodded vigorously. He glanced at Raven. "It was nice meeting you."

"What?" Raven answered, dumbfounded. "Okay, bye, Billy." *Asshole.*

"I guess it's just you and me now," Tony said. "How about if we have a dance?"

Raven smiled. "Yes, I'd love to dance."

Tony Bruno held out his hand and led Raven to the dance floor. As their bodies pressed together, it was like electricity was running through them. They both felt it, but neither of them acknowledged it. Lost in the moment, Raven didn't notice all the people watching the two of them as they melted into each other.

Chapter Seventy-Six

Raven was sitting on the porch next to Cecilia. They were drinking iced tea to battle the heat wave that settled over Philadelphia. There was one window air conditioner in Cecilia's bedroom, and the twosome had decided Raven would sleep in there with her that night.

Raven had a radio playing, and the old ladies on either side were chatting away. There were a few neighborhood kids from the end of the block throwing a ball on the sidewalk. She looked around her, content. She loved being part of the community, something wholesome and real.

A week had passed since her first and last date with Billy McLeary. She and Cecilia had laughed about it until their stomachs hurt. She had told the old woman she hailed a taxi from the restaurant, but what happened was Tony put her in a taxi and sent her home even though Raven insisted she could walk alone.

Raven hadn't thought about Tony much that week. After he didn't bring her home from Coletti's, she realized there was nothing there, and she didn't give the evening much thought.

Cecilia was saying something to Sofia when a black car pulled up in front of her rowhome. "Who the hell is that?" the old woman muttered. "Kids," she yelled, "get up on my porch right now."

The kids' feet pattered on the pavement and up Cecilia's steps. All eyes were on the car now. Raven was watching the car, and a few seconds later the engine shut off and the driver's door opened.

Tony looked over the roof of his car at Raven and gave her a bright smile.

"Hello, Miss Cecilia." He looked from left to right over the porches. "Hello, ladies."

"Oh, Tony," Cecilia screeched, holding her hand over her chest. She was delighted that Tony had singled her out by name. "You scared the bejesus outta me. I thought you were a pervert here to take the kids."

Tony swaggered to the base of the porch. "Now, come on, Miss Cecilia. You know if we had a jerk like that running in our streets, me and Vincent would take care of it." He moved his eyes. "Hey, Raven. How's it going? It's pretty hot out here tonight."

Raven raised a hand and waved. "Hi. Yeah, it's very hot. What are you doing here?"

Cecilia nudged her.

Tony chuckled. "Oh, well, I came to see if Miss Cecilia wouldn't mind if I took you to get an ice cream . . . seeing it's so hot and all. I thought it'd be good."

"Yes, Tony. That's perfectly fine with me. It would be good for Raven to get out. She's always hanging around us old women."

"Old? Who's old? I don't see no old women around here. All I see is beautiful, mature women who could make a man's heart stop."

All the women giggled.

"Go on," Cecilia told Raven.

"I'm sorry, Tony. I can't go." She stood up. She was wearing cutoff jean shorts and a black T-shirt she'd bought from the thrift store that said, *Rock On*. "I'm a mess and, well, maybe some other time."

Cecilia bared her teeth at the girl. "Are you crazy?" she hissed.

"Well, what you're wearing don't matter to me. We're going to get ice cream. We ain't going to a ball or nothing. If we was going to a ball, I would've given you more warning so you could change your T-shirt. I think you look great, by the way."

Raven grinned.

"Oh, go on," Sofia shrieked. "You'll have a good time and Tony will be a gentleman. Won't you? 'Cause our girl ain't got much experience with men."

"O my God," Raven said, dipping her head down and covering her face with both hands.

"Our girl?" Cecilia challenged. "She's my girl. She ain't got nothing to do with you. Do I claim your kids as my own?"

"Okay, okay, stop," Raven broke in before they gave Tony her bra and underwear size. "Tony, I'll go with you. Anything to stop this humiliation."

Raven slid her feet into her rubber flip-flops and walked down the steps. She looked over her shoulder and gave Cecilia a wave.

When Tony opened the car door for her, the women oohed and aahed from their porches.

Carmela, a woman who lived two doors down from Cecilia moved to the edge of her folding chair. "Look at that," she said. "Such a gentlemen. You don't see that shit no more. Not like when we were that age."

All the women grunted their agreement, remembering with fondness when they were Raven's age and being taken on a date. Looking back on those moments was blissful but tinged with sadness because they were over.

Tony looked up. "She won't be home late, Miss Cecilia."

"Okay, Tony. No rush. You two kids have a good time . . . eating ice cream," she said dreamily.

Inside the car, Tony gave Raven a nervous glance. "I didn't wanna come here and ask you to get ice cream like that, but I didn't have your phone number."

"I'm sure you have ways of finding out Cecilia's telephone number." Raven turned and gave him a sweet smile. Her hair was in a sloppy bun, and her T-shirt was baggy and washed too many times. But all Tony could see was her silky brown hair, her long, toned legs, and a face making him weak in the knees.

He shook off the dumb look he knew was plastered on his face. "Ah right. So tell me about yourself."

She shifted her body in the seat to face him. "No. You go first. You know things about me already, but I don't know anything about you. Well, that's not totally true, I've heard a lot of things about you, but that's all gossip."

"Well, let's see. I'll be thirty soon. I ain't got no wife, girlfriend, or kids. I love pasta more than breathing, and I take my work very seriously. Oh, and my sister Macie is the only family I got and I'll do whatever is needed to make sure she's happy."

"Yes, you and Macie are lucky to have each other. So, you work for Johnny Morano?"

He nodded. "That's right. Been under him since I was young. Worked my way up and now I got a pretty good gig going. I make a lot of money. I make my own hours, and I get to make most of the decisions. Ain't much more I can want out of a job."

"But isn't your job dangerous?"

Tony gave her a side-glance. "A policeman has a dangerous job, too, but it don't mean they don't do it."

She laughed. "That's a good point."

"What have people told you about me?" he asked.

"Well," she said, looking out the front window. "That you are in the mob ... part of the Morano mafia."

He chuckled. "The Morano mafia? I'm part of the Morano family."

"Okay, the Morano family. But you're in the mob, right?"

"I'm a member of the Morano family. Look, this conversation ain't going where I thought it would. How about if we don't talk about all that now? I promise we can talk about it later. Okay?"

She nodded. "Sure. So what do you wanna talk about then?"

"I want you to tell me how you came to work for Maria. Can we start there?"

"Oh." Raven smiled. "I had worked for Ava and Dante in North Philly for a summer. After the shootings, I was on my own ... no family or friends left. Nowhere to live or work. I didn't know what I was going to do. Some bad stuff happened and out of desperation, I called Ava. I didn't think she'd want to talk to me but was surprised that she was happy to hear my voice. She sent me to see Maria and that's how it all happened."

"Okay, that's good. I like to hear the Morano family is working like that. Ava and Dante are good people. They run that shop in North Philly. Helps us out a lot. They make money and we keep a pulse on what's going on there," he explained.

"That makes sense. After I was here for a while, I didn't understand why their shop wasn't in South Philly, around their friends. So they are there because of Johnny then?"

"Yeah, in a way. Nobody forced them or nothing if that's what you're wondering. Ava and Dante, like the rest of us, are committed to the Moranos. So they stepped up and volunteered."

Raven shook her head. "But what do they get out of it?"

"Financial help. Protection. A lifelong bond with Johnny Morano. The same things people get when they work in a big company. You know, they get a paycheck, they work in nice offices, and they get a lifelong pension."

Raven chuckled. "You make good points," she commented.

He smiled. "So last week, when I saw you with Billy McFeary ..."

"McLeary." She giggled.

"Yeah, him. I didn't like it too much. I think you can do a lot better than some junior accountant that blabbed to Vincent that his daddy got him a reservation at Coletti's."

Raven shrugged. "Why do you care who I'm with? I barely know you."

"Well, you did stay at my apartment for a week. That's gotta count for something."

She nodded. "I'm very grateful for that and for Macie taking good care of me."

"I know you are. I was just saying that after you stayed at my place, I took an interest in you," he hedged.

"An interest? What does that mean?"

"It means I wouldn't mind going out on a date with you."

"Then how come you didn't come and ask me out sooner? It's been a long time," Raven added.

"I don't know. I guess I was nervous."

"Tony Bruno was nervous? About me?"

O my God. I can die a happy woman right now.

He nodded. "What if you said no?"

Raven blushed. "Well, that's a good point. I mean, you're ten years older than me. That could've been a reason to turn you down."

"That ain't nothing in Italian years. What else?"

She gazed out the side window. "You have girls falling all over you. Throwing themselves at you. I saw them at Coletti's. I heard all about it, too."

"Yeah? So what? I don't pay them no mind. That don't mean shit to me. I'm the real deal and I don't want no broad hanging off my arm because I got clout in the neighborhood. I want someone real," he stated.

Raven's heart was fluttering in her chest. Here she was, Raven Ledger, in the confines of Tony Bruno's car talking about *him* being nervous about *her*. Tony Bruno, the most well-known mobster in all of Philadelphia.

"So? Are you going to ask me out or what?"

Tony smiled. "Yeah. You wanna go on a date?"

"Maybe." She giggled.

"Hey, that ain't no fair. You gotta give me an answer."

"Fine. When?"

"Fine? There ain't nothing fine about me. Fantastic, charming, good-looking, charismatic . . . all those will work, but not fine," he teased her.

"All right. I'd love to go on a date with you. When would you like to go out?"

"How about I take you to dinner tomorrow night? I know of a real nice place off the beaten path where we can enjoy a quiet meal."

"Tomorrow night works great. What time will you pick me up?"

He chuckled and shook his head. "Seven. And I want your telephone number. Make sure you tell Cecilia I asked you on an official date. I don't want her thinking this is a fling."

"Okay." She laughed nervously and found herself tongue-tied by his comment. "I'll tell her."

Raven rested the side of her head against the car window as they drove. *If this isn't a fling, then what is it?*

Chapter Seventy-Seven

The next night, Tony knocked on Cecilia's front door. The old woman pulled it open.

"Hello, Tony." She looked him over. "You look very nice. Come on in. Raven is still upstairs. She needs a few more minutes. I was just making espresso for myself. Would you like to have a cup with me?"

"No real Italian refuses espresso, especially when you're making it," Tony boasted. He gave her an undeniable, irresistible, adorable grin.

She went to him like a magnet to metal. "Tony Bruno, you're so damn handsome." She took advantage of being so close to him. She lowered her voice to a whisper and got on her tippy-toes, putting her mouth near his ear. "I wanna tell you something." She pointed to the ceiling, up at the bedroom where Raven was getting ready. "That girl has been through a lot in her short life. I think if you find you're not compatible you should break it off quickly. She can't afford to get emotionally attached and then have her heart torn out of her chest again."

Tony put his warm hand on the back of Cecilia's neck. "You know I haven't had a girl since Kate—not a serious one. I haven't had the stomach for it. That was twelve years ago. Raven is the first woman I met that I wanna get to know better. Something about her makes me wanna be around her. You know? But, Miss Cecilia, I barely know her. It's too soon to know if this can be something serious between the two of us. But I'll tell you this, there's something special about her."

"What do you think is special about her?" she asked, trying to determine his intentions.

"I ain't figured it out yet, but when I do, you'll be the first to know. Well, maybe the second or third. You know I gotta tell Vincent and Salvatore everything first or they'd probably disown me. They're pretty happy that I wanted to take someone out to dinner tonight."

"That's very sweet. But I'm not playing with you, Tony. I need her intact. I'm getting too old to put people back together." Cecilia's eyes filled with fiery tears. "She's like my granddaughter now. I don't even want to charge her rent. You know, I don't need the money. I got everything I want, but she refused. She wouldn't even hear of it, says she's gotta pay her fair share. That's the kind of person Raven Ledger is. You handle that shit with great care."

He leaned in and kissed her cheek. "You have my word."

Cecilia nodded. "Good." She patted his broad chest with the palm of her hand. "Now come have some espresso. I made some biscotti this morning, too, good and dry for dunkin'," she said.

"Oh man. Are you trying to ruin my dinner?"

She glared at him.

"I'm right behind you, Miss Cecilia."

By the time Raven walked into the kitchen, Tony and Cecilia were sitting at the kitchen table laughing.

"Oh, there she is," Tony said. He took her in. Her hair was pulled up on the sides with a barrette holding it in place on the back of her head. Her long hair cascaded down her back in thick, silky strands. She was wearing mascara, which Maria showed her how to apply, and a delicate pink lip gloss, also provided by Maria. Her body looked fabulous in the denim mini skirt, with a white blouse and white sandals. She was the image of youth and summer.

With his eyes on her, she asked, "Is this too casual? I wasn't sure how to dress."

Tony shook his head. "No, you look beautiful."

"You do," Cecilia added, admiring the girl's beauty. "You look perfect."

Raven blushed. "Thanks. Do you wanna get going?"

Tony stood, turned to the old woman, and bowed. "Miss Cecilia, thank you for the espresso and the best cookies in this whole city. Don't tell Maria I said that, though, okay?"

"It'll be our secret," Cecilia responded, beaming at the man.

Chapter Seventy-Eight

Tony and Raven sat at a corner table at an exclusive Mexican restaurant in Center City. The entrance was tucked away in an alley. Inside there were only ten tables, all filled.

Raven looked around at the warm décor and atmosphere. There were round tables. The ceiling was lit up like the night sky. It had been painted black and strung over the paint were thousands of pixie lights. The floors, bar, and tables were made of polished mahogany. The chairs were sturdy and plush, the seats and backs covered in a rich deep purple velvet fabric. The pictures on the walls were from various beaches and hillsides in Mexico. They were all in black-and-white, each with a spotlight on them.

"How do you know Cecilia?" Raven asked.

"I know almost everyone in South Philly. But I met Cecilia when I was young. She was best friends with a woman named Donata who took me in when I was a boy. Donata used to own the bakery where you work now. Donata got the cancer in her lungs, and before she died, she sold the bakery to Maria. It looks all different now. Anyway, Donata and Cecilia were good friends, so I spent a lot of time around those two women. They practically raised me." Tony shook his head. "Donata was a good soul. She helped me a lot. I still miss her."

"Oh, Cecilia never told me that story."

Tony grinned. "Did you ever ask her how she knew me?"

Raven shook her head. "I never thought to." She looked around the restaurant, admiring its beauty. "Do you come here a lot?"

"I come here on special occasions. I guess I should've asked if you like Mexican food before I brought you here, huh? That wasn't very thoughtful." He looked down at his hands.

"Are you kidding? I love Mexican food. But tell me, I thought Italians only eat their own food."

Tony pressed his index finger to his lips. "Don't tell anyone." He chuckled. "Believe it or not, me, Vincent, and Salvatore like all kinds of eats. Don't get me wrong, Italian is our favorite, but we love food from all over the world."

Raven opened her menu and she had to swallow a few times. Everything was so expensive. *Twenty-two dollars for a salad? A plate of lettuce?* The entrees were from one hundred to one hundred fifty a plate, and that included no sides. They were all separately priced. She looked up from the menu at Tony.

He glanced at her. "What's wrong? You don't see nothing you like? I can have the chef make you something special."

She closed her menu. "No. There's nothing wrong. I like everything. I-I don't know what I should eat for dinner. What are you getting?"

Tony rattled off his appetizer, salad, entrée, and side as Raven calculated over two hundred dollars for his food. She swallowed hard.

"How about you?" he asked. He could see her apprehension. "If you're worried about the prices, don't. I wouldn't bring you to a place I couldn't afford."

She nodded, then she smirked at him. "Now I know why they only need ten tables in the whole place. I'm going to have exactly what you're having."

Raven was at ease with Tony. It wasn't because he was one of the most feared mobsters in Philadelphia; it was because she sensed he'd suffered the same as her. There was a gentleness about him that she suspected most people never saw. That he reserved for moments like these.

Tony sipped from his wine glass. "So you ended up killing your brother?"

Raven choked on her iced tea. "That's hardly the way to ask someone something like that."

"Aw, come on. You know what I mean. I don't always have the right words. No matter how I ask it, you know it's the same question. But I'm curious. I don't know another woman who had to do something like that. Tell me about it."

Raven straightened her spine. She folded her hands together, elbows on the table. "Well, it was awful and so powerful all at the same time. He was my twin brother and I loved him, but don't tell anyone I said that because they'll stone me to death. Loving him was what made it so hard. But the powerful part was by pulling that trigger, I was able to stop him from killing more people. Everyone in that room was helpless. The room was chaotic, and Matthew was feeding off of everyone's fear. Then he hands me the very thing that could make all of the suffering stop." Her eyes filled with fresh tears. "So I used it and made the suffering stop."

Tony put his hand over hers. "You did good. You saved a lot of people that day. And even though it was hard, you stuck up for the people who couldn't fight for themselves. I admire that. It takes guts."

Raven shook her head. Her eyes pivoted to his. "Thanks for saying all of that. This is one thing I never get to talk about. You know, how I felt about my brother and having to kill him. Those thoughts never get to leave me. I mean, I get it, no one wants to know the gory details of what was going on in my head as I pulled that trigger. You're the first person who has asked me."

"Well, I ain't no stranger to a gun and what it can do to stop people. But see, I was raised on that shit, brought up to understand how to use a weapon. You never even held a gun before that day, right?"

She nodded. "Right."

"And you just pointed and that was that."

"Yeah, it's easy to kill when you're put in a situation that warrants it. But I think about it every day. The looks on people's faces right before he murdered them. The begging and crying everyone did, but all my brother did was laugh in their faces. It was disgusting. And then my brother's expression when he realized I was going to shoot him. I'll never forget the look of betrayal on his face."

"Did he say anything to you?"

She looked down at her hands resting on the table. "Matthew's last words to me were, 'I should've known better than to think you'd have the guts to do anything big with your life. Give me the gun or I'll blow your fucking head off.'" Raven lifted her sorrowful eyes to meet Tony's. "Then he lifted his rifle to shoot me, so I shot him first. It's not something I'm proud of. I know a lot more people didn't die that day because of what I did, but no one understands the toll it's taken on me . . . and my life," she added.

Tony nodded. "I understand. Believe me, I do. I know what it's like to be betrayed by someone in your family. But that's another story that's already been written." He put his hand on her slender shoulder. "Are you up for a walk? We can go to Penn's Landing, maybe get some coffee or dessert?"

Raven nodded. "That would be nice."

As they were leaving the restaurant, Tony reached for Raven's hand and their fingers intertwined. Raven realized being there with Tony, her hand wrapped in his, was as natural as breathing. She found comfort in his company.

As they walked, both of them hoped this could be the start of a bond between two people who desperately needed to be loved by the right person.

Chapter Seventy-Nine

Cecilia rushed to the door when she saw Tony's car stop in front of her house. She was twisting her hands together and held a nervous smile on her lips.

Raven unlocked the door and pushed it open.

"How was your date?" Cecilia asked.

Shocked to find the woman there, she jumped and slapped her hand over her heart. "Cecilia! You scared me." She took a couple of deep breaths. "The date was really nice. The restaurant was wonderful. They had these homemade tortilla chips—"

Cecilia cut her off. "I don't wanna hear about chips. I wanna know about Tony. Was he a gentleman?"

"Yes, he was."

"Sit down," Cecilia said, sitting on the sofa and pointing to the spot beside her.

Raven grinned. "Here we go."

The old woman angled her body toward the girl. "Did he kiss you?"

Raven shook her head. "We held hands."

"That's nice. Do you two get along well?"

"Cecilia, it was one date. We got along fine, but it doesn't mean anything."

"Did he ask you for another date?"

Raven gave her a bashful grin. "Yes," she mumbled. "Dinner on Saturday night."

She clasped her hands together. "Ooooh. Where's he taking you?"

The twenty-year-old unstrapped her sandals and slipped them off of her feet. "He's going to cook for me at his apartment." She gave the woman an exaggerated eye roll. "He claims to be a good cook. We'll see."

Cecilia narrowed her eyes. "His apartment, huh?" she grunted.

"Yeah, why are you saying it like that?"

The old woman shrugged. "I think it's too soon for you to be alone with him in his apartment. You don't wanna give him the wrong idea."

"Cecilia," Raven said, scooching closer to the woman until they were touching. "I can promise you I won't give him the wrong idea. I'm *not* going there to have sex with him. I'm going to eat dinner. Besides, I spent a week sleeping in his spare bedroom," Raven argued.

"Yeah, but Macie was there."

Raven pursed her lips. "Tony isn't going to force himself on me. He's not like that."

"I'm sure he wouldn't, but I'd feel better if the dinner was chaperoned."

The girl chuckled. "You know, this isn't 1910 when women needed escorts or they'd be called a slut. Besides, I've been called much worse than that so I'm already ahead. Listen, I trust Tony. I get a good feeling from him."

Cecilia nodded. "Your gut instincts are very important. How will you get there?"

"Tony must've known you'd ask that question."

"That's right." Cecilia nodded. "Because Tony was raised by an Italian woman."

"He's sending Vincent over to pick me up—and before you ask, Tony will drive me home."

"Vincent? Oh boy. Don't let that little devil drive too fast. And make sure he knows you're Tony's girl."

Raven yawned and stretched her arms out far. "I'm nobody's girl, other than yours."

Cecilia's face lit up with pride. "I like that. You hang on to that good sense you got in your head."

Raven stood, leaned over, and gave Cecilia a peck on her cheek. "You know I will. Good night."

***

On Saturday night, Vincent parked the car and honked the horn. He waited less than five seconds and honked again. He looked up at the house, tapping the steering wheel.

Cecilia opened her screen door and stood on the porch. Her hands were on her hips and when Vincent made eye contact with her, she lifted her eyebrows. Then she went back inside.

A minute later, Vincent knocked on the screen door with his head hanging.

Cecilia stood on the other side. "Vincent DeLuca, you honk for dogs to get out of the street. You honk when a car is about to back into you. There are specific reasons we use the car horn. To collect my Raven is not one of them. You have to walk up here like the decent man that you are and bring her to your car properly."

Vincent cracked a smile. "Sorry, Miss Cecilia. Hey, do you think we can keep this between you and me? Tony will get pissed if he heard what I did."

Cecilia nodded. "Yes, we can. As long as you never do it again." She turned and walked to the bottom of the steps. "Raven, Vincent is here for you."

As Raven descended the stairs, Vincent smiled. When Cecilia saw the admiration in his eyes, she whacked him. "Put your tongue back in your mouth," she hissed quietly.

"Hi, Vincent," Raven sang. "I have to grab my purse in the kitchen."

Vincent turned to the woman with urgency. "I wasn't drooling over her. I mean, I would if Tony didn't like her. I'm happy for my friend. Me and Salvatore have been trying to get him to get back in the game, but he refused until he met Raven. She's bringing our boy back to life. It makes me happy."

"Oh, well, that's very sweet. I like to hear that you're happy for your friend. But if I find out that this is a game for Tony, which he assured me it isn't, then somebody is going to be in trouble."

"Aw, come on, Miss Cecilia. I didn't mean it that way."

Raven came into the living room and hugged the old woman. "You don't have to wait up for me. Tony will walk me to the door. I promise."

Cecilia shook her head. "And I'll be waiting right here to make sure you get home safe."

Raven had overheard a lot of what Cecilia and Vincent said to each other. It was curious to her how these two mobsters, who terrified everyone, reverted to small boys under the scrutiny of an old lady. She smiled to herself and walked out the door.

Chapter Eighty

Tony chuckled at Raven's question about their behavior with Cecilia.

"What? You think because me and Vincent are respected in the neighborhood that we can do whatever we want? It don't matter who you are; it's all about respect. Donata taught me that to get respect, I had to give it. Most of the time it works out. Then I run across a few knuckleheads that it don't, and that's when things get tricky. I promise you, though, those who don't give respect ain't getting it either." Tony stirred his tomato sauce. "I told ya. I've known Miss Cecilia since I was a hungry, dirty kid with nobody to care for me. It doesn't matter how much power I got. Being rude to her would make me an asshole. Donata would turn over in her grave." He paused and made the sign of the cross. "God rest her beautiful soul. Vincent and Salvatore, we all feel the same way. We ain't better than nobody and we need to look out for the people in this neighborhood. That's what real men do."

"Wow, that's interesting. I was in a temporary foster home, and I wanted to stay with that woman forever, she was so kind. She told me the same thing about respect." Raven looked down at her hands, and a frown formed on her face. "Cecilia seems to like you, but I get the feeling she's afraid I'll get hurt."

Tony nodded. "That's Cecilia. She loves hard. See, I ain't got a strong record with women. I'm not like Vincent. I don't sleep around. I ain't a family man like Salvatore. I do my own thing. Don't get me wrong, I love being in the company of a woman, but I only had one serious person in my whole life. We was sixteen when we fell in love." He closed his eyes and pulled up the image of his first love. "Boy, I thought it was forever. By the time we were eighteen, we were married."

Raven's mouth dropped open. "You were married before?"

"Yeah, I was, and I loved it. There was something really good about that kind of commitment. To have someone that I knew would always be there for me." His eyes veered off to the window as he looked out over the neighborhood he loved and protected. "What me and Kate had was great. It was special and we was good for each other. I haven't let myself attach to another woman since she left. It took me years to get over her. Still today, I get mad sometimes that she's gone . . . that I ain't got that person who feels like home no more. Do you have a person that no matter where you are, if you're with them, it's home?"

Raven frowned. "No. I've never had that. Maybe my father when I was young, but it was so long ago I can barely remember the feeling."

Tony nodded. "Well, someday when you find home in a person, you're gonna remember this conversation 'cause you'll never wanna lose it."

"So you decided not to have any serious relationships after Kate?"

He shrugged. "I ain't that calculated. I guess I've been afraid, and I ain't never met another woman that interests me like that. Until I met you. I know it's kinda soon to say that shit to you, but I thought you should know it. So you understand where my head is at."

Raven was flattered and her heart fluttered in her chest. "What happened to Kate . . . I mean to you two?" She walked over and stood next to him.

Tony's eyes clouded. They went flat and he avoided her gaze. "I can't say too much about it without reliving it. All I can say is one day we were happy and the next day she was gone. It was the hardest time of my life. For years, I kept waiting for her to walk through our apartment door." He grinned. "Back then, we lived in a dump, but we didn't mind 'cause we had each other."

"How did you manage once she was gone?"

"Whew. That's a hard question. I was like a zombie for a while. I wished I was dead," he stated. "I was lucky to have Vincent and Salvatore there by my side to put me back together. If it weren't for them, I don't think I'd be here talking to you today. I'd be a different man."

She rubbed his arm gently, attempting to ease the pain that was deeply etched on his face. "I can't imagine what you've been through, but I think I understand what you're saying." She placed a hand on her belly. "That fiery burning in the pit of your stomach. Loneliness that's so intense you think you're going to die. I've had that before. It made me give up all hope."

Tony looked into her eyes. "Yeah, like that." He looked down at his feet, then back up at her again. "What about you? You ever been in love?"

Raven scoffed and shook her head. "No, I've never even had a boyfriend."

"Get outta here. You never had a boyfriend? I don't believe you. Someone as gorgeous as you are?"

Her face reddened. "Nope. Never. I wasn't popular in school, and I lived with a very strict, corrupt foster mom. I only had one friend, and we weren't accepted into the North Philly crowds." Her eyes ran over him and stopped on his plump lips. "I've never kissed a guy either."

Tony put his hand to his forehead. "And you're twenty?"

She nodded and laughed. "Yes. It's not the worst thing in the world. I'm young and I have plenty of time."

He lifted his palms toward her. "Hey, I ain't knocking it. I think it's amazing. Most people are experienced by the time they're fifteen. You ain't like the women I'm used to."

"You mean the ones that throw themselves at your feet?" she teased him.

Now Tony was red in the face. "I have no idea what you're talking about."

"Mm-hmm. Sure you don't. Anyway, what is Tony Bruno cooking for dinner?" she sang, happy with the connection they had.

"Well, let's see. I made us some veal scallopine with homemade pasta that Macie made. A little salad, some bread from a great bakery I know of," he joked.

Their eyes locked and Raven stepped into him. He put a strong hand on the small of her back, and she placed both hands on his shoulders.

His eyes moved from her lips to her eyes. "Is it okay if I kiss you? I know it'll be your first and I swear I'll do the best that I can to make it good so that you don't think you wasted it on me," he said in a raspy tone.

"Yes. I'd like you to kiss me."

Tony moved his head forward and angled his face as his lips met hers. At first, it was their lips pressed against each other's. But after a few seconds, Tony opened his mouth slightly and gently moved his tongue over her lips, easing her mouth open.

Raven could barely breathe. She didn't recognize the sensations running through her. She closed her arms around Tony's neck and pressed her chest against his. She allowed him to guide her as he edged her mouth open, letting his tongue slide inside and dance over hers.

When they parted, they were both panting heavily.

"How'd I do?" he asked with a glow in his eyes.

"Oh." She nodded, still holding fast around his neck. "You did great." She backed away and gave him a side-glance. "But you know, I don't have anything to compare it to," she teased.

"Maybe you can compare that one to the next one I give you later tonight."

The two shared a laugh as he took her by the hand and led her to the kitchen table.

Raven looked at the beautiful place settings and then at him. She pointed to it. "Macie?"

"Oh yeah. That's all her. I might be able to cook, but I can't do none of that girly, fancy, decorating shit. She makes things look beautiful. She can't fix herself up or pick out nice clothes, but everything else she does just fine." He threw her a look over his shoulder. "Macie thinks she's ugly, so she doesn't try to make herself pretty."

Raven didn't know what to say. It was true, Macie did nothing to enhance her appearance. "She did a beautiful job. Be sure to tell her I said so." She smiled. "How can I help with dinner?"

He pointed to a chair. "You sit. I got this covered."

Raven took a seat at the table, and all she could think about was that kiss, as Tony went over to the stove.

"So, did you cook this meal, or did Macie?" she asked in a light tone.

Tony slapped his hand against his heart like he'd been stabbed. "You're killing me. Macie wanted to cook this meal so that everything was perfect for you tonight, but I told her I had to do it myself. She likes you."

"I like her, too. She's very smart and so kind."

"Yeah, she is. I don't know what I'd do without her," Tony agreed.

He opened the refrigerator and brought over the salad and a basket of bread from the counter. Then he made each of them a plate.

"Mangiare," Tony said. "That means to eat."

Raven smiled and put a piece of veal in her mouth. "Oh, this is delicious."

"Thank you very much. I think so, too."

***

When they finished dinner, Tony took Raven into the living room. He put on music and poured them each a glass of wine. He handed her the glass.

"Oh," she said nervously. "Thank you, but I don't drink."

"Why? You a recovering alcoholic?"

Raven chuckled. "No, I mean I've never tried alcohol."

"Boy, there's a lot of firsts you're gonna enjoy with me . . . I hope. Anyway, this ain't drinking, Raven. It ain't like I'm offering you a glass of whiskey or grappa. This is a fine wine from Italy. You sip it. It's like a dessert, good for digestion."

"Okay, the digestion part? That was totally an old person thing to say." She giggled.

He laughed with her. "Shit, you're right, it was. Look, I ain't trying to get you drunk if that's what you're worried about."

Raven gave him a polite smile. "No, that wasn't what I was thinking." She lifted the glass and put it to her lips, pulling a splash of the purple liquid over her tongue. "Mm. Wow. That's so good."

"See, I told you." He sat down next to her, leaving only a few inches between them. "So I like you. What do you think?"

She nodded. "I like you, too."

"So you think you wanna have some more dates and see if this goes anywhere?"

"I'd like that," she murmured.

Tony took a sip of wine. "Me too."

Chapter Eighty-One

On Monday morning at the bakery, Raven was humming as she scrubbed away at the pans in the sink.

"Well, you're cheery this morning," Effie commented.

"What are you talking about? I'm always cheery," she bantered.

"Uh-ha. It wouldn't have anything to do with that date you had with Tony on Saturday night, would it?"

Raven shrugged and giggled.

"Oh, I see. You're a schoolgirl now." Effie made her way over to Raven. "So? How did it go? You haven't said a thing about it."

Raven's mood was light. "It was so nice. He's a good cook, too."

"I'm happy you had a good time. Remember what I told you about getting involved with a mobster? You recall that conversation?"

Raven's smile dimmed and her excitement drained. "Yeah, I remember. But I think I'm willing to take that chance. He's kind and funny and sweet. It's nothing serious right now, but I wanna see if things can work out with him. He and I talked about it and agreed that we would give it a try."

"Okay now. You said this ain't serious, but you already had that conversation. Sounds serious to me," Effie said, lifting her eyebrows. She searched Raven's face, a girl who lived so long without being loved. "It's okay to be happy, and I'm happy for you, but you have to be careful."

***

Later that afternoon when Raven was working the front of the bakery, Tony strolled into the store. He leaned over the counter and pecked her on the cheek. "How are you today?"

Raven's eyes moved around, watching the customers observing her and Tony. She cringed and gave him her attention. "I'm fine." She lowered her voice to a whisper. "People are staring at us. I don't know if this is good for your reputation. I'm not well-liked by some of the customers because of who I am. They saw you kiss me on the cheek."

"Oh really?" He turned and scanned the restaurant.

Then he looked at Raven, put his hand on the back of her neck, and pulled her face to his. When his lips met hers, Sienna and Beatrice were sitting against the far wall and gasped. When Tony heard it, he leaned his upper body closer to Raven's.

When they parted, Tony turned around and glared at the two women, who shrank under his harsh gaze. "Is something wrong, ladies? I heard you gasp. What? You see a spider?"

The two women shook their heads, gathered their things, and rushed out of the bakery.

"That wasn't very nice," Raven scolded him. "You know that they're afraid of you."

"You and me ain't going to do things because other people approve. People like us," he pointed from him to her, "we only do them if we want to. Capiche?"

"That's fine. But I'm not worried about me. I'm used to people acting like assholes toward me. It's you I'm worried about."

"Ah, fuck them." He grinned. "I can't be bothered caring about what people have to say about who I wanna kiss. I kiss who I like, that's it."

"As long as you're okay with it. Everyone in this town loves you . . ."

He raised his hand to silence her and wagged his finger. "You don't ever need to sacrifice something you want 'cause you're worried about me. I can take care of myself." His tone softened and his eyes danced. "You're into me, aren't you? I can tell you are," he said in a singsong tone.

Raven shrugged. "Oh, I don't know. I barely know you. We just said the other night we will see how it goes."

"Okay, well, how about this? You and me will have lunch together for the next two weeks. So that we can get to know one another real good. If at the end of those two weeks, you still like me and I still like you, we'll make it official. How's that sound?"

"It depends on what making it official means," she cracked.

"It means you'd be my lady and I'd be your man. Exclusive. No one else."

She leaned into him again. "I guess so."

He chuckled. "You guess so? I'll accept that. Since we missed lunch today, how about I come by when you're done work and we'll go get some pizza? I know a great place."

She smiled. "I bet you do. I'll be ready to leave here around three."

As Raven watched Tony walk out of the bakery, she saw men on the street rushing over to him. She hated the way some looked so feeble, walking up to Tony and shaking his hand, trying to get on his good side. One man practically bowed to him, and Raven's eyes moved up to Tony's face which was stone cold. The scowl was so pronounced it even made her nervous. She would find out later the bowing man had borrowed money from the Moranos to pay a gambling debt and wasn't keeping good on his promise to repay them.

Chapter Eighty-Two

Raven and Tony had lunch together for the next two weeks. Tony had also added six dinners over that same time. By the end of the second week, the couple had become good friends and had built trust in one another.

At the last lunch, Tony took her in his arms. "So, now that we know each other, I was thinking that maybe you and me could be, you know . . . just you and me like we talked about."

Raven smiled. Here was Tony Bruno, a respected mobster tripping over his words to *her*.

"Okay, so let me get this straight. That means we don't date other people?" she asked.

He nodded. "But I don't wanna call what we're doing dating no more. I want us to be more serious than that. I want you to move into my guest room. You know, we can try living together."

Raven pulled her head back and looked into his eyes. "Tony, I can't do that. There's no way I can leave Cecilia."

"Cecilia will be happy for us if she knows we're serious. It don't mean you're outta her life, just her house. My apartment is five minutes away." As he talked, his hands flew in the air like he was the conductor of a choir.

Raven shook her head. "I d-d-don't know. This is moving so fast." She rubbed the back of her neck to relieve the sudden tension. "We haven't even had sex."

He ran his hand over her butt. "So what? I know it's gonna be good. If it ain't, we'll work on it until it is. That's how I operate."

"That's not what I meant." Raven's voice was serious. "I don't know if I'm ready to take that step after what? Three weeks?"

"Did anybody say something about losing your virginity to me right now? I sure didn't." He looked behind him, twisting his head to the left, then the right. "Did anybody say anything about sex?" he yelled into the street and laughed.

"O my God, shut up. Stop it before someone hears you," she begged playfully, putting her hand over his mouth.

He kissed her palm. "I hope everyone hears me. I want all of South Philly to know that Tony Bruno is back. I'm getting a second chance at love." He looked into her face. "I don't know what's gonna happen between us, but I got a good feeling about this. I wanna be with you. That has to mean something, right?"

She nodded and laid her head against his chest. "Okay, but before I can agree to anything, we have to talk about some things first."

He ran his hand over her thick, silky hair. "Sure. What would you like to talk about?" he asked, leaning in and kissing her on the mouth.

"Well," she hedged, gathering the courage to be honest. "I've been working at the bakery long enough and I've heard a lot of things. I've watched Maria make sacrifices for stuff that Salvatore needs. She has to give up a lot of her time to do things for him in the middle of the day because he calls her out of the blue." She lowered her face. "That's all fine. I know that couples do things for each other. And I also know, just like Salvatore, that your loyalty will always be with the Morano family first."

Tony tilted his head and watched her expectantly.

She raked her fingers through her hair. "I ain't about to ask you to change when it comes to the Morano family. I know it's what you do and you love being part of the mob. But it scares me. It makes me nervous about getting too involved with you." She placed her palm on his warm cheek. "No one has ever put me first my whole life, but I'm ready for that now. I won't play second ever again. I want that with the person I love and dedicate my life to."

Tony leaned into her, pressed his lips against her forehead, and stayed there. After a moment he pulled his head back. "Look, everyone will tell you that my loyalty is with the Morano family. I pledged to the organization, and I love them and everything that I do. Even the parts that ain't that pretty. I will protect Salvatore and Vincent with my life. But you gotta know, I ain't like other mobsters. I mean, I'll just say it like it is if you and me are gonna give this a go." He leveled her with his gaze. "I will protect you with my life. You gotta understand something about me, I can be loyal to the mob and you. Nobody, I don't care who they are, owns Tony Bruno outright. You get me?"

Raven nodded. "Tony, I believe you, but I'm still afraid I'll get burned. Am I making a mistake? Are you going to turn into some other person once we're together?"

"Nah, Raven, this ain't no mistake. You'll never be sorry that you picked me. I think women are the most special creatures God put on this earth. They're the soul of a family. They hold things together in a way us guys can't. I really want this—to be with you. I lost my first love and I don't wanna lose my last."

"Are you saying you love me?" she asked, shocked.

"I'm saying I'm falling in love with you. I believe good, solid love takes time and effort. You have to be kinda like the same person, spend time together, and know each other through and through. That's why I want you to move in. So we can see how we are as a family. My parents were miserable. My father was a rotten alcoholic, and my mother was a woman broken by the weight of the times when women had a place under the rule of their husbands. I ain't giving her a pass for not protecting me, but I see things for what they are. I don't want that for myself. I don't want you and me to be two strangers who have the same address and telephone number fifty years from now. I don't want that for me, and I know you don't want that for you. If you agree to try and give us a chance, I promise you'll be my number one priority. As long as we have an understanding about my work."

She straightened her neck and pecked him on the lips. "I love that you're comfortable telling me things that are in your heart. I think I understand better now. But Tony, I need to get really clear about what would be expected of me. Say we stayed together and I let you marry me."

He chuckled at her words. "Okay, well, someday *if* you let *me* marry *you*, then I'll make you happy. It'll be like we both hit the lottery."

She looked down at her hands. "That's not what I'm talking about. What I mean is, what does the Morano family expect of Tony Bruno's live-in girlfriend or wife?"

Tony pulled his shoulders back and looked up to the sky. "Oh, I see what you're getting at. I can tell you that women married to guys like me, at least in the Morano family, are strong and opinionated. They're independent and modern. You would be my confidante. The person I turn to when my heart is in shambles. The one who gets to put me back together. You would show me love and respect all the time. In turn, I have to give you all the same things. A husband's disrespect of his wife, at the level I'm at, is not tolerated. That means the Morano top guns aren't allowed to cheat on their wives. But I ain't gonna lie to you, that one happens." He held his palms up. "But I can tell you that I ain't ever gonna cheat on you."

Raven grinned. "Well, none of that seems so bad. Now, when you say help you when your heart is in shambles . . . what does that mean?"

Tony kissed her neck. His warm lips were like hot coals. "I got a past just like you do. It ain't great neither. I had a real fucked-up childhood. Sometimes that gets the better of me, but nobody on the outside sees that. We're the same, you and me. We got hurt young when we didn't deserve it, and now all we want is to be loved."

"Yeah, I get what you're saying but why do you think some kids have to be put through so much bad shit?"

Tony smiled. "Maybe so when we get older, we can protect others."

Raven nodded. "Yeah, let's stick with that. Tony, I could never hurt anyone who hasn't done anything to me. You know that, right?"

Tony chuckled. "You ain't gonna ever be asked to hurt no one. You'll never be involved in any of that. You won't do my job, but you'll need to help me deal with it sometimes. What people see on the outside isn't always what's going on inside."

"Ha! Tell me about it. So, when you say words like respect, does that mean I can't curse you out or does that mean when you tell me something, I can't question what you're doing or where you're going?"

"Of course you can curse me out. I might yell back, but it won't mean I don't love you. But asking questions . . . I'll let you know about the things that I can. When I don't tell you something, it's because it's safer for you not to know. There are times when I'll need to go away for a while. When that happens, you won't know where I'm going."

Raven's eyes grew large. "You mean like leave for days?"

Tony pursed his lips and nodded. "Yeah, sometimes. It doesn't happen too often. Usually when I have to travel to New York or New Jersey with Vincent and Salvatore to meet with other people. While I'm gone, you'll have Maria to talk to. Or you can have a sleepover at Cecilia's. Or you can hang out with Macie."

Raven rolled her eyes. "Macie and Cecilia are fine, but Maria is my boss. And she's so—oh, I don't know, sophisticated. She's kind and totally has her shit together. I wish I had an ounce of her togetherness in me. I'm not seeing her and me hanging out while you're out of town."

Tony nudged her gently. "I've known Maria since she was a teenager. There was a time when she was a lot like you. She learned how to carry herself by being part of the family. Alessandra Morano, Johnny's wife that I told you about, helped Maria out a lot. Took her under her wing so that someday she'd be ready to support Salvatore as the head of the family. By embracing the values that are needed to live a good life, Maria has everything she always wanted. Now me on the other hand? I don't need to learn how to talk all proper and shit. There ain't a criminal within fifty miles that would take me seriously if I talked like Salvatore does. Besides, that ain't my thing. I do like the nice clothes, though," he said, tugging his shirt. "My talent is working with my hands and my mind. My temper helps a little here and there, too," he joked.

Raven rested the side of her face on his shoulder. "And what if something bad happened to you? Does that mean something bad happens to me, too? What would the Morano family expect of me then?" she asked with growing concern.

"Oh boy. First off, ain't nothing gonna happen to me 'cause I'm careful and have that crazy ass Vincent around me all the time. But okay, let's dig into it. It's best to get it all out there now. When a mobster dies, if the wife remains loyal to the family, the family takes care of her and her children until they die."

Raven cringed. "That sounds ancient. I don't want 'the family' to take care of me. I want to know that they won't force me to do anything I don't wanna do."

"Like what?" Tony asked.

"I don't know. Like, marry another mobster."

Tony laughed until tears rolled down his cheeks.

Raven narrowed her eyes. "I'm glad you find it so funny. I heard about gangs that make the widows be with someone else so they can't leave with any secrets."

She smiled as Tony continued to belly laugh. But when he didn't stop, she pinched her lips together and crossed her arms over her chest.

"Okay, okay." He patted his hand on his chest to stop himself from laughing. "No, you won't be forced to marry someone they pick. They ain't gonna arrange a marriage for you. We're not a knuckle-dragging gang. The Moranos know the person I pick to be with can be trusted. If something ever happened to me, the Moranos would expect that they could continue to trust you." He chuckled again.

Raven put her hands on her hips. "Is there anything else that I would have to do if I decide to be your girlfriend?"

Tony coughed to clear his throat. "Yeah, you'd be required to let me love you forever. To let me keep you safe." He looked up at the sky. "Oh yeah. You'd have to learn how to make some of Cecilia's recipes. That would be a definite requirement. And if we ever got married, you'd give me plenty of children. You want kids, right?"

Raven nodded as a small smile played on her lips. "Oh definitely. I've thought about children a lot since the shootings. Having no blood relatives left is an odd feeling. Could you imagine your life without Macie?"

Tony shook his head. "No, there's no way. I love her too much."

"Exactly. I want to build a family and raise my children the way I wanted my mother to raise me and Matthew."

"See, I think we're very compatible. I'll need you to give me an answer about moving in with me . . . say, by tomorrow."

Her eyes bulged. "Tomorrow? Tony, you can't put a timeline like that on this," she huffed. "Are you serious?"

He nodded. "I'm serious if you'll let me be serious."

Raven gave him a half grin. "I'll see what I can do. I have to talk to Cecilia before I make any decisions."

Tony placed his hand on her cheek. "That sounds reasonable."

***

Back at the bakery, Raven set out to finish her work. She thought about Tony and a warmth spread through her. Then a chill offset the warmth as she thought about the mob. She was worried that the Mafia would be more like a gang and that Tony couldn't see it because he was too integrated into their society.

She'd ask Cecilia. The woman had known Tony since he was a boy and knew all about the Morano family. Cecilia was the one person who could guide her on this decision.

Chapter Eighty-Three

Raven was sitting across the kitchen table from Cecilia, choking down her dinner. She was worried about discussing moving in with Tony. Her nervous jitters made her mouth dry and suppressed her appetite.

As the old woman chatted away, she asked, "When are you seeing Tony again?"

Raven smiled at her and nodded. "Yes."

Cecilia rested her fork on the side of her plate. "Yes? Yes, what? Is there something wrong with you? Did you hit your head today?" She reached over and touched the girl's hair.

Raven glanced at her, lowered her head, and shook it. "No, why?"

The old woman squinted. "Because I asked you when you're going out with Tony again and your answer was yes. Does that make any sense to you? 'Cause it sure don't to me."

"Oh." Her eyes were still downcast. "I'm trying to work through something. I have a decision to make and I want to talk to you about it—you know, get your advice. It's important what you think."

Cecilia abandoned her dinner and crossed her arms, resting them on the table. "Well, I don't know why you're fretting like that. You can talk to me about anything."

Raven's eyes met hers. "This is different than the normal crap I babble about. Me . . . me. Well, Tony asked me to move into his apartment with him."

"Oh, he did, huh?" The old woman looked down at her plate. "That sure as hell is different. Why so soon?"

"That's what I asked, and he thinks that if it's gonna work between us—for life—then we need to live as a couple and see how that goes. I see his point, but I don't know if it's the right thing or the right time."

Cecilia nodded. "Yes, I see his point, too. Look, I've known Tony for most of his life. He's a good man to the people he loves and cares about. To others, he is a ruthless, cruel man who will do whatever it takes to protect the mob or carry out his job."

"I know. I told him that's what scares me. He's been kind and gentle with me . . . never pressures me for sex." She wrung her hands together. "I have strong feelings for him. It's hard for me to say no. I want to be with him. I really, really like him," Raven admitted.

"Are you sure you're not attracted by his power? I mean, that can be awfully sexy. Plus the fact that every unmarried woman will be envious as hell," the old woman stated.

Raven shook her head. "No, that's not it. I can see how people will think that, but that ain't me. I saw what power did to my brother. Power can destroy decent people and power can be used to do good. I expect Tony to use it for good. The people kneeling to him, begging him, pleading and wanting to be on his good side—if anything, it turns me off."

Cecilia picked up her fork and dug it into her plate. "Tony won't change for you or anybody else. He's a mobster—what do you mean use it for good? How's he gonna do that?"

"He will help people that can't help themselves. I'm not talking about drug dealers and gamblers here. I'm talking about using his power to help everyday people. He's been doing that for a long time. You told me yourself he watches over this community."

Cecilia nodded. "Yes, he does. If you can live with both parts of him—the good guy and the bad guy—then I think you have your answer."

Raven's eyes grew wide. "What? What's the answer?"

"You are falling in love with the man, not the mobster. That's very important." Cecilia dragged her eyes to Raven's. "You have to love the man that Tony is because loving the mobster will only end in failure and disappointment. If you're asking for my blessing, you have it."

Raven leaned toward the woman and threw her arms around her neck. "Thank you." She pulled back. "So you don't think I'm making a mistake?"

Cecilia shook her head slowly. "I never said that. I've given you my blessing." She looked at her. "You will come back here and live with me if it doesn't work out with Tony. You don't need to be afraid that you'll lose what you have here with me. You're my family now, and this is your home."

Raven's eyes welled. She was overwhelmed with gratitude for the people who had come into her life. All the people who had stepped in to help her.

"Thank you. I'm gonna go call Tony."

Cecilia smiled. "Okay, you go do that. But listen, tell him you're not moving for two weeks to give me some time to get used to the idea."

***

"Tony? Cecilia gave us her blessing."

"I knew Miss Cecilia wouldn't let me down. She knows I need a woman like you in my life to keep me on the straight and narrow," he remarked.

"Excuse me," she said with a giggle. "I'm coming there to be your girlfriend, not your mommy."

"Oh boy. You got that right. So you want me to come pick you up tomorrow with your things?"

Raven shook her head even though Tony couldn't see her. "No. Cecilia said two weeks from now . . . so she can get used to the idea of me not being here."

***

Two weeks later, Raven and Cecilia clung to each other, saying their tearful goodbyes.

"Come on, you two," Tony said. "You're gonna see each other tomorrow. Cecilia's coming to our apartment for dinner, remember?"

Raven nodded and sniffled. "It's not the same, Tony. Visiting each other and living together are different. Isn't that why I'm moving in with you?"

Tony hung his head. "You're right. Take all the time you need."

Vincent nudged him. "You want me to bring her crap out to the car?"

Raven glanced at Tony. "I only have my duffel bag."

Tony looked it over. "This is all the luggage you got?"

"Yeah. It's all I need."

He gave her a warm smile. "And you're all I need."

Vincent grunted. "Aw, come on. That's sickening shit coming from a man like you."

Tony glared at him, then moved to Cecilia. He kissed her on the cheek. "See you tomorrow, Miss Cecilia."

As they walked to the car, Raven looked over her shoulder at Cecilia. It was the end of one chapter and the beginning of another. While she would see Cecilia frequently, there was nothing that could match living and loving someone under the same roof.

Chapter Eighty-Four: One Month Later

Tony was in his kitchen crushing tomatoes for sauce when Raven sauntered up behind him. She pressed her body to his.

"You can't be doing that shit, Raven. What are you trying to kill me? You're giving me blue balls and they're gonna explode soon." He looked over his shoulder at her. "You need to keep your distance."

Raven kissed the back of his neck. "How long are you going to be cooking?"

"Well, the sauce takes about an hour to simmer." He glanced at her again and saw something different in her eyes. They were a fiery green. "What's going on?" He put the spoon down and turned to face her.

"Nothing's going on. You're so suspicious." She let out a soft giggle. "I was thinking that maybe, you know, you and me can . . . you know."

"Wait," Tony chuckled. "Is this you seducing me?" He shook his head.

Raven blushed. "You mean it's not working? Oh darn." She smiled at him, placed his hand on her breast, and moved her lips toward his.

Tony met her halfway and they shared a kiss.

"Let's go into your bedroom," Raven suggested.

Tony lifted his eyebrows. "I ain't gonna say no to that."

Inside the bedroom, Raven sat on the edge of his bed. "Listen, I know I haven't been living here that long, but I love everything about it. I think it's working out well between us. What do you think?"

Tony stood over her. "It's been a long time since I've been this happy. We're right for each other. You know?"

While there had been a lot of kissing and touching over clothes on his sofa, they hadn't taken things further than that.

Raven stood and met his eyes. Then she lifted her dress over her head. She stood facing him. Thanks to Maria, she was wearing a white lace bra and matching thong.

Tony's eyes moved downward from her face to her breasts, her flat stomach, and then her toned legs. He stopped at her bare feet. "You're beautiful," he rasped.

She unhooked her bra and dropped it to the floor.

Tony moaned. "Jesus Christ, Raven. You're killin' me."

She smiled at him and moved closer. Raven placed both hands on his chest and he dipped his head, pressing his lips against her bare breasts. She dropped her head back and pushed her pelvis toward him.

Tony bent and took one of her breasts into his mouth, and his warm, wet tongue lapped softly on her hard nipple.

Raven let out an erotic whimper. Then she pulled his shirt off. She looked into his eyes as she unbuckled his belt, unbuttoned and unzipped his jeans, and then slid them down to his ankles as he quickly stepped out of them.

Tony was in a pair of boxer briefs, his stomach muscles rippling and the veins that ran through his arms plump by pleasure and his quickened heartbeat.

Raven reached her hand down and rubbed between his legs, feeling his hardness through the fabric.

"Holy shit, Raven. I want you so bad."

"I want you, too, Tony." Raven kissed him. Slow at first, then she pressed her mouth harder to his and gently pushed her tongue into his mouth.

Tony placed his hands on her butt cheeks and pulled her into him. He let out a groan. Then he brought a hand from her buttocks forward. Over her hip and down low on her thigh. He brought his hand up slowly, barely touching her skin. He moved the thong aside and slipped his fingers inside. He softly moved in and out, watching and loving the pleasure on her face. Her eyes were gently closed, and her mouth was slightly open.

Raven's voice sizzled from her throat. "Let's get on the bed." She moved on it and slipped on top with Tony sliding in next to her. She lifted her hips and removed her thong, tossing it to the side. "Get naked," she rasped.

Tony slid his boxers off and moved his body on top of hers. He licked one of her nipples while running his warm fingers gently over the other. He moved down her body slowly, stopping at her navel to lap at her belly button. He gradually made his way down between her legs and when his warm, wet tongue hit her in the exact right spot, she arched her back and let out a sound of pure erotic pleasure.

Raven dug her fingers into his thick hair, pulling his face into her, wanting him more with each passing second. He slipped his fingers inside of her again while stroking her with his tongue at the same time.

"Oh, God," Raven groaned. She grabbed his shoulders and pulled him up. Then she reached her hand down and guided him toward her.

"Are you sure?" Tony grumbled.

Instead of answering, she pushed her groin toward him, still holding on to his penis. She moved him toward her until they were touching. Then she put her hands on his butt and pressed him forward. As he entered her, Raven was filled with warmth, love, and lust.

They rocked at a steady rhythm. Each of them devouring the other. Each of them wanted more, wanted to get physically closer and closer. Then they both burst with sexual pleasure.

After, they lay in Tony's bed for a long time, holding each other, still connected at the groin.

"I love you, Tony."

He put his mouth over hers, giving her a passionate kiss, then pulled away. "I love you, too."

Chapter Eighty-Five

Effie ran from the kitchen and into the bathroom. "Oh shit!" she yelped.

Raven rushed after her. "What's wrong?" At the door, she could hear Effie retching. The toilet flushed and the door opened.

"I think I have the flu," Effie told her.

"Okay, well, you go home and I'll finish everything here."

Effie dabbed her forehead with a towel and placed a hand over her stomach. "Fuck, I think I'm gonna be sick again." She closed the door and went back into the bathroom.

"Shit," Raven said. "What can I do for you?"

"Blahhhhh." She spewed more vomit. "Nothin'."

Fifteen minutes later, Effie finally grabbed her purse and coat. "I don't know if I'll be in tomorrow."

Raven glared at her. "Stay home with your germs. I'll call Maria before I leave. We can cover for you tomorrow. I'll call you in the morning to see how you're doing."

Effie nodded and lifted her arm as she walked out the back door.

Raven looked around the kitchen. There were a lot of things to do. *This will take me at least two hours.*

She went into Maria's office and lifted the telephone.

"Maria? Hi, it's me."

Maria immediately concerned, raised her voice. "Is everything okay?"

"Yes, everything is fine. Effie has been puking for the past half an hour. She thinks it's the flu. I'll be here earlier tomorrow morning. I told her to stay home."

"Oh, that's awful," Maria said with relief in her voice, both that nothing was wrong at the bakery and that it was only the flu. "I'll be in an hour early and I can help, too. I'll call my mother-in-law now and see if she can spare a few hours to work the counter."

"Great. See you then," Raven said.

"Have a good night, Raven. Thanks for your help."

Raven hung up the phone with a smile. Then she lifted it again and put the receiver to her ear.

"Yo!"

Raven chuckled. "You do know that's not a very nice way to answer the telephone. Right?"

Tony snickered. "What? That's how I answer the phone."

"Well," Raven huffed. "It's not very welcoming."

"Exactly. I don't wanna welcome people in. I want them to keep their distance. Did you call here to teach me phone etiquette?" He was smiling.

"No, I called to tell you I'll be home late. Effie went home sick, and I have at least two more hours of work now."

"Okay, call me when you're done and I'll pick you up. I don't want you walking by yourself at night."

"Oh, please." Raven smiled.

"I ain't kidding."

She blew out a breath. "Okay. Sounds good."

"Ah right. Two hours."

"Yes, Tony. I'll call you when I'm done," she giggled.

"Yeah, but that's two more hours I gotta wait to show you how much I love you."

"I see. Well, maybe you'll appreciate me more."

Tony scoffed. "I already appreciate you more."

"Okay, gotta go. The bakery isn't going to clean or prep for tomorrow morning by itself."

Raven hung up the phone and went into the kitchen with a pep in her step. She was always happy talking with Tony.

She set out to work methodically, hoping to get everything done in less than two hours. Raven turned on the radio and cranked up the volume as she beeped and bobbed around cleaning and prepping ingredients that Effie would normally do.

Raven looked at the clock. She'd been at it for fifteen minutes. She was sweating and her hair kept falling in her face. She reached into her pocket but couldn't find her hair tie. Thinking she must've left it on Maria's desk she walked back into the office.

She switched on the light and smiled seeing the hair tie next to the telephone. She walked to the desk and picked it up. When Raven turned to leave, the lights snapped off and the office door slammed shut.

She froze. Her heartbeat accelerated. She tried to look around the room, but it was pitch black inside the windowless office. "Wh-wh-who's there?" she murmured. Her hands were waving out in front of her.

Out of nowhere, a flashlight turned on, giving the room a grisly glow. A man's face lurched forward. His parted lips were close to hers. He sucked in a long, loud breath, breathing in her terror and fueling his rotted soul. He was unrecognizable with only the whites of his eyes showing through the mask. He didn't blink. He was focused on her fear. She pulled her head back slightly. In the dim light of the tiny flashlight, Raven saw he was dressed in all black. He was even wearing black gloves.

Time stood still. The moment was too familiar, too much like being inside the high school. Raven had escaped death before, and she desperately wanted to escape death again. She'd seen this person, dressed exactly the same way when he was carrying a rifle and killing teenagers and teachers.

Her limbs were trembling. She brushed her fingertips over the desk behind her, feeling for something she could attack him with. The man was dressed like Matthew was on that day. The day that never stopped haunting her. Flecks of blood and flesh flashed before her eyes, the memories of the trauma storming back at her again.

Raven's mind rewound as though she was falling backward off the edge of a rocky cliff. The memories of all the people begging and pleading. The bodies. The color red . . . the color of death. Then the nauseating smell of sulfur laced with metal, like rotten eggs, was lodged in her sinuses again. That smell had stuck with her. The smell that reminded her of evil.

"Matthew?" she said, almost incoherently. The image of her brother's eyes recognizing her, pulling her into them was burned in her brain.

Raven was lost in her past trauma. She was fighting against the downward pull, clawing herself upward, to reach the surface and take the breath of air she desperately needed. She was stuck in the past, the horrible, unthinkable minutes that haunted her dreams and tainted her outlook on life.

The man's chapped lips turned up into a smile. An ugly, wicked grin. She stared at all of his crooked, brown teeth. His cruel, vile grin snapped her back to the present. She pulled her arms back and rammed them into the man's chest, but she had only pushed him two steps back.

His eyes were crazed . . . opened wide, bulging, red veins running through the whites. His eyes were fixed on her like a python assessing a mouse he was about to gobble down. His lips were now pressed into a straight white line. He cocked his head to the side and gave it a light shake. It was the same obsessed, faraway look that Matthew had in his eyes that day. Her fight-or-flight instinct kicked into overdrive and she ripped her body away, trying to dart around him. She knew getting out of that office was essential to her survival. He snatched her wrist, spun her around, and slammed her against the wall.

Both of his hands flew up and clasped around her throat. She couldn't breathe. His hands were so tight.

He's going to break my neck.

He squeezed tighter, gauging her level of consciousness.

Raven knew he wanted it to last . . . he needed to watch her suffer. After several seconds, with the lack of air to feed her lungs, she became subdued.

He took one hand away, reached into the waist of his black pants, lifted his arm, and pressed a gun against her temple.

"Your end is near," he hissed. His voice was hoarse and certain, leaving no room for her to doubt him.

He put the gun back in his waistband. Then the man placed one hand on her small breast, then the other, pressing her harder into the wall. Tormenting his prey, playing with her, controlling her. He slid his gloved hand over her stomach. When his fingers reached the top of her jeans, he found the button. He yanked at it several times until the button popped and she heard the small metal disk hit the floor. Then he pulled at the zipper.

Please, God help me. Don't let this man rape me. Please, she prayed silently. A whole new level of panic set in.

The masked man snickered. He was feeding from her terror, pulling the emotions from deep within her. His upper lip arched into a punishing, obscene smirk. "Gonna get me some lovin' tonight," he taunted. "Yeah, you're about to get loved on like you never knew." He let out a wicked chuckle.

"Please, I have twenty dollars in my back pocket. You can take it. Just let me go," she cried.

THE TWIN SISTER

"Let you go?" he screeched. "Oh no. You're my new bitch. But don't worry because when I'm done with you, I'm going to shoot you in the head and take you out of your misery. I would love to see the look on your little mobster boyfriend's face when he finds you."

"Oh, please. I swear. I'll get you a lot more money. Just tell me how much. You don't need to do this to me," Raven begged.

"Of course I need to do this to you, darlin'. See, my wife Michele is Sable Floyd's cellmate. You remember Sable, right? Your foster mom? You're the reason she's rotting in prison. Isn't that true?"

"N-n-no."

"Are you saying my wife is lying?"

"No, I never did anything to Sable."

"Oh, come now. Of course you did. All Sable wants is revenge on you for ruining her life. See, a while ago she came up with a great idea. She thought that I should mentor your not-so-bright brother. Sable told me all about what a pathetic weasel he was during a visit with my wife. Except Matthew fucked up. He was supposed to kill you . . . fucking coward. If that's not bad enough, the pussy lets you shoot him. Now that's a twist in the storyline. And you know what? I kinda miss the little cocksucker. He was a good ass kisser." He shook his head. "I'm gonna get five grand from Sable to kill you. Not bad for an hour's worth of work."

"I'll give you ten thousand if you let me go," she blurted, not caring where the money would come from. "Please, my boyfriend . . . he can help you. He can get you money."

His eyes burrowed into hers. Then he pressed his teeth into her shoulder, and as he gnawed through her flesh, a scream of agony emerged from her.

"Ahhhhhhhhh! Nooooooooooooo!"

When he released his jaw, she was panting. Raven's body trembled.

He looked into her eyes, and she saw his bloodstained lips through the hole in his mask. "Nah, I don't need you to double it. I want that piece of ass you got tucked in your jeans." He put his index finger over his lips. "Don't tell my wife, though. It wasn't actually part of the deal. Sable just wanted me to kill you. You know, a man gets lonely when his wife is locked up."

Raven shook her head frantically. She tried to kick and punch him but every time she did, he put his hands back on her neck.

"Shhhhh." His sour breath drifted up her nose. "Don't worry, after I get my lovin', I'm gonna take your life. Just like Matthew Ledger took all those other lives that had no meaning. You're no different. Your time has come, so if you want to go out with any style, stop fighting it."

Raven forced herself to appear calm. She gave him a simple nod. "Okay, I won't fight you," she choked out.

"Good," he said, releasing his hold from her neck.

Make him get to know me. Make him see me as a person.

"What's your name?" she managed, rubbing her neck.

"Oh, I'm sorry. I didn't introduce myself properly. I'm Jester."

Shock spit liquid panic through her veins. The floor dropped out from under her feet.

Fuck me!

"Jester, my boyfriend is coming to pick me up. If I'm not outside waiting for him, he's gonna know something is wrong," she lied.

Jester chuckled. "I came in when that Black woman left. I know you talked to the owner once and then your boyfriend. You told him you would call him in about two hours. So we have plenty of time. This won't take more than, oh I don't know, thirty minutes."

A heaviness settled over Raven. She was tired of fighting. She was sick of battling her way uphill. She had worked so hard to create the life she was living. There was no way she'd fight her way back from this one. Jester would make good on his promise. He would kill her.

Raven eased her eyes closed. *God, why did you give me this life? What was the purpose?*

Wanting to be strong, she came back into the present. Like her teacher, Mrs. Fisher did with Matthew, she would not give Jester the satisfaction of dying afraid and letting him feed off of her misery.

Her thoughts drifted to Tony, and she imagined being home with him, taking comfort in the safety of his embrace, nestled against his chest, and being at peace.

She opened her eyes and looked Jester squarely in the eyes. He wasn't the devil. Jester was a man who worshipped Satan, nothing more than flesh and bones. He was the pathetic creature who had helped Matthew plan the school shooting. Sable was behind all those deaths, too.

Raven moved her eyes around the room looking for something to use to bash Jester's head in. There were only papers and folders.

Life was ending for Raven. She'd crossed the finish line. She smiled thinking about all the people she knew and loved now. Then a gush of relief passed through her. There would be no more shrinking away from the common whisper she heard in the distance. *That's Raven Ledger, the shooter's sister.*

Raven gaped at Jester, her eyes wide and mouth hanging open as if she was witnessing him sprout sharp horns and black wings. Even as she tried to deny him access to her, Jester's dark energy and unsympathetic gaze filled her with dread. His eyes were dead. There was no life in them, only malicious intent.

Her time had come. Soon the worst would be behind Raven, and she would be off to a better place. That's what Raven believed—that in death, there would be a peaceful existence waiting for her. She would leave this world as Raven Ledger, the girl who fought her way through the horrendous life she'd been given, the girl who died at the hands of a stranger who'd been paid by Sable to inflict one last round of punishment on her.

Then something inside her head snapped, and with it, she had a rush of adrenaline.

Fuck Sable. I'm gonna give it one last effort, one final fight.

Chapter Eighty-Six

Raven lifted her knee and shoved it forward with the last of her energy.

Jester bent over, holding his crotch. His gun had been knocked out of his waistband and slid across the floor.

Seeing this as her opportunity, she kicked him on the side of the hip, sending him onto the floor. She moved around the back of him. He was rolled in a fetal position, and she kicked him many times. Then she pulled her leg back one final time and kicked him in the back of his head.

Breathing heavily, she glared down at him. "You can tell Sable Floyd to go fuck herself."

She turned to leave the office, and Jester gripped her ankle with both hands. Raven tried to use her other foot to kick him off, but she was too unstable and fell to the ground. He quickly crawled on top of her like a cockroach scurrying to consume crumbs. He sat on her stomach and put both hands around her neck. This time, he took no enjoyment in her suffering. This time, he wanted Raven Ledger dead.

Chapter Eighty-Seven

Raven scratched and swung at him until there was nothing left in her. Her arms dropped to the floor and she closed her eyes.

When the office door flung open, Jester was surprised and loosened his grip on her. Raven reared up on her legs and lifted her hips, and he fell next to her.

Then Jester was being lifted from the ground like he was floating. Raven rolled onto her side and glanced up at him. Marveling at how he was rising in the air. Her eyes moved up, and that's when she saw Tony.

Tony threw Jester against the wall. He lifted him again and slammed his back onto the floor.

Tony turned to Vincent. "Get our guys. I want him gone and I don't want anyone to find one fucking fingernail of this prick when they're done. Tell the crew not to make one mistake."

"Ah right. I got you." Vincent looked at Raven still on the floor, gasping for air. "I'm gonna go with the guys, make sure this gets done right. This is about family."

Tony nodded, and then he rushed to Raven. He squatted low to be at eye level. "Are you okay? You think anything is broken?"

Raven shook her head. "No." Her eyes met his. "I fought him, Tony. I would've been dead already, but I stopped him from killing me."

"It looked like he was pretty close to doing that when I came in."

"Yeah, but I stopped him long enough for you to get here." She reached her arms up, and Tony lifted her to her feet. She was wobbling but intact. "Why? How did you know to come here?"

Tony looked into her eyes. "When you called me . . . I heard movement behind you."

She shook her head. "That's impossible."

Tony smiled. "No, Raven. Nothing is impossible when you're trained how to hunt."

He held Raven around her waist. As they turned to leave the office, a handsome man stood in the doorway. "Hello, Raven. I'm Salvatore, Maria's husband. Are you okay?" he asked.

She nodded, her eyes glued to him, trying to process everything happening. "Yeah, I'm good. I'm a fighter . . . been fighting my whole life and I'm not about to stop now."

Salvatore gave her a broad smile, illuminating his classically striking face. "Take her home," he directed at Tony. "Vincent has Jester, and I have the rest of our things covered tonight. She needs to rest."

Tony nodded. "Yeah." He held on to Raven and hugged Salvatore with his free arm. He looked his friend in the eyes. "You know exactly what I want done."

Salvatore nodded. "Yes, Tony. We all want the same. You don't need to worry."

"Salvatore?" Raven's voice was weak.

He looked at Raven.

"You have to be careful. Jester's wife is in prison with my old foster mom, Sable Floyd. She hired him to kill me. Sable hates to lose. She might send someone to hurt you if she finds out you're protecting me."

Salvatore smirked. "I see. You two better get going."

***

Salvatore made one telephone call when he got home. His contact found out where Sable Floyd was jailed and ordered the hit on her. By the time the prison guards found her, she had been beaten and stabbed so severely they had to use dental records to make a positive ID on her. The Morano family connections inside the prison had stripped her naked, beat her with lead pipes, and stabbed her in the face more than twenty times. The guard who stood at the door to make sure no one saw the murder had received ten thousand dollars in cash for standing watch while two inmates tortured and then took Sable's life.

Jester's wife Michele, who helped Sable, was released from prison a week after Sable's murder. Michele only had to worry for a short time about her missing husband, Jester. On her seventh day after being released from prison, she was reunited with Jester in his final resting place—a blast furnace at a large steel plant outside of Philadelphia. Jester had gone into it still alive, while Michele's throat was slit and she had died before her body entered the 2800-degree furnace.

Chapter Eighty-Eight: One Year Later

Raven was in a room in the back of the church. She was pacing and touching her face.

"You better stop fidgeting and rubbing your hand on your face. You're gonna ruin your makeup," Cecilia said.

"I hate wearing makeup. It's itchy," Raven argued.

"It's for the pictures. Remember?" Maria added with a sweet smile.

Raven nodded. "Yeah. I know, but you wear it all the time. I think the foundation is gonna crack off my face as soon as I smile."

"I think you'll be fine," Maria remarked.

Raven smiled. "Okay. But I'm taking it off as soon as the pictures are done."

Maria scoffed. "Right. That will be at the end of the night. This is an Italian wedding. Your reception is being held in Johnny Morano's backyard. There will be pictures until you're ready to go to bed. Maybe one or two while you're lying next to Tony in bed," she teased.

"Aw, leave the girl alone," Effie chimed in. "She's a natural beauty and I agree with her. If she don't wanna wear it, then she shouldn't have to."

The door opened, and a woman poked her head in. "Is everyone ready?"

Raven nodded, gripping her bouquet tighter. She looked at Cecilia, Maria, and then Effie. "I can't believe this is happening. All of you got me to this point. Until you all came along, I had no family, and now I do. I will love you all forever."

"Aw." Cecilia sniffled, swiping at a tear. "We love you, too," she said, and the other two women nodded, holding back their tears.

"Okay, maid of honor," Raven said, looking at Cecilia. "It's time for us to go."

Cecilia looked at Maria and Effie in their matching bridesmaid dresses. Yes, her bridal party was older, but they were also wiser and had been her backbone over the past year.

***

Tony stood at the altar with his back erect, shuffling from one foot to another. He had his hands deep inside his pants pockets. Vincent and Salvatore stood on either side of him. Vincent put a hand on Tony's shoulder.

"We're real happy for you," Vincent said, his voice cracking.

Tony's head snapped toward Vincent. "What the fuck are you crying about?"

Vincent shrugged. "I don't know, man. It's real nice to see you happy again. You ain't like me. You're more of a one-woman man. So I like it, is all. I think Raven is a good dame."

Salvatore leaned into his friend. "This is a significant moment for you, Tony. The rest of your life is about to become richer. You picked a good bride."

"I'm nervous," Tony admitted.

Salvatore and Vincent shot each other a look.

Salvatore lowered his voice. "This isn't Kate. Raven will be by your side until you're old and have long, wrinkled balls."

Tony shook his head and scoffed. "Thanks for that image. Gives me something to look forward to." He turned and met Salvatore's eyes. "How do you know it won't be like Kate? I can't go through that again."

"Because you're older and know better now. Raven is different than Kate. She's more mature, more aware, and more committed. Raven is a fighter, like you. I've seen it . . . We all have."

Tony nodded. "Yeah, I love her a lot. I never thought I'd love another woman after Kate. I didn't know I could love somebody this much again." He looked down at his shoes, taking in several deep breaths to calm his nerves. Then the music started, and Tony lifted his head and watched the back of the church. He was jumpy until he saw Raven appear.

Chapter Eighty-Nine

Raven stood in the back of the Saint Joseph's Catholic Church with her arm looped through Johnny Morano's.

Raven had been taken by surprise after they got engaged and Johnny had approached her at the engagement party, with his wife Alessandra by his side.

"Raven, Alessandra, and I are so pleased to have you join our family. You have done wonders for this man," Johnny said, lifting his chin toward Tony.

"Whatever that means," Tony mumbled, and Johnny returned a stern look.

Johnny took Raven's hand in his own. "I know that your father passed when you were young. I wanted to ask if you would allow me the privilege to walk you down the aisle and give you away to someone"—his eyes moved to Tony—"I consider a son."

Raven's heart was racing. She was wrought with emotions of joy already. She was touched and so very grateful.

She smiled at him. "Yes, that would be really nice. I appreciate the offer. You're so kind." She lowered her face. "I was worried I'd look silly walking to the front of the church by myself."

Johnny opened his arms and Raven stepped into them. As he held her, his eyes met Tony's and the Godfather gave him a quick smile and nod.

"Thanks, Johnny," Tony said. "You accepting Raven as your own means everything to me."

It was rare for Johnny Morano to put forward that much respect for one of his men. But he had been honest with Raven. He considered both Tony and Vincent like they were his blood sons. But there was something bigger to his action. To be walked down the aisle by the Godfather of the Philadelphia crime family sent a warning to the other crime families and gangs—Raven Ledger was more than just Tony Bruno's bride. She was now seen like Johnny's daughter and the Morano family wouldn't tolerate anyone causing her harm.

***

A few feet from the altar, Johnny lifted Raven's veil and kissed her on both cheeks. He took her hand and turned to Tony.

"Your bride is to be loved and honored for all of her days," Johnny said, lifting her hand toward Tony. Then Johnny turned to Raven. "Your groom is to be loved and honored for all of his days."

Raven grinned and nodded. Then she placed her hand in Tony's and turned toward the priest who stood at the altar.

Tony leaned into her. "I'll love and protect you till the day I die, Raven Ledger."

Raven turned to him and smiled as though there was no one else in the church but them. "I love you the same. I've waited my whole life for you and I'm never letting you go. In you, I've found home."

Continue reading...

Read more about Tony Bruno in the novel **Mean Little People.** Tony is a bullied child who becomes a feared man in a Philadelphia crime family. Turn the page to read a sample.

The Beating Path

Seven-year-old Tony Bruno feared the strong hands of death were reaching for him. His small feet pounded against the hot pavement as he tried to get away from the boys chasing after him.

In midstride two of the seven-year-old boys snatched Tony by the back of his old T-shirt. His arms flailed spastically. He tried to make contact with his small fists.

One boy grazed by Tony's fist yelled, "Knock it off, Bruno, you little queer."

Tony was dragged through the trash that lined the city sidewalk.

"Leave me alone," Tony cried in a high-pitched voice.

"Shut up, Bruno. I swear if you open your mouth again, we'll kill you," Vincent snapped.

Tony twisted and thrust against the boys. He fought with everything he had in him, but he was no match for the kids who used bullying as an after-school activity.

Tony's eyes fixed on his surroundings as if seeing them for the first time. He looked into the open lot, taking in the small patch of trees and overgrown grass. On either side of the lot were brick buildings with broken windows that revealed the lifeless blackness within. Vines clung to the exterior as if they'd grown there from the inside out. Tony never walked between the buildings. It was taboo. This place scared him. This was the place where monsters lived. He'd heard the groan of drunks coming from deep inside the cavity of the broken-down buildings when he'd walked by months earlier with his mother.

Tony fixated on his mother's words now.

"There are googamongers that live in that place. Do you know what a googamonger is?" Teresa asked.

Tony had shaken his head, scanning the trees and buildings, waiting for a humanlike creature to come after him.

"They're real big. Bigger than your father. They got long claws for fingers and real sharp teeth. They like to eat children because every time they eat a kid, they grow stronger. So you keep your skinny ass outta there."

Tony was paralyzed with fear thinking about the googamongers. He kept fighting against his tormentors, but they dragged him deeper into the forbidden lot. Vincent and his friends forced Tony into the shadow of a small clump of trees. Tony peed himself, imagining the googamongers watching him, getting ready to eat him. His stomach turned with a wispy emptiness. Tony made one final attempt to free himself and got one arm loose. Vincent punched Tony in the gut, and a few seconds later, Tony's head slammed against a large oak tree.

Vincent poked his index finger into Tony's sternum. "Give us all your money."

"I ain't g-g-got no money." Tony stared into Vincent's rich brown eyes through the jet-black hair that fell in front of them.

Frankie grabbed Tony around the waist and threw him to the ground. Then he pulled Tony's T-shirt over his head and threw it off to the side.

"Look!" Frankie yelled, standing over the boy. "Bruno peed himself."

The boys stood in a circle around Tony and laughed.

Vincent turned to his best friend, Patton. "Grab the bucket we left in the grass."

Patton stared as if he were trying to read Vincent's mind. He jumped up and down and clapped his hands together. "Yeahhhhhh," he sang as he ran into the tall grass.

Patton raced back to the noisy circle of boys. Vincent pulled out an old plastic clothesline from the bucket they'd stolen from the neighbor lady they called Mrs. Mean. He handed the line to Patton, who threw it over a tree limb while another boy turned the bucket upside down.

A few minutes later, Tony stood on the bucket with the plastic cord around his neck. His fingers clawed at the cord with frantic desperation. His body shook. In the heat of the day, Tony's teeth chattered. He couldn't think. His mind went blank. While Tony didn't comprehend the possible consequences of the boy's actions, he felt he was in grave danger.

Vincent looked at Tony and smiled. "He looks just like that cowboy in the movie. They hung him from a tree. One of the guys smacked the horse he was sitting on, and the guy fell off. He was swinging by his neck. It was so cool—his legs were moving like he was riding a bike, and he was twitching and stuff."

The energy in the small group of boys was a blend of morbid curiosity and fear of the unknown. Tony's motions were jerky. His tongue stuck to the roof of his mouth. The more his fear showed outwardly, the higher the energy level rose through the circle of boys.

"I need to go home," Tony cried. "My ma will be looking for me."

"You'll go home when we say you can," Patton hissed. Then he picked up a long stick and whacked Tony on his bare back. The rough, bark-covered branches dug into his tender flesh and left bloated, red welts.

"Wow! Let me try that," Vincent said, picking up a branch and slashing it across Tony's abdomen.

Tony continued to pull at the cord around his neck. Each time one of the boys whacked him with a stick, he flinched, and the rope tightened. After a short time, Tony's muscles went limp, and he welcomed the numb feeling inside his head. His eyelids drooped, and he stopped fighting. His shoulders flopped forward, and his head hung. With a lack of oxygen, death crept upon him, bringing him the closure he longed for.

"Hey! What the hell are you boys doing over there?" A male voice boomed.

Vincent turned and saw a delivery truck driver at the edge of the lot. The man was heading toward them.

"Run!" Vincent screamed.

The boys took off in different directions, but Patton hesitated and then kicked the bucket from under Tony's feet before he ran.

The cord was long enough so Tony landed on his tippy-toes, but the initial fall tightened it around his neck even further, jarring him awake. Tony tried to suck in a breath, and when nothing came through, his panic heightened, and he lost his balance. He lost his battle against the strangling cord. His windpipe betrayed him, and the lack of oxygen comforted him again.

The deliveryman reached Tony right before he slipped out of consciousness. He lifted Tony's small body and held him on his hip, as though he were a toddler. The man quickly loosened the rope around Tony's neck. Tony gulped air into his lungs, and the bluish color on his face shortly returned to normal.

"What the hell happened here?" the deliveryman said. He pulled a knife from his pocket and cut the cord.

Tony rubbed his neck with his fingertips. He looked around with a pinched expression. Then he remembered. "Vincent and his friends followed me. And . . . and . . . they made me come here and . . ."

Tony sobbed from the memory that rushed into his mind.

"Okay, big guy. What's your name?"

"Tony."

"Well, I'm Mac. Let's get you home. Where's your shirt?"

Tony looked around the tall grass in a daze. It was gone, carried off by Patton.

"Forget the shirt. Are you all right?"

Tony nodded.

"You think you can stand?" Mac said, placing Tony on his feet.

Tony wobbled at first but then gained his footing.

"Where do you live?"

"Over that way," Tony said, pointing toward his row home.

Mac slowly walked Tony to his house and stood at the front door with him.

"Everything will be fine," Mac said. He softly rapped on the front door.

Tony's father, Carmen, yelled when he flung the door open. "What the hell did you do now?"

"Nothing," Tony replied timidly.

Carmen looked at Mac, whose mouth hung open.

"What the hell are you staring at, and who are you, anyway?" Carmen barked.

Mac adjusted his stance. His legs locked at the knees and his chest pushed forward. "I just found your kid being hung from a tree. A group of boys was hurting him. Those boys don't have any scruples. Your son almost died."

"My son almost died because he ain't got no backbone. Now, go on and deliver your packages. Stay the hell outta other people's business."

Mac stared at Carmen for a moment. Then he bent down and looked into Tony's eyes. "You take care of yourself. Stay away from those boys. You hear?"

Tony nodded. "Yeah, I wish they'd just leave me alone."

"Oh, for crying out loud! Get the hell in this house before I give you another beating."

Tony knew from his dad's squinty eyes that his father was having a worse day than normal. For a brief moment, Tony wished he could go live with Mac. He didn't want to face his father, not alone, not again.

After Carmen slammed the door, he turned to his son. His eyes pored over Tony's gangly body, and he bent slightly at the waist to look closely at the purple mark around his neck from the cord.

Carmen's upper lip lifted. "Where's your shirt?"

Tony bent his neck and sniffled, his fear ignited by his father's venomous stare. He took a few steps backward and crossed his arms over his abdomen.

"I asked you a question, boy."

"The kids stole it from me."

"Why did you let them steal it?"

"I didn't let them. They made me."

"That's because you're a little weasel. Ain't got no man in you."

Carmen grabbed a handful of Tony's thick brown hair and pulled his head back to look into his son's green eyes. "You're pathetic. Go to your room, and don't come out till I say so. While you're up there, I want you to think about how much you embarrass me. I swear your Ma cheated on me with another man because you ain't no son of mine. Look at you! Covered in all those scratches and bruises. The sight of you makes me sick. Get outta my living room before I slap the shit outta you."

Tony gimped up the steps as quickly as he could manage and shut his bedroom door gingerly. He pulled on a clean T-shirt and lay on his bed, waiting for his mother to come home. He rubbed his arms and legs with open hands. Pulling the blanket from his bed, he wrapped himself tightly and waited. He put his hand to his forehead, expecting it to be on fire, but it was cold and clammy.

Then his bedroom door flew open. He sat up quickly, and the blanket dropped to his sides when he saw the belt in his father's hand. Carmen's hand lifted into the air, and the belt came down on Tony with a hard crack. The beating went on for several minutes, and when it stopped, Tony lay in a ball wishing the boys had killed him.

BUY NOW: Mean Little People (Home Street Home Series: Book Four)

The HOME STREET HOME SERIES is a collection of novels that can be read in any order.

More books by Paige

Home Street Home Series (can be read in any order):
Believe Like A Child
When Smiles Fade
One Among Us
Mean Little People
Never Be Alone
My Final Breath

Rainey Paxton Series (must be read in order):
A Little Pinprick
A Little High
Girls Missing
Girls Found

Raven Ledger Duet (must be read in order):
The Shooter's Sister
The Twin Sister

A Note From Paige

Dear Dearth Reader,

I want to take a moment to thank you for reading and supporting my work. I appreciate you spreading the word about my books to family, friends and co-workers. If you enjoyed this book please go to Amazon and leave a short review so that other readers can determine if this is the right book for them . . . great reviews mean so much to me and keep me writing. Thank you!

~Paige

Made in United States
Cleveland, OH
01 July 2025